Former journalist S. D. Robertson quit his role as a local newspaper editor to pursue a lifelong ambition of becoming a novelist. An English graduate from the University of Manchester, he's also worked as a holiday rep, door-to-door salesman, train cleaner, kitchen porter and mobile phone network engineer. Over the years, Stuart has spent time in France, Holland and Australia, but home these days is back in the UK. He lives in a village near Manchester with his wife and daughter. There's also his cat, Bernard, who likes to distract him from writing — usually by breaking things.

STAND BY ME

Lisa and Elliot have been best friends since the day they met as children. Twenty years later, life has pulled the pair apart, and Lisa is struggling. Her marriage is floundering, her teenage kids are being secretive, and she's so tired she can't think straight. So when Elliot knocks on the door, she's delighted to see her old friend again. With Elliot back in their lives, Lisa's family problems begin to improve. As their bond deepens, she realises how much she's missed him, and prays that this is one friendship that will last a lifetime. But sometimes, life has other ideas . . .

S. D. ROBERTSON

◆

STAND BY ME

Complete and Unabridged

CHARNWOOD
Leicester

First published in Great Britain in 2018 by
Avon
London

First Charnwood Edition
published 2019
by arrangement with
HarperCollins*Publishers*
London

A catalogue record for this book is available from the British Library.

ISBN 978–1–4448–3962–3

Published by
F. A. Thorpe (Publishing)
Anstey, Leicestershire

Set by Words & Graphics Ltd.
Anstey, Leicestershire
Printed and bound in Great Britain by
T. J. International Ltd., Padstow, Cornwall

This book is printed on acid-free paper

For Claudia and Kirsten

Prologue

Pain. That was the last thing he remembered. Excruciating, relentless, all-encompassing pain. The kind that focuses your mind absolutely, driving out all other thoughts as it pierces through your defences with shuddering ease.

The past, the future. Neither existed at that moment. There was only the present, rolling in ultra-slow motion.

No air, no up or down. A rag doll on a spin cycle: his tears invisible; his cries unheard.

That pain, dwarfing every other feeling. Had it been there a moment or forever?

He just wanted it to end. And finally, after rising to a blinding crescendo of agony, it did.

Blissful nothingness swooped down from the heavens above and engulfed him.

★　★　★

His return to consciousness was gradual and unexpected. As he became aware of himself again, it was as a detached series of thoughts and memories floating in the darkness. The echo of his torment remained in the background: a low hum, gone but not forgotten.

It was this way for some time. Then, hidden within that low hum, he began to hear the faint murmur of something else.

Was that someone whispering?

1

He had to strain to hear it, so quiet was the sound. But the harder he concentrated — the more he strove to tune in — the louder it grew, until eventually he identified a voice, androgynous in tone.

It took longer still to comprehend the actual words, delivered in a sing-song manner that was neither quite human nor robotic. At first he heard what appeared to be gibberish. Another language perhaps, but not one he recognised. And yet as he focused his mind on the sound, piece by piece, word by word, he gradually began to understand.

It was one sentence, repeated on loop: 'Follow the light to its source and find yourself.'

Light? What light? There was only darkness here.

Wasn't there?

He looked all around. Saw nothing.

And then the briefest flicker of white in the far distance.

It was barely anything — and yet it was something.

Something that wasn't pain.

A purpose.

1

NOW

Friday, 20 July 2018

What time had Mike started drinking? He'd seemed merry when Lisa had got home from work, but she'd let it go. It had been nice to see him smiling for once, even if it was artificially induced, and she'd assumed he'd only had a couple of beers. It must have been considerably more than that, though, for him to be so far gone now.

It was no secret that her husband liked a tipple; in recent weeks, they'd spoken several times about how the frequency of his drinking had increased since he'd stopped working. She'd voiced her fears that it was getting out of control and he'd argued otherwise. At best, this had come in the form of calm reassurances that he wouldn't let it escalate too far. At worst, it had been a slanging match, with him shouting at her to get off his back and her calling him an alcoholic. Not that Lisa actually thought he was. Not yet. She just wanted to shock him into cutting back before it really did get out of hand. But maybe she'd misjudged the situation.

'What's wrong?' Mike asked. 'Don't you like it here?'

Lisa wanted to point out that he was slurring

3

his words, despite the fact it was barely 8 p.m. and they were still waiting for their starter to arrive at the restaurant. But at the same time she didn't want to ruin the evening. He'd arranged it as a surprise to celebrate their wedding anniversary: an unusually thoughtful gesture. So much so that when he'd told her this morning, before she'd set off for school, her initial response had been to wonder what he'd done wrong and was trying to make up for. She'd not vocalised this, thankfully. Nor had she expressed her concern about the cost of a decent meal out in Manchester. They could barely afford to get takeaway in their village; never mind get a taxi to and from the city centre for the privilege of enjoying overpriced food and drink. That was the cold hard truth. But she'd weighed up the matter at work, where it had been the final day of term before the summer holidays, and decided to throw caution to the wind for once and enjoy a rare night out.

So Lisa had dug a pair of heels and her favourite black dress out of the wardrobe; she'd used the curling tongs to add some life to her dull, limp blonde hair for the first time in ages, and made more than the usual cursory effort with her make-up. Mike had worn the smart navy shirt she'd bought for his birthday, swapping his usual jeans and trainers for chinos and tan brogues.

But she couldn't enjoy being with him when he was so plastered. He might be sitting up straight and behaving himself so far, but his eyes had gone — and that was never a good sign.

Being out with her husband in that state was like riding in a speeding car without a seatbelt on.

'Hello? Earth to Lisa.'

'What was that?' she replied at last, shaking her head in a bid to focus.

'I asked whether you liked it here or not, but you were miles away. What's up?'

'Oh, nothing. Sorry. I was thinking about work.'

'Anything I can help with?'

'No, it's not important,' Lisa fudged. 'It'll take me a few days to switch off, that's all.'

'I apologise if I'm boring you,' he said before taking a long swig from his pint of lager, his eyes darting around the restaurant, looking everywhere except in her direction.

Lisa took a deep breath. Things were on a knife edge already, which did not bode well. Thankfully, a young female waiter turned up with their starters. She beamed a toothy grin at them. 'Hi, folks. So who's having the butternut squash soup tonight?'

Lisa raised her right hand and smiled back as the girl presented her with the large white bowl, two-thirds full with its steaming orange contents and central swirl of sour cream. 'There you go. Enjoy.' She turned to Mike. 'And the beef carpaccio for you, sir?'

He smiled. 'Thank you.'

Lisa noted her husband's eyes lingering a moment too long on the waitress's ample chest, on display in a partly unbuttoned white blouse, as she leaned over the table with his plate. How embarrassing, she thought, her fingers squeezing her thighs under the table. The girl looked young enough to be his daughter, for God's sake. And Lisa couldn't remember the last time he'd looked at her with that degree of lust. They'd barely touched each other in months.

She bit her tongue, lowering her nose over the soup bowl instead to breathe in the aroma. 'Oh, wow,' she said. 'That smells delicious. Yours looks lovely too. Excellent choice coming here, love.'

'Don't sound so surprised.'

'Why not? You springing this on me is a lovely surprise. And of course I'm not bored. I just need a little time to get into school holiday mode. You know how it is.'

'Not any more,' Mike said.

'Oh, come on. Let's focus on the positives and enjoy ourselves. I'm very impressed. You thought of everything, even arranging for the kids to have sleepovers tonight. Anyone would think you were trying to get me alone.'

This made Mike smile, as she'd hoped it would. He'd always been a sucker for flattery. Feeling the tension dissipate, she allowed herself to sit back in her chair and enjoy a sip of her gin and tonic, trying to heed her own advice.

Things were all right for a while. Although it was still obvious to Lisa that Mike was drunk, he managed to behave himself throughout the starter and main course. This was partly down to her efforts to keep the conversation light and chatty, avoiding danger topics and even engaging in some light flirting with him. She did her best to appear relaxed and happy, although in truth she felt like a firefighter tackling a smouldering blaze near a petrol station. She went with his suggestion to get a bottle of red wine to accompany the steaks they'd both ordered, but drank more than she usually would in a bid to reduce his intake. This backfired when, without warning, he grabbed a passing waiter and ordered a second bottle.

Feeling tipsy now, Lisa couldn't stop herself from intervening. 'Wait a minute,' she said, grabbing the waiter's arm before he had a chance to leave and then looking at her husband. 'Is that really necessary, love? Don't you think we've had enough?'

The look Mike gave her in return was thunderous. 'Ignore my wife, please,' he said with feigned calmness, his eyes locked on to her face, daring her to contradict him again.

The waiter, not much older than his female co-worker and probably also a student, shuffled awkwardly on the spot, looking from one to the other. 'Um. What, er — '

'I said to bring me another bottle of red,' Mike snapped, raising his voice loud enough so that several nearby diners turned to look.

'Yes, of course, sir. Right away.' He shot towards the bar without looking at Lisa again and her heart sank.

Mike thumped his right fist into the top of the small dining table, causing a loud clattering sound that drew yet more inquisitive glances. 'What the hell was that?' he growled. 'Are you trying to make me look like an idiot?'

'You do that all by yourself when you thump

7

tables and raise your voice in public, Mike. Excuse me for daring to question whether we need another bottle of wine or not.'

Lisa realised at this moment, mortified by her husband's behaviour, that she barely recognised him as the man she'd married sixteen years earlier. Physically he hadn't changed that much. He still had the same broad shoulders, brown eyes, olive skin and thick stubble she'd fallen in love with when they'd met as trainee teachers. Even his short black hair wasn't that different, despite receding a little and gaining some flecks of grey. No, these changes were on the inside, which was worse. The very public collapse of Mike's career had mentally scarred him in all kinds of ways — and Lisa feared that the funny, kind, driven man she'd once adored may have disappeared for good.

'If I want another bottle, I'll have one,' he slurred.

'Don't you think that maybe you've had enough?'

'Oh, here we go. I was waiting for this.'

'Well, I wasn't going to say anything, but I could tell you were pretty plastered when we arrived — and now you're embarrassing me. How much did — '

'I'm the embarrassing one?' he replied. 'That's rich coming from you. I go to the effort of organising this, and how do you repay me? By making me look stupid in public. Thanks very much. You've ruined everything now. Bloody typical.'

Lisa shook her head. 'I think you'll find — '

8

She was interrupted by the return of the waiter, who avoided looking at her as he delivered Mike's wine and unscrewed the cap. 'Here you are, sir. Would you like to try it first?'

Mike shook his head and gestured for him to fill his glass. After he'd done so, the waiter's eyes fell on Lisa's glass; he hesitated before looking in her direction. 'Madam, would you, um, like me to — '

'No, thank you. My husband will be drinking the bottle alone.'

Lisa regretted saying this almost straight away — not because of how it made Mike look, but because it further embarrassed the waiter, who was just a young guy doing his job. He nodded awkwardly before leaving the bottle in the middle of the table, clearing away the unwanted remains of their main course, and scuttling off, leaving the pair of them scowling at each other.

Mike was seething. That much was obvious. But so was Lisa — and she'd not been the one to start the row. Usually she did her utmost to avoid such confrontations, but buoyed by the alcohol and a sense of injustice, she had no intention of backing down on this occasion.

'Well,' she said. 'I'm so glad we came out to celebrate our anniversary like this. How lovely.'

Her husband's reply was to empty his glass in one go before pouring himself another. 'Happy?' he asked her.

'Ecstatic,' she replied, standing up and removing her handbag from the seatback.

'Where are you going?'

'Toilet. Is that okay with you?' Then before Mike had a chance to react, Lisa grabbed his glass and threw the wine in his face. Leaving behind the sound of his spluttering and shouting, she sprinted for the exit, retrieving her jacket from the coat stand on the way and instructing the bemused receptionist that her husband would settle the bill.

The first thing she did after hitting the pavement was laugh. She howled like a maniac as she made her way to the nearest taxi rank, no longer minding that people were staring. She couldn't believe what she'd done, but she knew where it had come from. That was repressed frustration bursting out. Lisa knew the tiptoeing around her husband couldn't last forever. She'd desperately tried to give him enough space to lick his wounds. But there was only so much time she could wait for him to pick himself back up. For too long there had been a tightness in her chest; a knot in her stomach. She'd squashed down her feelings, like a coiled spring; it felt great to release them at last.

However, her elation began to fade in the taxi home to Aldham, giving way to the realisation that she and Mike had major issues to iron out. She didn't exactly feel guilty about throwing the wine, still believing her husband had driven her to it. But she was ashamed at how they'd behaved in public. She imagined how mortifying it would be if someone they knew had witnessed it.

'Late night at the office?' the driver asked her as they sped through the city streets.

Charming, she thought, wondering who would go to work in heels and a cocktail dress.

'I'm a primary school teacher, so no,' she snapped, pulling her mobile out of her bag to avoid further conversation. Luckily, he got the hint and turned on the radio.

It was 8.42 p.m. and still broad daylight, emphasising how strange it felt to be heading home so soon. At least she knew she'd have the house to herself when she got back. Until Mike followed her, of course, although she hoped that wouldn't be for some time.

Lisa looked down again at her phone and noticed she was gripping it so tightly that her fingertips had gone white. Mike hadn't contacted her so far. Her guess was that, despite the soaking she'd given him and the inevitable red wine stains on his clothes, he'd stay out drinking by himself, drowning his sorrows and telling his sob story to anyone who'd listen. She didn't want to think about the row they'd eventually have; it was as well that the kids were out.

At home she kicked off her heels, changed into her dressing gown and flopped on to the couch with a cup of tea. She had promised herself a large glass of white, but that was before the booze from earlier started to wear off, making her feel grotty. More alcohol was the last thing she wanted.

She was flicking aimlessly through TV channels when her phone vibrated on the coffee table. Rather than Mike, it turned out to be Sandra, a fellow teacher and her closest friend at work. She'd sent her a text message from the taxi, hinting at what had happened and hoping for a girlie chat.

'Hello?'

'Lise, hi. Are you okay?'

'Not really. Tonight's romantic meal turned into a disaster.'

'How come?'

She recounted the story, veering from tears to laughter and then back again in the process.

'Oh my God,' Sandra said. 'I can't believe you did that. Was it a full glass of red?'

'Yes. Was that terrible of me?'

Sandra giggled. 'Sounds like he had it coming. And he didn't say anything afterwards?'

'I didn't wait around to find out. I jumped straight in a taxi and came home. I'm sure he'll have something to say when he gets back.'

'When are you expecting him?'

'No idea. Do you think I should call his mobile or send him a message?'

'Gosh, I really don't know, Lise. Whatever you think is best. He's had some time to cool down now, but it's a tricky one.'

'He's probably getting plastered in a bar somewhere, moaning about his psycho wife.'

Sandra, who had only met Mike a handful of times, asked: 'Don't be offended by this, but, um, he's not likely to hurt you or anything, is he? You know, if he comes back in a state. Because if you need somewhere safe — '

'Mike would never lay a finger on me,' Lisa replied. 'He has his faults, but he's not that kind of man. Thanks for caring, though.'

12

'Well, you're always welcome here. You know that.'

'You're a good friend, Sandra, but I'll be fine. There'll be a big row at some point, I'm sure, but nothing I can't handle.'

Lisa felt better after ending the call. It was always good to chat to a friend for moral support at challenging times.

She finished her cup of tea and picked up the remote control to unmute the television. A programme about border control at Australian airports was showing. She was about to flick over but got hooked by the tales of people trying to smuggle in contraband.

Watching this made her think about her childhood friend Elliot, or El as she often called him. Although he'd lived down under for the past two decades, he still regularly popped into her thoughts. They'd been best friends throughout their years at secondary school, only for him to emigrate after their A-levels. They'd written regular letters to each other at the start, but eventually these had petered out as life got in the way.

Since Lisa had never been one for technology or social media, her only recent contact with her old friend had been infrequent emails and Christmas cards. All the same, she'd always dreamed of going to visit him one day. They'd been so close as kids — gone through so much together — she couldn't imagine them not getting along any more. She was confident that they'd carry on where they'd left off, chatting away nineteen to the dozen and making each

13

other laugh at silly things. Mind you, El was quite the success story these days. He'd set up a lucrative technology firm in Sydney and, according to the letter tucked into his card last Christmas, had recently created a popular app for smartphones and tablets. In fact, from what Lisa had read in the *Sydney Morning Herald* after searching online, this app was doing extremely well. It was some kind of fun educational tool for toddlers, which had already netted him a fortune, by all accounts. Maybe that meant he'd outgrown her.

Lisa was musing on this when the doorbell rang. Oh dear, it must be Mike, she thought, her heart sinking. Who else would call round so late on a Friday night? He was probably so drunk that he'd lost his key. She took a deep breath, turned off the TV and went to answer the front door. Time to face the music.

14

2

He was in a small, box-like room without a window. The plastered walls and ceiling were cream: smooth, unmarked and with no fixtures or fittings. A powder-coated white metal door was the only way in or out.

Somehow the room was brightly lit, although this puzzled him, since he could see no obvious light source.

He was sitting at a table in the middle of the room, struggling to grasp how he'd got there or, indeed, where that was. He needed time alone to review his thoughts and memories in order to try and make sense of this. But the man sitting on the other side of the table in the smart black suit and tie, the sort you'd wear to a funeral, kept staring at him and talking.

'Are you in any discomfort?' the man asked in a northern English accent. He'd introduced himself earlier, hadn't he? So why couldn't he remember his name?

'Sorry, what was that you just asked me? I don't seem to be able to, um — '

'I was asking whether you're in any pain. Sometimes, when people have been through such a major trauma, there's a sort of residual . . . well, yes, discomfort. It usually passes pretty quickly.'

That word *pain* had thrown him; diverted his mind to unwanted memories. 'Sorry to be

15

weird,' he said after taking a moment to regroup his thoughts. 'I'm struggling to focus. Please could you repeat that once more?'

'Wait. Bear with me.' The man picked up a tablet-like device from the table and tapped something into it. He scrutinised the screen, which was directed so that only he could see it, rubbing his light stubble with one hand and nodding his head occasionally. When he looked up, he spoke slowly: 'You're disorientated, right? Finding it hard to concentrate?'

He nodded in reply.

'That can happen, but it should also pass quickly. We need something to ground you. Cup of tea?'

'Yes, please.'

The man promised to return soon, grabbed his tablet and left through the metal door.

Alone in the room, he found himself tapping his fingers on the table and staring at the floor, which was coated in a shiny grey material with a hard yet rubbery feel underfoot.

His eyes wandered to the metal legs of the oak-effect table and the two brown moulded-plastic seats. They reminded him of school furniture.

But this wasn't a classroom. It was . . . somewhere else, the implications of which made him fidgety. His right leg bounced up and down under the table as his mind whirred, fighting to get back up to speed.

3

THEN

Thursday, 8 August 1991

'I hate it here!' Lisa shouted, slamming the door behind her as she stormed out of the house and down the steep concrete driveway.

'Where are you going?' her mum's voice called from an upstairs window.

'Out,' she replied without turning back.

She was so angry with her parents right now, she could scream. How could they do this to her? How could they take her away from all her friends at such a crucial time in her life? How could they dump her here — in the middle of nowhere — a boring old village where she didn't know anyone? It was so unfair.

Lisa had no idea where she was heading. She just needed to get out of that place: the house that wasn't her home; the bedroom with the manky brown carpet and the awful bright green walls. It was this that had caused the latest row. Jamie, her annoying younger brother, had been winding her up by calling it the Bogey Room. Not once, of course, but over and over again.

'I could come in here,' he'd said, 'wipe my bogeys on the wall and you wouldn't even notice. Bogey Room, Bogey Room.'

That had been the culmination of a series of

taunts by Jamie, who liked nothing better than winding up his sister. Lisa, who'd been doing her utmost to ignore him as she read the latest issue of *Smash Hits* magazine, had finally lost her rag. She'd hurled one of her trainers at him, delivering a perfect clip round the ear. Next thing, he was running to their mum in tears and Lisa was the one in trouble.

'He's fine. It hardly even touched him. He's a big crybaby.'

'You should never throw things at your brother,' Mum had replied, taking his side as always, oblivious to the fact he was standing behind her, grinning and sticking his tongue out at his sister.

'Tell him to stop winding me up, then. Look, he's doing it right now. There's nothing wrong with him. He's disgusting. He was just saying that — '

'I don't want to hear it.'

'He's the one who keeps — '

'Enough. I'm run off my feet trying to unpack and the last thing I need is you two squabbling. Stay out of each other's way if you can't get along.'

'Fine.'

Only it wasn't, of course; when Jamie had reappeared at her door a few minutes later, whispering the same taunt about the green walls, she'd had to get as far away from him and his wind-ups as possible.

Now where to go? They'd only lived in Aldham for five days and, although it was August, the rain had been almost constant, so

18

she'd barely stepped outside. It was drizzling at present; she ought to have taken a jacket with her. But there was zero chance of her going back for one, so she carried on regardless.

Her dad had mentioned something about a lane that led away from all the houses and into the countryside. He'd pointed it out from the car yesterday, saying it was popular with dog walkers and there was a nice little stream. It seemed as good a place as any to go, so that was where Lisa headed. It was only a short walk from the house and, within a couple of minutes, she found herself on the rough, moss-laden tarmac of Victoria Street.

There were a couple of grand-looking houses at the start, with big gardens and winding drives, but after that the track narrowed to barely the width of a car, with nettles and other wild plants and bushes on either side, flanked by tall trees. These did at least provide some shelter from the rain, although they also made it rather gloomy and creepy.

She thought about turning back, but then a kind-faced, elderly woman appeared from around the corner. Dressed in wellies and a cagoule, she was walking in the opposite direction, a chocolate Labrador at her heels. 'Morning, love,' she said, a quiver in her voice, as the tubby dog waddled forward and sniffed at Lisa's jeans.

'Hello,' Lisa replied with a smile, although she continued walking and resisted stroking the dog, not feeling in the mood for having a chat with a stranger. The woman's presence spurred her on, nonetheless, partly by reassuring her that this was a safe place, but also because it would look weird if she turned around and retraced her steps.

As it happened, once Lisa turned the corner from where the pensioner had appeared, the lane became far less eerie. The trees thinned out, letting in the light and revealing an open field on one side and the stream her dad had mentioned on the other, with more fields beyond. The drizzle was easing off too, so Lisa was happy to keep on going.

She strode along for a hundred metres or so, breathing deeply in a bid to unwind, to try to forget about her irritating brother and the disaster of relocating to a new part of the country, cut off from all her friends.

That was easier said than done, though. Since the move, she'd barely thought of anything else other than how much she missed the gang. They'd all promised to write regularly. She'd even spoken briefly to Paula, her best friend, on the phone yesterday evening after Mum had agreed she could call to pass on the new number. But it wasn't the same. Plus Paula had been in a rush, which hadn't helped. She'd been about to leave for the cinema with Zara, a likely candidate for new best friend, leading Lisa to feel even more cut off than before.

They were all getting ready to start at the same secondary school in September — Oak Park, where Lisa had always expected to go too. They were probably all together right now, chatting and giggling on the swings in the park and pretending not to notice the boys showing off on their BMXs. Meanwhile, here she was. Why did Dad have to get a stupid new job that meant they had to move? And why so far away? It had taken ages for them to travel by car from Nottingham, where there was loads to do, to this isolated village north of Manchester. She might as well have been on the other side of the world. She'd been popular before. Now she was a no-mates loser with nothing better to do than go for a walk alone.

Thinking about the injustice of it all brought tears to her eyes. Meanwhile, she reached a poorly maintained stretch of the road and found herself having to dodge an increasing number of rain-filled potholes and mud patches. Still she continued until, misjudging one particular spot, her trainer-clad right foot ended up ankle-deep in cold, mucky water.

'Yuck!' she shouted, lurching forward only to lose her balance, slip and fall flat on her bum in the mud.

It was too much. Rather than getting up, Lisa slumped where she was on the ground and started sobbing. She let out all her frustrations in one almighty wail and the tears gushed like waterfalls down her cheeks.

Eventually the moment passed and, coming to her senses, Lisa realised how ridiculous she must look. Keen to avoid anyone finding her in this state, she levered herself up and assessed the damage. Okay, her jeans, shoes and socks were filthy and wet; she'd probably also collected a few bruises. But despite her over-the-top reaction, it clearly wasn't the end of the world. Thank goodness there was no one around to see, she thought, when a voice cut through the silence.

'Ouch!'

The sound, which came from nearby, gave Lisa a fright. 'Who's there?' she snapped, scanning her surroundings but seeing no one in either direction on the lane, nor in any of the surrounding fields.

'Hello?' she said in the most confident voice she could muster. 'Can I help you?'

What a ridiculous thing to say, she thought, waiting for an answer that didn't come. She'd almost convinced herself that she'd imagined the sound, when there was movement and a loud rustling from a thick bush on the other side of the stream. Then: 'Ouch! Get off me.'

It was clear this time that the voice was high-pitched — a child's. To Lisa's ear, well-practised from seven years at primary school, it definitely sounded like a boy.

'I can see you there in the bush,' she said. 'What are you: some kind of peeping Tom, having a laugh at my expense? My dad's a policeman, you know. I'll report you to him, shall I? You won't be laughing then.'

'No, please don't,' the voice replied from the bush. 'I'm not spying on you or laughing.'

'Why are you hiding in that bush, then? Come out here and show yourself.'

There was a pause before the reply. 'I can't.'

'Fine. I'll go and get my dad.'

'No! Please, I'm begging you.'

Lisa was surprised how well her empty threat was working. She had no idea what this boy looked like, never mind his name or where he lived. And what were the odds of her being able to bring her dad back here in time to catch him? Whoever he was, he obviously wasn't very bright. How else could you explain it?

'Show yourself,' she said. 'Final warning.'

'Okay, okay. Give me a second.'

There was some more rustling, another 'ouch' and then a beetroot head appeared, peering out from one side of the bush, mole eyes beneath a shock of dark curly hair.

'There you are,' Lisa said to the boy, who looked a little younger than her eleven years. 'That wasn't so difficult, was it? So why don't you come properly out, then?'

He shook his head vigorously, causing his chubby cheeks to wobble from side to side. 'I can't, seriously. Please don't make me.'

'Don't be ridiculous. Of course you can. What — '

'I'm not wearing any clothes, okay,' he blurted out, his face turning an even deeper shade of red. 'They stole them — and my glasses. I can barely even see you, whoever you are.'

Lisa couldn't believe what she was hearing — and yet she knew without doubt that this boy was telling the truth. The pain in his voice was all too real. Then there was the look of misery and shame on his face. The look of a victim. Suddenly everything had changed.

'I'm sorry,' she said. 'I had no idea. Who did this to you?'

23

'Some boys from my class at school. They invited me out to play with them. I thought they were being nice at last. I should have known better.'

'So have they left you totally, um, naked?' Lisa asked, feeling her own cheeks burning.

'I'm in my pants and socks,' he replied.

Lisa let out a quiet sigh of relief. 'Any idea what they did with the rest of your stuff?'

He shook his head. 'Not a clue.'

'Why were you crying out before? It sounded like you were in pain.'

'I was. I still am. There are some nettles back here that I stung my legs on, and quite a few creepy-crawlies.'

'Oh dear.'

'It's my glasses I'm most bothered about. My mum will kill me when she finds out. I only just got them. They were a gift for finishing primary school.'

This got Lisa's attention. 'Wait. Do you start secondary school next month?'

'Yes.'

'You must be eleven like me. I'm Lisa, by the way. What's your name?'

'Elliot.'

'Nice to meet you, Elliot. I'm new in the village.'

'Oh, are you the girl who's moved into Christopher's house?'

'I think that was the name of the boy who lived there before us. Did you know him?'

'Yes. He was my best friend.'

Lisa wasn't sure how to reply. She almost felt

like apologising, but of course that would be ridiculous. It was hardly her fault. She'd never have moved here in the first place, if she'd had her way. She felt sorry for Elliot, though. The pickle he was in put her wet jeans and trainer into context. She decided to help him.

'Okay, Elliot. What can I do to get you out of here?'

A few minutes later she arrived back home, panting after running all the way. She burst through the front door without saying a word and headed straight for her bedroom.

'Lisa, is that you?' her mum called from downstairs.

'Yes,' she shouted back. 'I forgot something. I'll be heading out again in a second.'

She rummaged through her clothes, many of which were still in boxes, looking for something suitable. Elliot was shorter than her, from what she'd been able to make out, but he also looked a bit plump and boys usually had larger feet than girls. Eventually she came across a large yellow T-shirt, which Mum had bought her to wear as a nightie, plus a baggy pair of grey jogging bottoms. They'll do, she thought, throwing them into a rucksack along with a big pair of hand-me-down flip-flops she'd received from a cousin but never worn.

'Why don't you take your brother out with you?' Mum called. 'He could do with some fresh air.'

'I don't think so,' Lisa said under her breath. She grabbed the bag and raced past the closed door of Jamie's bedroom, heading downstairs before he had the chance to emerge.

'Bye!' she shouted as she passed the kitchen, where Mum was on her hands and knees loading something into the back of a large corner cupboard. She thought she heard her say something in reply but pretended not to, continuing on her way.

Shortly afterwards, having passed another couple of dog walkers going the other way, Lisa returned to the spot where she'd left Elliot hiding. 'I'm back,' she said. 'I'll find somewhere to jump across the stream, shall I? Then I can give you these clothes.'

Elliot's head reappeared, eyes wide with terror at the suggestion. 'No, don't do that. Can't you throw them over to me?'

Imagining herself in the same situation, Lisa understood why Elliot didn't want her to see him virtually naked. 'Yes, that's fine,' she replied. Removing the rucksack from her shoulders, she moved to the very edge of the stream and tried a few practice swings in the right direction. 'Right, I think I can make it. I'm going to aim straight for the middle of the bush. On three, okay? One . . . two . . . three.'

She threw the bag as best as she could, getting it across the water at least, but not as far as Elliot. It caught in the low-hanging branch of a nearby tree, a metre or so in front of the bush where he was hiding.

'Sorry,' she said as Elliot's face sank. 'That didn't go to plan. I can come over there and grab it, if you like.'

'No, I'll get it.' He paused before adding: 'But

would you mind looking the other way?'

This amused Lisa. At primary school, when they'd had to change for PE or games in the classroom, the boys had usually been happy parading around in their underwear. It was the girls who tended to be more self-conscious. 'No problem,' she replied. 'I'm turning around now.'

Lisa noted how peaceful it was down the lane as the noise of every movement Elliot made carried across the stream. By the sound of things, not least his various grunts and groans, he seemed to be struggling to pull the bag free. She was about to ask if he needed a hand when he shouted, 'got it.'

'Great. Can I turn around again?'

'Yes.'

He was back behind the bush when she did so, but a few moments later, he emerged with a look on his face somewhere between sheepish and relieved. He looked odd in the T-shirt and joggers, both of which were tight width-wise but too long in length.

She threw him a smile. 'Do they fit okay? They were the best I could find at short notice.'

'They're fine, thanks.' Elliot stepped forward in the flip-flops, which actually looked about the right size, and then almost tripped over one of the oversized legs of the jogging bottoms, barely managing to steady himself on a tree trunk. 'Oops.'

'Careful,' Lisa warned. 'Maybe you ought to roll up the legs a little.'

'Good idea,' he replied, bending forward to

follow her suggestion. 'I'm really not very good without my specs.'

He wasn't exaggerating about this, as Lisa discovered when she had to take back the rucksack and help him across the stream. Then they made their way back to the village.

'What do you want to do about getting your things back?' Lisa asked as they neared the start of the lane.

Elliot shrugged. 'Nothing, I guess. What can I do? They're gone now.'

'But your glasses.'

'I'll have to wear my old ones again and tell Mum I lost them.'

'Why not tell her the truth? She could contact the parents of these boys. Then they'd have to return them.'

'You're kidding, right? Then I'd be a telltale, which would only make things worse. It's not like I can prove what they've done. It's their word against mine. And there were three of them. I wouldn't want to worry my mum, anyway.'

He stopped walking, took hold of Lisa's arm and looked her in the eye. 'You're not going to tell your dad, are you? Please don't. I'd be dead meat.'

'No, of course I won't.' She grimaced. 'He's, um, not actually a policeman. I kind of made that up. Sorry.'

She expected Elliot to be angry with her about this, but instead he started to laugh, making his deep blue eyes sparkle. 'Really? Wow, I can't believe I fell for that. I'm so gullible.'

Lisa smiled. 'It's understandable. You did have other things on your mind at the time, what with being almost naked and all. I shouldn't have lied to you.'

'That's okay. You rescued me, which more than makes up for it.'

'True.' She looked over at Elliot, in her poorly fitting clothes and flip-flops; then down at herself, wet and caked in mud, and it was her turn to laugh.

'What?'

'I was thinking how ridiculous we both look, that's all.'

Her words set Elliot off again, in a fit of giggles this time, and the way he laughed — which reminded Lisa of a seal — was so contagious that soon she too couldn't stop.

She lost track of how long they stood there chuckling next to the Victoria Street sign. Several adults walked past in that time and the odd looks they gave the pair only served to make them laugh even more.

Eventually, Elliot announced that he ought to get home. 'Is it okay if I return your things tomorrow? I could bring them round to your house in the morning, if you like.'

'Um, sure,' Lisa replied.

'Cool.'

'Not as posh as you'd think, is it, this place?'

'What do you mean?'

Lisa nodded towards the sign. 'Victoria Street. It's a very grand-sounding name.'

'Oh, right. Yeah, no one actually uses that. Everyone calls it Vicky Lane.'

'Really?'

'Yep. Anyway, I'll see you tomorrow.'

'Wait. Before you go, you are all right, aren't you? You know, after everything that happened.'

'I'm fine, thanks to you. I owe you one.'

'I was glad to help.'

Lisa could tell that Elliot was itching to leave, no doubt keen to get some of his own clothes back on, so she said goodbye and they headed off in opposite directions.

He seemed a bit odd, she thought. Certainly not a typical boy of her age. But that wasn't necessarily a bad thing, and the laughing together at the end had been good fun.

Maybe they could be friends.

4

When the man returned to the room, the lapel of his black jacket bore a pressed metal badge, which stated that his name was Will.

Of course. How had he forgotten that?

'Here you are,' Will said, handing over a large white mug of tea. 'Sorry I took a while. It's hot, so be careful.'

'Thank you.'

'Sugar?' Will asked, opening his palm to reveal some sachets.

'No, thanks.'

Will, who hadn't brought a drink for himself, seemed happy to watch him sip the tea in silence. Meanwhile, he scrutinised him with his blue eyes, occasionally running a hand through his thick grey hair. Only when the mug was half empty did Will ask him if he felt more clearheaded.

'Yes.' The tea really seemed to have helped. He'd even stopped tapping his fingers and bouncing his leg up and down.

'Good. You've probably got a few questions.'

And of course he did, starting with where he was and how he'd got there.

It was a huge amount to take in, even though some of it was as he'd suspected or remembered. It was devastating and yet also strangely calming. For if the worst thing imaginable had already happened, what else was there to fear?

The last thing he expected was to be presented with a proposal. His unique circumstances and the transitory nature of his current position meant he could help with something, Will explained at length.

'Is this for real?' he asked eventually, still absorbing the details. It involved a person who meant a great deal to him — who he'd love nothing more than to help — and an incredible, impossible chance to return to the world he'd thought lost forever only moments ago.

Will responded with a solemn nod. 'Yes, and so you know, it's a rare privilege that you're being offered here. But it will only be for a short time — probably a matter of days.'

'What do I have to do? How does it work exactly? How would I even get there?'

'Give me the word and I'll take care of the details.'

'It's that straightforward?'

'From your perspective, yes. The situation you'd face there is . . . complex, but we'd provide you with all the necessary information.'

A wave of nervous excitement washed over him. His bouncing leg started up again, vibrating the remaining tea in his mug, as he gave Will his answer. 'I'm in.'

5

NOW

Friday, 20 July 2018

Lisa approached the front door, expecting an immediate verbal assault from her husband. She was poised to drag him inside, if necessary, to avoid sharing their inevitable row with the whole neighbourhood. And she was well prepared to fight her corner: to take on his drunken logic in a bid to explain her extreme actions.

She must have cut a strange figure in her dressing gown and smudged make-up when she jerked open the door like a lioness primed to defend her cubs — only to find it wasn't Mike at all.

A good-looking man in smart jeans and a red polo shirt stared back at her, illuminated by the motion-sensor light on the front of the house. He appeared startled, although that was hardly surprising considering her sudden, violent entrance. 'Lisa?' he asked, his big, deep blue eyes scanning her up and down.

'Who's asking?'

The man, who looked vaguely familiar, gave her a playful grin, showing off a perfect set of white teeth. 'That would be telling, wouldn't it?'

This was an odd answer and he had a strange accent to match, which Lisa couldn't put her

33

finger on. There was definitely some local in there, but mixed in with something else. It reminded her of that mid-Atlantic twang that US-based British actors sometimes adopted. But that wasn't it either. Scandinavian? No, she didn't think so. She'd need to hear him speak some more to work it out.

Wherever he was from — and whatever he wanted — Lisa's immediate temptation was to give him short shrift, based on the fact it was late on a Friday night to be showing up unannounced. But seeing him standing there on her doorstep, all tanned and muscular with closely cropped dark hair and a chiselled jawline, she hesitated. Could he be someone she recognised off the TV? She found herself looking behind him for a cameraman, but if there was one, he was well hidden.

'You don't recognise me, do you?' he said. 'That's understandable. It's been a long time. I wasn't totally sure it was you straight away, what with the blonde hair and all, but now I see it. Those gorgeous hazel eyes of yours haven't changed one bit. Come on, Lisa, have a guess.'

Then the penny dropped and her hands flew to her mouth as she gasped. 'No, it can't be!'

'Yes, it can.'

'But I was just thinking about . . . '

'Go on.'

'Oh my God. Is that really you, El? You're so different.'

Her friend beamed a warm smile at her. 'Same old me on the inside. Now come here and give me a hug.' He held his arms wide open and, a

34

moment later, Lisa found herself lost in his warm embrace, her troubles temporarily forgotten as her mind flew back to the last time they'd been together.

★ ★ ★

Tears were streaming down her face, although she'd been determined not to cry any more. Elliot was tearful too and she knew from the tender look in his eyes how touched he was that she'd made the trip.

They'd done this already the night before. He'd called around at her house and stayed for tea one final time. They'd spent ages chatting in her bedroom, focusing as much as possible on the excitement of their respective futures, rather than the obvious negative of them being apart. And then suddenly — far too soon — it was time for him to go. They'd said goodbye then, amid the obvious hugs, kisses, tears and promises to keep in touch. But it hadn't been enough and, after an awful night of barely sleeping, Lisa had found herself knocking on her parent's door at 5.30 a.m., begging to borrow the car to drive to the airport.

'I need to see him one last time,' she'd bawled. 'I can't bear it if I don't.'

Her mum had taken pity on her. Not wanting Lisa to make the journey alone, as a new driver in an emotional state, Christine had agreed to take the wheel, despite her husband's tired groans that it was ridiculous. They'd made it in the nick of time, with an out-of-breath Lisa

35

catching up to Elliot right before he and his mother disappeared through security into the departures lounge.

'Is everything okay?' Elliot asked, his face a cocktail of surprise, confusion and affection.

'Don't worry,' Lisa said, looking at Wendy, his mother. 'I'm not here to try and change his mind, but I had to say goodbye one more time.'

And so she did. They only got a few extra minutes together, but Lisa didn't regret going there for an instant. Before Elliot finally left on his one-way trip to the other side of the globe, she wanted him to know exactly how important he was to her; how much she'd miss him being around.

'Don't forget me.' That was the last thing she'd whispered in his ear as their wet cheeks pressed together and Wendy's voice softly insisted that they really had to go.

'Never,' he replied. 'How could I forget the girl who saved my life?'

And then she watched her best friend leave.

★ ★ ★

How had twenty years passed since that moment? So much had happened in Lisa's life since then. But the astonishment of seeing Elliot now — feeling his arms around her again — washed away the passage of time, so it felt only a heart-beat ago.

'When did you get so big and strong, El?' she asked as she stood back from their embrace and looked him up and down, marvelling at how

36

different he appeared, not least without his trademark specs. 'But more importantly: what's going on? How are you here?'

He started to laugh in that way that had always reminded Lisa of a seal: a welcome sound from the past, and one thing about her old friend that didn't seem to have changed at all.

'What's funny?' she asked.

'That name,' he said, still chuckling. 'El. No one's ever called me that but you. It's funny to hear it after so long.'

Lisa blushed. 'You don't like it? You never said.'

'It's fine. Hearing you say anything is music to my ears after so long apart.' He rubbed his hands together and shook his head in an exaggerated shiver. 'So are you going to invite me inside, or what? You might call this summer, but it feels like midwinter out here to me.'

'Of course. Sorry, come on in. Do you have any luggage or — '

'Oh no, don't worry. I've got a room at The Grange.'

'Ooh, very swish,' Lisa replied.

Elliot grinned. 'It also happens to be the only hotel in the neighbourhood.'

He had a point. Aldham wasn't exactly a tourist hot spot and The Grange, a grand four-star hotel and golf course, was the sole option for several miles. Located in spacious grounds on the edge of the village, it specialised in business functions and weddings. Hardly a cheap option, and yet it was probably exactly the kind of place Elliot was used to staying

37

nowadays, in light of his financial success.

Although Lisa protested that he would have been welcome to stay at the house, she was secretly glad to hear this. The spare room was choc-a-bloc with accumulated junk and in no current state for visitors — especially ones she wanted to impress. Plus, there was the ticking time bomb of her husband to think about. His eventual arrival home would be bad enough without having to explain an unexpected male houseguest. Not least one who happened to be her childhood best friend and the kind of good-looking guy who no doubt had women falling at his feet.

Lisa couldn't get her head around El's physical transformation from a plump, self-conscious schoolboy to the hunky man here in her home. No wonder she hadn't recognised him straight away. The only recent photo she'd seen of him, thanks to her aversion to joining Facebook and so on, had been a headshot accompanying the *Sydney Morning Herald* article she'd found online last Christmas. That obviously hadn't been a very recent or flattering photo, because although some weight loss had been evident, the picture really hadn't done him justice.

Was this why she felt so self-conscious as she led him into her lounge? Or did that have more to do with the kind of beachside mansion she pictured when she imagined his home in Sydney? He'd gone places — literally and figuratively. Meanwhile here she was, following in her mother's unexciting footsteps as a primary school teacher and still living in Aldham. The house was actually smaller than the one she'd grown up in. It was nice enough: a simple four-bedroom detached from the late sixties. But through Elliot's eyes it probably looked poky and cluttered.

'Sorry it's a mess,' she said. 'But at least it matches me in my scruffy dressing gown. Do grab a seat while I nip upstairs to change.'

'Gosh, I've made you feel awkward, haven't I? I knew I shouldn't have turned up unannounced so late. I ought to have waited until tomorrow and then called ahead. But the truth is that once I got here, I couldn't wait.' Elliot scratched his head. 'The whole trip back to the UK was a last-minute thing.'

'No need to apologise,' Lisa replied, tidying up some of the various remote controls, pens, magazines and newspaper sections strewn across the lounge furniture. 'It's fantastic to see you.'

'Please don't clear up on my account, Lise. You should check out my study at home if you think this is untidy. Honestly, it would turn your stomach.'

'Oh, it's nothing that didn't need doing anyway. Right, make yourself comfortable and I'll be back in two ticks. Can I get you a drink on my way: tea, coffee, something stronger?'

'I'd love a glass of water when you're ready, but no rush.'

'Coming up.'

'Where's the rest of the family?'

'The kids are out for the night, staying with friends; Mike should be back later.'

Lisa raced up to her bedroom. She scowled at her unruly reflection in the mirror: her messed-up hairstyle and exposed roots; her dumpy figure and pale, blotchy skin. Wishing this hadn't been Elliot's first impression of her, she eyed her black dress. It was still lying on the bed where she'd discarded it earlier. She considered putting it back on, only to accept that doing so would look even stranger than running upstairs to change. So instead she pulled on the light-blue linen trousers she'd worn to work, adding a fresh white T-shirt. After completing a brisk repair job on her make-up, she was on her way back downstairs when the doorbell sounded.

Shit. This time it had to be Mike for real.

She considered darting to the lounge to give El a heads up before letting Mike in, but then the bell rang again. Dammit. This was going to get messy. Heart in mouth, she swung open the door, only to find herself facing another man who wasn't her husband. What the hell?

'Can I help you?'

'I bloody hope so,' the man replied. He looked to be in his early forties, casually dressed, curly grey hair, stocky with a beer gut. 'Is this where Michael Adams lives?'

His brusque tone put Lisa on the defensive. 'Who's asking?'

'The knackered cabbie who foolishly agreed to bring him home.'

'What? Where is he?' Lisa asked, looking behind her latest visitor and seeing for the first time a black cab parked in front of the drive.

'He's sprawled out in the back, pissed up;

40

dead to the world. I can't shift him. Are you his missus?'

Lisa nodded.

'Here, take this.' The taxi driver handed her Mike's wallet. 'I had to get it out of his pocket so I could find out where he lived. Luckily, his driving licence is in there. And don't be thinking I've robbed anything. Some folk would. They'd have probably dumped his drunken arse at the side of the road too, but that's not me.'

'How much is the fare?' she asked, looking at the two ten pound notes still in the wallet and wondering if that would be enough.

'That's already sorted, love. I got him to pay upfront, seeing the state he was in. He was at least still conscious then. Are you going to help me get him out? If he spews in there, that'll cost you.'

Lisa heard footsteps behind her and turned to see Elliot in the hallway. 'Everything all right?' he said. 'Sorry, I couldn't help but overhear the conversation. Why don't I give this bloke a hand, instead of you? It sounds like heavy work.'

Putting her embarrassment aside, Lisa accepted his kind offer. It was at least better than the prospect of injuring her back by hauling Mike's boozy bulk out of the taxi.

After wrestling him off the back seat, the two men carried his lifeless form between them, one arm around each of their necks. He didn't even open his eyes. They were good enough to take him all the way inside and up the stairs to their bedroom, leaving him on the bed in something approximating the recovery position.

41

Lisa offered the cabbie an extra ten pounds for his trouble. He declined but she insisted.

'I'm so sorry about this, El,' she said once they were alone again.

'No worries. These things happen.' He asked if she'd rather he went back to his hotel, but she told him to stay. They hadn't had a chance to talk yet.

'Let me check on him and then I promise I really will be back with your drink of water. Unless you want something alcoholic. I could do with a nightcap.'

'Go on then. Whatever you're having, but I'll still take the water too, please.'

'Coming right up.'

In the bedroom, Lisa tried again to speak to her husband but got no response. Goodness knows how much more he'd had to drink after she'd left. She could smell the booze oozing out of his every pore. Oh well. As embarrassing as his arrival had been, at least their inevitable row had been delayed until morning. Hopefully they'd both be in a better mental state to deal with it then.

She'd also managed to avoid the potential car crash of the two men meeting for the first time when Mike was drunk and angry. She pulled off his trousers and socks but, despite her best efforts, was unable to remove his shirt. The idea had been to pop it straight in the wash, in a bid to shift the huge red wine stain on the front. But it had dried now and Lisa suspected there was little chance of removing it whatever she did.

Mike stirred, muttered something incomprehensible and then farted, which Lisa took as her cue to leave, tiptoeing out of the room and pulling the door to.

In the kitchen she filled Elliot's water from the tap and poured them both a large Baileys over ice. She took a deep breath and carried the drinks through to the lounge. Elliot was sitting on the couch, legs crossed, reading a computer magazine that belonged to her son, Ben.

'Here I am, at last,' she said, leaning over to place the drinks on the coffee table. 'I hope Baileys is okay.'

Elliot put down the magazine and smiled. 'Perfect, thanks. Everything all right?'

'With Mike, you mean? I think so. He's fast asleep. I'll check on him in a bit, but I'm sure he'll be fine. I suspect he might have a hangover in the morning. You're probably wondering what happened.'

Elliot held up his hands. 'Hey, everyone needs to get off their face once in a while, I reckon. Looks like he did it in style.'

'You can say that again.'

'Listen, if you want to talk about it, here I am. If not, no worries. I'd say we've got plenty of other stuff to catch up on.'

Lisa didn't feel like going into it now. What had happened between her and Mike tonight was far too complicated to explain in a quick conversation. It was the latest in a long line of problems; not a can of worms she wanted to open at the moment. She'd already blown it in terms of making a good first impression of the life she'd built over the last two decades. So instead she turned the conversation back on Elliot.

'Well, that's true,' she said. 'Such as what finally brought you back home for the first time in all these years. Are you here on your own, actually, or —'

'Are you trying to ask if I've got a girlfriend?' Elliot said, straight-faced, before bursting into a big grin. 'No, I don't. And yes, I'm here alone.'

To her annoyance, Lisa could feel her cheeks flushing, but she tried to ignore it, taking a sip of her drink before replying. 'I was actually thinking more about your mother. I thought she might also want to catch up with old friends and so on. How is Wendy? Still as gorgeous and glamorous as ever, I bet.'

Elliot grinned. 'Mum's good, thanks. And yes, time's been kind to her. She probably would have liked to come, but as I say, it was all very last minute. Boring business stuff, but at least it means we get a chance to catch up after so long.'

It seemed odd to Lisa that he would have business here — or even in Manchester, as opposed to London — but Elliot didn't seem especially keen to talk about that or his success in general. Despite several probing questions on her part, Lisa discovered very little, other than the fact that he was single with no kids and he wasn't sure how long his trip would last. It was almost like he had something to hide, or at least that he wasn't telling her everything. He seemed far more eager to talk about her life: how her job was going, for instance, and what Mike and the children were like. He was especially interested in Ben and Chloe, which she found surprising for someone without children of their own.

'So Ben's sixteen now?' he asked.

'Almost. His birthday's next month. That was his magazine you were reading, actually. He's very into computers and technology. He'll probably be in awe of you when you meet. I'm sure he'd love to have a job like yours one day.'

'Really? That's cool. And what about Chloe? What age is she?'

'Twelve. She's just finished her first year at secondary school.'

'So not much older than we were when we first met. That's the two of them in the photo on the mantelpiece, right? Wow, look at those lovely light green eyes of hers. What a striking colour. She looks an awful lot like you did at that age.'

'Don't tell her that, El. No girl wants to look like her mother.'

'Ben's a lot like his dad too, isn't he?' He laughed. 'It's like you've both got your own mini-me.'

Lisa giggled.

'Where do they go to school? Are they at King George's and Queen Anne's, like we were?'

'You're kidding, right? Like we could afford those fees! Did you hear that the two schools have merged now, by the way, so boys and girls are together? Queen Anne's has recently been converted into apartments and everything's based on the King George's site. They're calling it The Royal School, Westwich.'

'Seriously? No I hadn't heard that. Strewth.

So where do your two go, then: Waterside?'

'That's right. It's a very good school.'

'Hey, I'm no private school snob. I'm sure it's great. Plus they're following in the footsteps of their uncle.'

'That's right.'

'How is Jamie? Still local?'

'Good. Yes, he lives in the village.'

'Any family?'

'Two young daughters: Hannah, who's seven, and Emily, who's five. He's not with their mum any more, but they share custody.'

'What does he do?'

'He works in sales, for a chemical manufacturer. It keeps him out of trouble. You must see him while you're here. He'd love that.'

'Definitely. What about your mum? Does she still live in the old house?'

'She's fine. Still in Aldham; still teaching part-time. But no, she moved to a smaller place after Dad died. She's away on a coach trip around Eastern Europe at the moment.'

Despite Elliot's apparent reluctance to talk much about himself, Lisa really enjoyed their conversation. It flowed easily between them, as it always had when they were younger, which was great after so long apart.

And yet she still couldn't get over how much her friend had changed. After they'd said goodnight and he'd headed back to his hotel, promising to return the next day to meet her family, Lisa found herself thinking about this as she struggled to get to sleep next to a snoring Mike.

For one thing there was the voice: the strange accent she hadn't been able to place when she'd first answered the door. He didn't exactly sound Australian or English, but rather a hybrid of the two, occasionally more one than the other. It amused her how he often ended sentences with a raised pitch in his voice, as if asking a question when he wasn't, which she'd heard Australians do before. She wondered if this would change while he was here and, surrounded by his old countryfolk, whether he'd slip back into how he used to sound.

Physically, although she could now recognise her old friend from his facial features and the way he smiled, he was almost like a different person. He could easily walk past old acquaintances in the village without them realising. Part of that was the fact he'd got himself into shape and no longer wore the glasses he'd had to live in as a boy. (He'd had laser surgery, apparently, so no longer needed them.)

But it was also down to the way he held himself: so self-assured. When they were younger, he'd always been very chatty with her and other people he knew well, but he could be painfully shy around strangers. However, there hadn't been any sign of that around the taxi driver, or even with her, as there might have been after so long apart.

He had the confidence of someone successful, Lisa decided. So why hadn't he wanted to talk about any of that, or to elaborate on the details of his last-minute business trip?

Maybe she was the reason. Since she'd

obviously done so little of note with her life and was married to the kind of man who came home unconscious in a taxi on a Friday night, perhaps he was too embarrassed to discuss his own exciting world, not wanting to rub salt in her wounds. She really hoped that wasn't true.

It was on this depressing note that the tiredness lurking in the shadows finally took hold and Lisa drifted off to sleep.

6

THEN

Friday, 9 August 1991

Elliot had butterflies in his stomach as he opened the low wrought-iron gate at the top of the driveway. He half expected Boris, his best mate Christopher's pet Jack Russell, to fly around the corner from the back garden to greet him with barks and licks. But of course he didn't, because they no longer lived here. They'd moved away. Now this house, which he'd visited countless times before, belonged to a different family. Weird.

Walking into the unknown in a familiar setting was part of the reason he was nervous. There was also the fact that the new occupant he'd come to visit was Lisa. He'd yet to see her close up with his glasses on, but he was pretty sure she was gorgeous: the kind of girl he wouldn't usually dare to approach. He'd thought of little else since she'd rescued him yesterday.

Elliot pushed his old glasses up on his nose, wishing they fitted as well as the new ones he no longer had. He reached up and rapped three times on the shiny brass knocker. He remembered Christopher's dad replacing it and repainting the white door. 'It's the little things that help sell houses,' he'd told Elliot, who'd

49

hoped his efforts would fail, so his friend could stay.

Rather than Lisa, the door was answered by a slim woman around his mum's age with long and luscious wavy red hair, hazel eyes and a warm smile.

'Hello. Can I help you?'

'Um, yes. I'm here to see Lisa. We met yesterday. My name's Elliot Turner.'

He offered her his right hand, having swung his left — holding a plastic bag containing Lisa's clothes and flip-flops — behind his back.

'Nice to meet you, Elliot,' she replied, graciously accepting his handshake. 'I'm Mrs Benson, Lisa's mother. I didn't know that she'd already made a friend. How nice. Do you also live in the village?'

He nodded as Lisa appeared in the hallway behind her.

'Thanks, Mum,' Lisa said. 'I'll take it from here.'

'Of course,' Mrs Benson replied, backing away. 'But don't leave your new friend on the doorstep. I'm sure he'd like to come in, wouldn't you, Elliot? The house is a mess, but — '

'Muuum!'

Mrs Benson held up her hands. 'Sorry, I'm cramping your style, aren't I? I'll make myself scarce.' She disappeared into the kitchen.

Elliot handed the plastic bag through the open door to Lisa, glad to see her in focus this time, looking amazing. Tall and slim, dressed in denim shorts and a pink T-shirt, she had the same beautiful hazel eyes as her mum but with long, straight auburn hair. Way out of his league. 'Your things, as promised.'

'Great, thanks.' She lowered her voice. 'Sorry about Mum. Would you like to come in?'

'Sure, if that's okay.'

'Of course. Anything to get me away from unpacking.'

It was strange walking through Christopher's old home, seeing how much everything had already changed. Thanks to the different furniture and so on, it was like entering another house.

As he followed Lisa up the stairs, he wondered whether or not she'd moved into Christopher's old bedroom, where he'd spent so much time. It turned out she had — and that was the weirdest thing of all. Gone were the *Star Wars* posters and memorabilia; the stack of comics and books; the noticeboard covered in photos from the school trip to London; Herbie the giant gorilla won on a coconut shy. In their place were Madonna and Prince posters; a pink radio-cassette player; a large pile of *Smash Hits* and *Jackie* magazines; and a dressing table covered with brushes, combs, hairclips and beauty products.

'So this is my room,' Lisa said, leading him inside and dropping the bag of her returned items in a corner. 'It's obviously not finished yet. A lot of my stuff is still in boxes. I can't wait to get this old carpet changed and to have the awful green walls painted, but . . . what's up?'

'Sorry?'

'You look like you've seen a ghost.'

'No, I, um — '

She held a hand up to her mouth. 'Oops. I totally forgot that your friend used to live here. This used to be his bedroom, didn't it?'

Elliot nodded.

'Wow. That must be weird. Were you here a lot?'

'Loads.'

'Was he the one responsible for the lovely green walls?'

Elliot threw her a wonky grin. 'Yep. He used to be mad keen on the Incredible Hulk.'

'That explains a lot. I nearly let my little brother have this room, even though it's the biggest, because of the awful colour. Now he insists on calling it the Bogey Room to wind me up.'

Elliot, who had stopped noticing the garish colour long ago, couldn't help but laugh. 'I suppose it's not the best colour in the world, is it? It seemed like a good idea to Christopher at the time, although in his defence, it was a few years ago. What colour will you change it to?'

'I'm not sure, but Mum and Dad have promised they'll get a decorator in soon.' She sat down on her bed, the duvet cover all pink and white stripes, and pointed towards a cream beanbag on the floor near the window. 'Have a seat.'

'Cool,' Elliot said, glad of an alternative to standing awkwardly in the middle of the room. 'So you didn't tell your mum about yesterday?'

Lisa shook her head, reaching into a pocket of her shorts, pulling out a bobble and tying back her long hair. 'I thought it best not to say anything, since you said you didn't want to tell your parents.'

'Yeah, there's only my mum, actually. My dad died when I was little.'

'Oh, I'm sorry.'

'That's okay.'

'What was his name?'

'Gary.'

She nodded. 'How old were you when it happened?'

'Four.' Elliot was impressed. Most kids got embarrassed when they found out and changed the subject.

'No way. What happened?'

'He was killed in a motorbike crash.'

'How awful. Do you remember it?'

'A bit. But it's more what happened afterwards: people visiting a lot; Mum crying all the time. Suddenly everything was so different.'

'Sorry, do you mind me asking this stuff? You don't have to answer if you don't want to. I'm so nosey sometimes — and we barely know each other. Mum reckons I'll be a journalist when I grow up.'

Elliot laughed. 'I don't mind. It's nice to talk about him sometimes. It makes him seem more real. The truth is I don't have many memories, because I was so young. Most of what I know about him is stuff Mum's told me.'

'Do you have any brothers and sisters?'

'No, it's just the two of us. That's probably the reason she worries about me a lot, which is why I don't tell her everything.'

53

'Did she believe you about losing your glasses?'

Elliot wrinkled his nose. 'Yes, but she was mad. She made me turn my bedroom upside down, looking for them.'

'Your old ones don't look so bad.'

'Well, apart from the paperclip holding the right arm in place and the fact that they're always slipping down my nose. So you have a brother?'

'Yes, Jamie.' She sighed, shaking her head. 'He's eight — and incredibly annoying. He's not here at the moment. Dad's off work today; they've gone to the DIY shop.'

'Your dad the fake policeman?'

Lisa blushed. 'That's him.'

'What does he really do?'

'He sells BMWs. He's been promoted to manage his own dealership. That's why we moved here.'

'Cool. What about your mum?'

'She's a primary school teacher.'

Elliot nodded. 'Mine's a nurse. So you didn't want to move?'

'No, it's a nightmare.'

Lisa explained how they came from Nottingham, where she'd lived in the same house right through primary school. Her parents had sprung this on her during her final year and, before she knew it, the move to Aldham was upon them. She hadn't wanted to leave her friends behind; now she was dreading starting secondary school not knowing anyone. 'To make matters worse, it's a private girls' school,' she said. 'Mum and

54

Dad made me do this entrance exam. It's not even that close. I'll have to get a bus.'

Elliot sat up on the beanbag. 'Hang on. It's not Queen Anne's, is it?'

'That's right.' Lisa said, raising an eyebrow. 'In Westwich. How did you guess?'

'Because I'm going to King George's, the boys' school next door. We'll be on the same bus.'

★ ★ ★

A little later, Elliot grinned down at Lisa from the treetop. 'I told you it would be fun.'

She was perched a few branches lower down the ancient oak. He could tell she was enjoying herself from the exhilarated look on her face whenever she stared up at him, but she seemed like she was concentrating too hard to say much.

'You've really never done this before?' he asked.

'Nope.'

'Well, I think you might be a natural tree climber, in that case. Don't stop there, though. There's room for both of us up here. Come on, the view is excellent.'

Elliot loved climbing this tree. It was in a large field behind his house. He'd been doing so for years and could scale the branches in no time. He so enjoyed being up here among the leaves, watching the world below. It rarely failed to put into perspective whatever troubles he had in his day-to-day life. Even the biggest, meanest bullies looked tiny from such a height.

Earlier, when the two of them were chatting in Lisa's bedroom, she'd complained that there was nothing to do in Aldham compared to the urban life she used to lead. Elliot, who'd hardly spent any time in the city apart from the odd boring shopping trip with his mum, had only ever known life in this quiet village surrounded by hills and countryside. And he'd always found plenty to keep himself occupied. He and Christopher had never been bored, thanks to their bicycles, two overactive imaginations and more nature-packed open spaces than they knew what to do with. So when he looked at Lisa like she was crazy and she challenged him to prove his point, bringing her to this huge tree had been the obvious next step.

'Are you sure that branch is strong enough to hold us both?' Lisa asked as she edged her way upwards.

'Definitely. I've been up here loads of times with Christopher and he's taller than you. We used to call it the crow's nest when we were younger, like the lookout point on a boat. We'd pretend to be out at sea, checking to make sure there were no pirates on the horizon.'

'Okay, here goes.' She took a deep breath and then, arms quivering, she climbed the final few metres, following her new friend's instructions on the best route to take. Her left foot slipped at one point, causing her to let out a little scream, but Elliot reached down to steady her, offering calming words. Soon she sat down next to him, one leg on either side of the branch, and let out a long sigh of relief. 'Done it. Wow.

That was a bit scary.'

Elliot winked. 'You did brilliantly, especially considering the lack of trees in Nottingham. Did they cut them all down after Robin Hood, then?'

This made Lisa giggle.

'Now you know what you were missing out on. Look, you can see both of our houses from here.' Elliot pointed to give Lisa her bearings.

'Oh yeah. Hey, look: you can see my mum in the kitchen. Gosh, I hope she doesn't spot us. She'd have a heart attack. Does your mum know that you come up here?'

Elliot nodded. 'She used to panic and tell me not to, but I've been doing it so long now that she doesn't think anything of it any more.'

'It is a bit dangerous.'

'Only if you fall, which we're not going to.'

'I guess.'

Elliot felt happier than he had in ages: more than he'd ever thought possible in light of Christopher moving away. It was great to be up here with a new friend and, after needing her help yesterday, he was glad to be the one in charge now — the guide.

Elliot definitely fancied Lisa. Who wouldn't? Not that he expected her to be interested in someone like him: short and fat with glasses. There were lots of better-looking boys. That was one reason why he'd never had a girlfriend. But he liked spending time with Lisa — and it was more than her looks. He'd happily settle for being her friend, he decided.

The way she looked and her confidence reminded him of the popular girls from his class

57

at Aldham Primary, who'd all either ignored him or laughed when the popular boys had made fun of him. Perhaps that was what Lisa had been like in Nottingham. Maybe she'd only stay friends with him until someone better came along.

And yet Elliot had a feeling that Lisa wouldn't ever behave that way. Look at what she'd done for him yesterday: the effort she'd made to rescue a stranger. And it was so nice the way she'd asked him about his dad earlier when most people would have been too embarrassed to continue. He couldn't imagine any of the popular girls he knew climbing this tree. No, he hoped that she was different and they could keep hanging out together this summer. He was really glad they'd be going to neighbouring schools in September.

'Hey, look,' Lisa said, snapping him out of his thoughts. 'Two kids are over there in the field. I think they're coming this way.'

Elliot followed her gaze and his heart sank. Why, of all people, did it have to be them?

'We'd better go,' he said.

'What? I've only just got up here. I don't think I'm ready to — '

'Please? I really don't want them to see me.'

'Those kids? Why not?'

'I'll explain in a minute. Let's get down to the ground first.' Elliot had already started descending the tree. The last thing he wanted was to leave Lisa behind, but he needed her to grasp the sense of urgency.

'Wait for me,' she said, panic raising the pitch of her voice.

Elliot did his best to reassure her. 'I will. I'm not going to leave you, but we don't have long. Do the opposite of what you did on the way up, okay? Otherwise, copy me.'

'I can't see you to do that,' she replied. 'Slow down.'

Reaching one of the larger branches, he stopped to check on her progress. Thankfully, she wasn't as far behind as he'd feared. 'That's it. You're doing a great job. I'll wait here, so we can do the last bit together.'

'Thanks.'

Elliot looked over to where Lisa had spotted the kids. 'Dammit,' he said under his breath. They were heading this way and making speedy progress.

'There you are,' Lisa said, joining him at last on the large branch. 'What on earth is the — '

'Please, not now. You first; I'll follow.'

'Oh, I get it. It's them, isn't it? The ones who took your stuff yesterday.'

Elliot sighed. 'Fine, yes it is. Can we go now?'

'I can't believe I didn't guess straight away.'

'Please, Lisa. They'll be here any minute.'

'Why are you running away from them?'

'Do you really need to ask that? You saw what they did to me yesterday.'

'Yes, but I wasn't with you then. And now we have a chance to get back your stuff.'

Elliot couldn't believe what he was hearing. Lisa was crazy if she thought she could make any difference to the situation. The boys heading this way were Johnny and Carl, two of the three who'd stitched him up yesterday — and the

59

worst two at that. The biggest, toughest lads in his year, they'd been in his class right through primary school and he couldn't remember a time when they'd not picked on him, usually for being fat or clever. They loved to dole out 'punishments' like nipple twisters and wedgies. Nothing original — they weren't bright enough for that — which explained why they also used to find it so hilarious to say that he and Christopher were gay.

The only reason he'd gone along with them yesterday — foolishly buying their claims of wanting to bury the hatchet ahead of secondary school — had been because they were with Peter. Another Aldham Primary classmate, he and Elliot had been good friends in their infant years, often visiting each other's houses. They'd grown apart as they got older, developing different friends and interests, but Peter had never been nasty to him. He'd not been especially friendly with Johnny and Carl either. So seeing him with them had been a surprise and, feeling lonely in Christopher's absence, Elliot had decided to take a leap of faith and go with them. Big mistake.

★   ★   ★

Johnny and Carl were the ones who actually stripped him, who jeered at how he looked in his underwear, joking that he needed a bra for his 'boobies'. Peter stood to one side, looking awkward. But he didn't do anything to stop them. He didn't say a word. Then Johnny turned to him and asked why he wasn't getting involved, suggesting it was because he and Elliot used to be 'bum chums'. That was when Peter stepped forward and pulled Elliot's glasses off his face.

'Don't, Peter,' he pleaded. 'Please. They're new. You know I can't see a thing without them.'

But his former friend didn't listen. Instead he dropped the glasses on the floor, stamped on them countless times and then threw them into the distance. In his semi-blinded state, Elliot didn't have a clue where they ended up. What would be the point in looking, anyway? Peter had wrecked them.

Johnny and Carl seemed as impressed by Peter's actions as Elliot was aggrieved. The three of them left together, as thick as thieves, which was exactly what they were, since they took Elliot's clothes and shoes with them.

Once he was sure they'd gone, Elliot allowed himself to cry. He wept big fat tears. And then he pulled himself together, hid behind a bush and waited for help to come, as it eventually did in the form of Lisa. His one small consolation was that he hadn't broken down in front of the boys. He'd come close, but the shock of Peter's betrayal had actually hardened his resolve not to give them the satisfaction.

* * *

'I said that now we have a chance to get back your stuff,' Lisa repeated. Her voice returned Elliot to the present, away from yesterday's painful memory, still red raw in his mind. 'How

61

about instead of running away, we try something else?'

'I don't think that's — '

'Hey, you two!' Lisa shouted before he could stop her.

'What are you doing?' Elliot growled.

She winked. 'Trust me.' Then she stood tall on the branch and waved vigorously in Johnny and Carl's direction, shouting: 'Up here!' When they eventually twigged where the voice was coming from, she continued: 'Stay there, please. I need to speak to you urgently. Well, my father does. He's a police inspector. We've recently moved to the village and he's very unhappy about what happened to Elliot yesterday. You two will be in big trouble if he catches up with you.'

Soon, as Elliot looked on in utter bewilderment, she was asking which of them was the faster runner. Johnny said it was Carl and his friend nodded in agreement.

'Right. How about this, then?' she said. 'I'll race Carl across the field and back and, if he wins, I'll let you off the hook. It was me who told my dad it was you. Elliot didn't say anything, not wanting to be a grass. That means I could easily change my mind. I could tell my father I've made a mistake, simple as that. And do you know what? I'm still prepared to do so even if I win. But then it'll be on the condition that you both apologise to my good friend Elliot, return his stuff today and promise to leave him alone from now on.'

They took the deal. Elliot didn't have a clue what Lisa was up to. However, she'd done such a good job of pulling the wool over the boys' eyes so far, using her hypnotic status as the attractive new girl to maximum advantage, that he had no intention of interfering.

It turned out she was one heck of a fast runner. She easily beat Carl in the race and, after he and Johnny gave Elliot a reluctant apology, to his surprise that evening they also returned his clothes and shoes. No such luck with his glasses, but they'd been so badly damaged, there wouldn't have been any point in getting them back. Plus that was down to Peter, rather than them, which was a fight for another day.

7

Saturday, 21 July 2018

Mike came round gradually. For a moment or two there was a blissful nothing. No dreams, no reality, no real thoughts. Just a calm feeling of being half-asleep, half-awake; comfortable in his own bed. Then reality started to trickle in. It began with a dull pain in his head and a vague sickness in his stomach. Next he realised he was on top of the quilt rather than underneath it, which was unusual. Plus he was wearing a shirt, despite usually sleeping in just boxer shorts. And how come he could smell wine?

He opened his eyes and looked down to see, as feared, that he was still wearing the shirt Lisa had thrown red wine all over in the restaurant. Shit. The uncomfortable scene replayed in his mind. He remembered feeling shocked, embarrassed, furious as she left him there alone — all the staff and other diners watching him, like he was in a freak show. Had he really shouted out loud for everyone to stop bloody staring? Things got sketchy from that point. He hadn't stayed in the restaurant for long afterwards, he didn't think. He had vague memories of being in a couple of other bars, talking to whoever would listen. Did one of them have pole dancers or was

64

that a dream? And how had he got home? He had no memory at all of making that journey or of getting into bed.

Mike looked over at Lisa, who was lying in a foetal position under the quilt, facing away from him on the far side of the bed. At least she was there. That was a good sign, wasn't it? Hopefully that meant he hadn't said or done anything too stupid last night. Because God, he'd been furious at her.

Now, with the alcohol no longer raging through his veins, he felt stupid more than angry. He'd been a drunken pig. He could even understand why Lisa had done what she did. What a disaster of an evening. Not exactly the romantic night out he'd planned. He'd got carried away on the booze, as usual, and . . . oh no.

Mike leapt up from the bed and ran to the toilet to be sick. After he was done, his throat sore and dry, he washed his face in the sink and swilled his mouth out with some water before taking a drink. He could see in the mirror that his shirt was ruined. It looked like it had been soaked in blood. He considered shoving it in the dustbin, but since it had been a gift from Lisa, he dropped it into the washing basket instead. Better to let her make the decision to throw it away.

'Lisa?' he whispered, returning to the bedroom.

There was no answer, so he slipped on his dressing gown and tiptoed out of there, gently closing the door behind him. Leaving Lisa to sleep was a good idea, especially if he wanted

65

things between them to be okay again any time soon.

Mike was surprised to find two used tumblers resting in the kitchen sink. They both smelled of Baileys, which turned his stomach in its current state. Had he and Lisa had a drink together when he'd got back? He racked his brains, but there was nothing there.

After swallowing a couple of painkillers to ease the thumping headache that had developed since he rose, Mike headed to the lounge and sprawled on the couch. He felt horrendous. And once he was horizontal, he couldn't even muster the energy to get back up to turn on the TV. This was why he preferred to leave devices in standby, so you could turn them on with the remote, but Lisa was far too energy conscious for that. And these days, thanks to him no longer having a job, it was also a matter of saving money, so it wasn't even like he could argue against it.

As awful as Mike felt, he didn't think he'd be able to fall back to sleep. He was wrong.

★　★　★

'What am I going to do with you, Liam?'

The boy continued to stare out of the window, as if he was alone in the room and hadn't been asked a question. So Mike walked over to it and shut the blinds; cut off the view of the school playground.

'I asked you a question, Liam. It's polite to answer.'

'Go screw yourself.'

'I beg your pardon?'

'You heard.'

Mike could feel himself getting riled by this boy again. He'd been sent to his office countless times before. The head was currently away at a conference, so there was no passing him along on this occasion. As the primary school's deputy head teacher, the buck stopped with him today.

Liam Hornby was easily the school's most troublesome pupil. He was in Year Six now, which at least meant he'd no longer be their problem by the end of the school year. But it was only October, which meant months more of this nonsense ahead. He'd joined the school halfway through Year Five, after his parents had moved to the area, and he'd been a pain in the neck from the word go. But despite numerous incidents with other pupils and staff members in that time, he'd never quite done enough to allow them to get rid of him, like he knew just how far he could push the boundaries.

Liam's parents were much the same. When contacted, one or both of them would come into school eventually; often after cancelling a couple of times first. Then they'd be apologetic, pledging to take their son to task, but Mike could tell it was an act. Behind the facade, they didn't care. You developed an intuition for these things after years of teaching. They said and did what was required to keep Liam at school. They knew exactly how disruptive their son was but did nothing about it. Why? No clue. They seemed normal enough. They lived in one of the nicer parts of the catchment area and both had jobs. Some people didn't deserve to have kids. Had they taught him the foul language, Mike wondered, or was it something he'd picked up from being allowed to watch the wrong things on TV?

'Language like that is unacceptable, Liam. I won't tolerate it.' Mike tried to maintain a poker face; to hide his shock at what the kid had just said to him.

'Dunno what you mean. Can't prove it.'

Mike took a deep breath and fought to stay calm as he looked across his desk at Liam, who was tall for his age and overweight, making him quite an imposing presence for an eleven-year-old. Maybe this time they'd be able to get rid of him. A temporary exclusion was on the cards at the very least. 'Well, I can prove the reason you're here,' he said. 'Half the school witnessed you attacking poor Joshua with the stinging nettles at break time. He's in so much pain he's had to go home. Why would you do something so nasty to him? Where did you even get the nettles from?'

Liam looked up at him with dead, psycho eyes and a grin to match. 'What's a stinging nettle? I just chased him with some leaves. It was a game. A bit of fun.'

'Don't give me that, Liam. You knew exactly what you were doing. I asked you where the nettles came from. Well?'

The only answer he received was a shrug, accompanied by a smug look of defiance. For some reason it really got under Mike's skin. He felt himself getting angry. It wasn't the first time

68

this kid had wound him up in this way. His blatant lack of respect was infuriating. And yet Mike knew it was his job to stay calm, or at least to appear that way. Liam was trying to goad him and if he realised he was succeeding, it would only make him worse.

Joshua Banks, the boy who'd been attacked, was no angel. He'd been in Mike's office on several occasions too, although he was much easier to handle than Liam. At least he was able to acknowledge when he'd done something wrong. Mike had no idea how the attack had come to pass. Joshua, who'd suffered nettle stings all over his arms, face and torso, had been too distressed to explain. And there was zero chance of getting a confession out of Liam.

Mike couldn't get over the nastiness of the incident, which he was convinced was premeditated. Since he was unaware of any nettles growing in the school grounds, he could only assume that Liam had brought them with him from outside, presumably hidden in his bag. Wearing gloves to handle them, he'd also made a point of shoving the plants inside Joshua's T-shirt.

'What do we have to do to get through to you?' he asked, as calmly as he could manage. 'Why are you so determined to cause trouble at every opportunity? It's not for my good that you come to school, Liam. It's for your own. You're the one — '

Mike stopped mid-sentence when he saw Liam, the little shit, leaning back in his chair and yawning. What the hell was the point?

69

'You're a — '

It was the sound of his desk phone ringing that stopped him this time, although he was glad of the interruption. He'd almost said something he would have later regretted.

'Hello?'

It was Beth in the school office on the line, wanting to know if he had the key for the safe. He did and, although she offered to come and get it, he said that he would take it through to her instead. He liked the idea of getting a moment away from Liam. It seemed like a good way to cool down; to put things into perspective.

'Stay where you are,' he told the boy. 'And don't touch anything. I'll be back to deal with you in a moment.'

It was a stupid move, leaving him alone in his office like that. Mike was already thinking so as he headed back there a couple of minutes later. But it didn't prepare him for what he found — what happened and the terrible path it led him down — when he opened that door.

★　★　★

Mike woke with a start, a gasp for air, jolting upright on the couch as his eyes sprang open. His muscles were clenched and his body covered in sweat, eyes darting wildly around the room as he took in where he was — and where he wasn't.

A dream, thank God. An awful memory: the start of his downfall, his undoing, haunting him as it so often did.

He lowered himself back on to the sofa and, as

his hands kneaded the soft cushions, he took a series of slow, deep breaths. He focused on one spot of the swirling pattern in the ceiling above him, which had been wallpapered then painted white to hide the cracks. He stared upwards trailing the curves of the embossed lines with his eyes. And he fought to wipe his mind clean of all other thoughts. He fought to forget, or at least to compartmentalise, this recalled moment. But God it was vivid — so raw, so fresh — like he'd just lived it again.

This was the booze getting its revenge from the night before; so too the feeling of panic in his chest. But gradually it passed. It always passed eventually, he told himself.

And then he carried on. He stood up and walked through to the kitchen. He boiled the kettle and made two cups of tea, which he placed on a small tray and carried upstairs to the bedroom, where he could hear that his wife was awake and moving around.

It was time to face the music: to do his best to smooth things over with Lisa again.

8

THEN

Friday, 6 September 1991

'Hi, Mum, I'm home,' Elliot called.

'In the kitchen, love,' Wendy replied casually, as if that was where she'd been the whole time. In truth she'd just raced down the stairs of their small dormer bungalow, so that Elliot didn't know she'd been watching through her bedroom window for him to get back.

Her heart had swollen with pride when she'd finally spotted him down the road, making his way home from his first day at secondary school. Her little boy looked so grown up in his new King George's uniform: a maroon blazer with the boys' school's own crest, plus a green-and-grey striped tie, white shirt, grey V-neck jumper and black trousers. It was uncanny how much he looked like her late husband.

As Elliot closed the front door behind him and removed his shoes, Wendy picked up where she'd left off in the kitchen, preparing their tea. Right Said Fred were banging on about how sexy they were on the radio and she found herself singing along in her deepest voice.

'Muuum! Please don't. That's gross.'

'What?' She grinned, taking in the sight of her pride and joy, whose crisp smartness from this morning had taken on the ruffled look that a day at school inevitably delivered. 'It's a big hit. Might even knock Brian Adams off the top spot at last.'

'Hmm.'

She stretched her arms out wide. 'Come on then. Where's my hug?'

She ruffled his curls as she took him in her arms, squeezing him tight. He smelled like school, whatever scent that was: books, pencils and ink, perhaps, with a soupçon of sweaty socks thrown in for good measure.

'So, spill the beans,' she said, planting a kiss on his forehead before letting him go. 'How was it?'

'It was fine.'

'Fine? Is that all you've got? I'm going to need a lot more information than that about my boy's first day at secondary school. Let me get you a cup of tea and a biscuit. Then I want you to tell me everything.'

Although he sighed and made out it was a pain to have to recount the day's events, Wendy knew it was only an act. Unlike a lot of kids, from what other parents said, Elliot had never been one to shy away from sharing such things with her. Communication was one of the strongest things about their relationship. It had been just the two of them for so long that talking through their respective days and confiding in each other was second nature.

There were limits, of course. As grown up as Elliot could seem, Wendy would never bother him with work issues or financial concerns, of

73

which there were unfortunately a few as a single parent. And although she was intrigued by the new friendship he'd formed over the summer with Lisa, who was absolutely lovely, she knew better than to pull his leg about her being his girlfriend or even to suggest there was anything romantic between them.

Lisa had a funny habit of calling him El for short, which he'd told Wendy he didn't mind, although he feared it made him sound like a girl. She'd told him to say something if it bothered him, but she suspected he never had, for fear of offending his new pal. Wendy actually found it rather sweet, just like she did their whole friendship. And how funny that Lisa lived in Christopher's old house. Wendy had worried how Elliot would cope when his old friend had moved away, but it had worked out perfectly. Lisa had spent almost as much time at their home in recent weeks as Christopher used to. She'd even stayed for lunch or tea several times and, honestly, Wendy found her far more polite and chatty than her predecessor.

'So let's start with the bus journey,' she said. 'How was that? Did you sit with Lisa?'

'Yeah, it was fine. We sat next to each other on the way there and then on the way home we were on the back row downstairs with a couple of others.'

'Boys from your class?'

He shook his head and scratched his nose. 'No, I was the only one from my year. They were some new friends of Lisa's from Queen Anne's: Charlotte and Joanne.'

74

'Oh, that's nice. What were they like?'

'Um, one had blonde hair and the other one had brown.' He giggled. 'I'm not sure which was which, actually. I didn't say much to them. I felt a bit shy.'

'Oh, go on with you. What's there to be shy about? Look how well you get on with Lisa and you two only met a few weeks ago. Plus I'm sure there'll be lots more boys on the bus when everyone else starts next week.'

Elliot shrugged. 'I guess.'

He explained that the bus hadn't been particularly full, since it was just first years and sixth formers on the first day, to help the new starters settle in.

'What's the Queen Anne's uniform like?' Wendy asked. 'I've not seen Lisa in it yet. Is it green, their blazer?'

'Yes. Well, emerald they call it, apparently, with a matching jumper and socks and a white blouse.'

'What about the skirt?'

'Um, that's green tartan, a bit like a kilt. Pleated.'

His last comment made Wendy smile to herself. Not many boys Elliot's age — or older, for that matter — would notice whether a skirt was pleated or not. That came from having a mother who loved fashion and, lacking the budget to buy the kinds of clothes she wanted to wear, had learned to make them herself.

Wendy's late mother, a heavy smoker who had died a few years earlier from lung cancer, had been a seamstress. She'd taught her the tricks of the trade, as well as the importance of always being nicely turned out and applying make-up well, so as to make the best of oneself. 'You don't have to be rich to look good,' had been her motto, which Wendy had adopted for herself.

Elliot was only too familiar with the sight and sound of Wendy working her sewing machine in the lounge late at night. On occasion, he'd even helped her decide on which pattern or material to use. Her hobby provided them with a little extra income here and there, as friends and neighbours would sometimes ask her to alter clothes for them. However, she wasn't always good at accepting payment, especially from those she knew well; it felt mean to charge them for doing something she enjoyed.

In the kitchen Elliot had moved on to telling Wendy about the structure of his first day at school. The morning and early afternoon had been dedicated to meeting teachers and getting to know the other pupils in his form, followed by a couple of hours of sport.

Rugby try-outs, to be precise, which she knew Elliot — who'd never been much of a sportsman — had been dreading.

'And?' Wendy asked.

Elliot screwed up his face. 'Let's just say I don't think my Saturdays will be occupied by rugby matches any time soon.'

'What about getting changed?'

He'd confessed to Wendy beforehand that doing this in front of the other boys was something he'd been concerned about, having been teased a few times at primary school for being overweight. She knew Elliot was a little bigger than he ought to be, but she loved to feed him up and thought he was perfect as he was. 'It's just puppy fat,' she often told him, although the truth was that Gary, his dad, had been on the cuddly side too; she found it hard to discourage anything in her son that reminded her of him.

'It was okay,' Elliot said, answering her question. 'I didn't much like the look of the communal showers, but there was no time for anyone to use them today. The teachers were around most of the time too, so no one was being nasty.'

The boys were probably all still scoping each other out at this early stage, Wendy thought, hoping the situation wouldn't change. 'And the rugby?'

'I wasn't very good. I kept dropping the ball and I was one of the slowest runners. I got put into a group called Gentleman's Rugby, which is basically a nice way of saying we're the rubbish ones.'

Wendy stifled a laugh at this. 'Oh well. There's much more to life than rugby. But you made some new friends?'

Elliot ran his middle finger in circles around the rim of his tea mug. 'Kind of. The boy who sits next to me in our form room seems nice.'

'What's his name?'

'Neil Walsh. He lives down the road from school, close enough to walk.'

'Super. What's he like?'

Elliot shrugged. 'I dunno. Friendly.'

'And the others?'

77

'They're fine.' Changing the subject, which Wendy took to mean she'd probed enough about his day, he added: 'It sounds like Lisa's going to make the hockey team.'

'Really? How come?'

'She said she scored a couple of goals today. She used to play at primary school.'

'That's nice.'

Elliot frowned. 'Not for me. She'll be busy most Saturdays if she's selected, because that's when they play their games against other schools. I don't get why she'd want to give up so much of her free time.'

'Oh, Elliot,' Wendy replied. 'You should be happy for her if she makes the team. I know you're not particularly keen on sport, but life would be boring if we all liked and disliked the same things. What about tomorrow? I'm sure she doesn't have a hockey practice yet.'

'Not yet, no. We're going to meet up in the morning.'

'There you go. So that's something to look forward to.'

Elliot rolled his eyes. 'How long until tea's ready?'

'About forty-five minutes. Would you like grated or sliced cheese on your burger?'

'Grated, please.'

Burger and chips was Elliot's favourite meal, which was why Wendy had made it for him today. If he had his way, he'd visit McDonald's every week. But they could only afford to eat out as a rare treat. Her homemade Wendy Burger, as she liked to call it, always went down well.

She did feel bad sometimes that she wasn't able to spoil Elliot more, but her modest nurse's salary was the only household income, so there was never going to be a lot of money to spare. At least he had clothes to wear, food to eat and a roof over his head. Wendy was particularly proud of the fact that their home was detached, even though it was actually smaller than a lot of terraced properties: the upstairs in particular. It was plenty big enough for the two of them and she did her utmost to fill it with love and laughter.

Would she have preferred it if Gary was still with them and they were a complete family? Of course. He was a wonderful man, who she loved with all her heart. And the way he was taken from them — killed in a motorbike crash, gone in an instant with no warning — had always felt particularly cruel. A day didn't go by when she didn't think of him and wish that he and Elliot had got to spend more time together. Gary had adored his 'little man'. It was awful to think of everything he'd already missed out on as his son grew up. Today was yet another milestone his dad should have been there for. They kept on coming.

As for Elliot, he said he still remembered his dad, but she wondered how much of that was what she'd told him rather than actual memories. He'd only been four when he'd died, poor thing. She kept Gary as alive as she could in Elliot's mind by regularly talking about him, showing photos and recounting stories from their time together. What more could she do?

She would have liked to have kept in touch with Gary's parents. However, they'd made that impossible by cutting off all contact when she'd needed it most, soon after his death, inexplicably blaming her for what had happened. She'd never heard from them since, so apparently they had no interest in getting to know their grandson.

Wendy had learned long ago that you just had to make the best of things and focus on the positives rather than the negatives, like the fact that she and Elliot had such a close relationship and how incredibly proud she was of him. She was constantly telling her friends and colleagues about his amazing achievements, such as getting into King George's. He was her everything — the one aspect of her life that was perfect and she wouldn't change one iota. She couldn't have wished for a kinder, more loving child.

Elliot may not have been much of a sportsman, as today's rugby trials had shown, but he came into his own in the classroom. He'd always been one of the brightest in school: an all-rounder, as the teachers liked to put it, excelling equally at Maths and English and everything in between. It seemed to come easily to him. Wendy wasn't sure where this came from, since neither she nor Gary had been especially academic during their own school days, but of course she was delighted.

His Junior Three primary school teacher, Mr Armitage, had contacted Wendy to suggest Elliot ought to apply to somewhere more academically challenging than the local comprehensive. She'd taken some convincing, because of the distances involved and, most importantly, the fees. But after Mr Armitage had presented her with details of the various bursaries and scholarships available, even offering his services as a private tutor free of charge, she'd come round to the idea.

As kind and supportive as Mr Armitage was, Wendy had always suspected that part of the reason for his offer was down to her being a widow and him a bachelor with aspirations of marriage. He was a socially awkward chap. Although he had made a couple of attempts to ask her out, they'd been so clumsy and unclear that, simply by playing dumb, she'd managed to wiggle out of them without the discomfort of formally rejecting him. But she saw the way he looked at her when he thought she wasn't watching: the way so many men did when they learned her husband had died. Apparently there was something appealing about a young widow. She suspected that some liked the idea of sweeping in to rescue her, while others assumed she must be desperate and therefore an easy conquest.

The truth was that in between working, sewing, running the household and looking after Elliot, she didn't have much time for dating. Plus, she still couldn't picture being with anyone but her beloved Gary, which was why she continued to wear her wedding ring. She'd also made a secret pact with herself not to date anyone while Elliot was still at primary school, to avoid confusing him when he was too young to understand. That obviously no longer applied.

And yet, even with her thirty-second birthday just around the corner, she still didn't feel in a rush to do anything about it.

Anyway, whatever Mr Armitage's reasons were for helping Elliot, following several weeks of evening classes, he'd taken the King George's entrance exam and won a scholarship. He and Wendy had both been really impressed by the school during an earlier open evening, so he'd accepted.

'I have a little gift for you,' Wendy said now, as Elliot tucked into his burger. She opened one of the drawers and removed a small, rectangular parcel wrapped in brown paper, which she slid across the kitchen table into his hands.

'Ooh, exciting,' he said. 'What is it?'

Wendy beamed a broad smile in his direction. 'Well, you won't find out by staring at it.'

'No, but I mean what's it for?'

'Finishing your first day at secondary school, of course. I'm terribly proud of you. I know you'll do really well at King George's.'

'I'll do my best,' Elliot said, turning the package around in his hands and even giving it a little shake next to his ear before he finally unwrapped it.

'Fantastic,' he said, his eyes glowing when he found the new pair of specs she'd bought to replace the ones he'd lost while out playing over the summer. He put them on immediately and beamed at her with such joy that she knew they were worth every hard-earned penny they'd cost her.

'Thanks so much, Mum.'

82

'You're welcome. I couldn't have you in those old ones forever, could I?'

'I promise I'll take good care of them this time.'

'Yes, please do. No more taking them off while you're out and about. Okay?'

'Okay.'

'How do they fit?' she asked. 'If they're not right, we can pop to the optician's tomorrow and get them adjusted.'

Elliot stood up and walked around the table, giving her a bear hug that left her gasping for breath. 'No, they're perfect.' He grinned. 'No one will recognise me at school on Monday now. They'll be like: 'Who's this cool dude in the funky specs?' I'll have to introduce myself all over again.'

'Go on with you, silly sausage. Go and get changed out of your smart new uniform before you spill your tea down it.'

83

9

NOW

Saturday, 21 July 2018

Chloe was seriously freaked out. The minute she got up to her room, she messaged her best friend, Holly, whose house she'd stayed at the night before.

C: Are you still awake?

H: For now. Mum says I have to go to bed soon, seeing as we barely slept last night. It was fun, though, right?

C: Definitely! I'll ask my parents if you can come for a sleepover here soon. What are you up to?

H: Not much. Chilling, watching some YouTube videos. You?

C: Something seriously strange happened tonight. I have to tell you about it.

H: Sounds exciting. Btw, before I forget, you left your hairbrush.

C: Wondered where that was. Thanks. Will pop round for it sometime.

H: So what happened?

C: Mum had this old friend over for tea — a man called Elliot. They were BFFs when they were kids. (They didn't say so, but I think he might be gay.) Anyway, like twenty years ago, Elliot moved to Australia and they never saw each other again — until now. He turned up yesterday and surprised Mum. He's staying at The Grange.

H: What's he like?

C: Nice, I guess. He has an odd accent, somewhere in between English and Australian.

H: What's so strange?

C: Coming to that now. I was on my own with him in the kitchen when we were tidying up after tea. The two of us were emptying the dishwasher. I picked a sharp knife out of the cutlery rack and it slipped from my hand. It fell, blade first, straight towards my bare foot. There was no time to move. And this is what freaked me out: right at the last minute, the knife changed direction. Suddenly, without any obvious explanation, it went flying to one side, out of the way.

H: Eh? So it didn't hit your foot?

C: Nowhere near. It ended up on the other side of the room, like some invisible force had swiped it away.

H: What do you mean? Did it hit a cupboard or something on the way down?

C: No, definitely not. There was nothing between the knife and my foot other than air. That's what was weird.

H: And Elliot?

C: He was putting away some plates at the time. He wasn't anywhere near close enough to knock it away. But somehow I still think it was him.

H: You're confusing me.

C: I think he did it without touching it

— using his mind or whatever.

H: Is this a wind-up, Chloe?

C: Seriously. I looked over at him after it happened and he gave me this kind of embarrassed look, like he'd been caught doing something he shouldn't have. Then he smiled and said: 'Close call, kiddo. You need to be careful with knives.'

H: What did you say?

C: Nothing. I was too busy trying to wrap my head around it.

H: Did you tell your parents or Ben?

C: Of course not. They'd think I was crazy.

H: And you thought I wouldn't? Lol. Remember we basically had no sleep last night. It's probably your mind playing tricks. Sorry, got to go. Mum's breathing down my neck about having a shower. Chat in the morning?

C: Sure. Night. X

H: Night. X

Chloe placed her mobile on the bedside table. It was 8.32 p.m. Her parents were still busy entertaining downstairs. Better that than biting each other's heads off, anyway.

She hoped Elliot wasn't any more to Mum than an old friend. Chloe was already worried enough about her parents' marriage, without anything or anyone else to complicate matters. Certainly Dad hadn't looked as enthusiastic about their visitor as Mum had. And neither of them had been keen to chat about their evening out together last night, which suggested it hadn't gone well.

She thought back to Holly's words about how

tiredness might have led her to imagine the kitchen incident. Really? No, that wasn't possible. She knew what she'd seen.

So what did that make Elliot? A magician? A superhero? Some kind of supernatural being? A vampire, perhaps?

They'd studied Gothic literature in English class at school this year, looking at classic novels like Bram Stoker's *Dracula* and Mary Shelley's *Frankenstein*. She'd loved the idea of these books but found the reality hard going. Instead, she'd turned to something more modern: Stephenie Meyer's *Twilight* saga. She was hooked, currently enjoying the second book in the series, *New Moon*, which was next to her mobile on the bedside table.

Could Elliot really be a vampire? She laughed at herself for considering this option. And then she came back to it, since only a fantastical explanation could come close to explaining what she'd seen. And was it any more ridiculous, any more unbelievable, than the idea of him being a superhero?

The big argument against the vampire theory was the fact that Elliot had eaten with them earlier. In *Twilight*, Edward ate a small amount of pizza at one point, Chloe recalled, but it definitely wasn't a pleasant experience for him. He compared it to a human eating dirt, from what she remembered. Well, there was definitely no sign of that at the table tonight. Elliot had dug into Mum's lasagne with enthusiasm, commenting on how delicious it was, and even having seconds.

On the other hand, Elliot appeared younger and in better shape than either of her parents. He was good-looking, for an adult: the right combination of slim and muscular, with a jawline that actually reminded her of Robert Pattinson, who played Edward Cullen in the *Twilight* movies. (She was saving these for later but had seen plenty of photos.) Such things, together with that supernatural ability, were ticks in the potential vampire box.

What about the fact he'd used his power, or whatever it was, to stop her from being injured? Traditionally, vampires were considered evil, like Dracula, but Edward and the other Cullens weren't like that. Still, even they struggled with their instincts in the face of human blood. Maybe that was also why Elliot had stopped the knife, because if it had hit her foot, there would have been loads of blood.

Plenty to chew over. Chloe considered searching some vampire mythology online: something other than *Twilight*, since that was just one writer's take on it. But stifling a yawn, she realised this would have to wait for another time.

The bedroom door burst open and in walked her elder brother.

Chloe sighed. 'It's polite to knock first.'

Ben ignored this and asked her what she was doing.

'Nothing. You?'

'Not much.'

Chloe wondered what Ben wanted. He rarely came into her bedroom unless he needed a favour. Not that she minded. Secretly, she was fond of her big brother, but she'd fallen into the habit of pretending not to be. She found she got more respect from Ben this way than she did in the old days, when she used to follow him around, begging him to play with her.

There were almost four years between them. She had a June birthday and his was at the end of August. So now she was twelve to his fifteen, but that would only last another few weeks; then he would turn sixteen and the age gap would return to normal.

They'd never discussed it, but Chloe suspected that Holly, who was far more into boys than she was, had a crush on Ben. She was always batting her eyelashes at him; she would burst into laughter if the slightest hint of a joke left his lips. As annoying as this was, Chloe could just about understand why — not that she'd ever admit it.

Ben was relatively handsome, compared to other boys around his age, who tended to be gangly and awkward. Broad-shouldered with thick, wavy dark hair, brown eyes, olive skin and a clear complexion, he looked very different to Chloe. She had pale white skin, already showing a tendency for spots, plus light-green eyes and long, straight auburn hair. That was her mum's natural colour too. She'd been dying it blonde for years but wouldn't entertain the notion of her daughter doing the same. Totally unfair.

'What do you think of Elliot?' she asked Ben.
'Why?'

'I just wondered. He seems a bit . . . unusual to me.'

'What do you mean?'

She shrugged, not yet ready to trust Ben with what she'd seen. She needed more evidence first — and to re-evaluate the situation when she wasn't so tired. 'I'm surprised you're not down there chatting to him. He's a big deal in computers and stuff, right? Might be able to get an IT geek like you a job one day.'

Ben frowned, muttering that a post in Australia would be useless to him. Despite his sporty physique, the only games he tended to play were on his PC. He spent much of his spare time behind his computer screen, often tinkering with technical things that Chloe didn't understand. And yet Ben hated being labelled a nerd. He definitely wanted something. Otherwise he wouldn't have let her get away with what she'd just said.

He wandered aimlessly around her room, picking and poking at things on her shelves and desk, before finally getting to the point. 'Any chance you might be able to do me a tiny favour, Chloe?'

She smiled to herself. 'Depends what it is.'

'You know how Mum and Dad are going to see Aunt Jenny on Monday and they agreed we could stay at home?'

Chloe nodded.

'I could do with popping out for a bit, um, alone.' Ben scratched his head. 'Would you be okay here by yourself for a couple of hours?'

'Where do you need to go?'

'To meet a friend nearby. No one you know.'

'Ooh, a girlfriend?'

Ben's face soured. 'No. Bloody hell, Chloe.'

'What? You expect me to say yes without any questions?'

'What's the problem? You're always telling Mum and Dad that you're old enough to be left home alone. I thought you'd jump at the chance.'

'What if I need you for something?'

'I'll have my mobile.'

'I don't know, Ben. We'll both be in big trouble if we get found out.'

'I'll take the heat if that happens. But why would it? If we don't tell them, how will they find out?'

'Well, I don't see why you can't tell me where you're going and who you're meeting.'

Ben sighed. 'I knew you'd be like this.' He reached into the pocket of his jeans and pulled out a ten pound note. Chloe hadn't expected this, but knowing he was prepared to pay, she pushed for more and got him up to twenty.

'So it's a deal then?' he asked before handing over the notes.

'Yes, but if Mum and Dad find out somehow, it's on you.'

'Fine.'

Chloe was intrigued. What was Ben up to that was so secret — and worth paying her twenty pounds?

As she considered this, lying on top of the green and white striped quilt on her bed, she shut her eyes for a moment.

Twenty minutes later, the sound of a cat meowing woke her up. It was actually her phone's notification for receiving a text message. She'd installed the realistic sound for fun; since it had caught out so many people, leading them to look around for a noisy kitty in places like libraries and shops, she'd stuck with it.

Chloe wondered who it might be. Most of her friends tended to use messaging apps rather than texting, unless they were out of data or had no Wi-Fi.

The text was from a number she didn't recognise, which wasn't saved in her contacts. It read:

Chloe Adams? Be warned. I'm watching you.

10

NOW

Saturday, 21 July 2018

Saying goodnight to Elliot felt almost like travelling back in time to Lisa. It so reminded her of when they were both teenagers, having one last gab at the front door before going their separate ways.

'Thanks for tonight, Lise,' Elliot said, stepping outside and then turning back to face her. 'It's been ace.'

'Not at all. Thank you for coming. I was worried you might not want to after all the drama yesterday.' She lowered her voice before adding that she hoped Mike, who'd already gone up to bed, had made a better impression this time.

'Listen, I've already told you not to worry about last night. He was pissed. It happens. Trust me, it's nothing I'm not used to after twenty years in Oz. Forget about it. I've really enjoyed meeting your family after all this time.'

Next thing Lisa knew, El was offering to come back tomorrow afternoon to cook for them in return. She told him not to be silly, but he refused to take no for an answer, so eventually she agreed.

'Don't worry,' he told her with a smile. 'My

cooking's improved since you last tasted it.'

'You mean the only time you ever cooked for me?'

'Yes, beans on toast, I believe.'

She giggled, leaning forward and resting her hands on his shoulders. 'That's right. You burned the toast and the beans.'

'Exactly. So it's not going to be any worse, is it?' He winked. 'And if it goes wrong, I can always order us a takeaway, right?'

He gave her the kind of tight hug that banished all her troubles for a moment, filling her with warmth and hope. Then he set off for his hotel. 'See you tomorrow.'

'Night, El. What's that aftershave you're wearing, by the way? It reminds me of the sea.'

He shrugged, adding with a grin: 'I'm not. It must be Eau d'Elliot that you can smell.'

She remained at the door, shaking her head and smiling, watching her old friend walk down the pavement into the distance and thinking how wonderful it was to see him again. If someone had told her a week ago that this was going to happen, she wouldn't have believed them. So much time had passed since they'd last seen each other that she'd given up on it ever happening.

Lisa had been heartbroken when he'd emigrated. Before that she'd always imagined that they would be lifelong friends; that they would visit each other at their respective universities and regularly meet up after graduating, even if they didn't live in the same place. She'd hoped that as adults they'd get on with

94

each other's partners, be like honorary aunts and uncles to their respective kids, maybe even take their families on holiday together. It had never occurred to her that Elliot would be drawn to the other side of the world, forcing their lives apart.

And even after he'd left for Australia, Lisa had persuaded herself that he wouldn't be gone long: that the pull of home would bring him back before she knew it. This had been her way of dealing with the loss, essentially by burying her head in the sand, although as the years passed and he didn't return, she had no choice but to accept the truth.

Funnily enough, Elliot's absence had actually played a role in bringing her and Mike together. They'd met as teacher-training postgrads and had been good mates for some time before they eventually became a couple. Mike was the first really close male friend she'd had since El had left. He was nothing like him in terms of looks or personality. He was much more of a typical alpha male, for a start, and yet something about the dynamic between them was reminiscent of her relationship with Elliot.

Part of this was to do with how much fun they had together and how comfortable she felt with him. There were no games; she could just be herself. But it was more than that. It was like their differences were perfectly aligned to complement each other, making for a yin-yang type connection. The same could be said of her and Elliot as kids, although in that case she'd been the dominant one, whereas with Mike, who was a year older, the roles were reversed. Perhaps this explained why the latter friendship had been the one to develop into romance.

The reason they'd got married so quickly was more prosaic: an unplanned pregnancy while they were both still on the course. Not that they'd ever told Ben he was an accident. Her son knew that she'd been heavily pregnant with him at the time of the wedding, but the official line was that the ceremony had been planned before that.

Would they have got married eventually anyway, even without the pregnancy? Lisa thought so. They'd been madly, passionately in love ever since their friendship had blossomed into romance. And even now, with Mike stuck in a rut having lost his way career-wise, she still loved him deeply. He wasn't only the father of her children. He was her husband: for better, for worse, for richer, for poorer, in sickness and in health.

That wasn't to say it was easy at the moment. It was anything but. Just look how badly things had gone between them at the restaurant last night.

Locking the front door and turning off the lights downstairs, Lisa considered how many family meals had also been ruined by arguments since work had got so messed up for Mike. He'd been very happy in his job as a deputy head teacher. He'd been a natural in the role. The way things had turned sour so quickly, so forcefully, Lisa could totally understand how her husband had been broken by that. But then for everything to go wrong again — for him to screw up so spectacularly in another job, particularly one so beneath his abilities — that was the cruellest blow of all.

Not that any of this excused Mike's behaviour in Manchester yesterday. But it did go some way towards explaining it. The big question now was how to help him move forward; to find a new purpose in life. Because no matter how happy Lisa felt at this moment, following a lovely evening with her old friend, she knew the feeling was temporary.

She was also painfully aware of how everything they'd been through as a family of late had impacted on the kids. She'd seen the worried looks on their faces over some of the more fiery arguments between her and Mike. Lisa did try to shelter them from these things, but it wasn't always possible when they all lived under one roof, especially when Mike could be so volatile.

She felt that Ben and Chloe had become more withdrawn at home, sharing less of what was going on in their own lives. She didn't like that at all. She wanted to be there for them whenever they needed her, and hoped that spending time together while school was out this summer might improve things. If only they'd been able to afford to go on holiday.

Mike had been in one of his better moods this evening, but Lisa knew from experience how quickly that could change: how fast he could sink into depression. Luckily, he'd been the one to eat humble pie after last night's catastrophe. She had feared he would take the hump over her throwing the red wine over him and leaving him alone there. But waking up in bed this morning with little to no memory of how he'd got home had been quite the reality check. He knew he'd drunk far too much and he'd apologised profusely for that and his boorish behaviour.

He'd been tiptoeing around her since then, although she could sense some tension regarding the arrival of El. It probably didn't help Mike knowing, but not remembering, that he'd helped the taxi driver carry him up to bed. But of more significance was the way her old friend had turned up unannounced, totally out of the blue, in great shape, oozing confidence and success.

Lisa wasn't stupid. She could see how this might be threatening to her husband, especially in his current circumstances. She hoped he'd be able to deal with it. Elliot probably wouldn't be around for long, anyway. He'd remained vague about the length of his stay so far, or the exact reason for it, but as fantastic as it was to see him, Lisa couldn't imagine him having the spare time to be here for more than a few days. Hence she was keen to see as much as possible of him while she could.

As Lisa trudged upstairs for the night, she felt a wave of tiredness wash over her. When she looked in on Ben and Chloe, they were both fast asleep, or at least doing an excellent job of pretending to be. Mike, on the other hand, was sitting up in bed with his nose in a paperback.

'Still awake?' she said. 'I thought you came up because you were tired.'

Mike shrugged, placing the open thriller novel

down on the quilt. 'Once I was up here I felt like reading.'

'Elliot's coming over to cook for us tomorrow,' she said.

'Since when?'

'He offered after you went upstairs, love. He really wanted to do it in return for today. I thought: why not?'

'Nice of you to consult me.'

'Why, is there a problem? Did you have something else planned? If you'd rather do the cooking, then be my guest.'

Lisa almost added that this would make a refreshing change, but she bit her tongue. They'd already had plenty of rows about the amount that Mike did around the house; she was far too wiped out for another of those now. Instead she went to the bathroom to wash her face and brush her teeth.

When she returned, Mike put his book down again and eyed her quizzically without saying anything.

'What?' she asked eventually.

'Oh, nothing,' he replied.

'Well, it clearly is something. Spit it out.'

And so he did, although it wasn't what she was expecting.

'I was just wondering if Elliot was, um, gay.'

'What? Where did that come from?'

'I don't know. The way he carries himself, I suppose. And the fact you two were such good friends growing up.'

'You thought I was his fag hag?'

'Sorry, his what?'

Lisa couldn't help but laugh. 'It's a slang expression for a woman who enjoys hanging out with gay guys. You've seriously never heard of that?'

He shrugged. 'Not that I recall.'

Mike definitely wouldn't be the first person to think that Elliot was gay. He'd always been in touch with his feminine side. Part of it was probably down to his close relationship with Wendy and the lack of a father figure growing up. But she'd only ever known him to be attracted to girls.

Bizarrely, Mike said his gay theory was also related to the fact that Lisa often abbreviated her friend's name to *El*, confessing that he'd originally thought he was a girl because of this.

'I remember you talking about the close friend you had growing up,' he said. 'But I always assumed it was *Elle*, as in the girl's name. Not a shortened form of *Elliot*.'

Lisa found this a little hard to believe, suggesting Mike hadn't listened too closely to any of her stories about the two of them. She also wondered why exactly that had led to her husband concluding he must be gay. But it reminded her of Elliot's recent comment about the nickname — giving her the impression he'd never liked it — so she made a mental note to try to use his full name more often.

'So is he gay or not?' Mike asked.

'No, he's not.'

'Okay.'

'But there was never anything romantic between us, if that's what you're getting at.

100

Contrary to popular belief, it is possible for members of the opposite sex just to be good friends. El and I are living proof of that.'

What Lisa didn't tell Mike was that she remembered how Elliot used to stare at her when he thought she wasn't looking, especially in their early teens, when hormones were all over the place. He'd even kissed her once when he'd got drunk at that crazy party when they were sixteen. It hadn't meant anything, though, so why give Mike something to be needlessly jealous about? There really hadn't ever been anything romantic between them. And yet as she thought this, a mental picture formed of the all-new Elliot: handsome, masculine and confident. She wondered how things might have been different if they'd met later in life.

Mike sighed. 'That wasn't why I was asking, Lisa. I was actually thinking that if he was gay, we could talk to him about . . . oh, never mind.'

Lisa knew what Mike was getting at. She understood the way he thought. But she didn't have the energy to go into that with him right now. His heart was in the right place, though, bless him.

Climbing into bed, she leaned over and gave her husband a kiss goodnight. 'Sorry, I'm shattered, love. Can we carry on this discussion tomorrow?'

'Sure, I'm wiped out too.'

As Lisa made herself comfortable, snuggling into a foetal position under the quilt, Mike placed his book on to the bedside table and turned off his lamp.

101

A moment later he was cuddling up to her from behind and planting a few tender kisses on her neck. 'Don't worry,' he whispered. 'I'm not trying to get frisky. I know I still don't deserve that after yesterday and I doubt either of us has the energy.'

You're right there, Lisa thought, although all she actually said was 'hmm'.

'Can I just say, again, how sorry I am about what happened in the restaurant?' Mike added. 'I was horrible to you and, well, there's no excuse. It might not seem like it sometimes, but I do love you, Lisa . . . more than anything.'

'Good to know,' she replied, reaching over with one arm to ruffle his hair and relishing the closeness between them. 'I love you too.'

She did love him, with all her heart, which was why she put up with the kind of nonsense he'd pulled yesterday. He was a good man: a kind and loving husband and father. He'd just had a hard time of it recently. Life had dealt him some bad hands. Every day she hoped for some light at the end of the tunnel to help him finally move forward.

The fact they were going to visit Mike's Aunt Jenny over in Harrogate on Monday, at his suggestion, was a good example of his caring, family-focused nature. A retired midwife, her husband had died a few years earlier and, since they'd never had children, she didn't have many family members nearby. They were about the closest. After hearing that she'd suffered a fall and was recovering in hospital, Mike hadn't hesitated to arrange a visit to cheer her up.

Lisa had agreed to go too. But Ben and Chloe, who'd only met their great aunt a handful of times, had asked to be excused. Lisa's inclination had been to bring them along regardless. However, Mike had argued that it was the start of their summer holidays and there was no harm in them staying behind, on the condition they remained together, since Chloe was still too young to be home alone.

Lisa hadn't been entirely comfortable with this, particularly since her mum was away on that coach trip around Eastern Europe and their Uncle Jamie would be out at work, meaning no family safety blanket. But she knew she had to let the kids grow up at some point and a hospital visit wouldn't be much fun for them, so she'd reluctantly agreed.

As these thoughts swam around Lisa's head, Mike's body did the involuntary twitching thing that indicated he was in the process of nodding off. She loosened herself from his grip, suddenly feeling too hot, and he grunted something inaudible before rolling away in the other direction.

He'd be fast asleep in moments. So why wasn't she? How could she feel so tired and yet her mind remain so awake?

The next thought that popped up to bother her was their lack of a family holiday this year. Lisa wished they'd been able to afford to go away, but with Mike still not working, it simply wasn't doable. The other day she'd overheard Chloe's friend Holly telling her about her family's planned trip to Sicily, where some family friends apparently owned a house next to the sea. Holly had been moaning — surprise, surprise — about how it would be too hot and she'd rather not go. Chloe had replied by saying: 'At least you're going somewhere nice. I checked Sicily out on the Internet and it looks amazeballs: gorgeous beaches and all kinds of awesome food. We're not going anywhere this year, which totally sucks.'

When Holly had asked why, Chloe had lied and said it was because they were saving for a really good holiday to Florida the following year, which had broken Lisa's heart.

Although she and Mike tried to avoid discussing financial matters in front of the kids, sometimes — often to explain why they couldn't do things — it was unavoidable. Like when they wanted takeaway when there was plenty of food in the fridge, or when they came home with a letter about an expensive school skiing trip that was never going to happen.

Money was tight on one salary, something Lisa wished she hadn't had to teach Ben and Chloe. They also had a better grasp than they ought to of what a tough time Mike had been through, having experienced so much of it alongside him.

The ordeal had been hard on all four of them. Both of the kids had mentioned being teased at school. Then there was that one awful occasion when they'd been out on a family walk and some horrible man had recognised Mike from the news reports and spat at his feet, calling him a 'damn disgrace'. Lisa had leapt to his defence, sending the man packing with a torrent of abuse in return. But it was Mike's behaviour afterwards that was most upsetting. He'd turned deathly pale and barely spoken a word for the rest of the day. He'd looked beaten and broken, which isn't how any child should have to see one of their parents.

At least all of that was over now — and had been for some time. But Mike wasn't over it. Not by any stretch of the imagination, especially in light of his one disastrous attempt at getting back on his feet and doing something else. So where did he go from here? Something had to change, for the good of the whole family. The problem was that Lisa had no idea what that might be. She was well and truly stumped.

11

THEN

Tuesday, 12 May 1992

Elliot's heart sank as soon as he saw Paul Samson, or Samo as he was widely known, heading towards him further down the corridor. Shit.

It was a warm, sunny day, so most of the boys were enjoying the weather outside on this lunch break. For some that meant taking part in official cricket and athletics sessions; others were kicking a football on the back field, with blazers as goalposts, or simply shooting the breeze with their mates.

Elliot was alone, as usual. He'd grown accustomed to this early on in the school year. It didn't even bother him too much any more. The problem was that Neil Walsh, the boy who sat next to him in form room, and the closest thing he had to a best friend at school, was a keen sportsman. For the first two terms, Neil had been busy at rugby practice most lunchtimes. Now he could usually be found in the cricket nets, practising his batting and bowling with the rest of the team.

They didn't have much in common at first glance, Elliot and Neil. If they'd not been placed alongside each other in class, simply because of the location of their names in the register, they probably wouldn't have been friends. But they had been — and, despite their differences in terms of athleticism, academically they were well matched. A friendly rivalry had developed between them, with each trying to outsmart the other when it came to test scores and marks for homework. King George's had a habit of ranking the boys at every available opportunity. The aim was clearly to foster a competitive streak in them and thus promote achievement. In Elliot and Neil's case, it definitely worked. The pair tended to feature in the top ten in most subjects — and beating each other was always a priority. The fact that they shared a similar sense of humour and were both into computers didn't do any harm either.

The problem was that Elliot hadn't especially clicked with any of the other boys. Neil was pally with a lot of his rugby and cricket teammates, but most of them weren't like him. They tended to be the more boisterous types — and Elliot struggled to find common ground with them, quickly learning that they were more likely to make fun of him than be genuinely friendly. There were obviously plenty of other boys like him, who weren't sporty. But after contracting a nasty bout of the flu in mid-September, which had kept him off school ill for nearly three weeks, he'd returned to find various social groups had formed that didn't include him. It didn't help that he had no old friendships to fall back on either, being the only one to come here from his primary school. So when Neil wasn't

107

around, he'd got into the habit of spending his lunchtimes in the school library and the computer room, or sometimes traipsing around the grounds alone.

On this particular occasion, he'd planned to go to the computer room. But after heading up there once he'd eaten his lunch and Neil had gone to cricket, he'd found it to be closed due to a staff meeting. He was on his way outside when he saw Samo, who was looking straight at him and grinning as the pair made their way towards one another in the otherwise empty ground-floor corridor.

Samo was two years older than Elliot, meaning he was also significantly bigger and stronger. He took the same bus as Elliot to school and back every day, getting on two stops after Aldham in the mornings. Unfortunately, he was a bully and one of his favourite things to do was to pick on Elliot, who he'd taken to calling E.T., after Steven Spielberg's famous alien. The main reason for this was because of his first name, which he shared with the boy in the film, despite spelling it differently. But Samo had also cottoned on to the fact that due to his surname, Turner, E and T were actually his initials.

It wasn't the worst name in the world to be called. But when you had it thrust unwanted upon you several times a day, always used in a jeering manner, it soon became annoying. The irony was that when he was younger, Elliot's mum had called him the same thing for a while, although in an affectionate way. It was after they'd watched it together for the first time and, for fun, she'd claimed to have named him after the boy in the film. It wasn't true; E.T. hadn't been released until 1982, well after his birth in June 1980. The real reason for him being called Elliot was the fact it was Wendy's maiden name.

Samo, nasty piece of work that he was, liked to use the nickname in a way that suggested Elliot was some kind of freak who didn't belong.

'E.T. phone home,' he called along the corridor in a stupid impression of the voice from the film. 'E.T. phone home.'

Elliot wanted to turn around and run back the way he'd come, but he knew that would make things worse. If only there was a different way to walk that didn't take him right past Samo. But there wasn't. Nor was there anyone else around. It was just the two of them, a row of wooden lockers on one side and several locked classroom doors on the other.

He looked straight ahead and tried not to make eye contact. His plan was to keep walking and simply to ignore Samo, who was alone too, thankfully. He was usually worse around his mates, as he liked to show off.

'E.T. phone home,' Samo called out again, a few metres ahead of him now.

Elliot said nothing; kept on walking.

And then Samo was there, right in front of him, blocking the way with his bulk and holding both arms out like a scarecrow. His whole body reeked of cigarettes and his breath, as he bent forward, getting right in Elliot's face, was a foul mix of tobacco and Juicy Fruit chewing gum.

'Where do you think you're going, E.T.?'

Elliot said nothing. His heart was pounding like a drum roll and he felt like he was about to open his bowels. Refusing to meet Samo's glare, he stepped to the left and then to the right, but both times his assailant moved with him.

'I asked you a question, bender,' Samo continued. Speaking in an exaggerated, slowly enunciated manner, he added: 'Where do you think you're going?'

Elliot still said nothing. He concentrated on breathing and not soiling his pants.

'Have you forgotten how to talk, lard boy? I swear, if you don't answer me, you're going to be sorry.' As he said this, Samo glanced up and down the corridor, making sure they were still alone, and then he grabbed Elliot by the throat with his right hand, which smelled even more strongly of smoke. It felt like it was made of iron and Elliot started to panic as he struggled to breathe.

'Outside,' he strained.

'Good,' Samo replied, loosening his grip a little. 'So you can talk after all. I don't speak alien, though. What did you say?'

'I said I was going outside.'

'Really? Who said you could do that?'

'I . . . don't know what you mean.' Elliot's eyes, looking all around, desperate for someone — preferably a teacher — to turn up, fell on to a piece of graffiti carved into the front of one of the nearby lockers. 'Carter is a tripod,' it read, which meant nothing to him and provided little comfort.

'Didn't you get the memo?' Samo said with a

nasty grin. 'You have to pay to go outside and I'm the one who collects the money. That'll be fifty pence, please.'

'What? I don't have any money.'

'Liar.'

'Honestly.'

Samo released him from his grip. 'Prove it.'

He shoved Elliot towards the lockers and told him to empty his pockets, which he promptly did. He was telling the truth about having no money, so all that came out was his bus pass and hymn book, two pencils, a biro and an unopened pack of Polo mints. As he was doing this, the door Samo had come through swung open and Elliot thought for a moment he was saved. In fact, the opposite was true. It was two of Samo's pals: lads he went smoking with behind the games hall. Elliot didn't know their names.

'What are you up to, Samo?' one of them called as they made their way towards them.

'Chatting to my friend E.T. here,' Samo replied. 'He wanted to go outside and I was telling him about the new charge that's been introduced. Problem is he doesn't have any money.'

'That's a shame,' the other new arrival said. 'He'll have to pay in another way, then, won't he?'

'My thoughts exactly.' Samo pocketed Elliot's Polos, adding: 'This will do for starters, but it's not enough. Come on, lads. Let's carry him to the bogs.'

'No, get lost!' Elliot shouted, twisting loose and trying to run away. But it was no use. The three lads were far too strong. One clamped a sweaty hand over his mouth and together they lifted him off the ground and ran with him on their shoulders in the direction of the toilets.

Moments later they bustled him into one of the cubicles, ordering a couple of other boys present to get lost and keep their mouths shut or else. Elliot fought frantically to resist, biting at the hand over his mouth and then, when it was pulled away, shouting as loudly as he could for them to leave him alone. It was futile. They forced his head into the grimy, smelly bowl regardless and flushed it.

The boys were laughing hard, apart from the one moaning about his hand being bitten. But unfortunately that wasn't Samo, who found it hilarious to point out that Elliot's curly hair, which was now soaking wet, made the perfect 'bog brush'.

Then came the sound of a male teacher shouting at someone outside for kicking a football against a window. His proximity was enough to break the spell and the boys let go of Elliot, who slumped on to the tiled floor, gasping for breath and face soaked with a mixture of tears and disgusting loo water.

Before they finally left him alone, Samo growled: 'Don't you dare say a word about this to anyone, freak, or it'll be a whole lot worse next time.'

Then he was alone.

He stayed on the cubicle floor, hugging his knees and desperately trying to calm himself down, for several minutes. Eventually, he heard the teacher from outside come in and ask if everything was all right in here, but he held the door shut with his hands and stayed silent until he'd gone. When it sounded like the coast was clear, he stood up and let himself out. He spent several minutes scrubbing his face and hair with soap and water at one of the sinks, ignoring a couple of other boys who came in to use the urinals and wishing himself invisible. He took a clump of paper towels from the dispenser and made a feeble attempt at drying his hair before heading outside. He walked around alone for the remaining time until the bell sounded, not wanting to meet anyone's eye; trying to blank out what had happened.

★   ★   ★

It wasn't until he went to catch the bus home that afternoon that Elliot realised he hadn't recovered the stuff from his pockets, including his bus pass.

As he tried to explain the situation to the driver, who was new, Samo shoved his way past, making a sniffing sound and commenting that something 'smelled like crap'. To make matters worse, before disappearing upstairs, he told the driver: 'Don't listen to him. He doesn't usually get this bus. He's a chubby little liar.'

Fortunately Lisa, who was sitting in her usual spot on the bottom deck, came to her friend's aid. 'Is there a problem?' she asked, smiling sweetly at the driver.

'This lad doesn't have a bus pass. He says he's

113

lost it, but the other boy tells me he's lying and doesn't normally take this service.'

'Well, I can vouch for the fact that Elliot gets this bus every day,' she said, tucking her hair behind her right ear and flashing him a doe-eyed look. 'He gets on and off at the same stop as me, I promise. Please could you let him on? Otherwise he'll be stranded and his mum will be beside herself.'

'Fine,' he nodded. 'Go on then.'

'Thanks,' Elliot said, sitting down next to his friend and greeting Charlotte and Joanne, who were on the row in front.

'What happened?' Charlotte asked, slipping off the head-phones she'd been using to listen to her personal stereo.

'I lost my bus pass,' Elliot said.

'You're joking. Nightmare.'

'Any idea where it might be?' Lisa asked.

'I have a good idea where I lost it, but I doubt it's still there. Hopefully someone will have handed it in.'

'I see Samo was being his usual helpful self,' Joanne said.

Elliot nodded and yet couldn't bring himself to say any more. The girls knew Samo was a nasty piece of work. They'd seen him in action plenty of times before on the bus, but what had happened earlier that day was on another level. There was no way he was telling them about that. He hadn't even told Neil. It was too damn humiliating and, truth be told, he couldn't trust himself not to burst into tears in the process. All he wanted was to blank the incident out of his mind and do his utmost to ensure it never happened again. That was easier said than done, though, when Samo decided to come downstairs halfway through the journey, as he often did, to show off to the older girls sitting on the seats at the back.

Elliot, who'd been keeping one eye on the stairs for this very reason, felt his heart rate quicken when the bully appeared. Discretely, hoping to avoid getting shoved, he shuffled as far along the seat as he could without squashing Lisa, who was sitting next to the window. He still ended up with a flick to the earlobe that made him yelp.

Lisa, who was locked in a debate with Joanne about who was better looking out of Patrick Swayze and Keanu Reeves, turned to look at him. 'What's wrong?'

'Nothing,' he replied, silently fuming while imagining ways he could one day exact his revenge on his persecutor.

As the bus journey continued, Elliot hated having to listen to Samo's bragging voice booming out from behind him, telling various feeble attempts at jokes to the girls too stupid to see through him. They laughed, although none of it was remotely funny, as far as Elliot was concerned. He feared that Samo would also tell them what he'd done to him at lunch break. Thankfully he didn't, although Elliot suspected the only reason for this was because he didn't want to run the risk of getting into trouble. He did, however, make another comment about there being an awful smell as he made his way

115

off the bus. 'I think alien boy filled his pants,' he said, flicking Elliot's earlobe again as he walked past. 'Or maybe he's been bumming one of his gay pals. E.T. phone home.'

'Hey! Leave him alone,' Lisa snapped, clocking what he did this time. It only served to amuse Samo, who turned and blew a kiss in her direction as he waited for the doors to swing open.

'Is that why you cried out before?' Lisa asked Elliot. 'Did he also do that last time he walked past?'

Elliot nodded. 'It doesn't matter. Leave it.'

But before he could stop her, Lisa stood up and opened the window. As the bus pulled away and Samo walked along the pavement, she banged on the glass and shouted: 'The only thing that smells bad round here is your dog breath.'

The funny thing was that he hadn't been looking in their direction at the time and the noise made him jump. Charlotte and Joanne both laughed; even Elliot had to smile, although he hoped it wouldn't be something he ended up paying for later.

'You shouldn't let him talk to you like that, El,' Lisa said when it was just the two of them walking home.

'What am I supposed to do? He's massive. You're safe enough because you're a girl: he's never going to do anything to you. But he'd pummel me without a second thought.'

'Does he bother you much at school?'

Elliot looked the other way and shrugged.

116

'What does that mean?'

'Dunno.'

Lisa stopped walking and grabbed his hand. She pulled him towards her so he couldn't avoid her gaze. 'Dunno? Don't give me that, El. Not me. What's going on? I thought you were quiet on the journey home today. Plus there was that business with your bus pass. Something happened, didn't it? What did he do?'

'It's nothing. Don't worry about it.' But even as he said the words, his tears betrayed him.

He told his friend everything and, by the time he'd finished, Lisa was spitting feathers.

'That bastard!' she said. 'No way he's getting away with this. We're going to make him pay.'

The look in her eyes was ferocious, like a wolf baring its teeth. Elliot had only seen her that way once before — when he'd eventually told her about how that turncoat Peter had broken his glasses on the day they met.

And, boy, had Peter paid the price for that betrayal.

12

NOW

Sunday, 22 July 2018

'Breakfast's ready!' Lisa shouted up the stairs again. 'If you two don't come in a minute, your eggs will be cold.'

'I'll be down in a second,' Ben called in reply, presumably still in his bedroom. Meanwhile Chloe appeared at the top of the stairs, looking bedraggled in her pyjamas and tatty lemon dressing gown, hair all over the place.

'There you are,' Lisa said. 'Why are you wearing that old thing?'

Chloe frowned. 'What do you mean?'

'That dressing gown. It's far too short and looks ready for the bin. That's why we got you the new turquoise one. Any particular reason you don't seem to like wearing it?'

'Muuum! Not now. I'm still half-asleep.' She walked past Lisa and took a seat at the kitchen table next to her dad.

Still watching the staircase for Ben, Lisa went on: 'It's nearly ten thirty, young lady. A couple of years ago you'd have been up for three hours by now. What time did you go to sleep?'

'Not that late.'

'And the night before, at Holly's house?'

Chloe mumbled something inaudible.

'Ben?' Lisa called up the stairs again.

'One second, Mum. Seriously.'

'You already said that, and it was a lot more than one second ago, love. Come on now. It's bacon and eggs — and yours will be cold.'

Ben eventually joined them a couple of minutes later. He was at least dressed, in jeans and a T-shirt, but he didn't appear to have showered or shaved. Although not quite sixteen, he already had a thick beard growth. This was something Lisa wished he hadn't inherited from his father. Since he'd been out of work, Mike's face had been more or less permanently covered in that thick stubble of his — and Lisa hated it. For one thing it looked slovenly, especially in the half-beard, in-between stage that Mike favoured. It certainly wouldn't help him find the kind of professional work he needed. Plus it was so coarse and prickly that it hurt when they kissed or were in bed together. Not that this was too much of an issue at the moment. Mike's ongoing problems weren't exactly doing wonders for their love life.

'You look like you're growing a beard,' she told her son. 'Does this mean you're going to let it get all long and bushy over the holidays?'

'Don't be embarrassing, Mum,' he said. 'I just didn't fancy shaving today. Anyway, what's wrong with a beard? Dad usually has one.'

'Do I?' Mike piped up, getting involved at last and rubbing his dense stubble with the palm of his right hand. 'I don't plan it that way. I see it more like a by-product of not shaving.'

'Who made the scrambled eggs?' Ben asked before digging in.

'Guess,' Lisa replied, eyeing the others and placing her right forefinger in front of her mouth.

Ben chewed for a few seconds, screwing his eyes up in mock concentration, before declaring: 'Definitely Dad.'

This made Mike chuckle. 'How did you guess?'

Ben shrugged. 'Your scrambled eggs are better than Mum's. Sorry, Mum, but they are. It's about the only thing Dad cooks better than you, so don't take it to heart. But he does make delicious scrambled eggs. Can I have the ketchup, Chloe?'

'Please,' Lisa chipped in. 'Manners cost nothing.'

'Fine. Please, if it's not too much trouble, could you pass the ketchup, sister dear?'

She did as he asked.

'Thank you,' Ben said. 'And, darling Chloe, would you mind please talking a little less? All your chitter-chatter is hurting my ears.'

'Leave her alone,' Mike said, leaning over and planting a kiss on his daughter's head. 'You know she needs her fuel in the mornings to get going. Do you like my scrambled eggs too, love?'

Chloe nodded, her mouth full from her last bite. Then when her mouth was empty, she said: 'But Mum's are nice too.'

'That's my girl,' Lisa replied.

'Creep,' Mike and Ben said in unison. 'Jinx,' Ben added first, making everyone laugh.

Mike started talking about some cricket match to Ben, who played along and joined in the discussion, although Lisa suspected he wasn't particularly interested. She was glad to see her son in such jovial spirits for once. He'd been very moody of late, but this morning the cloud seemed to have lifted — or rather shifted to his sister.

Chloe clearly wasn't in the mood for talking at all. She was on the cusp of becoming a teenager, so this wasn't too surprising. Lisa wondered if it was anything to do with her friend Holly, whose house she'd stayed at on Friday, but she didn't dare to ask. Somehow Chloe had already cottoned on to the fact that her mum didn't like her (Lisa found her shifty), so any such question would simply cause her to bristle up. Consequently, she left her daughter to eat her breakfast and zoned out, enjoying a rare moment of relative peace.

Lisa had always been a big fan of family meals: everyone sitting down together at the table and talking to one another. Sunday breakfast was a particular favourite. It was the time of the week when everyone was least likely to be in a rush to do something else. It was the right distance away from Friday afternoon and Monday morning for all four of them to be at their most relaxed, which meant less chance of an argument.

'What's for tea tonight?' Ben asked her out of the blue.

Lisa shook her head. 'What? You've barely finished your breakfast and you're already asking about that.'

'Why not? Can we get takeaway pizza?'

Chloe's eyes lit up. 'Yeah, Mum. Go on. We've

not had that for ages.'

'That's because it's expensive,' Lisa replied, wishing she wasn't always the one who had to say these things. 'Plus it's full of junk. Anyway, we're doing something different today.'

Both kids groaned.

'Elliot's coming to cook for us,' she said. 'He'll be over mid-afternoon.'

'What's he cooking?' Ben asked.

'No idea. He said he'd bring whatever he needed with him.'

'Maybe it'll be something Australian,' Chloe chipped in.

Ben grinned. 'Like kangaroo or crocodile? He might struggle to find that in Asda. Mind you, they like eating bugs and stuff over there, don't they? Maybe we'll have to eat live spiders or something, like a Bushtucker Trial on *I'm a Celebrity*.'

'Yuck,' Chloe said.

'I wouldn't worry, you two. He was telling me about how much he'd missed certain English foods during his time away, so you'll probably find it's something familiar.'

Mike stayed silent, neither laughing nor joining in with the banter. He'd been pleasant enough to El yesterday; Lisa really hoped that wasn't about to change.

★ ★ ★

'G'day, cobber,' Elliot said in an exaggerated Australian accent as Lisa opened the front door.

It was just before 3 p.m. and, after a dry but

122

overcast morning, it had started to spit with rain.

Lisa greeted him with a hug and a kiss on the cheek. 'Come on in before you get too wet.'

Elliot, holding a large brown paper bag in one arm, stepped inside, wiping his shoes on the doormat. 'How are you going?'

'Fine, thanks. You?'

'Great. Shame about the weather, but. And there's stupid old me planning a traditional Aussie barbie.' His eyes shot wide open. 'Hold on. You have got a barbecue, right? And somewhere under cover where I can cook?'

Leading him through to the kitchen, Lisa winced. 'We do, but I'm not sure we have any, um, charcoal or — '

His tanned face broke into a smile and he gave her an affectionate squeeze with his free arm. 'Don't worry, Lisa. I'm pulling your leg. I've gone for a traditional English roast, instead. When in Rome.'

'I can't believe I fell for that. A roast sounds lovely. What meat have you gone for?'

'Beef, naturally. I know it's usually more of a winter meal, but I thought: what the hell. It's not exactly summery weather, is it?' He wrinkled up his nose. 'And if I'm totally honest, it's what I fancied, being back here and all.'

'Where did you go shopping?' Lisa asked, puzzled by the paper bag.

'Details, details,' he replied with a flamboyant wave of his hand. 'Come on. Let's get going. If you could give me a quick walkthrough where everything is and how the oven and hobs work, then you can leave me to it.'

123

'I'm happy to lend a hand.'

'No need, although I'd love to have your company and maybe the odd cup of tea along the way. Where's everyone else?'

'The kids are up in their rooms and Mike's, um . . . well, I'm not sure where he is, to be honest.'

He raised an eyebrow. 'Everything all right? I'm not stepping on any toes, am I?'

'No, don't be silly. It's lovely of you to come and cook for us like this.'

The next hour or so flew by as Elliot whipped around the kitchen like a pro, refusing any help and yet still finding time to chat, while deftly avoiding answering anything too probing about himself.

'You've certainly progressed from burning beans on toast,' Lisa told him.

'I enjoy cooking,' he replied. 'I took some classes when I first got my own place.'

'I thought single guys were all about microwave meals, takeaways and eating out.'

'Not this one.'

'What about the extra numbers?'

'What, cooking for five?' He looked at Lisa, who at his insistence was sitting out of the way at the kitchen table, and slowly shook his head. 'Just because I'm single and don't have any children, that doesn't mean I'm some kind of loser with no friends.'

'No, I didn't — '

He winked. 'I've got it covered. Don't worry.'

'No, it looks and smells fantastic, honestly. Sorry, I feel bad now.' She lowered her voice.

'I'm not used to a man who's quite so handy around the kitchen. You remember what my dad was like. He could barely cook oven chips.'

'And Mike? Doesn't he like to — '

She shook her head but said nothing as she heard someone coming down the stairs. Chloe and Ben had both popped in at different points to greet their visitor; Mike had been conspicuous by his absence. According to Ben, he'd gone out for a run — something he rarely ever did these days — but he'd not told her anything about this, nor said hello or goodbye when he'd slipped out and back in again through the front door. Now he walked into the kitchen fresh out of the shower, hair still wet and wearing a clean polo shirt and shorts.

'How are we doing?' he said, avoiding Lisa's eye as he headed straight for the fridge.

'Hello, Mike,' Elliot replied, throwing him a warm smile and standing to one side. 'Sorry to impose myself on you again.'

'You're all right. Beer?'

'Only if you're having one.'

Mike removed two bottles of Heineken from the fridge, opened them and handed one to Elliot before asking Lisa if she wanted anything, which she didn't.

'Where have you been?' she asked.

'For a run.'

Lisa tried to convey to him with probing eyes that this was unusual. 'Yes, Ben told me. But where did you go?'

'Smells good,' he said to Elliot rather than answering her.

125

'Thanks. Hopefully it'll taste even better.' He raised his bottle of beer. 'Cheers.'

'Cheers. Anyway, I'll leave you to it.'

'Aren't you going to stay and chat for a bit?' Lisa asked, widening her eyes at him.

He avoided her gaze. 'I have a couple of things to do.'

'Hey, you'll never guess who I saw earlier,' Elliot said once they were alone again.

'Who?'

'Peter Webber. Well, I'm ninety-nine per cent sure it was him. I passed him on the pavement walking here. I don't think he recognised me, so I didn't stop to chat.'

Lisa gave him a blank look, to which he replied: 'You know, the kid who broke my glasses the day we met. The boy I thought was my friend, who turned on me to impress Johnny and Carl.'

'Oh God, that Peter!' Lisa said, raising a hand to her mouth. 'Does he still live in the village? I wouldn't know him from Adam.'

Elliot shrugged before opening the oven door, prodding the meat and turning some of the vegetables. Then he walked over to the table and leaned on the back of one of the seats. 'Do you remember what you did to him for me?'

'How could I forget?'

13

THEN

Friday, 23 August 1991

Elliot hadn't seen Peter since the day, just over a fortnight earlier, when he'd so cruelly stomped on his glasses. He'd probably been away on holiday, judging by the tan he'd picked up in the meantime.

Elliot spotted him from Lisa's bedroom window. He was walking along the street, wearing shorts and a Manchester United shirt.

'Bastard,' he muttered.

'Who's a bastard?' Lisa asked, looking up from painting her toenails on the bed.

'Oh, no one.' He'd not yet told his new friend about Peter's involvement in the incident.

'So you shout that out of the window at everyone who walks past?'

'I didn't shout. And the window's closed, so he won't have heard me.'

Stuff it, Elliot thought. He told Lisa everything — and was surprised at the ferocity of her reaction.

'What? He really is a bastard! Why didn't you mention this before? We're going after him.'

'What about your nai — '

'They can wait.' She wiped the wet bits away with a tissue and grabbed some socks.

127

Outside it was overcast but dry and warm.

'Which way did he go?'

Elliot felt somewhere in between nervous and excited about what Lisa had planned. 'He looked like he was heading towards Vicky Lane.'

'Perfect. Come on.'

'What are we going to do?'

'I'll work that out when we catch up with him.'

As it turned out, that didn't happen until they were a good way down the lane, at a point where the track was more dirt than tarmac; well past the scene of Elliot's humiliation, which still stung every time he walked by. This far down, Vicky Lane was often impassable after heavy rain, when it became a water-logged mud bath. But the weather had been kind for the past week, so today it was fine.

'There he is,' Elliot said, pointing to a figure a hundred yards or so ahead of them, who was leaning forward at the side of the track, hands on his knees and panting. 'He must have been running. That explains how he got so far ahead.'

'Do you think he was running from us?'

Elliot shook his head. 'He likes running. He was the fastest at school and he's in some kind of athletics club. Best not challenge him to a race, like you did the other two, because you might not win.'

Lisa frowned. 'No faith in me, have you? Don't worry, that's not what I have in mind for Peter. He doesn't look much, does he? He's all skin and bone; definitely shorter than I am.' She nodded. 'Good.'

Next thing she told Elliot to hide in the

undergrowth at the side of the track in a position where he could watch what happened without being seen. Meanwhile, she strode on towards Peter, who was busy doing stretches.

Elliot crept forward through the long grass and shrubs that provided his cover, careful to stay out of sight. Once Lisa was within a couple of metres of her target, he stopped where he was, maintaining a crouch position, and waited.

'Hello,' Lisa said in a friendly voice. 'Peter, isn't it?'

Peter, who'd been facing the other way, turned around with a look of surprise on his face. 'Yes. Who are you?'

She held out her right arm, which he met with a handshake. 'Lisa. Pleased to meet you.'

'Hello, Lisa. Nice to meet you too. I'm sorry but how — '

'I know Johnny and Carl. You're a friend of theirs, aren't you?'

He nodded gingerly. 'Yeah, I guess. Are they around, then?'

'That's right. We're hanging out in the field over there.' She pointed off to the side of the track, back the way they'd come, giggled, and bit her bottom lip. 'I saw you running past and asked them who you were.' She placed a hand on his shoulder, maintaining eye contact. 'You, um, seem really fit. Do you go running a lot? And how come you're so lovely and tanned. Have you been away?'

Elliot smiled to himself at what an outrageous flirt Lisa was being. It made her seem so much older than him: so self-confident and aware of

129

the power she could wield over unsuspecting boys. It was clear that Peter, whose cheeks were crimson as he told her how much he liked running and how he'd just returned from a family holiday to Corfu, was already putty in her hands. He was almost drooling.

'The only thing is,' she added, 'as I was rushing to catch up with you, I felt my favourite bracelet slip off my wrist.' She nodded towards a patch of grass a little along from where Elliot was hiding, but on the opposite side of the track. 'Would you mind giving me a hand finding it? I haven't got my glasses on today and I'm useless without them.'

What are you up to, Lisa? Elliot thought, remaining in his hiding place as he watched Peter nod and agree to look for the fictional bracelet.

They walked over to the spot she'd indicated and both spent several minutes bent over, scouring the long, thick grass for something that wasn't there.

'Are you sure it was here that it fell off?' Peter asked eventually.

She looked like she was about to cry. 'I think so. I'm pretty sure. Please don't give up. It was a gift from my nana. I'd be heartbroken if I lost it.'

This spurred Peter on and, as he continued to look in the grass, Lisa discretely turned to where Elliot was positioned and winked.

'What are you doing?' he mouthed.

Her only reply was to hold a finger up to her lips and look away.

She had Peter eating out of the palm of her hand. He was down on all fours, crawling around like a dog, while she stood to one side, suggesting different spots for him to try. This went on for a good ten minutes. Eventually, an exhausted Peter stood up to stretch his back and shake his legs. 'I'm having no luck. What does it look like exactly, this bracelet?'

'It's a very thin gold chain with a small heart pendant attached. The catch is a bit dodgy, which is why I think it came off. I should have stopped straight away when I felt it fall, but I was worried you might run off before I had a chance to speak to you. I didn't imagine it would be so difficult to find. Maybe it was a little bit further along.'

This was enough to convince Peter to have another look; if he wondered why he was doing all the work while Lisa watched, he didn't let on. It was all Elliot could do not to burst out laughing.

'Watch out,' she said. 'There's a big pile of dog muck near your right leg.'

'Eww!' he replied, shuffling away from it, then carrying on searching.

'You don't know anyone with a metal detector, do you? That might be the answer, but I've only recently moved to the village, so I don't — '

'Good idea. Um, I can't think of anyone, but my parents might be able to. Would you like to come back to my house so I can ask? Dad's at work, but Mum's home.'

'That sounds nice. But won't your girlfriend mind? If you were my boyfriend, I know I wouldn't like the idea of another girl going home with you.'

A red-faced Peter, falling hook, line, and sinker for her con, said: 'I, er, don't have a girlfriend at the moment.'

This amused Elliot, who knew for a fact that Peter had never had a girlfriend in his life.

'Oh, that's good.' Lisa smiled, batting her eyelids like she'd been doing it for years. 'But would it be all right if we looked here a little bit longer first? It sounds stupid, but I'm afraid that if we go now, someone else might come along in the meantime and find it. I love it so much.' She looked down at the ground, playing her role with aplomb. 'And it's all I've got left to remind me of poor Nana since she died.'

Thus she convinced Peter to continue. The search carried on for so long that Elliot felt his own crouching knees start to seize up, forcing him to silently shift into a seated position. He was beginning to wonder where Lisa was going with this when suddenly everything changed.

One minute she was standing over Peter, smiling sweetly and encouraging him to continue. The next she pounced on him from behind, wrapping her right arm all the way around his neck to her left bicep, and pressing down on his head with her left hand. Her face was pure concentration and aggression, while Peter's eyes were wide with shock and fear.

'What the hell?' he whined, struggling to free himself but not getting anywhere.

'Every move you make to get away, it'll get tighter,' Lisa said through gritted teeth.

'Why are you — '

'Quiet. You don't speak unless I say so, right?'

She must have increased the tightness of her grip at this point, because now Peter's eyes looked ready to pop out of his beetroot face.

'Right?' she repeated.

'Yes,' he replied in a tiny, terrified voice.

'This should make things crystal clear,' Lisa said as she jerked herself and her captive to one side and then pushed his face down towards the ground, causing him to yelp.

'Come over here, El,' she called, looking in his direction.

Elliot jumped to his feet and walked over, not knowing what to say or do. When he got there, he saw that Lisa was holding Peter's head above the pile of dog muck she'd warned him about a few minutes earlier.

'Anyone coming?' she asked, keeping her eyes locked on Peter.

Elliot looked up and down the lane. 'No.'

'Doesn't smell nice, does it, Peter?' She inched his head closer to the foul mess.

He shook his head. 'Please don't.'

'Listen, there is no lost bracelet. Do you know what this is really about?'

Elliot felt awkward standing there in the middle of the lane, watching this bizarre drama unfold. He had no idea that Lisa was capable of this and part of him wanted to tell her to stop; to let Peter go. He looked so pathetic, trapped like he was. Surely she wouldn't really lower his face into the dog dirt, would she?

Peter mumbled something inaudible in

response to Lisa's question, which led to her squeezing his neck even tighter and him letting out another yelp.

'So we can understand, please,' she said.

'Elliot,' he whined. 'What I did to his glasses.'

'Good. Now we're getting somewhere. So what do you have to say to my good friend here?'

'Sorry,' he spluttered, snot dripping out of his nose and his mouth drooling.

'I don't think he heard you. You'll have to speak up. Or maybe you'd rather have a mouthful of — '

'Sorry! Sorry! I didn't mean it.'

'And you'll never do anything like that to him again, will you?'

'No, no. I promise. Never.'

She turned to Elliot. 'Up to you. Do we accept his apology, or shall I keep on going? Maybe we should make him buy you a new pair of specs.'

Elliot shook his head. There was no way Peter would be able to afford to replace his glasses. Besides, even if he could somehow raise the cash, it would only create a difficult situation with Elliot's mum, who thought he'd lost them. She'd end up questioning where the money had come from and — well — it wasn't worth the hassle.

'No, I think he's had enough.' He couldn't believe it, but somehow he felt sorry for Peter, despite what he'd done to him. He looked so scared and helpless. Plus they had been friends once. Just because Peter had chosen to forget that fact when he was so desperate to impress Johnny and Carl, it didn't mean Elliot had to be the same. He was better than that.

'Are you sure?' Lisa said. 'Maybe I should give him a taste of this dog muck, all the same.'

'No, please!' Peter cried out, wriggling and shaking in a last desperate attempt to get free.

'Do you really want me to squeeze tighter?'

He stopped.

She patted his head. 'Good boy. Now I'd like to hear you say sorry to Elliot one more time.'

'I'm sorry.'

'Like you mean it.'

'I do! I'm really sorry.'

'Stay well away from him, okay? Otherwise, I'll be back for you. And next time there'll be no letting you off.'

As quickly as she'd grabbed him in the first place, she let him go, flinging him to one side like a rag doll. 'Get out of here.'

And he did. He ran off as fast as his shaking legs would carry him, only slowing down when there was a safe distance between them. He turned around at this point and it looked for a moment like he might shout something at them. But when Lisa raised a hand and made as if to come after him, he had second thoughts and carried on going.

Neither Lisa nor Elliot said a word until he was out of sight, at which point they both burst into laughter.

'Where on earth did that come from?' he asked her, open-mouthed. 'You were like Rambo meets the Terminator or something. How did you know — '

'I went to judo every week where we used to

135

live,' she said. 'They ran classes at my old school on Saturday mornings. I started at like five years old and I was pretty good.'

'No kidding. You were vicious. I didn't think you had it in you. What was it called, that move or whatever you used on him?'

'I had him in a choke hold. I'd get into trouble for using it like that, to be honest. You're only supposed to use it in self-defence outside competitions and training, but — well, I was never going to hurt him. It got the message across, anyway.'

'You can say that again. So are you going to carry on with judo here?'

She shook her head. 'Doubt it. I stopped about six months ago. It was time for a change.'

'Would you really have pushed Peter's face into the dog muck?'

'Of course not. That would be disgusting. It wasn't part of the plan, but after I spotted it, I improvised.'

Elliot chuckled. 'You had a plan?'

Lisa rolled her eyes. 'Well, kind of. I sized Peter up and decided I could probably take him. I maybe ought to have asked you first whether he knew any martial arts, as then he might have been able to escape. But I took a gamble and it paid off. He's not the kind of person who's likely to try to get revenge, is he?'

Elliot shook his head. 'I doubt it. He'll probably want to forget the whole thing ever happened. I don't expect he'll tell anyone that you got the better of him like that.'

'Because I'm a girl?'

'I didn't say that,' Elliot replied with a grin. 'But since you did, then yeah. Thanks for standing up for me. It means a lot.'

'That's what friends are for.'

'I'll pay you back one day.'

'Don't be silly. There's no need.'

Elliot took Lisa's hand in his and, looking her in the eyes, he squeezed it. 'I will, though. I don't know how yet, but I definitely will.'

14

NOW

Sunday, 22 July 2018

'Wow, this is delicious.' Lisa raised her glass of wine and proposed a toast. 'To our visiting chef. It's wonderful to see you again after so long. You're very welcome to come around here and cook for us whenever you like. Cheers.'

'Cheers,' everyone said in unison.

'You're too kind,' Elliot added. 'It's my absolute pleasure to be here and I'm delighted to cook for you all.'

A moment later Ben grabbed his throat with both hands and jerked to his feet, making a guttural choking sound as his chair tumbled backwards on to the kitchen floor.

Lisa jumped to her feet, the terrified look on Ben's face filling her with panic. Her pulse was racing and she screamed something unintelligible, even to her, as her arms reached desperately across the table to her son. But before she or one of the others had a chance to respond, Elliot was standing behind him, circling his arms around his stomach. He administered a series of upward thrusts with a fist below Ben's chest until the piece of beef lodged in his throat popped out on to the table.

The sound of Ben gasping for air filled the

room — and time started again. Lisa looked at the deathly pale, saucer-eyed faces of her husband and daughter before remembering to breathe again and, finally, rushing to her son's side.

'Are you okay, love?' she said, as Mike and Chloe also leaned in, both repeating the question and looking equally shocked.

Ben replied with a slow nod of his head, making a thumb sign with one hand, as he rubbed the top of his chest with the other and cleared his throat several times, gradually catching his breath.

'He'll be right,' Elliot said, patting Ben on the back before returning to his seat. 'He just needs to chew on his meat a few more times in future, rather than trying to gulp it down whole.'

'Thank goodness you were here,' Lisa said, remaining at Ben's side and keeping her eyes fixed on him, part of her refusing to believe it was over; fearing he might start choking again. 'You used the Heimlich manoeuvre, right? That was incredible, El.'

'I only did what anyone else would have done. Glad to help.'

★ ★ ★

Later, after Chloe and Ben had disappeared up to their bedrooms and the three adults were drinking coffee in the lounge, Lisa brought up the choking incident again.

'I can't thank you enough for what you did,' she told Elliot. 'I keep thinking what might have

139

happened and, well, you saved his life. How did you get to him so quickly? It was like you were there, helping him straight away, while the rest of us were still processing what was going on.'

He shrugged. 'Right place, right time, I guess.'

Mike, who'd been quiet ever since, was staring at his mobile. Eventually he looked up and asked if Elliot had performed the manoeuvre before.

He nodded. 'I have, believe it or not. This is the second time. The first was a bit more hectic. It took a lot more goes until it worked. So much so that I feared I was going to lose him at one point.'

'When was that?' Lisa asked.

'About twelve months ago. I was working late, alone with a colleague, and he started choking on some pizza we'd ordered. I had been shown what to do once, years earlier, on a first aid course, but theory and practice are very different. You have to get your hands together in the right place and go pretty hard with the thrusts. Ben might be a bit sore tomorrow, but that's better than the alternative, right?'

'Definitely.'

'I thought Heimlich was only recommended as a last resort these days,' Mike said in a flat voice. 'Aren't you supposed to start with back slaps, working up to that if necessary?'

'Are you kidding, Mike?' Lisa snapped. 'You're seriously going to start criticising Elliot's technique after he saved Ben's life. Is that what you've been looking up on your mobile for the past however long? You're unbelievable.'

'I'm just — '

'Well don't. I didn't see you doing anything to help.'

'I didn't see you doing anything either.'

'Come on, guys,' Elliot said, clearing his throat, his hands kneading the sofa cushion. 'You're both in shock, which is totally understandable. I, um — '

Before he could finish, Mike let out an angry sigh, stood up and left the room. As Elliot and Lisa stared at each other in stunned silence, they heard the front door slam shut.

Lisa rolled her eyes. 'Sorry about that. Mike's not in a good place at the moment and it doesn't take much to set him off. He had no right — '

'Don't worry. No offence taken. So what's going on with him? How do you mean he's not in a good place? I thought the start of the summer holidays was every teacher's favourite time of year.'

'That's the thing.' Lisa paused to have a drink from her coffee mug. 'Mike isn't a teacher any more. He was doing well. He was a deputy head with excellent prospects, but that didn't work out. Now he's, um, in between jobs.'

'You're joking. I had no idea. Why didn't you say?'

'It's complicated. Things happened and . . . Mike's still very raw. The point is that he probably finds you a bit of a threat, what with your successful business and glamorous life in Australia. I imagine that's why he said what he did.'

She could have told Elliot this before. There had been plenty of opportunities. But the truth was that she hadn't wanted to tell him. It wasn't that she was embarrassed or ashamed about her husband no longer having a job. It was more that she didn't want her old friend, who was doing so well, to see how imperfect her life was now. And Mike's joblessness — as well as the awful career-wrecking allegation that had led to it — was at the core of the family's problems.

She'd always intended to tell Elliot eventually. God knows, it would certainly explain a few things, like Mike coming home blind drunk in that taxi on Friday night. But she'd knowingly put it off as long as she could.

It was like that school reunion she'd attended a few years ago, at a point in her life when things had been going smoothly. All the people in attendance had done their utmost to show everyone else how well things had turned out for them, papering over the cracks; in several instances, these started to show through once the booze was flowing. A case in point was Joanne, who used to get the bus to school every day with Lisa and Elliot. She'd shown up looking fabulous, crowing about how she was making stacks of cash in some high-flying business role in London. Three hours later, Lisa had found her sobbing in the toilets, cheeks lined with mascara. She'd confessed how unhappy she was after years of trying and failing to have children, only for her long-term boyfriend to leave her for a twenty-year-old, who'd since fallen pregnant.

At the time, Lisa hadn't understood why people felt the need to hide the truth; why they cared so much what people they hadn't seen in years thought. But she'd been in a position of strength then. She and Mike had both been content at work and happy as a couple. The kids had been younger and less sulky. Ben and Chloe had still enjoyed doing family things, rather than spending so much time in their bedrooms, glued to their mobiles, which they guarded like state secrets.

Then that little shit had come along and poisoned everything.

El had always been a good listener. It had been one of the first things she'd liked about him all those years ago: an unusual trait in a boy, which had no doubt been fostered by Wendy. From what Lisa knew of him as a thirty-eight-year-old, it was a quality he'd retained. So she decided that now was the right time to tell him what had happened.

For her the nightmare had begun when she'd received that phone call from a shell-shocked Mike. Just thinking about it now, so long after the event, still made her stomach churn. Lisa took a deep breath before she started talking.

★ ★ ★

Liam Hornby.

Lisa had heard Mike moan about him on several occasions. He was a troublemaker. This wasn't unusual, though. There were certain kids from her own school that she complained to Mike about too. Every school had its problem children. Most classes had one, although of

143

course the level of the problem could vary considerably.

Liam Hornby was definitely in the top tier of trouble-makers. He was a problem that needed dealing with on a weekly, if not daily, basis. So by the time he decided to take things to the next level, turning Mike and his whole family's lives upside down in the process, his was a name with which Lisa was only too familiar.

It was very unusual for Mike to call her at work. When she saw his number pop up on her mobile as she was chatting to Sandra over coffee in the staffroom, she feared there must be a problem with Ben or Chloe.

'Hello? Is everything all right, love?'

'No,' he replied in little more than a whisper. 'The shit's hit the fan.'

'What do you mean? Are the kids all right?'

'Yes. It's nothing to do with them.'

'What is it, then? You sound so serious. You're scaring me.'

And then came that name. 'It's Liam Hornby. He's accused me of attacking him.'

What had happened, as Mike recounted it to her, was that Liam had been sent to his office after he'd badly stung another pupil with some nettles. It appeared that he'd brought these into school with the specific intention of hurting someone.

Mike had been called away for a moment and had made the mistake of leaving Liam alone there. When he'd returned, just minutes later, the boy had ransacked the room, throwing files and paperwork all over the place, knocking his

144

computer off the desk and even urinating all over the carpet.

A furious Mike had started yelling at him, for everyone nearby to hear, at which point Liam had smashed his own face down on to the desk, breaking his nose and spraying blood all over the place. Mike, frozen in horror at the nightmare scene unfolding before him, hadn't been quick enough to stop Liam darting out of his office and through the main entrance, leaving school. Mike had immediately sent the caretaker and another male member of staff after him, but they hadn't been able to catch up. Next thing, as Mike was trying to make sense of what had happened, he'd received a phone call from Liam's father, screaming blue murder. His son had turned up at his work in tears and covered in blood, he'd said, claiming that Mike had smashed his head into a desk. Mr Hornby had pledged to do everything in his power to ensure Mike 'went down' for what he'd done, informing him that he'd already called the police.

Of course Mike had tried to reason with him; to explain what had actually happened. But Mr Hornby had hung up on him.

This was the moment that Mike, desperate for support and advice, had phoned his wife at work.

'But you didn't do it,' she said, looking away from Sandra, who'd obviously picked up on the fact that something bad was going on, and was staring at her with a look of concern.

'I know that,' Mike replied. 'But how the hell do I prove it? He and I were the only ones in there.'

Lisa walked out of the staffroom and into the corridor, not wanting anyone to overhear her side of the conversation. 'Well, what about the fact he's a known troublemaker and you're a respected deputy head? Look at what that little scrote did to end up in your office in the first place and the awful mess he made in there. He's obviously deranged. No one's going to believe him.'

'Well, his father does and, after he's said his piece, I expect the police will too. God, how am I going to explain this to the head?'

'Wasn't there anyone else around who could act as a witness?'

'Someone might have heard me losing my rag and screaming at him, but that's hardly going to help. That conniving shit planned the whole thing. He set a trap and I walked right into it. His dad even said something about him wetting himself because he was so distraught.'

Unfortunately, Mike's fears came true and the allegation led to a police investigation as well as a local authority probe. In the meantime, he was suspended on full pay. Not that the money helped when he and the rest of the family had to put up with members of the press on the doorstep, asking uncomfortable questions; when Ben and Chloe got teased by classmates about their dad being a child beater. Of course Mike proclaimed his innocence. He did so to anyone who'd listen. But his name got dragged through the mud nonetheless, while Liam Hornby and his family retained their anonymity, even when the case against Mike fell apart a few weeks later.

It turned out that Liam wasn't quite as clever as he thought. His parents immediately moved him to another school nearby and, of course, he continued to cause trouble. But his big mistake came when his new head teacher called him into her office and he threatened to 'get her sacked', like he'd done to Mike. He gleefully told her how easy it had been to convince everyone he'd been attacked when he'd actually slammed his own head into the desk, warning her that he would do the same again if she didn't treat him right. What he didn't know was that this particular head made a point of recording all such meetings as a way of protecting herself. She came forward with this damning evidence and Mike was off the hook.

Except he wasn't. Not in his own head, anyway; not after everything he'd been through by that stage. The ordeal had eroded Mike's confidence, his faith in the teaching profession and his purpose in life generally. He told Lisa that he felt like no one at his school had stood by him in the way that they should have. So when they invited him back he refused, instead choosing to resign.

Lisa supported this decision. She even understood it to a degree, having witnessed first-hand the hell he'd been through. However, she did assume that in time, once the dust had settled, he'd find another teaching or deputy head role elsewhere. But it soon became clear that this wasn't going to happen.

'I reckon I'm done with teaching,' he told her in bed one night, soon after tendering his resignation. 'The way I feel now, and knowing what I do, I don't think I could ever go back to it.'

'Give it time, love,' she replied, thinking back to when they'd first met on the teacher-training course and how impressed she'd been by his talent and enthusiasm. 'I'm sure you'll feel different eventually. Teaching is your whole life. I know you've been through an awful thing, but please don't make any hasty decisions.'

However, time didn't make any difference. Nor did clearing his name in the press, despite several newspaper and radio reports discussing the ordeal he'd been through. It was too late. The damage was done.

★ ★ ★

'Strewth,' Elliot replied as Lisa finished recounting the story. 'Poor Mike. What a bloody nightmare. And how long ago was it that all this happened?'

'It'll be two years in October since the allegation was first made against him.'

'And he's not worked since?'

'Well, there was one other job that lasted a short while, but that's a story for another day.'

'Of course,' he said. 'You've been through it too, haven't you? Not easy trying to hold it all together, I bet. How are things at the moment?'

'Um.' Lisa shuffled in her seat, willing her eyes not to tear up but feeling them defy her nonetheless. She blinked, hoping Elliot wouldn't notice and that her voice would hold firm. 'They're okay.'

Next thing she knew, she was sobbing uncontrollably and Elliot was at her side, holding her, comforting her.

'Sorry,' she said, once the worst had passed. 'I didn't mean to do that. Things really aren't that bad. I don't know what came over me.'

'Shh,' Elliot whispered, squeezing her hand and looking her in the eye. 'It's all going to be okay. Trust me.'

'I just want us to get back to where we used to be as a family. Before all of the crap we've been through. We were so . . . normal then. So happy.'

'Sure,' Elliot said. 'I can understand that.' He paused before adding: 'How are you guys managing, um, financially, if you don't mind me asking? It can't be easy raising a whole family on one salary.'

Lisa was taken aback by the directness of the question, which she hadn't expected. 'Oh, er, no. We're fine,' she lied. 'We have savings and stuff.'

'Good,' he replied. 'Glad to hear that.'

Lisa pulled away from his embrace, using the palms of her hands to wipe dry her cheeks. 'Listen, I hope you don't think this is me asking for a handout, because it's not. We're fine, honestly. I know your business is doing well and everything, but we don't need your help.'

Elliot held his hands up defensively. 'Whoa there. Chill. I didn't mean it like that. I was asking after my friend, that's all.'

'Okay. Sorry. I probably overreacted.'

'Not at all. It's my fault for being nosy. Thanks

for telling me about Mike. It can't have been easy.' He paused before adding: 'Where do you reckon he's gone?'

'To the pub, at a guess. He'll probably be there for ages.'

'Until I'm out of the way, you mean?'

'Don't be silly.'

But Lisa knew that Elliot was right. She desperately wanted the two men to get along, although with Mike as he was at the moment, she couldn't see it happening.

15

THEN

Friday, 20 November 1992

Elliot thanked Lisa's dad for the lift and stepped out of his latest swanky car. As a BMW dealership manager, Graham Benson seemed to get a new one every few months. Not that Elliot was complaining. It made a pleasant change from riding in his mum's temperamental Vauxhall Nova with its fading red paint.

'Thanks, Dad,' Lisa said, leaning over to kiss him on the cheek before opening the front passenger door and climbing out.

'My pleasure, love,' he replied, smoothing one hand across his comb-over. 'I'll wait here for you at the end.'

As much as Elliot appreciated getting a lift with Mr Benson, as he still tended to call him, he never felt at ease in his company. Despite not being especially tall, his portly figure and booming voice gave him a big presence that intimidated Elliot.

He was always nice enough, but Elliot got the impression that he didn't especially approve of his friendship with Lisa. A traditional man's man, into football, drinking and gambling, he no doubt struggled to understand how the two of them — a boy and a girl — got on so well together. And since Elliot had zero interest in sport and very little knowledge about cars, finding a topic of conversation that lasted more than a few seconds was tricky.

It was fine as long as Lisa was there too. She'd skilfully kept them both chatting throughout the journey to King George's, where they were attending a disco for pupils from their two schools. Elliot hadn't planned on going. He'd made excuses not to attend any of the previous ones. But this time, now they were in their second year at the Westwich schools, Lisa had managed to convince him. Ever since the date had been announced last month, she'd gone on at him about it, promising how much fun he'd have. Eventually he'd given in, although he had no idea why she wanted him there, cramping her style.

She looked amazing, dressed under her winter coat in a floral babydoll dress with black Doc Martens — and more make-up than he'd ever seen her wear before. Like most of the boys, Elliot was wearing T-shirt, jeans and trainers topped with a plaid shirt. The latter, in red and navy, was one of Wendy's creations, although it looked as good as a shop-bought version, he had to admit. He'd made an attempt to lick his unruly curls into shape with some hair gel and even splashed on some of the Brut aftershave he'd received in last year's Christmas stocking.

'Looking sharp, El,' Lisa told him as her dad drove away.

'Thanks. You too. You look, um, lovely.'

She smiled and pecked him on the cheek. Her

152

hair, long and luscious, smelled of coconut combined with the peachy scent of her perfume. God, how he wished at times like this that she looked at him differently: like he secretly felt about her. At least he got to arrive with her. That definitely wouldn't do his street cred any harm.

'So, have you got your eye on anyone tonight?' she asked.

Her question caught Elliot unawares. 'Um, no. Not really. You?'

She smiled mysteriously. 'Maybe. We'll see.'

After queuing up to get inside together and checking their coats into the cloakroom, they entered the hall. In its darkened, music-filled state, it was almost unrecognisable from the space where the boys gathered for morning assembly. Almost immediately, Lisa bumped into a group of her friends and, although she made efforts to introduce Elliot to the girls he didn't already know, he struggled to keep up, thanks to a combination of the pounding bass and his own inhibitions.

'I'm going to the toilet,' he shouted into Lisa's ear.

She grinned, her teeth glowing bright white in the flash of the disco lights. 'Okay. See you back here in a minute.'

He didn't really need to go. It was an excuse to escape feeling awkward and get his bearings. Luckily, on the way back, he bumped into his friend Neil Walsh. He was with another boy from their form, Toby Jenkins, who was also on the rugby team and had been to primary school with Neil. They only lived a couple of streets apart from each other and had cycled together to the disco, as they often did to and from school. Elliot wasn't particularly friendly with Toby; he could be a pain when egged on by the rest of the rugby lot, but he wasn't too bad on his own.

'All right, Turner?' Toby said. 'Who's this hot friend of yours that Walshy won't stop talking about?'

Elliot hadn't taken to the custom of calling boys by their surname, although the practice was prevalent at King George's. It came from the fact that the teachers always referred to them that way, but he found it impersonal and preferred to do otherwise, particularly for his friends.

He realised straight away that Toby was talking about Lisa. Neil had met her a few times when he'd come over to stay the night at Elliot's house. He had noticed him making rather a lot of effort to chat to her on the last occasion, a few weeks earlier. But Neil had never specifically come out and said that he fancied her. Not to him, anyway.

Elliot raised one eyebrow and looked from one classmate to the other. 'I'm not sure what you mean. Neil?'

'Um, yeah. Could you give us a minute, mate?' a red-faced Neil said to Toby.

'Sure. See you in there, Romeo.'

Neil, also in a plaid shirt, screwed up his face and placed a hand on Elliot's shoulder. 'Well, this is awkward. I, er, kind of have a bit of a crush on Lisa, as you've probably now gathered.'

'Hmm,' Elliot replied, arms crossed, having fun watching his friend squirm.

154

'I was going to tell you before, but . . . I guess I wasn't sure how you'd react. I know you two are close and, um, I didn't want to step on your toes or anything. Despite what you just heard, I've not been saying anything disrespectful. She is gorgeous. I mean I wouldn't. Not, if you were . . . you know. But you're not. Right? Help me out here, mate.'

'It's fine,' Elliot said after a dramatic pause. 'Lisa and I are just friends. If you like her, go for it. Better you than some idiot. But I can't believe you didn't say anything before. I could have put a good word in for you.'

Neil let out an exaggerated sigh. 'Thank goodness. I thought you were mad at me for a minute there.' He paused before adding: 'Do you think she might be interested, then?'

'Why don't you ask her? I left her with some of her friends a few minutes ago. She's probably dancing now.'

'Excellent. Let's get in there.'

★　★　★

An hour or so later, with the disco in full swing, Elliot felt far from excellent. He was standing in a corner with a group of classmates. He'd given up trying to talk to any of them, due to the impossibility of hearing what they had to say, or being heard, over the deafening thud of chart hits by the likes of Charles & Eddie, Snap! and The Shamen. He wished he hadn't come to this stupid do. He'd have rather been at home watching TV. But the real reason he was feeling blue was because of what had happened between Neil and Lisa — what still was happening.

He tried not to keep looking at the two of them, together on the bench on the other side of the dance floor, arms around each other and lips locked. It was hard, though. He couldn't believe how long they'd been like that, barely coming up for air.

As suspected, Lisa and her friends had already been dancing when he and Neil had gone into the hall together. She'd spotted them and gestured that they should join in; reluctantly, Elliot had agreed. But a few songs later, feeling self-conscious and uncomfortable about how flirty Neil and Lisa were being with each other, he'd made an excuse about getting a drink. When he'd returned, he'd spotted Lisa's friends but not the other two. And then he'd seen them, snogging each other's faces off.

And despite everything Elliot had told Neil earlier, he wasn't happy about it. He was jealous. Even though Elliot had now developed a few other friendships with classmates, meaning he wasn't the lunchtime loner any more, Neil was still his best friend at school. He was a nice guy. But that didn't mean he was right for Lisa.

Or maybe it did, Elliot thought sulkily. He and Neil had a lot in common — that was why they got along well — and yet in Neil's case, it was better packaged. He was a sportsman, which everyone knew went down well with girls. Plus he was taller and better looking than Elliot, what with his floppy blond hair, warm smile and shoulders so broad it looked like he'd left the coat hanger in his shirt. He knew how to talk to girls too. He did it effortlessly, like it was no big deal. Elliot had noticed this when Neil had come home with him on the bus: not only talking to Lisa, but all the girls.

He could probably have any of the girls here, Elliot mused. So why did he have to choose Lisa? Arriving with her was the one thing he'd had going for him tonight — and Neil had to go and ruin it.

So why had he told him it was okay? He'd taken Neil over to dance with her. What had he expected?

He'd considered telling Lisa how he felt lots of times. But he knew it wouldn't make any difference. She clearly didn't feel that way. He'd never got that vibe from her. And if he did say something, he ran the risk of wrecking what they already had.

He looked over again at the happy couple and was surprised to see that they were actually talking now. And holding hands. For Christ's sake. Seeing that was arguably worse than all the face eating.

Elliot was thinking about going outside again when 'Jump' by Kris Kross started playing. This suddenly drew lots of boys to the dance floor, jostling each other and bouncing up and down like their lives depended on it. Elliot didn't bother. He hated the song and thought they all looked like imbeciles — especially the ones who turned their T-shirts back to front — but that probably had something to do with his bad mood. The good thing was that several spaces came free on the benches alongside the dance floor; seeing as most of the lads he'd been standing with had gone, he decided to sit down. Nowhere near Lisa and Neil, though. That would have been weird.

It was a little awkward sitting there on his own, but he'd felt that way for most of the night, anyway. Plus there wasn't too long left. He was essentially waiting to go home.

Then, to his surprise, up walked Charlotte from the bus. He knew that she and Joanne were supposed to be at the disco, but this was the first time he'd seen either of them.

Charlotte, a brunette, had recently cut her hair into a short bob. Lisa thought it had looked better long — not that she told her so — but Elliot liked it.

She smiled and took a seat next to him, shouting into his ear: 'There you are. Where've you been hiding?'

Elliot shrugged. 'Nowhere. I even danced a bit earlier. How's it going? Having fun?'

'Not as much as those two.' Charlotte nodded towards Lisa and Neil, who were busy sucking face again. 'Are you okay with it?'

'Yeah, why not?' Elliot was glad of the darkness as he felt his cheeks flush. 'They'll probably look good together when they're not pretending to be Siamese twins.'

Charlotte gave him a puzzled look. 'Sorry?'

'You know: because all they've done is snog.'

'Oh, I see what you mean.' She laughed. 'Lisa was, um, a bit worried that you might not like it. That it might be weird, seeing as you're good friends with both of them. That's why she didn't tell you that she fancied Neil, although it was pretty obvious from the way they were chatting on the bus, right?'

Elliot nodded, wondering how he hadn't noticed. Plus he was disappointed that Lisa hadn't felt able to discuss it with him, although she'd obviously talked about it at length with Charlotte. Was the reason really that he was friends with the pair of them, or was it more down to the fact that she realised how he felt about her?

'What are you doing sitting here all alone, anyway?' Charlotte asked.

'Yeah, I was with some mates, but . . . well, that's them over there, dancing. If you can call it that.'

The DJ had decided it was time to please the male crowd, so he kept them on the dance floor with popular songs by Guns N' Roses and Ugly Kid Joe. To Elliot's surprise, Charlotte remained talking to him the whole time. She looked pretty in a denim dungaree dress and white blouse; every time he spoke into her ear, he couldn't help but notice her perfume, which was lovely and sweet, like vanilla ice cream. He started to wonder . . .

'I wanted to ask you something,' Charlotte said, the tickle of her breath in his ear taking on a sensual note as the cogs of Elliot's mind whirred.

'Please do.'

'There's a friend that Lisa and I wanted to introduce you to tonight. A girl in our form.

159

We've told her all about you and, er, she's keen to meet you. Lisa was supposed to be the one to make the introduction, but she's busy. What do you reckon? Are you up for it?'

This unexpected twist in the conversation totally threw Elliot. He didn't know what to say. Part of him was disappointed, after allowing himself to think that Charlotte might be interested in him. He also feared a brain freeze at the prospect of chatting to a girl he'd never met before. And yet what did he have to lose? What was the worst that could happen?

'Um, where is she?' he asked. 'And who is she? Why do you think we might like each other?'

'She's called Nicola. She's on the dance floor. Come over with me and I'll take care of things from there.'

Elliot decided to go for it, even though it set his pulse racing. He wiped his clammy palms on the back pockets of his jeans and fought to keep his breathing steady as Charlotte weaved her way through the bobbing mass of bodies and he followed, mumbling apologies to everyone he bumped into.

They reached a small group of girls dancing in a circle when 'Vogue' kicked in, welcomed by several high-pitched screams.

'That's Nicola,' Charlotte shouted into his ear, nodding towards a slender redhead with pale skin, rosy cheeks and plaited pigtails, wearing ripped jeans and a Pearl Jam T-shirt. 'I'll introduce you after this song, okay?'

He nodded, pleasantly surprised, and spent the next five minutes watching those around him

160

demonstrate their knowledge of Madonna's dance routine while he stepped from side to side, hoping he didn't look as awkward as he felt. As subtly as possible, he kept one eye on Nicola, noting with interest that she didn't join in with the 'Vogue' routine and, although she must have known who he was, barely looked in his direction.

Then the song was over, replaced by a dance tune he didn't recognise, and Charlotte had an arm around his waist, leading him over to Nicola. There was smiling and nodding and, before he knew what was happening, Charlotte and the other girls had moved away, so it was just the two of them dancing opposite each other. The whole thing was weird and Nicola looked as uncomfortable as he felt.

'This is strange,' Elliot said.

'Sorry?' she replied, leaning forward. 'What was that?'

'This feels strange, doesn't it?' he said as close to her ear as he dared. 'Not us two dancing together, but the way they all moved away.'

Nicola nodded and gave him a pursed smile, but the blank look on her face suggested she hadn't heard any of that.

For a few more minutes they danced in silence, eyes darting around and only occasionally meeting. Eventually, Elliot felt like he had to say something else.

'You like Pearl Jam, then?' was the best he could come up with.

'Yes.'

He nodded for longer than felt natural, feet

moving in time to the music. 'What's your favourite song?'

'By Pearl Jam?'

'Yes.'

'Probably 'Alive'.'

'Maybe the DJ has it. Perhaps we should ask him.'

She nodded, but showed no sign of wanting to do so now or to continue the conversation.

It went on like this for a few more songs: Elliot saying something, Nicola giving a brief reply or nodding like she hadn't heard him, and then more silent dancing. His mind was racing, not a clue what he was supposed to be doing. Was it acceptable to dance in silence, as Nicola seemed happy to do? Or was she as uncomfortable as he was? Maybe she couldn't bear the sight of him and was dying for the whole interaction to be over.

Elliot was about to suggest that they should move to somewhere quieter, so they could hear each other speak, when things took on a whole new level of awkwardness.

The DJ took to the microphone and announced: 'Okay, guys and gals, we're getting towards the end of the night. It's that time the lovebirds among you have been waiting for. Let's slow things down and get romantic with the new one from Whitney Houston, 'I Will Always Love You'.'

And with that everyone suddenly paired off or left the dance floor, so the only people remaining were couples pressed up against each other, slow dancing.

Oh dear. Elliot had never done this before. He looked around, dumbstruck, watching what everyone else was doing. And then he turned back to Nicola, whose expression was also one of terror, and gave her an awkward smile. 'Shall we?'

She nodded, thank goodness. He had feared that someone into Pearl Jam might not take kindly to slow dancing to Whitney Houston, but luckily that didn't seem to be a problem. They moved closer together and, both apparently copying those around them, she put her arms around his neck and he put his around her waist. This meant their faces were looking in opposite directions, over the other's shoulder, which came as a relief to Elliot, who'd feared even more discomfort if they'd had to gaze into each other's eyes.

They remained in this position, silently swaying from side to side, for the entirety of that song and the three further slow ones that followed. Nicola smelled nice. She didn't seem to be wearing any perfume, so it was subtler than with Lisa and Charlotte, but pleasant nonetheless: a lightly citrus scented shampoo mixed with fresh laundry. Initially, Elliot's main concern was that having the curves of Nicola's body pressed against his own might cause him to get excited and embarrass himself. He found himself counting down from one hundred and pretending he was dancing with Prime Minister John Major, which had the desired calming effect.

As he was starting to relax and even to enjoy the moment a little, he felt a tap on his upper right arm. He looked over and saw Lisa's face beaming a huge smile at him from its position on Neil's shoulder. He smiled back, although it felt weird, and then the other couple swung around so it was Neil's face now grinning at him. His classmate even gave him a thumbs-up and then, a moment later, they were snogging again, causing Elliot to look away.

He'd noticed a few of the couples around them had moved from dancing to kissing, despite the watchful eyes of the teachers standing alongside the dance floor. Apparently they didn't mind, as long as it went no further. He'd only seen them intervene on one occasion all night — and that was in the case of an older couple who'd been getting frisky on a window ledge, behind a thick set of curtains.

So the next thing to occupy Elliot's mind was whether he should move in for a cheeky snog. He had no idea whether or not Nicola was up for it, as despite their close proximity, he hadn't seen her face for several minutes. She was still there with him, which was a good sign, he supposed. She hadn't made any obvious indication that she wanted him to kiss her, but she was pretty timid, from what he'd seen so far. Plus it was the boy's job to make the first move, right?

The problem was that he'd never kissed a girl before. He was desperate to do something about that; to find out what all the fuss was about. In his imagination, it had been Lisa he'd pictured himself kissing for the first time, but things had changed. He knew almost nothing about Nicola. However, she was pretty and seemed nice enough, albeit a little shy, so he realised he probably ought to strike while the iron was hot.

At the same time, he feared making an idiot of himself. So he waited, swaying from side to side and keeping his hands firmly in place around Nicola's waist, careful not to slip too low, as some of those dancing nearby had, for fear of offending her. And then suddenly, as the DJ faded out Vanessa Williams's 'Save the Best for Last', it was all over. The lights came on, the doors swung open and Elliot knew that he'd missed his chance.

Nicola's hands slipped from around his neck and, in turn, he dropped his from her waist. They stood apart and Elliot felt a bizarre need to rub his eyes, as if he'd just woken up. Instead he grinned at Nicola and, receiving a sweet smile in return, decided on the spot to lean forward and give her a quick goodnight kiss. Unfortunately, at the very moment he opted to do this, something to Nicola's side caught her attention and she looked away, meaning his lips landed on her ear.

'Um, goodnight,' he mumbled, so mortified that he wished the dance floor would swallow him up. 'Lovely to meet you. I've, er, got to go. Goodnight.'

Nicola, whose cheeks had turned a deep pink, looked down at her trainers and nodded. 'Bye.'

Before he could make any more of a fool of himself, Elliot headed for the door, hoping desperately that no one else had witnessed his humiliation.

'What an idiot I am,' he muttered under his breath. 'What a loser.'

16

NOW

Monday, 23 July 2018

'Careful!' Lisa said. 'You nearly hit that wall.'

'What? No I didn't.' Mike frowned at his wife, who was sitting next to him in the front passenger seat of their silver Octavia estate.

Lisa hadn't been such a backseat driver when she'd had her own car. Now they were down to one, meaning she drove the Skoda to and from work every day during term time; she seemed to think she knew how to drive it better than he did.

'If you'd rather drive, be my guest,' he said, knowing full well that she wouldn't want to do so. Lisa had always preferred to be driven, which suited him fine, apart from when she made such comments. Thank goodness for satnav. Mike could still remember the blazing rows they used to have in the car when they were reliant on maps.

'Better I tell you than you damage the car,' Lisa said. 'I'm the one sitting on this side and, trust me, you were really close.'

Mike sighed.

Neither of them spoke for the next few minutes as the car raced along the winding road through the hilly countryside to Harrogate. The views on either side were lush, sprawling and spectacular, despite the clouds above granting just fleeting moments of sunshine.

He had always enjoyed driving this route. It was so much more satisfying than a boring motorway journey. He turned up the stereo. It was tuned into Radio 2, although Lisa would have preferred Radio 1. He couldn't understand why she liked listening to all that chart pop stuff at her age, but there was no changing her mind. She said she found Radio 2 stuffy.

Their tastes were so different these days. Sometimes Mike wondered what the two of them still had in common, apart from the kids. Mind you, he remembered reading an article in a newspaper supplement about how the most successful couples often had very different interests and temperaments. It was the old opposites attract thing, apparently.

Glancing over at his wife, who he still found hugely attractive, Mike reminded himself how lucky he was to have her. She'd put up with a lot from him in recent times, not least his awful behaviour at the restaurant last Friday, which he was still supposed to be making up for. And then there was his disappearing act to the pub yesterday after he'd suggested that Elliot shouldn't have employed the Heimlich manoeuvre on Ben. Boy had that led to a tongue lashing later on. Honestly, he was surprised she'd still come along with him to visit Aunt Jenny today.

Also, as Mike regularly tried to remind himself, Lisa had been and continued to be amazingly understanding about him not working. He couldn't have wished for someone more sympathetic and supportive when he went through the Liam Hornby nightmare. And how had he repaid her? By jacking in his teaching career no sooner than he'd been cleared of the charges.

And then when he'd eventually found another job, he'd messed that up too. Seeing a white van shoot by in the other direction was all it took to cast his mind back to that fateful day a few months earlier.

* * *

Mike was in the third week of his new job as a delivery driver. It was quite a step down from what he was used to doing professionally, but it felt good to be out there again, having a function.

Battling through school run traffic on a Wednesday around 3 p.m., with only a handful of stops still to make, he found himself whistling along to the radio. For the first time in ages, he felt happy.

Why had he chosen this job? Because apart from being able to follow a satnav and to drive quickly without picking up speeding tickets, it didn't involve much hard thinking or tough decisions. He simply had to turn up on time and deliver everything he was expected to in a timely fashion. He didn't even have to worry about what to do when people weren't in, as most of his packages were to other businesses. And

168

unlike plenty of other driving jobs on offer, he wasn't required to provide his own vehicle. He had a white van, with the small but busy company's colourful logo emblazoned on the side.

In other words, he could do most of it on autopilot, leaving his mind free to think about more pleasant things, such as that screenplay he was going to write one day.

After shadowing another driver for a few days, he'd been let loose. And so far, apart from almost running out of diesel once because he'd forgotten to take the fuel card, things had gone pretty smoothly.

Even before the shitstorm that had led to him leaving teaching, his job as a primary school deputy head hadn't always been easy. He had enjoyed it, for the most part. He'd been good in his role and on track to become a head in the not-too-distant future. But it wasn't the kind of job you could switch off from when you got home. Even during the long holidays that non-teachers envied so much, he'd often had to work. And when he hadn't been working, school-related matters had often remained on his mind: anything from problem pupils to cutting his way through the latest red tape.

Lisa could compartmentalise things. She was far better than Mike at leaving work issues at the school gate. However, she'd never been a deputy head, and a lot of Mike's extra hours had come from trying to juggle the managerial side of things with the teaching. Lisa said this was why she wasn't interested in rising through the ranks, despite being tapped up several times. It certainly wasn't down to a lack of ability.

Despite the workload and stress, Mike had never thought of leaving the profession until he saw the dark side of things. Until he experienced what it was like to be falsely accused by a psycho pupil; to be hauled before the court of public opinion and presumed guilty. He'd expected much more support than he'd received from the head and his other colleagues. They'd known the truth about what Liam Hornby was like — and still he'd felt cut off by them.

Driving a van from one destination to another — handing over a parcel in return for a signature — was bliss in comparison. Plus it was infinitely better than stewing at home, wondering how they would be able to make ends meet as a family. The money wasn't great — nowhere near what he'd earned previously — but it was a start.

Stopping at traffic lights, his van dwarfed by a lorry behind him, Mike remembered wanting to be a truck driver for a while as a child. A friend had shown him the film *Convoy*, starring Kris Kristofferson, and the two of them had spent weeks afterwards pretending to be truckers with CB radios. He'd sit in one room, using the handle Hot Dog, with his pal in the next, calling himself Popcorn; they'd chat using a wired walkie-talkie.

That probably had something to do with the fact that Mike's initial plan for a new job had been to learn to drive a HGV. Lisa had talked him out of it on the grounds that he'd always be away from home. So he'd chosen this instead.

Although Lisa had never said so, Mike knew she thought the job was a waste of his intelligence and qualifications, seeing it as a stopgap until something 'more appropriate' came along. He, on the other hand, could see himself doing it for a while.

The lorry driver honked his horn and Mike snapped out of his daydream, realising the lights had changed.

He pulled away and, obeying the satnav, arrived at his next destination minutes later. It was an independent stationery shop on a busy high street. He'd been here before and knew he'd be lucky to find parking.

Crawling along the road, hoping to find a space, he spotted one a little way ahead on the other side, only for a large black 4x4 to pull into it. Dammit. Next thing, he was outside the small store. He cast his eye up and down either pavement for traffic wardens and, not seeing any, decided to risk double parking for a moment to get the job done. It was only one parcel. He looked over at it on the front seat next to him, having taken it out from the back at the last stop in case this happened — to speed things up. They were never very busy here, from what he'd seen previously, so he expected to be in and out in seconds.

Unfortunately, once he got inside, there wasn't a member of staff in sight. The place was deserted apart from him, so he called out: 'Hello? Anyone around? I have a delivery.'

No reply.

He was tempted to leave the package on the

shop counter and fake a signature. Several of the other drivers had told him they did this from time to time, but he was still new to the job and he didn't feel comfortable doing so.

'Hello?' he shouted, louder this time. 'Delivery! I'm double parked and in a rush.'

There was a door behind the counter. Mike put the parcel down and, having first peered through the window to check the van was still okay, he went to open it, hoping to find someone out back. It was locked.

He was about to give in, weighing up whether it was better to fake a signature after all or to return the parcel to the depot. Then he heard the sound of a toilet flushing somewhere nearby, followed by a door slamming shut and footsteps on stairs. Next the door behind the counter swung open and a gaunt elderly chap with bright red cheeks, unruly eyebrows and wild curly white hair appeared. The man, who Mike recognised as the proprietor, was still in the process of tucking his shirt back into his trousers.

'Oh, hello,' he said. 'Sorry, I didn't know anyone was waiting. Call of nature.'

'You want to be careful leaving the shop unattended,' Mike replied. 'I could have helped myself to anything.'

'Yes, yes. You're quite right. I usually put the front door on the latch, but I'm getting forgetful.'

'Never mind. It was just me this time delivering a parcel for you. If I could get a quick signature, I'll be on my way.'

As he was saying this, Mike cast another glance out of the window to check on the van

— and nearly had a heart attack as he saw it pulling away with a strange man at the wheel. Cursing loudly, he dropped everything and ran for the door. But by the time he got outside, the van was disappearing at speed into the distance.

He swore again — shouting with such volume this time that various people walking along the pavement turned to look. A young mum with a toddler scowled at him as they scuttled past, but Mike was in no state to apologise.

How the hell? He dived into the pockets of his trousers for the van key. But it wasn't there. He must have left it in the ignition, with the cab door unlocked for anyone to come along and help themselves, as they just had. This was the very reason you needed the key to access the parcels in the back: to make sure you took it out with you. Being a smart alec, he'd found a way to override that by taking the package out at the previous delivery.

He felt a horrible sinking, sickly feeling in his stomach. This was instant dismissal. He'd had that hammered into him at his induction less than a month ago. You were never, under any circumstances, to leave the key in the ignition when you weren't behind the wheel. Not even for a second. God, how was he going to explain this to Lisa after everything else they'd been through?

★ ★ ★

'Please slow down. You're scaring me.'

Mike blinked away the memories and, seeing

173

that his wife was right about his speed, lifted his foot off the accelerator.

'Sorry,' he told her, rubbing his eyes with one hand. 'I was away with the fairies for a minute there.'

She frowned. 'That doesn't sound very safe. Maybe I should drive. What's wrong? Didn't you get much sleep last night? You do look tired.'

'I'm fine. Just went into autopilot. They say you do your best driving in that state.'

To Mike's left, Lisa raised a sceptical eyebrow. 'Please get us there in one piece.'

He nodded. 'You can change the radio station for a bit if you like.'

'Thank you,' she replied, reaching forward to do so.

Placing his left hand on her lap, Mike added: 'Thanks for coming with me today, love. I really appreciate it.'

He got a pursed smile in reply.

'So, funny thing,' Mike said. 'I was chatting to Alan in the Swan last night — '

'Alan?'

'You know, the landlord.'

'I don't really, Mike. How many times have I been there with you? Two? Maybe three?'

He wondered whether mentioning the pub was a good idea. Especially after what Lisa had said last night about him spending money that they couldn't spare. Anyway, it was too late now, so he carried on regardless. 'So I was telling Alan about this unexpected visit from Elliot — '

'Moaning about it, you mean.'

'I wasn't, love. Honestly. I was just saying how

he'd appeared out of the blue and all that. Anyway, as I was telling the story, this other guy I've not seen before was getting a drink at the bar. He asks if I'm talking about Elliot Turner, who grew up in the village.' Mike paused for a moment for a little chuckle before continuing. 'The thing is, and I still can't quite believe this. I mean, he was pretty pissed, to be honest, this guy — '

'What was his name?' Lisa asked.

'Um, Peter something. I didn't catch his surname. He grew up here but lives in Manchester now. He said he was back visiting. Anyway, he knows you, or at least he did when you were a kid. That's what I'm getting to, if you'll give me a chance.'

Lisa sighed, but Mike continued: 'So this Peter starts talking about how Elliot was a bit of a nerd as a boy, who used to get bullied, and then one day this new girl moved to the village and became like his minder. He said if anyone gave him any grief after that, she used to beat them up for him. He even compared her to that female warrior on *Game of Thrones*. You know, the tall one.'

'Yes, I know who you mean.' Lisa scowled. 'He was talking about me, right?'

'Exactly,' Mike said, belly laughing despite his wife's angry face. 'My wife the warrior woman. I mean: what? He mentioned something about a fire and then he skulked off after I told him I was married to you, refusing to say any more. I was going to tell you when I got in last night, but it obviously wasn't the right time. Now I'm dying

175

to know if there's any truth in it. Were you really such a bad ass as a kid? And what about Elliot needing protecting? That doesn't sound like the guy I've met.'

Lisa gave a flippant wave of her hand. 'Whatever. Sounds like a load of drunken nonsense.'

'Fair enough,' Mike replied, knowing her well enough not to push any further.

'How much longer until we get to Harrogate?'

'About forty-five minutes.'

'Right, I'm going to close my eyes for a bit. I didn't sleep well last night.'

Lisa turned the radio down a notch and reclined her seat, shuffling around before settling on a position with her face looking out of the side window, away from him. As the jolly DJ played what he referred to as another 'summer banger', Mike wished he hadn't let her switch stations.

There was clearly more to that story than she was letting on. He knew she'd done judo at primary school, although he couldn't imagine her beating anyone up.

And what about Elliot? His tanned, muscular frame had shamed Mike into going out running yesterday for the first time in ages. Could it be true that he was once a wimp, relying on a girl to defend him from bullies? He couldn't help but smile at this idea.

So far — not that he'd admit this to Lisa — he'd found her old friend a bit of a threat. Who wouldn't? Elliot had flown over without warning from the other side of the world and had everything going for him. He was wealthy, successful and in great shape; he had a shared childhood with Lisa that Mike knew little or nothing about. Oh yeah, and he'd effortlessly managed to save Ben's life yesterday in between cooking a fantastic meal and being an all-round nice guy.

Mike's life, on the other hand, was in pieces. He was overweight, jobless and pretty useless around the house. He drank too much and bit Lisa's head off far more frequently than he bought her flowers or behaved romantically. He was stuck in a rut. The idea that someone like Elliot could potentially swoop in and steal all he had left — his wife and kids — terrified him.

Not that Elliot had given Mike the impression he was here to do that. One of the most infuriating things about him was that he was so amiable. Despite the potential threat he posed to Mike, even he found it hard to hate him. And if anything, hearing that Elliot hadn't always had things so easy actually increased his likeability factor.

No, it was jealousy rather than hate that Mike felt towards Elliot. Embarrassing but true. That was the reason he'd tried to criticise his actions yesterday. That and guilt for not being the one to save Ben himself.

But there was something else about Elliot too: something Mike couldn't quite put his finger on. He got the sense that there was more to this sudden visit back home than business. Why choose to return now, unannounced, after staying away for two decades? And if he was here about important matters relating to his company, how come he had so much free time on his hands to catch up with Lisa?

Wouldn't a last-minute trip to the other side of the world signal something of crucial importance? So how come he hadn't been fielding calls or emails on his mobile every few minutes? Come to think of it, Mike couldn't ever remember seeing Elliot use a mobile. Was that normal for a guy who ran a successful tech firm?

What if he was here for another reason altogether and the whole business thing was a cover story?

Whatever it was, something didn't add up.

17

NOW

Monday, 23 July 2018

Ben stuck his head around Chloe's open bedroom door. 'Right, I'm off. I'll be home before Mum and Dad get back.'

'Wait,' his sister replied. 'You said it would only be a couple of hours.'

'That was before I had to pay you twenty quid. Now I'm getting my money's worth.'

'When are Mum and Dad due home?'

'Around seven this evening.'

'And you'll be gone all that time?'

'We'll see.'

'You're really not going to tell me where you're going?' Chloe frowned. 'What if something happens to you? What if something happens to me?'

Ben had a bus to catch. 'Don't be a drama queen. I've got my mobile.'

'Is that aftershave I can smell?' Chloe walked towards him and made a stupid sniffing noise. He took a step backwards before she did something annoying like ruffling his carefully crafted hair or putting greasy hands on his new T-shirt. Then she started gibbering about him going on a date.

'You're pathetic,' he said, heading for the stairs.

'Charming. You should be nice to me if you want me to cover for you.'

'I don't remember that being part of the deal.' Ben continued towards the front door, opening it a crack and then turning back to Chloe, who was standing on the top stair. 'I'll see you later. Don't get into any trouble.'

'Bye, Romeo,' she replied, waving sarcastically, which Ben took to mean she was still on board. So she should be after what he'd paid her; hopefully it would be worth every penny.

He shut the door behind him and flashed a look at the time on his phone. Good. Still ten minutes until the bus was due. Damn, he felt nervous.

Ben's mobile, still in his hand, vibrated.

H: You left?

His finger darted across the screen, a trained courier of his thoughts.

B: Walking to bus stop.

H: Nice. :-) Let me know when you're on it.

Ben tried to regulate his breathing as he covered the last few metres to the bus stop. He wanted to calm down, but the butterflies in his stomach weren't easily tamed.

As he arrived at the shelter, a bald head jerked forward, like a tortoise peeking out of its shell, scanned the road and then disappeared back inside. It was an old man he vaguely recognised but didn't know personally. This was good, as it meant less chance of his parents finding out about the trip.

When the bus pulled up, Ben bought a return to Manchester and climbed the stairs to the upper deck, glad not to recognise any of the few faces already on board. He sat down in the rear corner — one row in front of the long back seat — wincing as he felt a strain in his stomach muscles. They were bruised from the scary moment at the dinner table yesterday when Elliot had rescued him from choking. Just thinking about that again sent a shiver down his spine, so he tried not to, concentrating instead on connecting to the bus's free Wi-Fi. Once that was done, he pulled his earplugs out of his pocket and stuck on the first playlist he could find.

He sent a message saying that he was on the bus. A moment later his phone vibrated with a response.

H: Nice. Can't wait. What time will you get into the city centre?

B: Just over half an hour.

H: Shall I meet you off the bus?

B: No need. I know where I'm going. Already looked it up.

H: Get you, Mr Resourceful. Buzz me if you have any problems. See you soon. X

Ben slipped his phone back into his trouser pocket and took some further slow, deep breaths. The nerves weren't improving. In fact, as the bus drove on, gradually filling up with passengers, they were only getting worse. He needed to hide this before he got there: to give the impression that today was no big deal.

He stared at his reflection in the window, wondering how old he looked to those around him. Although his sixteenth birthday wasn't until the end of August, he was confident he could already pass for that, if not seventeen. Eighteen might be a push, but his stubble helped. He had way more than most of the lads in his year, which was why he rarely went clean-shaven; he liked to think it gave him an edge.

A couple of girls around his sister's age giggled their way up the stairs and took a seat a few rows ahead of Ben. He thought they might have checked him out, which was funny. What would Chloe think if she found out what he was up to? Worse still, what if his parents found out? That didn't bear thinking about.

He knew he was taking a big risk doing this today, but it was the best opportunity to have presented itself — the only one on the horizon — so saying no hadn't been an option. He was confident that Chloe wouldn't get herself into trouble. She was a smart kid most of the time. He was actually pretty fond of her, when she wasn't annoying him. And he'd been secretly impressed by her enterprising nature, squeezing twenty pounds out of him to keep quiet. Not that he let on. It was more fun to be the aloof older brother.

A trippy dance tune he recognised came on. He turned the sound up and squeezed his eyes shut, doing his best to blank out everything else; let the music wash over him. He started to feel calmer.

Then, to his horror, he felt someone take a seat next to him. What the hell? Unless literally dozens of people had got on at the last stop, since he closed his eyes, there were plenty of other seats. If he'd thought there was any chance of someone sitting by him, he'd have spread himself out more. A moment later he smelled a gag-inducing stink of body odour and alcohol.

He didn't dare to open his eyes straight away, although he was itching to. He feared it might be someone he knew. But who did he know that reeked like a tramp? It was disgusting. He barely registered the sound of the music on his earplugs any more. Instead, he concentrated on shallow breathing, through his mouth rather than his nose, so as to minimise the foul smell.

When he could bear it no longer, he opened his eyes and stretched. The idea was to make it look like he'd just woken up, while hopefully also gaining some extra space. He noticed from the view out of the window that they'd entered one of the smarter northern suburbs of Manchester. A melange of shops, cafes and restaurants gave way to a large green park, flanked by rows of semi-detached houses. Not too far now.

'Hello,' a croaky voice snapped, loud enough to penetrate the sound of Ben's music. 'Nice snooze?'

Ben looked over to see a scrawny middle-aged woman grinning at him. She had nicotine-stained yellow teeth, long greasy grey hair, and a large whiskery mole on one cheek. Bizarrely for summertime, she was wearing a thick parka coat, snot green and covered in stains, plus a manky pair of lilac jogging bottoms and tatty trainers. It was all he could do not to recoil against the window.

Why was she sitting next to him? There were

loads of other seats available.

He pointed at his earplugs, pretending not to have heard her, but she stared back at him expectantly, until he removed one of them.

'Sorry, do you have the time?' she asked.

He pulled out his phone to check and told her, hoping that would be the end of the conversation.

'I hope you don't mind me sitting next to you,' she said, to which Ben pursed his lips in response. 'I always sit on this seat if I can. It's my favourite.'

Ben nodded, still breathing through his mouth.

'I can't explain why, but I definitely like it best. You must know what I mean. You chose to sit here too.'

'Mmm.' Ben realised he was a captive audience now — and this was one lonely lady, desperate to chat.

That was how it continued for the rest of the journey: a one-way conversation, with him pretending to be interested. She told him all sorts, from how she had a hospital appointment because of her bad knee, to the fact that she owned a cat called Pussy. It was all Ben could do not to burst into laughter at that last piece of information. So she wasn't homeless, although she clearly had an aversion to taking baths. He also suspected that the water bottle she kept swigging from held something far stronger than its original contents.

He should have got up and moved to the lower deck, pretending that it was his stop, but he

184

didn't have the heart. Part of him felt sorry for her.

At least it took his mind off where he was heading — what he was going to do — and that was a welcome relief. So he stayed there, hoping she didn't have nits or fleas that she might pass on to him, and humouring her.

Apparently she was a bit loopy, or some kind of religious nut, as at one point she started jabbering about how he had the mark of an angel on him.

'Right there,' she said, pointing a bony finger towards his stomach. 'I can see these things. I have psychic genes. My mother, God rest her soul, was a fortune teller. People would travel from far and wide to have her read their tea leaves. I could do it too if I wanted to.'

Ben smiled and nodded. Soon she moved on to telling him about how she'd been 'quite the looker' at his age. Then finally the bus reached the city centre and it genuinely was time for him to get off.

'This is my stop,' he said, pressing the bell.

'Have you got the time again before you go?'

Ben checked and she thanked him, standing up to let him out.

'It's been lovely chatting to you,' she said, clamping both of her skinny hands around his. 'You're a good boy, although you're a bit conflicted, aren't you? Look after yourself today. You might have someone watching over you, but you still need to be careful.'

'Okay. See you.'

'Sooner than you think.'

Stepping off the bus, he took a big gulp of fresh air, shuddering at the memory of that woman's awful stench and hoping it hadn't passed to him.

Ben's nerves returned with a vengeance — like an iron fist to his stomach — as it dawned on him how close he was to his destination. He'd be there on foot in a matter of minutes. He gulped. Then a loud banging noise from behind caught his attention.

18

NOW

Monday, 23 July 2018

The third key Lisa tried was the correct one. It turned in the lock and the outside door swung open, letting them inside the shared entrance hall of Aunt Jenny's flat. It felt a little strange that she thought of her by that name, when she was Mike's aunt rather than hers, but as he'd always referred to her that way, Lisa had fallen into the habit of doing the same.

They'd spent a couple of hours with Aunt Jenny at the hospital that morning. Now they were calling in at her home to pick up a few things she'd requested, which they would take to her when they visited again that afternoon.

Eyeing the concrete steps up to the second floor, where the flat was located, Lisa winced at the thought of her falling down them. No wonder she was so black and blue. They didn't look very forgiving. If anything, she was lucky to have only broken her arm and not something else. The cuts and bruises she'd suffered looked awful but would heal soon enough; the break would take some time to mend. An arm was better than a leg, in terms of self-sufficiency, but it was still serious in someone elderly — and Aunt Jenny was seventy-six.

187

They weren't showing any sign of wanting to discharge her from hospital yet, for which Lisa was thankful. Just as well the injury had happened in summer rather than winter, when beds were always in far higher demand. Then she might not have been so lucky.

Mike made for the stairs.

'Hang on a minute,' Lisa told him. 'I promised to empty her mailbox. Let me do that now before I forget.'

She waved the big bunch of keys in his face. 'Any idea which one it is?'

Mike shrugged. 'Not a clue. Why does she have so many keys? She lives in a two-bedroom flat. How many locks can there be?'

It took a couple of minutes to identify the right one and to pull out the post, which was dominated by colourful leaflets advertising double glazing and takeaways. Mike grabbed the lot and she followed him up to the flat.

'How did she fall again?' Lisa asked.

'She lost her footing, apparently, and missed a step. She was probably busy chatting to one of her neighbours and not paying attention to what she was doing.'

Lisa frowned. 'That's not very nice, love.'

'I'm only joking, although you know I'm probably right.'

Aunt Jenny certainly was a chatterbox. She had been when her husband was still alive, but she'd grown even more so since his death. She could happily gab away to anyone about anything — and usually did whenever she got the chance. She enjoyed company, which was understandable considering she lived alone nowadays.

So it hadn't been a surprise to find her bending a young cleaner's ear when they'd arrived at her bedside earlier, recounting stories of her own time as a hospital midwife in days gone by. The cleaner had looked as relieved to see them as she was, darting off as soon as they arrived.

Lisa for one had always enjoyed talking to her. She was such a vibrant, positive person. It was a shame that she didn't have more family living nearby. But like Mike, she was originally from the Milton Keynes area, where most of their relatives still lived. She and her late husband hadn't been able to have children; they'd retired to Harrogate having fallen in love with the town on their honeymoon decades earlier. Now she refused to move away.

Lisa had expected the flat to be in a mess, bearing in mind Aunt Jenny's sudden, unexpected departure and the fact she'd more or less begged her to run the vacuum around. In fact it was pretty tidy apart from a few unwashed cups, plates and cutlery next to the kitchen sink. It was a typical elderly woman's flat: carpet throughout, apart from the kitchen and bathroom, which had tiled floors; floral wallpaper with several framed photos and paintings; plenty of houseplants and trinkets.

Pulling out the list she'd made of items to take back to the hospital, Lisa asked Mike: 'Could you wash up those few things while I gather her stuff?'

He nodded, starting to run the hot water. He hadn't had much to say since the car journey. Something appeared to be on his mind, although that was pretty much par for the course with Mike. Maybe she shouldn't have cut him short when he'd started recounting what he'd heard in the pub about her and Elliot as kids, but it was such exaggerated claptrap. She hadn't been in the mood. She was still annoyed by the fact that he'd gone there in the first place: slipping out on their guest after being rude to him, then wasting money they didn't have on unnecessary alcohol. And all that so soon after their romantic meal from hell last Friday. So much for making it up to her.

She had considered not coming today as a result, but it hadn't seemed right to punish Aunt Jenny for Mike's bad behaviour. Lisa cared for her and didn't want her to think otherwise. Plus, she wasn't confident in her husband's ability to get his aunt everything she needed, such as clothes and underwear. Some things were best done yourself.

Mike peered in the fridge and pulled out a milk bottle, eyeing the expiration date before giving it a sniff. 'Fancy a brew? The milk went off yesterday, but I think we can get away with it.'

'Make yourself at home.'

'What? It's only going to go in the bin otherwise, Lise. Aunt Jenny's not going to mind, is she? Not after we've come to help her.'

'Not for me.'

'Suit yourself.'

Once she'd gathered Aunt Jenny's things together and vacuumed while Mike watered the plants, Lisa was ready to return to the hospital.

'I'm a bit peckish,' Mike said, 'but the only bread she has is in the freezer.'

'Stop rooting around. We can grab a sandwich on the way.'

'What? I thought we could save a couple of quid by making something here.'

'With someone else's food? If you wanted to save money, you should have stayed away from the pub last night.'

Mike sighed, running a hand through his hair. 'Not this again. Can we go?'

'Where? To the pub?' Lisa asked. Before she could stop herself, she added: 'Need a drink already, do you?'

She regretted saying this even before the thunderous look had swept across Mike's face. But by then it was already too late.

'Bloody hell, Lisa!' he shouted, slamming his open palm down on to the kitchen worktop. 'Why are you trying to wind me up? I'm not a damn alcoholic! I'm just a guy having a hard time of it, trying to cope. Do I like a drink? Yes, I do, because it helps me to forget how messed up my life is. Do you see me swigging a bottle of whisky at ten in the morning? No, you don't. Because I'm not an alcoholic. So stop suggesting that I am.

'You want to know why I went to the pub yesterday? Fine, I'll tell you. It was to get away from the Elliot love-in. Yes, Lisa, we can all see how brilliant he is; what great shape he and his

191

business are both in; what a fantastic catch he is. Well, guess what? As a guy who's messed up not one but two jobs and finds himself washed-up and ready for the scrapheap before he's even hit forty, that's hard to watch.'

Lisa, standing in the doorway of the small kitchen, hadn't uttered a sound as Mike was speaking. His voice had gradually trailed away from the initial angry bellow to a hobbling near whisper. Once he stopped, all she could hear was the sound of his heavy breathing. Both of his hands were now gripping the edge of the worktop, white knuckles on display like he was holding on for dear life.

She moved towards him, keen to offer some comfort, to let him know that things weren't as bleak as they felt.

'Don't,' he growled, stopping her in her tracks.

'I'm sorry, Mike. I didn't — '

'Don't,' he repeated. After several long seconds of cavernous silence, he announced that he was going outside for some air.

'Can I get past, please?' he said without emotion.

'Sure,' she replied, moving back into the hallway, unsure what else to do or say.

'I'll meet you at the car in fifteen minutes,' he added.

And then he was gone.

Still reeling from the dramatic scene that she had unwittingly sparked, Lisa poured herself a glass of tap water and took a seat in the lounge.

She knew she shouldn't have wound Mike up like that — and yet she was genuinely concerned that he was drinking too much. The fact he'd admitted to using alcohol as a crutch proved she was right to worry. He had put weight on too and, as her husband and father of her two children, she was concerned for his health — both physical and mental. How could she not be when her own father, who was overweight and drank too much, had died from a heart attack? And boozing hadn't even been his major addiction. That had been gambling, the selfish legacy of which had been to leave his family without any financial safety net when he died. And boy could Lisa have done with a safety net now.

But how could she help Mike? He was usually so closed. It was rare to see such an outpouring of emotion from him, which was no doubt why he'd gone to cool down alone. In a way, she was glad of it. Sometimes these things needed to come out — to be said rather than thought. But it concerned her to see how much anger and frustration there was bubbling away under the surface — especially so soon after his public display of fury in the restaurant. And no surprise that alcohol was at the heart of both incidents.

She did understand what Mike had said about Elliot. She could well imagine how she'd feel if the shoe was on the other foot and a good-looking, successful female friend from his past turned up when things weren't going well for her. But what was she supposed to do: turn her old pal away?

The fact was that a small part of Lisa was envious of Elliot too. The foundation of their

193

friendship as kids and then teenagers had always been that she was the more fortunate, popular one, there to rescue him when he got into trouble. She'd enjoyed that and the way he'd always doted on her as a result. Now things were different. Elliot was the fortunate one, while she had grumpy children who didn't even seem to like her, plus a depressed husband with no job and a burgeoning alcohol problem. Oh yeah, and without Mike's salary, an impending financial black hole that regularly gave her sleepless nights.

When Lisa went down to the car, Aunt Jenny's bag of things slung over one shoulder, Mike was already behind the wheel.

He didn't say a word as she put the holdall on the back seat and then got into the front passenger side. But once she was sitting down and had her seatbelt on, he announced that there were two pre-packed sandwiches in the glovebox.

'There's a tuna mayo and a ploughman's,' he said, looking straight ahead rather than at her. 'I'm happy with either. Take your pick.'

Lisa smiled, appreciating her husband's gesture. 'Thanks, love. Where did you get them?'

'There's a corner shop a couple of streets away. I probably should have got us a drink too, but — '

'No, this is perfect. I had a glass of water inside.'

Taking the sandwiches out, Lisa suggested: 'Why don't we each have half-half? I can feed you bits while you drive, if you like. Aunt Jenny will be wondering where we got to.'

Mike, who still hadn't met her eye, nodded his agreement and started the engine. He'd switched the stereo back to Radio 2, Lisa noticed, but as soon as it came on, he turned it off again, opting for silence.

Having passed him a chunk of sandwich and waited until he'd popped it into his mouth, she placed a hand on his lap and said: 'I love you, Mike. That's the reason I said what I did in there. It's because I worry about your health. I want you to be around long enough to enjoy your grandchildren — unlike my father.'

She looked across at her husband, who was still chewing his sandwich. Eventually, he glanced away from the road and met her gaze for a brief moment. There was a subtle nod.

She fed him another bite before continuing: 'Elliot's an old friend, nothing more. I've already told you that. I look at him in the same way I look at Jamie, like a brother. It hadn't even occurred to me to compare the two of you, so you shouldn't either. He's come a long way since I first met him and he's earned everything that he has. I'm pleased for him; proud of him. But he doesn't have what we do: two great kids and each other.

'Remember that next time you feel washed-up or ready for the scrapheap, because you're neither of those things. I have faith in you, even if you don't. That's why I married you. And I know you'll bounce back soon enough, stronger than ever. You just need to put all the crap that's happened behind you and start believing in yourself again.'

She was sure that Mike swallowed a few times more than was strictly necessary to finish his piece of sandwich. Then, pulling up at a red traffic light, he turned to her, hands still tight on the wheel, and said: 'Thank you for saying that, Lisa.'

'You're welcome,' she replied, giving his left leg a firm squeeze before handing him some more of his lunch and then digging in herself.

That was a good speech, she thought. It was what Mike needed to hear, even if it wasn't entirely truthful. She desperately wanted to believe in him, but he wasn't making it easy for her. And could she hand on heart say that she didn't fancy the new-look Elliot even a little bit? Hmm. She was only human . . .

'I wonder how the kids are getting on at home,' she said. 'I hope they're not squabbling or doing anything they shouldn't be. I think I'll give them a quick call to check.'

Reaching into her handbag for her mobile, she dialled the home phone. 'No answer,' she announced eventually.

'They're probably in the garden,' Mike said, already sounding more cheery. 'Or more likely too busy doing other things to bother answering the phone.'

Lisa's finger hung over the touchscreen. 'Shall I try one of their mobiles or send a text?'

'No, don't bother, love. No news is good news. Leave them to it.'

She put the phone down and, flashing him a smile, turned back to eating her sandwich. 'You're probably right.'

19

NOW

Monday, 23 July 2018

Chloe was brushing her teeth for the second time that day when the front doorbell sounded; then the home phone started ringing too.

The two sounds were unexpected and, coming at the same time, they shocked her. She dropped her toothbrush into the sink and crept to the top of the stairs so she could see the door.

Lines of sunlight streamed through the obscured glass on to the oak-effect laminate of the hallway, the cream walls and the light beige carpet that ran up towards her. She could see the rough shape of the figure standing there. They appeared to be wearing a navy top, but that was all she could make out.

She felt her heart rate quicken; her breaths were fast and shallow. Who was it? What did they want? And why was the phone ringing too?

It didn't help that a few minutes earlier she'd received another nasty text message.

There had been six in total now since the first had arrived on Saturday night, warning her that she was being watched. Three more had arrived yesterday:

It must really suck to be you!

Still watching you. How does it feel to be such a loser?

What's it like to look in the mirror and see a pig staring back at you? Oink, oink!

There had been another this morning, soon after Ben had left:

You're disgusting. Thinking about you makes me want to puke.

She'd tried to ignore this, keeping busy by watching some TV, rooting around Ben's bedroom for non-existent clues about where he'd gone, and trying on some of her mum's jewellery.

Then the latest message — the worst so far — had landed about half an hour ago:

There's no magic potion to stop you being a lonely loser with slimy yellow teeth.

For the first time the sender had attached a photo, showing Chloe doing a science experiment at an open day. It had appeared in the last school newsletter. She was wearing a pair of protective goggles and holding up a smoking test tube, but this version of the picture had been altered, so there was a big red 'L' on her forehead and her teeth had been coloured in bright yellow.

This had felt so targeted and malicious that it had tipped Chloe over the edge. The comment about her teeth had preyed on her insecurity that they weren't perfectly white. Not like the ones everyone had on TV and in movies. She brushed them as best as she could, even convincing her mum to let her try some whitening toothpastes, although they made little difference. The dentist

198

had told her they were perfectly healthy; that her natural colour just wasn't as white as some. But to have that anxiety paraded in front of her like this by some anonymous bully was horrible.

That was why she'd been brushing her teeth for the second time that day, tears running down her face in frustration and fury, when the phone and doorbell had started up.

Cowering now at the top of the stairs, she was terrified it might be the sender, here to goad her — or worse — in person. She felt so vulnerable, wishing she'd never said anything about being old enough to stay home alone. Bloody Ben and his mysterious outing. Why had she ever agreed to go along with it?

The phone finally stopped ringing, thank goodness, only for the front doorbell to sound again. Shit.

Chloe didn't know what to do. Part of her thought it best to ignore whoever was there; to wait it out until they went away. But what if they didn't go away?

She'd been through a similar dilemma regarding the nasty messages. She'd thought several times about blocking the number on her phone, but for some reason, she hadn't done so. She hated receiving them; knowing someone hated her enough to send them made her miserable. But somehow she felt more in control this way. If she did block them, Chloe had a feeling she'd only be wondering if any more had been sent and what they might say. Now at least she was on top of them. And if they got too much, she could always change her mind.

She had also considered replying. She'd drafted several texts in response, from a simple query about the sender's identity, to counter-insults and even threats to go to the police. But ultimately it had felt more powerful to do nothing. Chloe had some experience of bullies from school and they tended to thrive on their victims' responses: especially fear and anxiety. Whoever was sending her these texts wanted to upset her. So there was power in not letting them know they'd succeeded.

Chloe had tried ringing the number once, although not straight after receiving one of the texts and not from her mobile. She'd used the home phone and dialled 141 beforehand to hide that number. However, it had gone straight to a standard pay-as-you-go voicemail greeting and she'd hung up without leaving a message. She assumed whoever was doing this wasn't using their main number but rather some anonymous sim card they'd picked up from a supermarket or phone shop.

Not responding could go one of two ways, Chloe felt. They might get bored and stop. Or it could lead them to step up their campaign, like by coming to the house when she was home alone.

Calm down, she thought. How could they possibly know that she was by herself?

Holly was still the only person Chloe had told so far about the messages. She had invited her best friend over today, but she'd already had a shopping trip planned with her Mum that she couldn't skip. Chloe had exchanged messages with her earlier, as Holly was in the car on her way to Manchester, but the picture message hadn't arrived at that point, so she hadn't mentioned that one yet.

Chloe suspected that the sender was someone from school: most likely one of the girls who'd bullied her in person at some point, of which there were a few. She could handle that. But what if it wasn't one of them? What if it was someone altogether more creepy, like a stalker or something?

When she'd mentioned this to Holly, her friend had suggested she ought to tell her parents. Maybe she was right. But they had so much of their own stuff going on. They hadn't seemed happy together for a while now. Since Dad had stopped teaching, basically. The idea that they might split up and get divorced, like the parents of many other kids at school, terrified her. The last thing she wanted to do was bug them with her problems and give them something else to worry and argue about.

For what felt like ages Chloe remained there at the top of the staircase, frozen and hugging the wall to avoid giving herself away. The doorbell rang again — the last time, surely — and then the figure moved at last. Instead of going away, though, they dropped down and next thing the letterbox rattled. Fingers were reaching through, flipping it up on the inside and revealing two beady blue eyes.

Chloe gasped, raising her hands to her mouth to hush herself and wishing she was invisible. She didn't dare to move, for fear of giving herself

201

away, but she knew all the eyes had to do was look up in order to see her.

Then came a voice. 'Hello. Is anyone there?'

Chloe recognised it straight away and immediately felt a wave of relief wash over her. There was no mistaking that part-Australian, part-northern English accent.

'Elliot,' she said instinctively.

The eyes looked up at her, guided by the sound, and she caught a glint of a toothy smile. 'Chloe! What are you doing hiding up there? It's only me.'

Despite the whole special abilities thing — the fact that he might be a vampire — Elliot didn't scare her. Quite the opposite, in fact. She'd never felt anything but comfortable in his presence, despite only meeting him two days ago.

Yesterday he'd saved Ben's life when he'd started choking. There hadn't been any really obvious special powers involved this time. And yet it had felt like Elliot's reactions were super-fast: as if he was able to see the danger ahead of everyone else and get to her brother's side in almost no time. One minute he was sitting eating and the next, before Chloe had even realised what was happening, he was doing that whatsaname manoeuvre on Ben.

No, there was an aura of safety and reassurance about Elliot, which hit Chloe as soon as she recognised his voice.

It never crossed her mind to do anything but open the door to him.

She was also interested to see what he looked like in direct sunlight, bearing in mind that the skin of the *Twilight* vampires was said to sparkle like diamonds in this situation. In other vampire stories, according to what Chloe had discovered so far online, vampires could actually be weakened or even killed by the sun.

As it turned out, Elliot's skin didn't sparkle. He looked very comfortable in the sun's warm rays. Come to think of it, he was also pretty well tanned, whereas vampires were supposed to be deathly pale. Chloe pushed these thoughts to the back of her mind and explained that she was the only one home.

'Is everything all right?' Elliot asked, looking at her eyes, which she guessed were still red from crying.

'Hay fever,' she lied, before offering Elliot a cup of tea. Because that was what adults expected when they called in somewhere, right?

20

NOW

Monday, 23 July 2018

Elliot took a seat at the kitchen table and watched Chloe put the kettle on. He wondered if he ought to offer her some help, since she was only twelve, but she looked comfortable enough and he didn't want to sound condescending. He was more concerned about the fact that she'd clearly been crying before he arrived and hadn't dared to answer the door, although she seemed much brighter now.

'I'm sorry for calling in unannounced,' he said. 'Now I think about it, your mum did mention that she and your dad would be out today. It totally slipped my mind.'

'Don't worry,' Chloe replied.

Elliot asked her how Ben was doing after his near miss at the dinner table yesterday.

'Yeah, he's good,' she said, avoiding his gaze. 'He's just popped out for a few minutes, but he'll be back soon. How do you take your tea?'

'Milk and strong, thanks.'

'Coming up.'

'So how long do you get off over summer?' Elliot asked, tapping his fingers on the table.

'Six weeks.'

'Nice. And you're only at the start now, right?

That's the best time of all. I remember it well: the whole holidays spread out before you. Nothing better.'

Chloe nodded, lifting two mugs out of the cupboard and dropping a tea bag into each before walking over to the fridge to take out the milk.

'It was early in the summer holidays that I first met your mum,' Elliot said. 'We were both eleven, a year younger than you, in between primary and secondary school. It's a bit of a funny story, actually. Did Lisa ever tell you?'

'No, I don't think so.'

'Well, believe it or not, she found me hiding in a bush with nothing but my underpants and socks on,' he said, getting an open-mouthed stare in response. 'Not out of choice. Some bullies had stolen all my clothes.'

Having recounted the tale to Chloe, Elliot added: 'It all came good in the end, thanks to your mum. But it didn't feel that way at the time. Not when I was standing there, shivering my arse off in the bush, wondering how the hell I was going to get home. It wasn't the last time I was bullied. Not by a long way. I was an easy target as a kid: chubby with glasses and curly hair; no father.'

'What happened to your dad?' she asked, handing Elliot his tea and joining him at the dining table.

'That looks great, Chloe. Thank you. My dad died when I was a sprog. Motorbike crash. So it was just me and Mum.'

'How awful.'

205

'I never knew any different. Mum did a great job by herself, although of course I would have preferred him to have been around.'

'Sure.'

Elliot took a sip of his tea. 'Oh, that's a lovely brew,' he said, grinning. 'They don't make them like this in Australia.'

'Glad you like it,' Chloe replied, blushing as she took a sip from her own mug.

'I guess your dad's around heaps these days,' Elliot said. 'That must be nice for you and Ben. Terrible how it came about, mind. What a nightmare he's been through.'

Chloe nodded rather than replying, giving Elliot the impression that she wasn't happy chatting about this subject. 'So where's that brother of yours got to?' he asked instead.

'Um, I'm not sure. I thought he'd be back by now. He probably bumped into a friend or something.'

'Where did he go?'

'Er — '

At that moment Elliot heard the sound of a cat meowing, which caught him off guard and almost caused him to spill his tea. 'Where did that come from? I didn't know you had a cat.'

Chloe giggled. 'Sorry, we don't. It's just my mobile receiving a text.'

'Seriously? I can't believe how realistic it sounds.'

Chloe pulled her mobile out of her pocket and, angling the screen away from Elliot's view, she unlocked it. He saw the blood drain from her face as she read it.

'Everything all right?' he asked after a long moment of silence.

'Um.'

Her eyes flicked from side to side as she appeared to weigh up internally what to tell him. He said nothing further, giving her space to make whatever decision she was wrestling with, and then she said: 'Could you excuse me for a minute? I really need to make a quick phone call.'

'Of course. Give me a shout if there's anything I can do to help.'

'Thanks.' She disappeared into the lounge, shutting the door behind her.

When she re-emerged a few minutes later, she looked even more flustered.

'What's the matter, Chloe?'

'Um, I think I might need your help. Well, it's Ben actually who needs it.'

She showed Elliot the text message he'd sent her:

Help. In big trouble. Can you call me NOW? No credit.

'Oh dear,' he said, looking up from the phone. 'And that's what you just did, right? Is he okay?'

She nodded. 'He says so, but he's stranded in Manchester without any money and no way to get home.'

'Manchester? I thought he'd just popped out for a few minutes.'

Chloe looked at the floor. 'Sorry. I promised not to say anything.'

* * *

207

'Can you see him anywhere?' Elliot asked Chloe a couple of hours later.

They were now at Manchester Piccadilly, the city's principal railway station.

'No,' she replied, frantically scanning the busy area around the ticket office again.

As Elliot also looked around, he observed a sea of faces: some saying hellos and goodbyes; some glued to arrival/departure screens or mobile phones; others staring blankly ahead. But not the face they were looking for.

His eyes darted from a man ordering a baguette at a food stall to a mum bending over a buggy to retrieve her little one's dummy. There were people of all ages everywhere — waiting on benches, finding change to enter the toilets, sipping from disposable coffee cups — but no Ben.

'Don't worry,' Elliot told Chloe, whose wide eyes and heavy breathing suggested she was on the verge of a major panic. 'Ben will be here somewhere. This is where you arranged, right? No chance of any confusion?'

Chloe took a deep breath. 'This is definitely it. One hundred per cent. He suggested it, because we've both been here before. It's where we had to pick up our train tickets when Mum and Dad took us to London for the weekend.'

'Why don't you try calling him?'

She did so, only to jerk the phone away from her ear a moment later, head shaking. 'Voice-mail. It's either turned off or he's got no signal. What if something's happened to him?'

'No need to panic. He was fine the last time you spoke to him.'

'We wouldn't have had to come here to get him if that was true. Mum and Dad will go ballistic if they find out about this. You're not going to tell them, are you?'

Elliot pursed his lips. 'Let's concentrate on finding Ben and getting him home.'

As discreetly as possible, while Chloe was busy scouring the crowd for her brother, Elliot stretched his right hand across his forehead, so his thumb and middle finger were pressed into his temples. His eyes flickered shut for a brief moment before he announced: 'Over there.' He stretched out his right arm, pointing across the train station into the distance.

'Where?' Chloe asked him, keeping her eyes trained on the crowd. 'Are you sure? I don't see . . . Wait. There he is!'

Chloe tore off towards the public toilets, where Ben's face had just appeared out of the door of the gents as he took his turn in the line at the exit turnstile.

Elliot watched with amusement as Chloe greeted her elder brother first with a kiss on the cheek and then thumped his arm. By the time he caught up with the youngsters, Chloe was still berating Ben for not being at the meeting place on time or being contactable on his phone.

'Calm down, sis,' Ben told her. 'I was desperate for the loo, that's all. I had to beg someone for a coin to get in first. Then I guess there was no signal in there.'

Ben's eyes looked a little puffy and red around the edges. Elliot got the impression he'd just splashed water over his face, which was still wet

209

in places, to hide this fact.

'Are you all right?' he asked, to which Ben replied, somewhat unconvincingly, that he was fine.

'Let's hit the road, then.'

Chloe protested. 'I'm just trying to find out — '

'Not now. We can talk in the car.'

'But — '

'No buts. Both of you: follow me.'

The car park was nearby. Before unlocking the light blue Fiesta, Elliot turned to Chloe and Ben. 'Cash?'

'Well, we all know that he hasn't got any,' Chloe replied.

'We wouldn't be here otherwise.'

'Good point. What about you?'

Chloe shook her head. 'I didn't think of it.'

Elliot raised his eyebrows.

'What? I'm twelve years old. I don't have much money. I'm usually with adults who pay for things. You have money, right? A credit card?'

Elliot frowned. Shuffled his feet.

'Hang on?' Ben piped up. 'Isn't this Nana's car?'

'We had to get here somehow,' Chloe snapped. 'Elliot's car is in Sydney. Probably at the airport, I'd guess. What would you have suggested?'

'Not nicking Nana's car, that's for sure.'

'Why's it nicking? Don't be ridiculous. She's on holiday. We borrowed it so that we could rescue her grandson. What's the problem?'

Elliot, who'd been watching the pair argue with arms folded across his chest, took his

210

chance to intervene. 'Are you two finished? How about we all get in the car and head home?'

'But we can't leave the car park without any money to pay, can we?' Chloe replied.

'Leave that to me.'

Elliot pulled the car up to the barrier and wound down his window to speak to the grumpy-looking female attendant in the booth.

'G'day,' he said, flashing his warmest smile. 'How are you this afternoon?'

'Ticket?' she replied.

'This should be fun,' he heard Ben mutter from the back seat, as Chloe, who'd called dibs on the front passenger seat, twisted round in her belt and shot daggers at her brother.

Meanwhile, Elliot reached into the side pocket of his door for the ticket they'd got on arrival at the car park. 'It's a freebie,' he said, injecting false confidence into his voice and waving the ticket in front of her before handing it over. 'Nothing to pay.'

The parking attendant frowned. She looked at Elliot, who kept his eyes locked on hers. Then she stared down at the ticket and her expression changed to a smile. 'Of course, sir. You have a nice day.'

'You too,' he replied, trying not to look too relieved as the barrier raised and he drove off into the road.

'What the hell?' Ben said once the attendant was out of earshot. 'How did you do that? It was like a Jedi mind trick or something.'

Elliot laughed it off, claiming it was because they hadn't been there very long and there was a

211

free grace period. However, judging by the looks on Ben and Chloe's faces, neither was convinced. Elliot had noticed Chloe in particular studying the car park charges sign on the way out, but fortunately rather than saying anything, she turned her attention on her brother. 'So are you going to tell us what happened today, Ben?'

Elliot pulled the car up at a red traffic light as Chloe asked this. He twisted round in his seat to see Ben's response, only to get the shock of his life when a strange grey-haired woman in a green parka coat started thumping on the rear side window next to where Ben was sitting.

21

THEN

Saturday, 12 February 1994

Wendy was heading out on a date. She was playing it down as dinner with a friend, but Elliot wasn't stupid. That friend was a man; it was the Saturday before Valentine's Day and she'd been behind the sewing machine all week making a posh new dress.

He wasn't sure what he thought about it. His mum attracting interest from the opposite sex was nothing new. For some time now Elliot had noticed the way that men looked at her, with her long black curls, big brown eyes and dainty figure. They went out of their way to help her with things: in the supermarket, the post office, you name it. Even Mr Armitage, his primary school teacher who'd coached him to take the King George's entrance exam, had fallen under her spell. Elliot had found it hilarious to see him stumble over his words in her presence, while constantly trying to compliment her on everything from the colour of her nail varnish to her choice of net curtains. Not that it had done him any good.

Elliot had never known her to have a boyfriend. He had asked her about it once or twice, as a few kids he knew had parents who'd remarried, but her stock response had always been that he was the only man she needed in her life.

Apparently that was no longer the case.

The weird thing was that Wendy had asked Elliot if he minded.

'What do you mean?' he'd replied, wondering if he'd heard her correctly.

'A man I work with — his name is Dr Nesbit — has invited me out for dinner next Saturday. How would you feel about that?'

'I dunno,' he'd told her, confused. 'What's it got to do with me?'

'Well, I wouldn't want to do anything that might upset you, darling. Nothing's more important to me than you and I don't want you to think I'm trying to replace your father or anything, because that's not it at all. It would just be a nice evening out with a colleague whose company I enjoy, who happens to be a man.' She paused before adding: 'Also, if I go, I obviously won't be around that night. You're a bit old for a babysitter, but I'd rather not leave you home alone. We'd have to sort something else out.'

'Like what? Where would you be going and what time would you get back?'

'I'm not sure yet, but I thought perhaps you could spend the evening at Lisa's house.'

'I guess. It depends if she has anything else on.'

'Would you like me to contact her parents?'

'Okay.'

Within an hour she'd spoken to Christine,

Lisa's mother, who'd offered to put him up for the night. So that was that. The speed with which Wendy had made these arrangements showed how keen she was to go on the date. So Elliot found himself carried along with it. How could he say no? What kind of a selfish idiot would that make him?

'Have fun, love,' she said, kissing him goodbye as he set off for Lisa's house with his sleeping bag and other overnight gear squashed into the Head holdall that usually contained his school books.

'Thanks, Mum,' Elliot replied. 'See you tomorrow.' Part of him wanted to wish her a good night, but he couldn't get the words out, so instead he waved and smiled.

Walking the short distance to his friend's house, daylight already starting to fade, he questioned what exactly he was worried about. Wasn't it about time that his mum did something for herself, rather than for him? He knew it was, but still the whole idea of her going on a date freaked him out. What if she fell in love and, next thing, she wanted to settle down with this Dr Nesbit? Elliot didn't like the sound of that. He was happy with things as they were. They'd managed fine so far, the two of them. He had no need of a stepfather.

And yet he was getting older. He'd be fourteen in June. In a few years, if everything went to plan, he'd be leaving home for university. If his mum hadn't met someone by then, she'd be left all alone.

Calm down, he told himself. He knew that he

was overthinking matters. It was just one little date.

But then Lisa made a joke about it soon after he arrived at her house, asking what his new daddy was called.

'Oh, come on,' his friend told him, lying on her front on the bed, chin resting on her hands. 'I'm only joking. No need to look so miserable.'

'I'd rather not think about the whole date thing. That's all.'

'Why not? It's nice for your mum to get out for once. Who's it with, anyway?'

Elliot shrugged. 'Some guy she works with. Dr Nesbit, he's called. I've not met him.'

'A doctor? Ooh, very nice. He'll have plenty of money, then.'

He scowled. 'Please don't.' Then he made a point of changing the subject by asking Lisa how that morning's hockey match had gone.

'We lost,' she replied. 'So that wasn't good. But I got chatted up by a cute boy afterwards, which made up for it.'

'Oh? Who was that?'

'Sean Ferguson from two years above us. Do you know him?'

Elliot, sitting on the edge of the camp bed Lisa's mum had made up for him, fought not to wince. 'Sure. What was he doing there?'

'He should have been playing on the rugby team, but he was on the bench after spraining his ankle during practice. Their match finished a bit before ours, so he and a couple of other lads came over to watch us.'

'And he asked you out?'

216

Lisa rolled on to her back and giggled. 'Maybe. He's really funny, you know. He was doing all these impressions of the other lads on the team. I always thought he was fit, but I'd never really spoken to him before.'

'So did he ask you out or not?'

'Yes,' she admitted eventually. 'There's a funfair on near school next Friday evening and he asked if I wanted to go with him.'

'And?'

Lisa lowered her voice. 'Don't say anything to Mum or Dad, because I'm not going to tell them why, but I'm hoping to stay at Hayley's house that night and we'll go together. She fancies one of the other boys who came over to talk to us — this lad called Mark who goes to Westwich High — so it'll be like a double date.'

Hayley was one of Lisa's hockey teammates. Elliot had met her a handful of times and hadn't taken to her. She'd always looked straight through him, presumably because he wasn't on the rugby team or in any way fanciable to her. She lived in Westwich, a stone's throw away from Queen Anne's, and Lisa had stayed there several times previously, ahead of early Saturday matches.

'Why not tell them the truth?' Elliot asked, making patterns in the deep cream carpet with his feet. Doing so cast his mind back to the original brown carpet and green walls — long since painted white — from the time of his old pal Christopher, who he hadn't heard from in ages. But Lisa's reply jerked him straight back to the present, the memory fading as quickly as it had emerged.

217

'Because we're playing away in Blackpool the next morning and it'll be an early start to get there on the coach. I know for a fact that Mum and Dad wouldn't let me go out if I asked them. But Hayley's mum is dead relaxed, so she won't care — and she won't tell them either, if I ask her not to.'

'Right.'

Elliot was taken aback by this, although he didn't let on. He couldn't imagine himself deceiving his mum in this way. Technically Lisa wasn't lying to her parents, but the avoidance of truth was deliberate enough to amount to the same thing.

And all because she was desperate to go on a date with Sean Ferguson. If Elliot had been given a choice of boys to select as decent potential partners for Lisa, Sean wouldn't have even been on the longlist. He was renowned as one of the toughest in his year. So far their paths had never crossed. However, Elliot had seen him brawling in the yard with other lads on several occasions, usually surrounded by boys chanting 'fight'.

The last time had only been a month or so earlier and had been a particularly brutal clash between Sean and another scrapper. There had been lots of proper punches thrown, unlike most fights Elliot had witnessed at King George's, which were usually more like bad wrestling matches. A teacher had eventually broken it up; the next day both lads had been covered in cuts and bruises.

Sean also had a reputation as a loose cannon

on the rugby pitch. This and the fact he'd once dislocated his arm had earned him the nickname Riggs, after Mel Gibson's character in the *Lethal Weapon* movies. Not that he looked anything like Mel Gibson. Despite being in good shape physically, Sean was ugly, as far as Elliot was concerned. He had these strange ears that were small but still managed to stick out too far and his nose was slightly bent in the middle, presumably from being broken at some point.

Elliot was sure he'd also seen Sean hanging around with his friendly neighbourhood bully and bus enemy Samo, although he didn't have the heart to mention this. Neither did he tell her that Sean was the typical kind of lad who'd find it hilarious to tease him for being fat or to allege that he was gay.

Elliot had long since given up trying to second-guess Lisa when it came to the boys she liked. They were usually sporty and often a little older than her, but there the similarities ended. At one point she'd gone out with his friend Neil, of course. But to Elliot's relief, that relationship hadn't lasted more than a couple of months. He'd found the whole thing rather uncomfortable, but with hindsight, Neil was the best of a bad bunch.

Not that Elliot would say that to Lisa. He'd learned to avoid passing judgement on her boyfriends, even after they'd split up, having told her that one such ex was a loser, only for them to get back together. That had made things awkward between them, including a short period of not

219

speaking. So these days Elliot knew to bite his tongue.

Secretly, he still fancied her, but it wasn't like he ever expected to do anything about it. He'd never told a soul either, sticking to the line Lisa sometimes used that they were best friends and didn't see each other that way. She clearly meant it. Sometimes she even behaved like he was one of her female friends, walking around in her underwear in his presence, for instance; asking him questions like if he thought her boobs had grown or whether they looked good in a certain bra. He played along in these instances, pretending to be totally at ease, although inside he felt anything but.

Wendy and Lisa's parents were totally blasé about the pair of them hanging out together. Despite being teenagers now, it was still normal for them to stay the night at each other's houses, sleeping in the same room, as they would tonight. Elliot knew for sure that Graham and Christine wouldn't allow a boyfriend to do the same. Neither would his mum, in the unlikely instance that he invited a girlfriend over to stay the night. The only reason either of them had ever been threatened with having this privilege revoked was when they'd been caught chatting too late into the night.

Even Jamie, Lisa's younger brother, had long since grown bored of making jokes about them being in love. There had been a time when he'd seemed to enjoy nothing more than pretending to snog his fist at the door of his sister's bedroom to wind her up. Now he barely blinked an eyelid whenever Elliot called round. He was usually too busy playing football, if not crowing about how many goals he'd scored that week and how he planned to go pro one day.

Despite not understanding the football obsession, Elliot had grown fond of Jamie, who he considered like a stand-in younger brother of his own. He was always full of beans and made mealtimes at the Bensons good fun with impressions of his teachers and a range of celebrities, from sports pundit Jimmy Hill to Will Smith, star of the *Fresh Prince of Bel-Air*, his favourite TV show.

'Do you know Sean much, then?' Lisa asked, twirling her hair with her right hand, still lying on her bed.

'Not really.' Elliot stood up and looked out of the window at the road below, where the early evening darkness was interspersed by orange pools from the street lights. 'I've seen him around school and that, but I doubt he knows who I am.'

'Is he a bit of a joker?'

Elliot shrugged, not having the heart to tell her that he was best known for fighting. 'I'm not really friendly with many of the boys in that year,' he said. 'And he's in the rugby crowd, which I'm not. I could ask Neil, if you like. He might know.'

'No, thanks,' she replied, as expected. Who would want their ex's opinion on their new love interest?

'So where's your mum going on this hot date of hers?' she went on.

'Oh, not that again,' he said with a sigh. 'Some Italian in the city centre, I think. I don't know what it's called.'

'He's taking her into Manchester? Must be serious.'

He turned back from the window to look at his friend. 'Don't joke about it, Lise. I feel weird about the whole thing. Mum going on dates isn't something I'm used to.'

Lisa wrinkled her nose and sat up on the bed. 'Hasn't she had any boyfriends since your dad died?'

He shook his head. 'And that suits me fine.'

'So why now?'

'Because I'm getting older, I guess. I don't need her as much as I used to.'

'You want her to be happy, don't you?'

'Of course. It's going to take some getting used to, that's all.'

He was distracted by the sound of someone — almost certainly Jamie — running up the stairs. Sure enough, a moment later Lisa's little brother appeared at the door, dressed in tracksuit bottoms and a Liverpool FC shirt. That was his team, much to the disapproval of Graham, his dad, an ardent Nottingham Forest supporter. 'All right, losers. Tea's ready.'

'Hello, squirt,' Elliot said. 'How's it going?'

'Don't you 'squirt' me,' Jamie replied with a grin, raising his fists like a boxer, then ducking and weaving at the door. 'I'll be bigger than you soon. Then you'll see.'

'That's big talk for a little guy,' Elliot replied, holding his own hands up in a martial arts style.

'You know I'm a black belt in karate, right?'

This made Lisa laugh. 'Is that an honorary award for watching *The Karate Kid* enough times?'

'Damn. My secret's out. What's on the menu tonight?'

'Pizza, of course,' Jamie replied. 'What do you think? It's Saturday.'

22

NOW

Monday, 23 July 2018

'You!' Ben yelled at the woman banging on his car window.

It seemed a strange response to Elliot, who'd got over the initial shock of the noise and was now more concerned that she didn't cause any harm or damage. Who the hell was this crackpot, with her yellow teeth and whiskery mole, and what did she want?

'Get lost,' he said, waving his hand at the window, signalling for her to leave them alone. Then he told Ben and Chloe not to worry. 'It's okay. The doors are locked. She can't get in.' He turned back to look at the road ahead. 'The lights will change in a minute and I'll be able to pull away.'

'No, don't,' Ben cried out, drawing Elliot's attention to the back of the car again. 'I know her. She was on the bus with me earlier. I think she has my — '

Before Ben could finish his sentence, the scruffy woman answered it for him by reaching inside her grimy parka and pulling out a brown leather shape. She held it up against Ben's window and mouthed something Elliot couldn't understand.

'Yes, look. She's got my wallet! Could you pull in?'

Elliot and Chloe eyeballed Ben in unison.

'Seriously, mate?' Elliot asked, open-mouthed.

'Yes!' He was scrabbling for the window winder — a manual one, which his hand eventually grasped — but it must have been seized up, as he didn't seem to be able to get it open.

A sudden angry din of car horns drew Elliot's attention back to the traffic lights, which he saw were now green.

'Crap. The lights have changed,' Elliot said. 'There are heaps of cars behind me. I don't think I can pull over.'

Before anyone could stop him, Ben unlocked his door and swung it open. 'Quick. Jump in,' he said to the woman, sliding across to the other side of the back seat. 'We can't stop here, but I'm sure we can pull in around the corner or something.'

She did as he said, to the accompaniment of more blasting horns, and then finally Elliot was able to pull the car away, waving an apologetic hand in the rear-view mirror in a bid to placate the angry motorists behind.

'Hello again,' the woman said calmly to Ben, as if getting in a car with him and two strangers was the most normal thing in the world. Handing him the wallet, she added: 'I believe this is yours. You dropped it on the bus. I did try to tell you that after you got off, but — '

'Yeah, I'm so sorry about that,' Ben replied. 'I totally got the wrong end of the stick. I thought — '

'Um, is anyone going to tell me what's going on here?' Elliot piped up, having opened his window to counter the eye-watering reek that had entered the car along with Ben's odd guest.

He'd taken a right turn after the traffic lights into a quieter road and was now scouring the vicinity for somewhere safe to stop.

'He's got an unusual accent on him,' the woman said to Ben, unfazed. 'Where's he from?'

'Elliot's from here originally,' Ben replied, 'but he's lived in Australia for the past twenty years.'

'So you know my name now,' Elliot said, glancing at her in the rear-view mirror as he indicated right and turned the car into a small pay and display car park. 'But I'm afraid I've no idea who you are and how you ended up with Ben's wallet.'

He pulled into a parking bay and stopped the engine, before turning to face the two of them in the back seat, as Chloe did the same. 'So?'

'I'm Cassandra,' the woman replied in her croaky voice, giving him a little wave and a smile. 'But everyone calls me Sandie. Ben and I met on the bus into town earlier. He dropped his wallet; I picked it up. By chance we happened to run into each other again. I spotted him through the car window as I was walking by. What are the odds? Funny old world, isn't it?'

He turned to Ben. 'Is that right?'

'Pretty much. She sat next to me on the bus and we chatted. I thought — '

'That I'd nicked it off you, right?'

Wincing, Ben looked down at his feet. 'I really am sorry about that.'

226

'Why did you think I was trying to get your attention after you got off?' Sandie asked him.

'I, um, thought you were rubbing it in. You know, that you'd tricked me or whatever.'

She took a swig from a water bottle that Elliot suspected had been refilled with either gin or vodka, since there was a strong whiff of alcohol about her, mixed in with body odour and other unpleasant smells he preferred not to identify.

'Goodness,' she said. 'I must have made a great impression. At least that explains the lovely hand gesture you gave me.'

Elliot had no idea what she was talking about, but Ben did, judging by the beetroot colour of his face.

'I feel like a right idiot,' Ben said. 'Thank you for returning it. How did you —'

'Find you?'

He nodded.

She winked, placing a scrawny hand — long, grubby fingernails and all — on his knee. 'Like I said to Elliot here, just chance, isn't it? What else?'

Elliot was wondering what on earth to make of all of this when Sandie suddenly reached forward with those unpleasant claws of hers and grabbed one of each of his and Chloe's hands. Her eyelids fluttered shut and she turned her face up to the padded ceiling of the car like some kind of eccentric medium.

Ben shrugged, pulling a 'don't ask me' face.

'Poor thing,' Sandie said to Chloe in a low, trance-like voice. 'Don't listen to those nasty words. You'll be rid of them soon enough.

Jealousy is an ugly worm capable of twisting even — '

Elliot was about to pull his hand away and end this nonsense when Sandie took a sharp intake of breath, breaking off mid-sentence, as her head shot in his direction. Her eyes snapped open, the whites threaded with scores of tiny red blood vessels that Elliot was sure hadn't been there before. The hairs on the back of his neck prickled and a shiver ran down his spine, like an alarm had been triggered in his body.

'You!' she exclaimed. 'You're — '

'In a bit of a rush, yes,' he said in a loud voice that stopped her in her tracks. Elliot feared what she'd been about to blurt out, getting the distinct impression that somehow she'd just discovered far more about him than he wanted her, let alone Ben and Chloe, to know. But how was that possible? Was she like him? No, he didn't think that was it. So what then?

He stared her down, taking control before things got out of hand. 'We all appreciate you returning Ben's wallet. It's very good of you. But I need to get these two home as soon as possible. Is there somewhere nearby I can drop you off, or is here close enough?'

Sandie's eyes remained fixed on him; she looked ready to say more, but no further words came out. The expression on her face was strained and, looking down, Elliot noticed the knuckles of her hands, both now clamped on to his, were ghostly white, in sharp contrast to his tanned skin.

Get out, he thought, his eyes guiding her

towards the car door in a silent command. Leave us alone. There's nothing here for you.

'Yes, I'll get out here,' she said a moment later, her voice taking on an almost robotic tone. 'Thank you.'

'No, thank you, Sandie,' Elliot said. 'Right, Ben?'

'Definitely.' Ben nodded, although his face was contorted with confusion. 'Thanks a million for returning my wallet. And apologies again for my behaviour earlier.'

Sandie showed no sign of having heard him. She didn't even look at Ben as she let go of Elliot's hand, reached for the door handle and climbed out of the car.

Who or what are you? Elliot thought. And then the pain hit: a sudden vicious stabbing feeling in his chest. Elliot froze, squeezed his eyes shut and leaned into the steering wheel, gripping on to it like the edge of a cliff, fighting to keep his breathing steady. This had happened before and, assuming it followed the same pattern, Elliot hoped it would pass quickly. He didn't have time to think about why it was happening or what it meant. He just wanted it to stop.

He felt Chloe's hand on his arm as she asked if he was all right.

'Yep. Just give me a second. Indigestion.'

The pain ended as abruptly as it had started. He snapped open his eyes and took a deep breath, shaking his upper body and exclaiming: 'Okay, guys. Let's make tracks.'

As he pulled the car back on to the road,

minus the extra passenger, Chloe said: 'Well, she was weird. And boy did she need a shower.'

Elliot looked at Sandie out of the rear-view mirror and felt a twinge of guilt. She was standing still in the car park, a confused look on her face.

Meanwhile, Chloe was holding her right hand — the one Sandie had grabbed — out in front of her, turning it around and examining it. She wrinkled her nose. 'I don't suppose anyone's got any hand gel, do they?'

'Sorry, no,' Elliot said, almost in perfect sync with Ben. 'By the way, I might need some help finding my way back. It's been a while. Straight on for now, right?'

'Um, yeah, I think so,' Chloe said. 'Ben?'

Her brother looked around in all directions before confirming: 'Yes, straight on. But I think you need to take a right before that big, weird-looking glass building up ahead. If there's a sign for the M60, then it's definitely that way.'

Not bad for a kid still too young to drive, Elliot thought.

Meanwhile, Chloe twisted round in her seat and stared at her brother. She looked about to say something when Ben beat her to it.

'Is it weird driving here, compared to Australia, Elliot?'

'It's not bad, to be fair,' he replied. 'We also drive on the left there, although our cars tend to be a lot bigger and they're usually automatics. It took me a while to get to grips with the stick shift on the way here. Isn't that right, Chloe?'

'No comment,' she said with a coy smile.

230

'Anyway, stop trying to shift the attention away from yourself, Ben.'

'What do you mean? It was you and Elliot that Sandie was saying stuff to. What was all that about a jealous worm or something?'

'Er, hello!' Chloe snapped back. 'She was your weird friend — and you're the reason we're here in the first place. Have you forgotten about the whole 'come and rescue me' thing? What happened? We know about you losing your wallet now, but that can't be it. You were really upset when I got your text earlier and phoned you back. Why were you even here in the first place? Who were you meeting?'

This is going to be interesting, Elliot thought.

23

NOW

Monday, 23 July 2018

'Well?' Chloe said, staring at Ben, waiting for a reply.

She looked across at Elliot, behind the wheel, and nudged him with her elbow.

'Ouch. What was that for?' he said. 'I'm driving here, love. It's not a good idea to start poking me.'

'It was a nudge.'

He rolled his eyes. 'Oh, that's all right then.'

'Aren't you going to back me up?'

'Oh, right. I see.' Elliot looked at Ben through the rear-view mirror. 'Come on, mate. She's right. Spill the beans. I'm going to need something if you want me to keep this hush-hush. By rights, I ought to tell your mum and dad.'

That got Ben's attention. 'No, please don't.'

The mere thought of his parents finding out what he'd been up to turned Ben's stomach. But telling Chloe and Elliot was little more appealing.

The secret to telling a believable lie was rooting it in the truth. He'd read that somewhere.

Digging his nails into the fabric of the car seat,

Ben racked his brains for a plausible explanation for how he'd got himself into such a mess. But even as he started to speak, sticking to the facts initially as he told them how he'd used up all his phone credit, all he could picture in his mind was the ugly and embarrassing truth of what had actually happened earlier.

★ ★ ★

Ben flicked the Vs at the bus — and that bloody con artist who'd stolen his wallet — as it pulled away down the road.

No sooner had he got off the double decker than she'd appeared at the upstairs window, near where they'd been sitting together, gleefully waving his wallet at him. So that was what she'd meant by the strange parting comment about seeing her again sooner than expected.

That woman had some nerve! She obviously took great delight in pickpocketing her unsuspecting victims, lulling them into thinking she was harmless and then pouncing. He figured that must have been why she'd sat down next to him in the first place, when he'd appeared to be asleep and thus an easy target.

So at what moment had she swiped it? It could have been when she'd stood up to let him out, what with all the clamping her hands on his and asking the time. Or maybe it was earlier: perhaps when his eyes had still been shut, or the first occasion he'd pulled his phone out to tell her the time.

He had tried running after the bus for a few

233

seconds, only to realise he didn't have a chance of ever catching up. Instead he'd unleashed his fury with a string of expletives, which had turned more than a few heads, plus the only hand gesture that had felt appropriate in the circumstances.

Not that any of this made him feel any better.

Dammit. How had he been so stupid as to fall for her trickery? He'd actually felt sorry for the woman, mistaking her cunning act for genuine loneliness. He'd thought that by talking to her — listening to her prattle on — he'd been doing his good deed for the day. Now she had all his money.

Then it struck him: his student ID card was in there too, plus his return bus ticket and — shit — his bank card. How had he not thought of that straight away? He'd have to cancel that, wouldn't he? Brilliant. How on earth did that work?

He managed to figure this out after getting a number off the Internet and phoning the bank up on his mobile, which luckily hadn't also been swiped. Unfortunately, thanks to spending a long time waiting in a queue to get through, he managed to drain what was left of the pay-as-you-go credit on his phone, leaving barely enough to send a couple of texts.

'Bloody hell!' he shouted, smacking the palm of his free hand on to the wooden bench where he'd sat down; only just stopping himself from hurling his mobile into the distance. This was exactly the reason he needed a contract, like all of his friends. But would Mum and Dad listen?

Of course not. They wouldn't even let him get an iPhone. He had to make do with a damn Android.

What was he supposed to do now? No money. No phone credit. He was screwed. The bank had also said something about reporting the theft to the police, but stuff that. What was he supposed to do: ring 999?

'Are you okay, lad?' an elderly passer-by asked him, his eyes squinting with concern. 'You look — '

'I'm fine,' he snapped, still smarting from his last run-in with a stranger. 'Leave me alone.'

And although he didn't retract his words, the look of shock — maybe even hurt — that he saw as the old man took a step backwards and continued on his way, jolted Ben to his senses. He had a friend nearby, who was no doubt wondering where he'd got to; there was no need to panic.

He knew where he was going. He'd memorised the directions after looking at a map online at home.

After a few tiring minutes of weaving through city folk, all of whom appeared to be in a rush, Ben turned into a quieter side street, and another, until he found himself at the entrance of the apartment block that was his destination.

It looked the same as it had online: a grand converted warehouse, eight storeys tall, with a suitably majestic arched entrance. The heavy wooden outer doors were open but, as he'd been forewarned, the glass ones inside were locked, requiring him to be buzzed in.

He pressed the silver button for apartment twenty-three and, a moment later, a familiar voice answered. 'Hello?'

'It's me — Ben.'

'Oh, at last. I was worried something had happened to you. Come on up. It's the sixth floor. Best take the lift.'

'Thanks.'

A buzzing noise and he was in. The empty lift was waiting and, as it rose, Ben adjusted his hair in the mirror and did his best to smooth out the creases in his T-shirt. His heart was pounding as he sniffed his armpits, glad to still smell his deodorant, before noticing the camera above him and hoping no one was watching.

'It's going to be fine,' he told himself under his breath as the silver doors slid open and he found himself in an empty corridor facing apartment number twenty-one. The door of number twenty-three was ajar when he got there; hoping he didn't look half as nervous as he felt, Ben knocked and walked inside. 'Hello?'

'Come in, Ben,' a voice called from somewhere out of sight. 'Grab a seat. Make yourself at home. I've just got out of the shower. I'll be with you in a minute.'

This seemed odd to Ben, considering his late arrival, but he was too busy being impressed by the roomy loft-style apartment with its wooden floors, exposed beams and large cityscape windows. It was immaculate. Everything in the open-plan space, from the pair of brown leather couches and huge TV to the classy kitchen area, looked brand new.

'Great place,' he called, staring out of the window at the sprawling rooftops of central Manchester.

'Thanks,' the reply came. 'Put some music on, if you like. There's an iPad with Spotify on top of the hi-fi. They're already connected up.'

'Great. Will do.'

'What took you so long to get here from the bus? I thought you might be having second thoughts.'

'No, nothing like that. I had a bit of a nightmare, to be honest. I'll tell you all about it later.'

'Sounds intriguing. With you in a minute.'

Ben walked over to the stereo, on a neat but solid-looking oak unit near a window, and raised an eyebrow at the brand — B&O — as were the enormous floor-standing speakers.

Ben had expected a nice place, but nothing like this. It was a long way from his bland family home in Aldham. He could picture himself living somewhere similar one day, but he'd have to land himself a decent job first.

He picked up the iPad and, taking it back to the nearest couch, started scrolling through. What to go for? This felt like a test. He decided the best bet was to choose a saved playlist, but before he could pick one, he heard footsteps behind him.

'Close your eyes, Ben.'

'What? Why?' he replied, almost turning around but managing to resist the urge.

'Please. Just for a minute. It'll be fun.'

Ben felt a bead of sweat trickle down his lower

back. Nodded. And closed his eyes.

He heard the footsteps again, walking past and in front of him, and then a loud creak of the floorboards that made him gasp and almost open his eyes.

'Sorry. Only me. Almost there.' The voice came from right in front of him now. He could hear breathing that wasn't his own. He could smell a mixture of things: toothpaste, shower gel, deodorant and a zingy, citrus-style fragrance. Underneath all that, subtle but still noticeable, was a hint of cigarettes. Not great, but not the end of the world.

'Okay. Now before you open your eyes, I need to say something.'

Ben felt his heartbeat quicken. 'Like what?'

'We've had a great time messaging each other and chatting on the phone, haven't we?'

'Yes, of course. You know we have. That's why I'm here. Can I open them now? This is getting weird.'

He felt a warm hand press gently on to his own, which was resting next to his leg on the cool leather of the couch. 'Please, a moment longer. I need to tell you something. I — '

Ben couldn't handle this. After everything he'd been through on the bus, he wasn't in the mood. It didn't feel right.

He opened his eyes and his jaw hit the floor.

There was a strange man kneeling in front of him who he'd never cast eyes on before in his life. He was small and skinny; pale and balding, with the remains of his ash-blond hair cropped short.

Ben jumped to his feet, knocking the man's hand away. He felt like he was about to throw up. 'What the — '

'Wait,' the man pleaded, remaining on his knees and holding his hands together in front of his face like he was praying. 'It's me, Henry. I know I don't look like you expect, but everything else is — '

A shiver ran down Ben's spine. 'Don't look like I expect? I thought you were seventeen! That you lived here with your dad. But you're . . . old.'

'I'm only thirty; people say I look younger.'

'Only? That's twice my age. Bloody hell! What are you: some kind of paedo? Have you been grooming me? Oh God, I can't believe this is happening.'

'No, Ben. You've got me all wrong. That's not it at all. Come on, you know me. You recognise my voice, right? I'm everything you thought I was — just . . . not physically.'

Ben's mind was racing. His thoughts were in a whirl. He ran a hand through his hair, no longer caring about messing it up. He needed to feel something — anything — to try to ground himself. To get to grips with what the hell was going on.

He and Henry — if that was even his real name — had been chatting online for weeks. They'd spoken on the phone countless times. But they'd never actually seen each other in person until now. They'd not even had a video chat. Henry had told him he felt uncomfortable talking to a camera and, although Ben had found that odd initially, they'd been getting on so well,

239

he'd accepted it — brushed his concerns under the carpet like some kind of idiot.

What terrified Ben most of all was how much he'd told this man. Henry was literally the only person who knew his actual identity that was aware of the biggest secret in Ben's life: the fact that he was gay.

He'd known this for some time now. And although he'd been open about it to others online — even done intimate things via camera with them — that had been anonymous. He'd never shown his face or given his real name.

Meanwhile, in his real day-to-day life, with his family at home and his friends at school, he'd never uttered a word or given a deliberate hint to anyone about it. He hadn't known how to or dared to even try, for fear of what the reaction might be.

At first Ben hadn't been a hundred per cent sure that he was gay. He'd hoped it was just a phase that he was going through. Now, although he still felt a long way from having the confidence to come out, there was no longer any doubt in his mind — and a lot of that was down to Henry.

Their relationship had been different to all the others. Despite meeting on a gay chat room, things had never got overtly sexual between them, as they had so quickly with other guys. It had never been about the thrill and release with them. There'd been plenty of flirtation, but it hadn't ever gone further. Something deeper had developed: a close bond — a friendship — that Ben had convinced himself might be something

240

more. He'd even toyed with the L word in the privacy of his own mind.

God, he'd been so looking forward to this moment. He'd been nervous, of course, but only because meeting Henry in person for the first time had meant so much to him. He'd thought today might be the first time he would actually kiss another boy; have the real physical contact that he so desired.

But that was when he thought Henry was a teenager like him. Sure, he'd seemed wiser and more comfortable with his sexuality than Ben. Come to think of it, there had even been times when the tone of his voice — expressions he'd used — had sounded unusual to Ben's ears. But he'd put that down to Henry, who was already 'out', being slightly older than he was — and perhaps a little eccentric. Now the truth had emerged — and it was horrifying, shattering everything that had gone before into a million little pieces. He wanted to pinch himself to check he wasn't in a nightmare, but he knew that wouldn't help. This was reality, right enough, and it was awful. Today was a genuine contender for the worst day of his life.

Ben had a million questions he wanted to ask Henry, but he could barely bring himself to look at him, never mind hold a conversation. It made his skin crawl to hear the voice he recognised — that he'd confessed some of his deepest, darkest secrets to — coming out of the mouth of this creepy guy he was seeing for the first time.

The photo Henry used online, of a hot seventeen-year-old Ben had hoped might be his

241

first boyfriend, didn't look remotely like him.

'That's not even a younger version of you in your photo, is it?' he spat, remaining on his feet and sliding to the right, so the couch was no longer blocking his exit.

'I'm so sorry, Ben,' Henry replied, his bottom lip wobbling like a toddler.

'So who is it in the picture?'

Henry shook his head, breathing heavily. 'I don't know. It was a random photo I found online. I didn't think anyone would be interested in talking to someone like me, so I — '

'Lied. That's what you did. Don't pretend it was anything else. God, I can't believe all the personal stuff I told you. You stole that from me. You're disgusting.'

Henry moved to get up from his kneeling position on the floor, making Ben panic. 'Stop. Don't come any closer,' he said, pulling out his mobile and brandishing it like a weapon. 'Seriously, if you do, I'll call the police and report you. I'm sure they'd love to hear how you tricked me into visiting you; how you imperson-ated a teenager.'

'No, no, please don't do that,' Henry said, crumbling back on to the floor, squeezing his head in his hands and rocking backwards and forwards. 'I didn't mean for this to happen. I wanted to tell you the truth ages ago, but I could never find the right moment. I was afraid you'd freak out.'

'Well, you got that last bit right.'

'I'd never do anything to hurt you. You have to know that. We had such a strong connection. I couldn't stop myself. I felt like I was falling in love with you.'

This comment was the final straw for Ben. He'd continued to back away and there were several metres between them now. Without warning, he darted for the door. His fingers fumbled with the latch as his eyes remained on Henry, who was on his feet and moving towards him, pleading even as Ben shouted warnings for him to stay put.

Then the door was open and Ben inhaled the cool stale air of the windowless corridor. He raced back towards the lift, saw a flight of stairs and hurtled down that instead, two steps at a time, not daring to look back to see if he was being followed.

Reaching the ground floor, he tore past the lift, terrified it might open and spit Henry into his path, and headed straight for the front door.

Ben shoved both palms against the cold glass, his panicked face reflecting back at him, but the door merely rattled in place.

'What the hell is this?' he said, looking back over his shoulder, relieved to see that he was still alone, and then pushing the door again in desperation.

Nothing. Shit. What did this mean? Did he need a key or someone to buzz him out?

Frantically he scoured the area around the door for some clue, his eyes finally landing on a large green button on the wall. Of course. He pressed it and, without another backward glance, pushed his way out on the street and ran at full speed back the way he'd come.

Ben didn't stop until he was several streets away, by which time he was panting and coated in sweat. Still he scanned the area around him for any sign of Henry, checking each of the dozens of faces passing by.

He changed direction and ran again, continuing this time until he reached the busy open space that was Piccadilly Gardens. Only here was he finally happy to stop — to grab a spare spot on a bench and catch his breath. He wiped his brow with the thick hair on his forearms and, despite the very public setting, couldn't stop himself from bursting into tears.

Once he'd calmed down, Ben spotted an icy can of lemonade changing hands between a drinks vendor and a passer-by. It reminded him of how thirsty he was. He wished he could gulp it down in one. But he wasn't going to be buying any drinks without his wallet. He didn't even know how he would get home. So he did the only thing he could think of: he used the small amount of credit left on his phone to text Chloe, begging for help.

★   ★   ★

Back in the present, still in the car heading home, Ben finished telling Elliot and his sister the heavily edited, fictionalised version of what had happened.

'So you went to meet this guy to buy computer parts?' Chloe asked, screwing her face up like she wasn't convinced by his improvisation. 'Why didn't you get them off eBay or something?'

244

'They were crazy cheap,' Ben replied. 'It didn't occur to me until I met him, stupidly I know, that they were probably off the back of a lorry. We've chatted a few times before on this IT forum and he's always given me good advice.

'I thought he was all right, but in the flesh he seemed shifty. And when I told him about having my wallet stolen, I don't think he believed it. He started having a go at me, saying I was a timewaster and asking me to turn my pockets out to prove it, which is when I got freaked and ran out of his flat. I overreacted really, but — you know — after what I thought had happened on the bus . . .'

Elliot hadn't said much so far, which Ben was glad about. He had feared he might start asking him for specifics about the made-up computer parts, which could have proved awkward. But when he did speak, it was to point out that Ben ought to be more careful meeting people from the Internet.

'It was dangerous meeting someone you didn't know like that, mate,' he said. 'Especially not telling anyone where you were going. There are some weirdos out there.'

'You're not going to say anything to Mum and Dad, are you?'

'By rights, I ought to. Especially knowing what I do now.'

'Oh, come on. That's not fair. I only told you because — '

'Hold your horses. I didn't say I would, did I? Are you going to learn from what happened today and do things differently — safer — next time?'

'Definitely.'

'That's good enough for me. What about you, Chloe?'

'Sorry?'

'I want you to learn from this too. I don't want you making similar mistakes one day.'

'I won't.'

'Good. You've only got one life, kids. Don't put it at risk needlessly. Now I'm not going to lie to your parents, but if they do find out what happened, it won't be from me. That's my best offer.'

'Thank you,' Ben replied. 'What about you, Chloe?'

She'd just received a text — as indicated by that ridiculous cat meow she insisted on using for her notification sound. After frowning at her mobile for a long moment, she turned to him with hazy eyes. 'Sorry. What was that?'

Ben resisted the temptation to snap. 'You're not going to say anything to Mum and Dad, are you?'

She shook her head. 'Of course not.'

'That wasn't them, was it? The text.'

'No.'

He breathed a sigh of relief. 'Good. Cheers, sis.'

24

NOW

Tuesday, 24 July 2018

Elliot was running out of time. He could feel it. He didn't know how. He just could. Like he could sense so much that had happened recently, such as that weird Sandie woman in Manchester somehow perceiving the truth about his presence here.

Yesterday, despite that particular near miss, he'd relished the opportunity to get closer to Ben and Chloe. Hopefully he'd done enough to gain their trust — at least to some degree. Mike, on the other hand, was going to be a harder nut to crack. The clock was ticking and he needed to step things up.

How many days did he have left? This wasn't a question he had the answer to, and yet he knew it wasn't many. He imagined a taut piece of string gradually being pulled tighter and tighter, destined to break.

As he pictured this, his mind jumped back to before his arrival here: to the place that was nowhere and everywhere; the bright room with no light source and the man in the black suit called Will.

★ ★ ★

'Why's this place so inhospitable?' he asked as Will returned to sit down opposite him at the table. 'It feels like an interrogation room.'

'Really?' Will frowned. 'I'm sorry about that. People don't always perceive it in the same way. Is there anything I can do to make you more comfortable?'

'No, it's fine.'

'You'll be out of here soon, anyway. I've had the final go-ahead for your return to Aldham. I just need to brief you about a few matters.'

Firstly, he brought Elliot up to speed on Lisa and her family, giving him an almost omniscient insight into their various circumstances. This knowledge came with a warning. It was crucial he didn't draw attention to or reveal the truth about his presence there. Will advised him to brush up on his acting skills to hide how much he now knew. He emphasised that failure to comply could bring his visit to an immediate halt, before running through a list of other rules and instructions.

But it was the last thing he mentioned that really piqued Elliot's interest: 'During your visit, you'll be able to interact with people normally. However, you'll also have certain, um, extra abilities to help you along the way.'

'Sorry, I don't understand.'

Will let out a short sigh. 'I'd like to tell you more, but I can't. Rules. You'll understand when you're there and the time is right.' He lowered his voice. 'What I will say is to use these gifts wisely and, er, sparingly. Everything has a cost.

And remember: this whole trip is a rare privilege.'

Well, that's as clear as mud, Elliot thought. 'How will I contact you when I'm there?'

'You won't.'

* * *

Since then he'd learned not to question too much about the here and now. He had to make the most of it while he could. That was his focus. The rest, like the great unknown waiting in the wings, he compartmentalised — a skill honed while running his company in Australia. He had to live in the now, focusing on the task in hand. Otherwise he'd fail, which wasn't an option.

It was a balmy summer evening. The warm sun remained high in the sky and the meaty, chargrilled smell of multiple barbecues floated in the breeze, accompanied by the happy cries of children splashing in paddling pools and having water fights.

Good weather like this meant so much more here than it did in Sydney, where hot summers were taken for granted. In the north of England, it was a rare treat: a fleeting moment of good fortune to be embraced and cherished. Not than any northerner worth their salt would admit this, particularly to a southerner. But Elliot knew the truth from his years of growing up here. Grown men would take their tops off in the street at temperatures considered coat weather down under. He'd even passed a couple today, the sight making him smile.

Weather-wise, Elliot had been spoiled for the past two decades. But since this was the first glorious day he'd experienced since his return to Aldham — and potentially the last — he appreciated it like the local he used to be.

He strolled up the drive of the small modern semi, six-pack of beer tucked under his left arm, and rang on the bell. As he waited for the door to open, he wondered whether he'd recognise his host — the closest he'd ever come to a younger brother — after so long. Like his sister, Jamie wasn't much of one for social media; Elliot had seen a couple of photos of him, but they only ever told half the story. Then the door swung open and the years tumbled away as that cheeky smile he knew of old beamed back at him.

'As I live and breathe,' Lisa's younger brother, now a strapping thirty-something with thick stubble and a receding hairline, boomed. Arms stretched out wide, he threw them around Elliot and pulled him into a bear hug, slapping him on the back.

'Lise told me you'd changed a bit, mate, but bloody hell. If I hadn't been expecting you, I'm not sure I'd have recognised you.' Releasing his grip and taking a step back into the hallway, he added: 'What about me? Have I changed much?'

Jamie, dressed in khaki shorts and a fitted polo shirt, did a model-like pose as Elliot looked him up and down. 'Your hair's darker than I remember and there's not quite as much of it.' He winked. 'Other than that, I don't know. You seem to have aged pretty well. Do you still do *Fresh Prince* impressions?'

250

'Haha. You remember those? Depends how much I've had to drink. Ask me later. Anyway, get your arse off that doormat and come in. Why the hell are you wearing jeans on a day like this?'

'Hey, it's not that warm. I'm used to Sydney summers.'

'Bloody show off.'

'Here,' Elliot said, handing over the beer as he stepped inside. 'Let me give you this. It's not cold, I'm afraid, but — '

'Cheers. I'll stick it in the fridge. Don't worry, there's plenty chilled for now. Lisa and the others are here already. They're in the back garden.'

He gestured for Elliot to follow him into the house, adding: 'I'd ask you how life in Oz was treating you, but I think that's pretty obvious. Aren't you a millionaire now?'

Elliot laughed at Jamie's directness. 'My company is doing all right.'

'You've created some kind of mobile app, haven't you?'

'Yes, it's an educational game aimed at pre-schoolers. It teaches basic maths and literary skills on smartphones and tablets. It's been very popular in Australia and America. Hopefully it will be released over here soon too.'

'Nice one,' Jamie said, loading the new beers into the fridge and handing Elliot a cold one. 'Where did you get the idea from? Have you got kids?'

Elliot shook his head. 'No, I'm single. I've never settled down. We did a lot of market research when we were developing the app, but I

251

do also have quite a few friends and colleagues in Sydney with young children. The germ of the idea came from spending time with them.'

'Oh, okay. Have you never fancied having any of your own?'

'I have, actually. I love kids, but it just hasn't happened. Work's kept me very busy.'

'There's still time, mate.'

If only, Elliot thought. From here he could see Lisa, Mike and Ben sitting on deckchairs in the small garden, while Chloe chased two screaming younger girls around, squirting them with a brightly coloured water gun. A black kettle barbecue was smoking away next to the rear fence. 'Those must be your two,' he said, picking up a bottle opener from the worktop and flicking the cap off his beer.

Jamie nodded proudly. 'That's right, mate. Hannah is seven and Emily is five. They always love seeing their big cousins. I only have them three nights a week. I don't know if Lisa told you, but their mum and I split up a while ago.'

Elliot nodded, raising his beer in the direction of a framed photo of the girls, all blonde hair and blue eyes, like Jamie had been back in the day. 'They're cute. Must take after her.'

Jamie laughed. 'Very good. So this is the kind of banter I can expect from you these days, is it? You're a bit of a player now, I suppose, since you got so buff. What's your secret, anyway?'

'The warm weather and the beaches help. It's more appealing to get out there and do something active: running, swimming, surfing and so on. Ian, my stepdad, was the one who got me into keeping fit, initially. He taught me that changing your whole lifestyle — developing a good daily routine and sticking to it — was the key.'

'Nothing to do with impressing all those hot chicks in bikinis, then. Unless . . . you've not started batting for the other team, have you? It's fine if you have. There'll be no judgement from me. I'm a modern man. That would certainly explain — '

'Explain what? Why I have no kids? You know that gay guys do that too these days, right? But no, I'm still straight.'

Jamie winked. 'Are you sure? I thought I caught you checking out my bum. It's fine. I'm used to it. Happens a lot at the gym.'

'Yes, yes. I can see that you work out, Jamie. No need to drop hints about the gym.'

'Touché.'

Elliot smiled at how easily he and Jamie had slipped back into their old habit of ribbing each other. He was sure the two of them would have stayed close had he not moved to the other side of the world. Mind you, Jamie needed to be careful with the gay comments around his nephew. Clearly he had no idea, but that was hardly a surprise bearing in mind how careful Ben was about concealing the truth. Not that it was doing him any good. Elliot was going to have to talk to him about that soon. But first he had to work out a way to explain how he knew; 'I just do — I can't explain it,' was unlikely to wash with him.

'Come on then,' Jamie said. 'Let's get out in the garden with the others. I'll introduce you to my girls, but don't be offended if they pull a face at you and run off. They're not good with strangers.'

★ ★ ★

A few hours, several drinks, lots of food and a shared clean-up effort later, Jamie announced that he needed to put his girls to bed.

'Do we have to, Daddy?' Hannah, the elder sister, protested. 'It's not dark yet and there's no school tomorrow.'

'I'm afraid so. You might not have school, but I have work — and I need to get you over to your mummy first thing. I can't be returning two sleepy moles to her now, can I?'

'Can't we skip a shower?'

Jamie pulled her over to him and sniffed her hair. 'Yuck! You smell like a barbecued sausage. What about you, Emily?'

The younger daughter smelled her own hair and, blowing a raspberry, replied: 'I smell like a burger.'

'Oh dear,' Jamie said, scooping them up, one in each arm. 'It's a bathroom emergency.'

He carried them, wriggling and giggling, into the house and up the stairs, leaving Elliot in the garden with Lisa, Mike and Ben. Chloe had disappeared earlier to visit her friend Holly, who only lived a couple of streets away from her uncle.

'He makes a good dad, doesn't he?' Elliot said to Lisa. 'What happened between him and the girls' mum?'

254

'He blew it. Cheated on her with a friend of hers.'

'Ouch. Were they married?'

'No. They used to live together, though. The girls were still tiny at the time of the breakup. Jamie claimed they were getting all the attention and he felt pushed out. Not very original.'

'They were always arguing,' Mike piped up. 'You wouldn't believe the shouting and screaming that went on.'

'Is Jamie still into his football?' Elliot asked. 'I remember he was mad on it as a boy.'

Lisa pulled a face. 'He still supports Liverpool, but he hasn't played for years. Dad pushed him so hard as a kid, I think he ruined it for him. He got his hopes up about playing professionally when it was never realistic.'

Lisa's phone buzzed with a text message. 'It's from Mum,' she announced. 'She says hi, El, and sends her love. She's gutted to have missed you.'

'That's nice. Is she having a good holiday?'

'Sounds like it.'

'Where is she now?' Ben asked, looking up from his phone for the first time in a good while.

'Budapest. Next stop Bratislava.'

Ben nodded.

'Bratislava being the capital of?' Mike asked him.

'Slovakia.'

'And Budapest?'

Ben sighed. 'Hungary. What is this: summer school?'

'I'm just checking if you've being paying attention in Geography. Well done, son.'

Ben threw his dad an unconvincing smile before returning to staring at his mobile. 'I think I'm going to head home,' he announced soon after.

'Okay, love,' Lisa replied. 'Have you got your key with you?'

'Yes.'

Elliot feigned a yawn. 'Do you know what? I think I might head back to the hotel too. I'm feeling bushed all of a sudden. Must be jet lag still. Do you mind if I walk with you, Ben?'

'If you like.'

Lisa placed a hand on Mike's shoulder. 'Maybe we should go too.'

'I thought you promised to read a bedtime story to the girls, love.'

'That's true. Best hang on.'

Elliot breathed a silent sigh of relief.

Ten minutes later, goodbyes and thank yous out of the way, Elliot and Ben hit the pavement. Jamie's house was right on the other side of Aldham from Lisa's, which gave them several minutes to chat. It was exactly the kind of opening that Elliot had been looking for with Ben.

'How's it going?' he asked the teenager.

'Fine.'

'Have you got some credit on your phone again now? I saw you using it earlier.'

'Yeah, but I was mainly on Uncle Jamie's Wi-Fi.'

'Of course.'

'Don't you have a mobile? I've never seen you with one.'

'Um, no. Not at the moment. I usually do, but —'

'Seriously? How's that possible with your job? Don't people need to get hold of you?'

Elliot thought on his feet. 'I'm at the hotel, aren't I? They can contact me there or leave a message. It gets tiring when people can contact you all the time. I guess I needed a break.'

'But I thought you were here on business.'

'That's right,' Elliot said, backtracking. 'I do have a mobile, of course, but I've switched it off and left it in the safe at the hotel.'

'Were you working earlier?'

'That's right.' Elliot decided it was time to change the subject. 'So have your mum and dad been okay today? No indication that they know anything about yesterday?'

Ben stopped walking and eyeballed him. 'Why? Have you said anything?'

'No, of course not. I told you I wouldn't. Parents can sometimes — I don't know — sense things. That's all I meant. Come on. Let's keep going.'

'Right. Sorry.'

'How about that Sandie woman? Have you heard anything more from her?'

'What?' Ben threw him a perplexed glance. 'How do you mean? I only met her for the first time yesterday. It's not like we exchanged details.'

'No, of course. Never mind. She was just a bit . . . unusual, wasn't she?'

'You can say that again.'

Elliot paused for a moment, the clomping of

257

their shoes on the pavement the only sound as they walked on. Then he added: 'I know at your age it sometimes feels like you have to deal with everything yourself; that your parents won't understand. But you'd be surprised. It's not healthy to have too many secrets.'

Elliot looked over at his companion as they crossed the road, but Ben kept his eyes firmly on the ground and lips sealed. Nodding at a passing dog walker, Elliot chewed the corner of his mouth before continuing: 'I knew a boy once who had this big secret he didn't think he could share with anyone. He thought his family and friends would judge him for it; that it would colour their view of him.

'But keeping that secret — holding it in and living a lie — was harder than he figured. It was like a gradual build-up of pressure inside his head, until one day it was unbearable; it had to come out. And do you know what? Once he told people, it was fine. Those that loved him didn't care. They accepted him for who he was. And the handful of people who did care weren't worth bothering with.

'He told me afterwards how great the relief felt to not have that secret hanging over him any more. And he wished he hadn't punished himself for so long by holding it in.'

Elliot stopped talking and looked over again at Ben. His face had turned several shades paler and remained pointed firmly down at the ground as they continued to walk in the direction of his house.

Elliot wondered if he'd gone too far with his

clunky story about a fictional friend, but it was the best method of addressing the issue — or at least skirting around it — that he'd been able to come up with in the time available. He hadn't predicted this opportunity to chat with Ben emerging as soon as tonight, so without having settled on a final approach, he'd more or less had to wing it. It wasn't like he had any real experience of dealing with kids. Not since being one himself.

'What do you think about that, Ben?'

There was a long pause and then: 'Dunno.'

'Any idea why I might have told you that story?'

Another pause. 'Not really.'

They were on the main road now, where the buses to and from Manchester ran. Ben had upped his walking pace. He was striding ahead, so Elliot almost had to jog to keep up. Meanwhile, they were fast approaching the point where their paths would diverge as Ben went home and he continued to the hotel. Part of him wished he could use one of his new-found abilities to get through to the teenager, rather than having to rely on traditional powers of persuasion. But this didn't work that way.

Elliot reached forward and placed a hand on Ben's arm.

'What the hell are you doing?' Ben spat, twisting around and coming to a sudden halt; shooting daggers at him. 'Why are you touching me?'

'I was trying to get you to slow down. I want to talk to you about something.'

259

'Well don't! I've no idea what you're on about. It sounds like you're trying to groom me or something.'

'Calm down,' Elliot said, noticing a middle-aged couple on the other side of the road staring at them. 'I know what actually happened to you in Manchester yesterday. Not the story you made up, but the truth. I want to talk to you about it. I want to help.'

Ben's jaw dropped. He gaped at him for a moment, eyes stretched, and then tore across the road without another word. He narrowly avoided a passing car, its horn blaring, and disappeared down a ginnel.

Elliot found himself rooted to the spot, horrified at the near miss he'd witnessed — and arguably caused. He shook his head and cast his eyes up to the vast emptiness of the sky.

'I wish someone would tell me how this works,' he said under his breath eventually, once it was steady again. 'A sign pointing me in the right direction or whatever. Anything. Clearly I don't have a clue what I'm doing.'

25

Then

Saturday, 25 June 1994

'Happy birthday, sleepyhead,' Wendy said, waking him with a kiss on the forehead. 'How does it feel to be fourteen?'

'What?' Elliot groaned. 'It feels like the middle of the night.'

'Nonsense.' She walked to the window and threw open the curtains, soaking the room with sunlight. 'Glorious! It's only your birthday once a year. You shouldn't waste a minute.'

Elliot stole a look at his alarm clock and, shuddering, pulled the covers over his head. 'What on earth, Mum? It's not even seven o'clock. Surely a guy is allowed a lie-in on his birthday.'

'Not this year, love. A little bird tells me you might have a visitor in a few minutes.'

'A visitor? Who on earth would come to see me so ridiculously early?'

'Someone who feels bad about not being able to come to your party later.'

He let a little light into his cocoon, wincing at the brightness. 'Really?'

'Yep. She'll be here at seven. I thought you'd appreciate a warning.'

Sure enough, by the time Elliot had thrown on

some clothes and splashed his face with water, he heard the doorbell. And when he came down to the kitchen, Lisa and Wendy were chatting away.

'There he is,' Lisa said, beaming a big smile at him. She was dressed in her emerald Queen Anne's tracksuit, with her hair tied back in a tight ponytail. 'Sorry to get you up so early on your birthday, El. I feel awful not being able to make your party this afternoon. You know I'd be there if I could.'

'It's fine. I told you that yesterday. I understand.'

Lisa, whose speed on the hockey pitch had caught the eye of the athletics coach, was due to compete in the one-and two-hundred-metre running races at an interschool competition in Birmingham that afternoon. Hence she wasn't able to make his birthday do — ten-pin bowling with a group of school friends.

Had she been able to come, Lisa would have been the only girl, but that had never bothered her. It had been that way in previous years and, if anything, had always worked to Elliot's advantage, raising his kudos with the other boys, who were only too happy to spend time in her company. The fact she was going out with hard nut Sean Ferguson at the moment would have probably increased her desirability to them, although it was still something Elliot struggled to comprehend or accept. He felt the relationship had driven a wedge between them; not least because of the fact it had altered Lisa's stance on their one-time shared enemy Samo, who she'd now started talking to on the bus, since he was one of her boyfriend's mates.

Elliot still remembered the ferocious look in Lisa's eyes when, two years earlier, she had sworn to make Samo pay for bog-washing her friend. And so she had, The ace up her sleeve had been the fact that she was friendly with a girl he'd been out with and had dumped unceremoniously shortly beforehand. Catherine, a fellow hockey player from Samo's year, had been only too happy to share some of his secrets with Lisa as a way to get her own back for the way he'd treated her.

★ ★ ★

After speaking to Catherine on Saturday morning, Lisa had gone shopping. She'd discovered that Samo, the supposed big hard man, was terrified of spiders, so she'd bought a realistic-looking fake. On the bus home the following Monday afternoon, she surreptitiously placed it on the seat next to him and, much to her and Elliot's delight, it worked a treat. Upon spotting it, Samo jumped to his feet and shrieked like a little girl, sending everyone on the lower deck into hysterics.

Then, as Elliot watched open-mouthed, Lisa struck while the iron was hot. She jumped to her feet and, facing Samo, declared in a loud voice, so everyone could hear: 'In case you were wondering who did that, it was me. It was to get you back for what you did last week to my friend Elliot, who had no idea what I was

263

planning, by the way.

'Now let me make something clear: if you ever lay one of your bully hands on him again or attack him with one of your pathetic insults, there's plenty more where that came from. I've been chatting to your ex-girlfriend, Catherine, and she told me some very interesting things about you, I'll say. Unless you want them shared with the rest of the bus — and spread around both of our schools — I'd suggest that you and your cronies steer well clear. *Capeesh?*'

Elliot couldn't quite believe what he was witnessing. Lisa's performance was a tour de force, right down to the Italian-American slang at the end, which she later admitted to stealing from a movie. And the best thing of all was that everyone clapped afterwards. Well, everyone apart from Samo, who was left speechless for once, his face resembling a giant tomato. Even the driver, who'd been turning his head every so often to watch the spectacle, joined in. It was something else.

'You're incredible,' Elliot told Lisa afterwards. 'There you go, saving me again. How can I ever repay you?'

'You don't need to repay me, El.' She landed a playful punch on his arm. 'That's what friends are for.'

'One day I will, if it's the last thing I do.'

★　★　★

Smiling at the memory, Elliot recalled how Samo had left him alone from that moment forward.

No more calling him 'freak' or 'E.T'; no more bog-washes; no more bullying, full stop.

The only disappointing thing was that Lisa had never told Elliot the details of Samo's embarrassing secrets. Apparently she'd promised Catherine, who also stood to be left red-faced by them, that she wouldn't. It had been one huge bluff, which in Lisa's hands had been transformed into a magnificent slice of revenge.

So how had they gone from there to here? Elliot wouldn't go so far as to say that Lisa and Samo were now friends. But why even pass the time of day with him? It wasn't like he'd really changed in the two years since then. He might have left Elliot alone, but he was still a bully to lots of other boys. He was still an idiot. But so was Lisa's boyfriend.

'Happy birthday, El,' she said, walking over to him in the kitchen and planting a kiss on his cheek before handing him an envelope and a small wrapped parcel.

'Great, thanks.'

'Aren't you going to open it?' his mum urged.

So he did. He started with the card, which contained a message reiterating Lisa's apology for not being able to attend his party. Then he moved on to the present and found, to his surprise, that it was a CD of the new Blur album, *Parklife*. 'Wow. Thank you,' he said, looking it over at length in a bid to hide his confusion. Lisa knew that neither he nor Wendy had a CD player. So why on earth had she bought this for him?

When he eventually looked up, he was faced with two big grins.

'What's going on?' he asked, although by that point he'd already guessed. He didn't dare to say it, in case he was wrong; his heart skipped a beat when his mum suggested opening her present next. 'It's in the lounge,' she said. 'Go ahead.'

He darted through the house, the others at his heels, and found a large brown box with a red bow around it sitting on the sofa. 'It was too big to wrap,' Wendy said, looking every bit as excited as he felt. 'I hope you don't mind.'

'Of course not.' He was already busy tearing it open. To his absolute delight, he found an all-in-one hi-fi with a double cassette deck, radio, separate speakers and — best of all — a CD player.

'Thanks so much, Mum,' he said, giving her a big hug and kiss.

'You like it, then?' she asked, eyes twinkling and a grin from ear to ear.

'Are you kidding? I love it.' Looking over at Lisa, he added: 'And you knew? I can't believe you kept that from me.'

Lisa shrugged, flashing him another smile. 'Sorry, El. What can I say? Wendy swore me to secrecy.'

'Lisa was great. She was my chief technology consultant. Without her assistance, I don't think I'd have had a clue. You know what I'm like with these things.'

'Well, thanks so much, both of you. I'm over the moon. Is it for down here or — '

'Don't be silly,' Wendy said. 'It's your present. It belongs in your room. I'm fine with my antique stereo and my LPs down here.'

266

'Brilliant.'

Lisa had had a CD player in her room for some time, but Elliot had never dared to ask for one. He knew money was tight at home, so he'd made do with his old tape player. He realised that buying this for him on top of forking out for his bowling party must have been a stretch for his mum — and he massively appreciated it.

Lisa wasn't able to stay for long, as she had to get to Queen Anne's in time to catch the coach for Birmingham. Elliot waited until she'd left to tell his mum how much her generosity meant to him.

'Don't be silly,' she replied. 'You're my only son. Nothing makes me happier than spoiling you.'

He was glad to see his mum so cheery. She'd been a bit down for the last couple of weeks after recently splitting up with the man she'd been seeing from the hospital, Dr Nesbit. While they'd been an item, she'd encouraged Elliot to call him by his first name, Alistair. However, he'd never felt comfortable doing so. He'd found him aloof and hard to talk to.

Wendy hadn't gone into detail about why they'd split up. But after overhearing her side of their heated final phone conversation, he had a good idea that Dr Nesbit had been cheating on her. This left Elliot conflicted. On the one hand, he was glad. It justified his lack of enthusiasm and meant he had her back to himself. And yet he could tell how much she'd enjoyed dating and having a life of her own again. The brief relationship had made her happy while it had lasted. Days like today served to remind him what a great parent she was — and how she deserved the best from him.

'How are you doing, Mum?' he asked her at the breakfast table while tucking into the bacon, sausage and eggs she'd fried up for him as a birthday treat.

'What do you mean? I'm fine.'

'I'm talking about, um, Alistair,' he said, forcing himself to use that name.

Her eyes widened as she finished chewing a mouthful of bacon before replying. 'I see. I didn't think you liked him, anyway.'

'I didn't really know him well enough to form a proper opinion, Mum.'

She nodded. 'Fair enough. I suppose I tried to distance you from the whole thing, in case it went wrong. Turns out I was right to do so.'

'This isn't about me. I asked how you were doing.'

'Yes, that's true. You did. I, er, I'm feeling a lot better now.'

Elliot dipped a chunk of sausage into his egg and chewed it slowly, not quite meeting Wendy's eye. 'That's good. You deserve to be happy.'

His mum choked up at this, which he hadn't expected. She didn't cry, nor did she say anything straight away in response, but the glistening of her eyes and her sharp, heavy breaths said enough.

Elliot emptied his plate in silence.

Eventually, Wendy dabbed the corners of her eyes with a tissue from her sleeve and, breathing more naturally again, reached across the table to

268

take Elliot's hand. 'I love you so very much,' she said, smiling. 'No one makes me happy like you do. Your father would be so proud to see what a lovely young man you've grown into. You really remind me of him sometimes, you know, especially around your eyes and in your smile. I like to think he drops by to watch over us from time to time; that he's somewhere nearby on important days like these.'

'Thanks, Mum. I love you too.'

'I know.' She gave his hand a tender squeeze before letting go, took a deep breath, then clapped her palms together above the table. 'Now back to more important matters. We've got several hours between now and when the others arrive for your bowling trip. What would you like to do? It's your day.'

'Well, first of all I need to finish setting up my amazing new hi-fi. Then I'd like to listen to my CD all the way through.'

'And afterwards?'

'Hmm. I'll have to give that some thought. It's not every day I get to decide these things.'

As the words left his mouth, Elliot felt a wave of sadness crash over him at the thought that he wouldn't spend the day with Lisa, as he had done his previous two birthdays.

Her birthday, which fell in May, had been different this year too. She'd spent the day out clothes shopping with her mum, rather than with him; that evening she'd hired out a church hall in Westwich, down the road from their schools, and held a big disco.

He'd barely spoken to her all night. She'd

spent most of it dancing or sucking face with Sean. Luckily, she'd invited some of Elliot's school friends too, so at least he'd not been alone. He'd even danced with a couple of girls, still chasing that elusive first snog, but unfortunately it hadn't happened. He was so shy when it came to girls he didn't know. He always ended up falling over his words and making a fool of himself. It made no sense, considering how easy he found it to talk to Lisa, or even Charlotte and Joanne on the bus.

That worried him less, though, than what was happening with Lisa. Were they really starting to grow apart, as he feared? God, he hoped not. He prayed that her relationship with Sean wouldn't go on too much longer. He wasn't worthy of her. Why did she have such weird taste in boyfriends?

At least she'd made the effort to come to see him this morning. That was something, wasn't it? And she'd picked a great present. Things between them were bound to change a bit as they got older. That was to be expected.

'We'll be fine,' he told his reflection in the bathroom mirror later, while squeezing an annoying spot that had appeared on his chin. 'She'd have come this afternoon if she could. We're Elliot and Lisa — friends for life. We'll be fine.'

But as often as Elliot told himself this, a part of him remained unsure.

26

NOW

Tuesday, 24 July 2018

'What was that all about?'

Elliot jumped at the sound of Chloe's voice behind him. He was still standing at the side of the main road following Ben's sudden departure. 'Hello,' he said, turning around and offering her the best reassuring smile he could muster.

'Hi. What's up with Ben? That car only just missed him.'

'I know.' Elliot shook his head. 'I was talking to him about what happened yesterday and then he darted off into the road.'

'That's weird. Was he worried you might tell Mum and Dad?'

'Maybe. I don't know why he'd think that, though. Has he said anything to you?'

Chloe laughed. 'You're kidding, right? He's barely said a word to me since we got back from Manchester. I'm surprised he came to Uncle Jamie's barbecue, to be honest. It was probably to keep an eye on us; to make sure we didn't blab.'

'Are you heading home?'

'Yeah. Holly wasn't feeling well. I went back to Uncle Jamie's, but Dad said that you two had just left. I thought I'd follow.'

271

The sound of a loud cat meow made Elliot jump for a second time. It was only when he saw Chloe reach for her mobile that he realised what it was.

'It's a menace, that cat noise of yours,' he told her with a grin.

She frowned at her phone and shoved it back into the pocket of her shorts.

'Everything all right?' Elliot asked.

'Yes, fine.'

He knew she was lying. He'd have been able to tell that even if he wasn't privy to extra information about her than he should have been. It was written all over her face. Maybe now was the time to talk to her rather than Ben. He'd spent more one-on-one time with Chloe, anyway, so perhaps he would be more successful. Mind you, he didn't want her doing anything stupid like running out in front of a car. He'd have to be careful.

'Come on,' he said. 'Let's walk together.'

'Are you not going back to your hotel?'

'I was going to, but I think I'd better come to the house. I want to check on Ben.'

Chloe scrunched her nose up at this. 'How come?'

'You saw what he did. I'd like to make sure he doesn't do anything else stupid.'

'Like what?'

Elliot shrugged. 'He's your brother. You tell me.' Turning to check the traffic situation, he added: 'Come on. Let's cross while there's nothing coming.'

As they continued on their way, Elliot was

wondering how best to get Chloe to open up when she turned the tables on him. 'Elliot, can I ask you a question?' she said.

'You just did,' he replied, immediately regretting how much that answer made him sound like one of his old school teachers. 'But no, seriously, fire away.'

She hesitated. 'It's a bit, um, awkward.'

'Okay.'

'The thing is, I've noticed that . . . well, let me put it this way, I know what you did with the knife in the kitchen.'

This immediately grabbed Elliot's attention, although he did his best to remain poker-faced. 'I'm not with you. Do you mean at Jamie's house?'

She shook her head, eyes wandering all over the place, refusing to meet his gaze.

'No, the first night we met, when we were emptying the dishwasher together and that sharp knife slipped out of my hand. It was heading straight for my foot and then, well, suddenly it wasn't any more. It changed direction for no obvious reason — went flying to one side — and . . .'

Her voice trailed away.

Elliot fought to keep his breathing steady. 'Sorry, I don't understand.'

Chloe took them down the same narrow ginnel Ben had used. It ran between the generous rear gardens of two large modern houses. It was too narrow for them to walk side by side, so Chloe continued ahead, talking as she went without looking back.

'If it was only that once,' she said, a new confidence in her voice, 'I'd maybe forget about it. You know, strange stuff happens sometimes that you can't explain. But it's more than that. I've noticed several other weird things.'

'I see.'

Emerging from the other end of the zigzag alley into a quiet residential street, she strode ahead in a way that reminded him of her brother a few minutes earlier.

She continued: 'So at the train station in Manchester I remember how you knew where Ben was even before he came out of the toilet. Like you were psychic or something. Then there was that trick in the car park where you convinced the woman working there that you didn't need to pay when you did. And look at the way you saved Ben when he was choking. How did you react so quickly? You were at his side, helping him, before the rest of us even knew what was going on.'

Chloe stopped in her tracks and turned to face him, almost leading them to collide with each other. 'You turned up out of nowhere. I've never seen you with a mobile or a wallet. There's something strange going on, I'm sure of it. And it's not just me. That weird woman who got into the car in Manchester saw it too. Then you did something — you stopped her somehow. How can you explain all that?'

Elliot nodded at Chloe and smiled, as if unfazed. He'd feared a moment like this ever since he'd arrived here. However, until a few minutes ago, he hadn't expected Chloe to be the

274

instigator. She was a lovely, bright little thing, so similar to Lisa at that age, although he hadn't pegged her as being quite so feisty. This direct challenge of an adult she'd only known for a few days said otherwise. He was impressed. It made him feel bad about the way he'd have to respond — and yet there was really no choice at this stage.

The shrill sound of a panicked female voice cut through the air. 'Somebody help!'

Saved by the bell. 'Where did that come from?' Elliot asked Chloe. 'Sounds serious.'

'The park maybe?' She pointed to her left, where the road curved around to what Elliot remembered as a small green between the houses. It was just out of sight — and to call it a *park* was going a bit far — but he knew where she meant.

'Help! I think he's going to jump.'

Elliot and Chloe looked at each other in horror and ran towards the voice.

Turning the corner, they saw a pasty-skinned young mum with a pram standing on the pavement next to the green, staring up at a large tree. She was holding a mobile phone to her ear and said: 'Yes, it's an emergency. There's a boy at the top of a big tree, threatening to jump . . . I'm in Aldham.'

'Oh my God, it's Ben!' Chloe cried out, running ahead to the foot of the tree.

'Do you know him?' The woman looked at Elliot, mobile still to her ear.

'Yes, I'm a family friend. Why do you think he's going to jump?'

'Wait,' she told the person on the other end of the phone. 'There's someone here who knows the lad.'

She looked back at Elliot. 'Because he told me so. I was walking past when I saw him climbing that tree. I told him to be careful — and he said it didn't matter, because he'd be jumping off in a minute.'

Elliot waved a hand in front of her face and, looking her in the eye, spoke in a level voice. 'It's fine. He's not going to jump. Tell them you made a mistake, then go straight home and forget this ever happened.'

Her eyes glazed over, which Elliot knew was a good sign. Leaving her to do exactly as he'd instructed, he continued after Chloe, who he could hear shouting at her brother. 'What's going on? Why are you up there? Why is she saying you're going to jump?'

'Go away, Chloe,' Ben replied. 'This is nothing to do with you.'

Elliot held his palm up towards Ben in the tree and commanded: 'Don't move a muscle.'

Then, before Chloe could say anything else, Elliot waved the same hand in her direction, leaning into her ear and whispering: 'Everything's fine. You're going to turn and walk home now. You've got a key, right?'

She nodded.

'Let yourself in and stick on the TV. None of this ever happened, okay?'

'Okay.'

'Good. You met me by the main road; we spoke for a few minutes and then we went our

276

separate ways. You asked me some questions: things that have been bothering you about me. I answered them to your full satisfaction. You no longer have any concerns about me. I'm a normal guy. Got it?'

'Got it.'

'Off you go.'

Elliot watched her walk back in the direction they'd come from as he gathered his thoughts. What he'd just had to do saddened him, but what other option was there?

He sighed and looked up at Ben, who literally hadn't moved a muscle. Then he did something he hadn't done in many years: he climbed the tree. This wasn't one he'd scaled much as a kid, as it hadn't been particularly big then. But it had grown a lot in the last two decades. When he joined Ben at the top, the hairs on his arms standing up in the cool breeze, he discovered a nice panoramic view of the village.

'This reminds me of my childhood,' he said. 'I used to climb trees all the time. Your mum and I went up quite a few together. Luckily, I haven't forgotten how. I didn't know it was your thing.'

He looked at Ben, on the branch above him, and wondered why he wasn't saying anything in response. Then he remembered the whole 'don't move a muscle' thing.

Waving his hand in front of Ben's face, he said: 'You can talk again now, but I want you to stay where you are on the tree until I say otherwise. Definitely no jumping off. Oh yes, and you'll have no memory of not being able to move.'

Elliot hoped that would be that in terms of having to use his powers of persuasion. It wasn't something he enjoyed doing, especially with those he was here to help. On this occasion there was no choice, but for his mission here to be a genuine success, he needed them to do things of their own volition — not because he told them to.

Ben blinked. 'What the hell? How did you get up here?'

'More to the point, what are you doing up here, telling people you're going to jump?'

'I only said that because I was angry. I came here to think — to get away from everything — and she started moaning about how I shouldn't be climbing this tree; that I could fall off.'

'Not a smart move, Ben. She nearly had the emergency services out.'

'Really? God, that would have been embarrassing.'

'Sure would. Anyway, mate, what's going on? First you run away from me, darting across a main road, nearly getting hit. Now this. And don't get me started on that grooming nonsense you were spouting.'

'Where's Chloe gone?'

'Home.'

'What about Mum and Dad?'

'Still at your uncle's, as far as I know. Listen, how about you stop asking me questions and answer mine. Why did you run away?'

Ben looked at the ground below. He let out a long sigh and closed his eyes. 'Because of what

278

you said. That you knew the truth about what happened in Manchester. And the rest.'

'The rest?'

'That stuff you made up about a friend with a secret. That was you, right? I'm not stupid. I presume Mum knows. How come she's never mentioned it?'

'Sorry. Knows what?'

'That you're gay. I guess that's how you knew about me. Gaydar and all that. But I'm scratching my head to see how you can really know what happened in Manchester. Was that bit bullshit? Were you guessing that it had something to do with meeting a guy?'

Elliot weighed up how best to answer. The clumsy, spur of the moment story about his fictional friend had back-fired. He hadn't been talking about himself.

He'd been called gay on plenty of occasions over the years — particularly at school, when it had been a stock insult for someone who didn't behave like everyone else. But the simple fact was that he found women, not men, attractive.

All the same, as a man who took care of himself physically and was in touch with his feminine side, people had genuinely made that mistake before. He'd been approached in bars and clubs; some of his gay friends in Australia had wondered before getting to know him. So it made sense why Ben might believe this. But Elliot knew he had to tread carefully, particularly in light of the fact that the teenager had just confirmed that he *was* gay.

'I can see why you might think that,' he said,

279

'but the truth is I'm not gay. I know lots of people who are. Sydney is very gay-friendly.'

Ben's face turned beetroot red. 'But I thought . . . shit, I can't believe I — '

'Listen, I think it's fantastic that you said it out loud. I'll be honest with you, I was tempted to go along with it and say that you were right about me. That would have been the easy thing to do, but it wouldn't have been fair on you, and it wouldn't have been the truth.'

Ben fell quiet.

'So you came up here to think,' Elliot said. 'I get that. It was one of the reasons I used to climb trees a lot. There's something powerful about being high up, with the world spread before you in miniature. It's liberating and helps put things into perspective.'

'I guess.'

'Is it something you do often?'

'Not really.'

Elliot patted the wide trunk with one hand, enjoying the feel of the rough bark against his palm. Would this be the last time he ever climbed a tree? If so, he wanted to remember it. He took a deep breath, sucking in the fresh evening air, and relished the silence that had fallen between him and Ben, instead of being daunted by it.

Why had he stopped climbing trees? It wasn't something you saw adults doing. But why not when it was so much fun and good exercise?

He scanned the village of his childhood from this unique perspective and welcomed the memories it sparked within him. It was great to be back in Aldham again, having spent so long away on the other side of the world.

He adored Sydney. He'd fallen in love with it from the moment he'd arrived. He still remembered the feeling of endless possibilities it had awoken in him when he'd first cast eyes on the magnificent Opera House from across the water. Living there — the people, the weather, the beaches — had never grown old.

And yet this was where he'd grown up. It held a place in his heart. He might not have returned before, but there simply hadn't been a pressing enough reason to travel so far. Building a tech firm from the ground up was a gigantic, all-consuming task. Making a success of it had taken its toll, not least on his personal life. That was the main reason he'd never settled down and had a family of his own.

He had thought about coming back here plenty of times over the years; about seeing Lisa. Did he regret that it hadn't happened? Yes, with hindsight, knowing what he did now about the unforeseen path his life would eventually take. But who was he to complain? He was here now, which was incredible.

At the top of the tree, the silence continued. It had been several minutes now. Elliot had decided not to be the one to break it, hoping that if Ben did so, he might finally open up. It was a policy he'd used successfully in business, usually to get the other party to concede something as part of a deal. Ian, his stepdad, had taught him this when he was first starting out, based on the principle that most people find silences uncomfortable. Whether or not it would work here, he had no idea. But it was worth a try.

'So how did you know I was gay?' Ben asked eventually. 'Have you told anyone?'

Elliot chose his words carefully, accepting that the truth wasn't an option. 'I didn't know for sure, Ben, until you confirmed it, but I had a strong suspicion. I have a sense for such things.'

Ben balled his hands into fists and pressed them into his forehead, rocking precariously on the tree branch. 'What? So you tricked me into telling you?'

'Can you please be careful?' Elliot shuffled closer to the teenager. 'Don't forget we're pretty darn high up. And, no. In answer to your other question, of course I haven't told anyone.'

'Not even Mum?'

'No.'

Thankfully Ben returned his hands to holding the branch.

'What about Manchester? You said you knew the truth about what happened.'

'I also have a knack for knowing when people are lying,' he replied, feeling such a hypocrite. 'When you were recounting the story in the car, your body language more or less screamed out that you weren't telling the truth. Parts were true, I think, but I'm pretty sure that the real reason you were there had nothing to do with computer parts.'

'So what do you think happened?'

'I was hoping you might tell me.'

'Why?'

'Because you were clearly upset by it — and a problem shared is a problem halved. I think you need someone to talk to. Life's tough enough as a teenager without the pressure of living with secrets.'

Ben stared into the distance, his Adam's apple jerking up and down several times as he swallowed; his breathing heavy and irregular. Eventually, lips quivering, he told Elliot: 'I didn't ask to be gay. If I could be straight, I would. I've tried, believe me. But I am what I am.'

'I understand.' Elliot's heart swelled with empathy as he took in the boy's strained, broken words. 'It's only natural to feel that way. Being different from what's considered normal is hard at your age. It can feel impossible. But you'll learn to embrace it — to be proud of who and what you are.

'I was a misfit at school and I got torn apart for it by some of the other kids. If it wasn't for your mum's friendship, I don't know how I would have got through it. I couldn't have managed alone, which is why I don't want you to. So know this: I'm here now. You can talk to me.'

He paused before adding, in his most gentle voice: 'But I'm only a visitor. When you're ready, I think you should consider telling your parents. You're their son. They love you. They can support you; help you through difficult times. The same goes for Chloe. Maybe even some of your close friends at school, when you feel the time is right.'

'I think I want to go home now,' Ben said in a flat voice.

'Of course, Would you like me to come too?'

'No, thanks.'

'Go ahead. I'll follow you down in a few minutes. That cool?'

Ben nodded and started to climb back to the ground. 'Thanks,' he said from a few branches down. 'And sorry about before.'

'You're welcome.'

Soon after Ben had gone, Elliot felt a sudden stabbing in his chest. Not now, he thought. Not again. Steadying himself against the thick tree trunk before the pain drove out all other thoughts, he squeezed his eyes shut. He took deep, heavy breaths, praying for it to pass quickly. A groaning sound escaped through his gritted teeth as the attack — definitely the worst one yet — ripped into him, the pain increasing before it got better.

Once it had passed, calm descending on him like a cold compress, he took heed of the clear message he'd been delivered, which only confirmed his fears.

He was living on borrowed time — and it was fast running out.

27

NOW

Wednesday, 25 July 2018

Chloe rolled over on her bed and looked out of the window. So much for summer. Yesterday's great weather had vanished overnight. Today it was overcast and raining.

She looked at the time on her phone: 11.02 a.m. God, she was bored. She'd sent Holly several messages so far this morning and got nothing in reply. If she didn't hear back soon, she'd phone her. Mind you, Holly hadn't been feeling well yesterday. Maybe she'd had a bad night and was sleeping it off.

Chloe hadn't slept well. It had been muggy, even with the window wide open, and she'd woken up loads of times. Now she felt grotty and grumpy. So she'd returned straight to her bedroom after breakfast to veg out. She had at least got dressed, in a fresh pair of shorts and T-shirt, but that was as much down to the heat as anything else. Stupid weather. If it was going to rain, it could at least have the decency to cool down a bit.

Chloe glanced over at the copy of *New Moon* on her bedside table and thought about picking it up to read a bit. Then she sighed and rolled over again, unable to summon up the energy.

She heard the toilet flush. Soon after came a gentle tap on her bedroom door. It was her mum. 'Are you sure you don't want to come, love?'

Chloe shook her head. 'No, thanks.'

She and Elliot were going to visit the posh school they used to attend. It was two schools back then, apparently — one for boys and one for girls, which sounded weird to Chloe — but these days it was mixed and the girls' school had been turned into flats. They'd discussed the idea at the barbecue yesterday and, bizarrely, had both got excited at the prospect of going back. Chloe couldn't ever see herself wanting to revisit her school as an adult.

At breakfast Mum had asked them all along. 'It'll be a fun trip out,' she'd promised. But the three of them had declined.

'What are your plans for the day?'

Chloe shrugged. 'Might see Holly later, if she's feeling better.'

'What about your other friends? I never hear about anyone apart from Holly these days.'

'She's my best friend. What's your problem with her?'

'There's no need to take that surly tone with me, Chloe.'

'I'm not.'

'All I'm saying is that it's good to have a group of friends — '

'I do, but most of them are away on holiday.'

This wasn't entirely true and, as soon as she'd said it, Chloe felt bad at the shadow it cast over her mum's face. The lack of a family vacation this year was a sore point — and it was wrong of her to highlight it.

'What about Saima?'

'What about her?'

'You used to be such good friends.'

'At primary school. Things change.'

Saima had been her best friend for years, but they'd grown apart since moving to Waterside High, where they'd first met Holly. The three of them were all in the same form, and — unlike Saima — Holly was in most of the same sets as Chloe, meaning they had nearly all their lessons together. Holly had lived a few miles away initially. Then her family had moved to the village, bringing her and Chloe even closer. Eventually, this had led to a row with Saima, who'd felt pushed out, and their friendship had never recovered. These days they barely said hello when they saw each other in school or on the street. Chloe couldn't remember the last time they'd met up or had a chat.

She hadn't thought about Saima much at all recently. But after her mum had gone, leaving her home alone with her dad and brother, Chloe found herself wondering more and more about her old friend. What if she was the one behind the nasty texts? This possibility hadn't occurred to her before now. Of course she'd wondered who was sending them, but she'd been thinking about people she'd had recent run-ins with, while her falling out with Saima had been ages ago. She thought they'd both moved on, but what if Saima hadn't?

As she was weighing this up, her phone pinged

with a message: Holly at last.

H: *Morning! Sorry for the slow reply. Mum made me turn my phone off to get some sleep.*

C: *And? Did it work?*

H: *Guess so. I only just woke up.*

C: *Feeling better?*

H: *So-so. Puked a few times after you left.*

C: *Really? :-(Guess you're not up for doing something today then.*

H: *Don't think Mum will let me out of her sight or allow me any visitors. She keeps going on about me being contagious. The anti-bacterial spray is basically glued to her hand.*

C: *Never mind. Hope you feel better soon.*

H: *Thanks. Hey, have you said anything to Edward yet?*

C: *Don't call him that! It's Elliot.*

H: *You know who I mean. And?*

C: *Yes, I caught up with him on the way home yesterday. I asked him some questions and he answered them to my full satisfaction.*

H: *What the hell does that mean?*

C: *It means I no longer have any concerns about him. He's a normal guy.*

H: *Seriously? So how did he explain everything?*

C: *Let's chat about that later. I need to tell you something else.*

H: *Like what?*

C: *It's about the dodgy texts.*

H: *Have you had any more?*

C: *One last night. Usual nasty stuff. Called me a 'skank whore' this time.*

H: *That's horrible.*

C: Yeah. Anyway, I think I might have an idea who's been sending them.

H: Who?

C: Saima.

H: Your dorky friend from primary school?

C: Bit harsh, but yes.

H: How's it harsh if she's been sending you those texts?

C: Well, I don't know for sure, do I? It's a guess, based on the fact that she has my number and almost certainly hates me. Plus she knows me well enough to press the right buttons: like the thing about the yellow teeth. What do you reckon?

H: You know her loads better than I do. If you think it's possible, it probably is. What a bitch!

C: What should I do?

H: Confront her? I'd ask her straight out.

C: You're right. I'll go to her house today.

H: Do it. Wish I could come with. Give her a slap from me.

C: Haha. Get well soon.

H: Thanks. Good luck. Let me know what happens. X

C: Will do. XO

28

NOW

Wednesday, 25 July 2018

'Anyone want a tea or coffee?' Mike shouted up the stairs. There was no reply.

Sighing, he tried again. 'Hello? Anyone there?'

He heard the muffled sound of activity and then Chloe's face appeared at the top of the stairs. 'What's up, Dad?'

'I was trying to ask my favourite two children if they wanted a brew.'

'No, thanks. I'm popping out in a few minutes, if that's all right.'

'Sure. Are you meeting Holly?'

'No, she's still not feeling well. I'm going to see if Saima's around.'

'Saima? Not seen her for a while. I thought you two had fallen out.'

Chloe shrugged.

'Whatever. Just make sure you have fun.'

She squinted at her dad. 'You're in a good mood today.'

'Maybe I am. Where's that brother of yours? Can you ask him if he wants a brew?'

'He's in his room. One sec.'

Chloe was shaking her head when she reappeared. 'He's fine.'

'What's he up to?'

'Who knows? He wouldn't let me inside. He's probably on his computer, as usual.'

'Right.'

Mike returned to the kitchen, made himself a mug of tea and took a seat at the table in front of his laptop, which finally appeared to be finished updating itself.

'Right,' he said to the empty room, before interlinking the fingers of his two hands and stretching his arms out in front of him to crack his knuckles. Not that they actually cracked. He only made the gesture because he'd seen writers do it in movies — and he immediately decided not to bother again, as it actually felt uncomfortable. Clearly he wasn't a knuckle-cracking kind of scribe.

He opened up the word processor and proceeded to stare at the blank screen for what felt like ages. Where to begin? He'd been here before, only to disappear down the Google rabbit hole; spending ages reading about how to write a screenplay rather than doing it.

Today's objective, which was what had got him out of bed feeling so chipper, was to draft a plot outline. So what was the problem? Why were no words coming out?

He drained the rest of his cuppa and then jumped up to make another. As he was doing so, Chloe called out from the hallway that she was leaving.

'See you later, love. Have you got your mobile?'

'Of course. Bye.'

Mike poured milk into his tea and watched the

light-brown cloud it created billow across the surface of the hot liquid, before stabbing it with his spoon and stirring it into submission. Walking back to the table with a renewed sense of purpose, he sat down again in front of the laptop, woke the screen with his hand and started typing.

★ ★ ★

'What are you doing?' Ben asked with his head in the door of the fridge.

Mike looked up, blinked and wondered how he'd missed him entering the kitchen. 'Um, just writing some ideas down.'

He watched his son root through the chilled items, half-expecting and perhaps even wanting a further probe into exactly what he was writing, but Ben appeared to have lost interest. 'Have we run out of coke? I thought there were a couple of cans left.'

'There might be more in the cupboard.'

'I want a cold one.'

'Can't you add ice?'

'That makes it watery.'

'Guess you're out of luck, son.' Looking down at the cold, untouched mug of tea next to him on the table, Mike added: 'If you stick the kettle on, I'll make us a brew.'

Ben scowled, in full teenager mode. 'I need something cold.'

'Could you put the kettle on anyway?'

'Fine.'

'What are you doing, Ben?'

'Computer stuff.'

'You should get some fresh air. I'm going for a run in a bit. Why don't you join me?'

Ben curled up his top lip. 'In this rain? Yeah, right.'

'You're not made of sugar, are you?'

'Very funny. Where's Chloe?'

'Out. At Saima's.'

'You mean Holly's?'

'No, Saima's.'

'Weird.'

As Ben disappeared back upstairs with a glass of cordial, Mike wondered if his and Lisa's suspicion about their son being gay would turn out to be true and, if so, when he would finally tell them. Lisa had been the first to suggest it and, although he still struggled to put his finger on exactly why, Mike had a feeling she was right. Ben certainly didn't seem to be into girls in the same way that he'd been at that age, when bikini-clad women had lined his bedroom walls. Ben could also be very secretive and moody at times, although weren't all teenagers?

When Mike had first met Elliot and mistakenly thought he was gay, he'd hoped that might be of some help to Ben in coming out, if that's what he needed to do. Now it was a waiting game again, since he and Lisa had agreed to give Ben space to tell them of his own accord, in his own time. Mike really didn't mind either way, but it would be nice to know for sure.

He clicked the keyboard to wake his laptop screen, feeling chuffed to see it full of words. He'd written almost his entire plot synopsis in one fell swoop. He'd started typing and let himself go. No muddling over the exact wording of each sentence. No over-thinking. Just words — nearly two thousand — banged out at the quickest pace he'd written anything in years, probably since writing a last-minute English essay at university.

It helped that the subject matter was close to his heart: a teacher wrongly accused of attacking a pupil. He planned to move the action to a secondary school and to change the false allegation, made now by a female pupil, to one of sexual assault. That way it ought to be different enough from his real-life experience. It was an idea he'd been mulling over for ages. He hadn't got a clue whether anyone would ever be interested in turning it into an actual film, or even if it would be any good. But at the very least it would be a decent learning exercise. Hopefully it might also help him to move on from the nightmare experience and to purge himself of some of the hang-ups he'd been left with as a result.

He realised that the copy was probably littered with mistakes, but that didn't matter. He could address those later. The important thing was that he had something down at last. He'd made a start.

Unfortunately, thanks to his son's interruption breaking his focus, the last few sentences didn't come as easily. Mike got there eventually, but at the expense of making that fresh cup of tea he'd asked Ben to put the kettle on for. The stone-cold one next to him looked even less appetising than it had previously, the milk forming a dandelion puff-ball image on the tan surface.

He was mulling over a working title — something he'd thought about plenty of times before but never settled on — when his eyes drifted across the screen, landing on the text *Document1*. Shit. That meant he'd not saved it yet. In his rush to do so, Mike's right hand jerked forward, catching the handle of the mug next to him on the table and spilling its entire contents all over the laptop keyboard.

The fact that Ben raced down the stairs, wondering what the hell was going on, was testament to the amount of shouting, swearing and table thumping that went on.

When he entered the kitchen, his father was directing his anger at the kitchen sink, shaking the laptop over it while frantically wiping the keyboard with a fistful of kitchen towel.

'Dad, what's happening?'

'What does it bloody look like, Ben?'

'Like you've lost your mind.'

'I've spilled tea all over the keyboard. I didn't save what I was doing. I'm in a mess, in case you hadn't noticed. Can you help?'

Mike thrust the laptop into Ben's open arms. 'You're good with computers, aren't you? Can you rescue it? The screen went all weird and then turned off. Now I can't get it to do anything. I didn't save — '

'Yeah, you said that already. Let me have a look.'

He placed the laptop back on the kitchen table

and took a seat. 'Can I have some more of that kitchen towel?' He raised his left hand and held it there until Mike passed him the depleted roll.

Mike stood behind him, grinding his teeth, his hands gripping the back of the chair. He watched Ben dab, poke and prod the laptop, praying that he'd miraculously make it whir back into life. But as the minutes passed and Ben tried various things, from removing the battery and messing around with the mains cable, to pressing certain key combinations, Mike started to lose faith.

'It's not happening, is it?' he said when he could hold it in no longer. 'It's totally dead, right?'

'No luck so far. What was it you had on there that you hadn't saved?'

Mike pressed his palms on to his cheeks, rubbing them up against his stubble and letting out a long sigh. 'Don't worry about it, son. It was a pipe dream. Clearly it wasn't meant to happen.'

'We could try putting it in a warm place, like the airing cupboard. It might be fine once it dries out. And even if the laptop itself is broken, that's not to say we won't be able to recover what's on the hard disk.'

'Including the file I was working on? Even though I didn't save it?'

'Maybe,' Ben replied. But his face said otherwise.

He patted his son on the back. 'Don't worry. Thanks for your help. It's my own stupid fault. I think I'm going to head out for that run now.

You're not planning to go out anywhere, are you?'

Ben shook his head.

'Great. Keep an eye out for your sister until I get back, will you?'

'Sure. You said she was at Saima's, right?'

'Yes.'

'Are you okay, Dad? You look — '

'Oh, I'm great, son. I'm fandabidozi!'

Mike left a puzzled-looking Ben in the kitchen and trudged upstairs to change into his running kit, desperate to inflict some pain on himself by pounding the pavement.

A single thought ran through his head over and over again: once a loser, always a loser.

29

THEN

Tuesday, 14 February 1995

Lisa raced down the stairs as soon as she heard the letterbox, making sure to get there before her mum or Jamie.

To her delight, among the various letters addressed to her parents were three red envelopes with her name on the front. She grabbed them, ditching the rest of the post on the doormat, and ran back upstairs, shutting her bedroom door behind her.

A moment later it swung open again and her brother was standing there, smirking.

Lisa tried to hide the envelopes behind her back, but she wasn't quick enough.

'Has someone been getting love letters on Valentine's Day?' he said in a sing-song voice.

'Get lost, Jamie.' She snatched at the nearest thing she could find — a hairbrush — and threw it at him, only for him to close the door in the nick of time, avoiding it.

Not that this kept him away. He opened it again a second later, grinning like the village idiot.

Jamie was also now at secondary school. He'd taken the exam for King George's but hadn't made the cut. So he'd gone to Waterside instead, the local comprehensive, and was now more than halfway through his first year there. As a result, his and Lisa's holidays didn't always match. But this half-term they both had the same week off.

At least the main sport at Waterside was football, which Jamie was still very keen on. That said, his confidence had taken a bit of a knock after discovering he was no longer the best player on the pitch, as he had been at primary school.

Lisa hadn't heard him talk about wanting to go pro for some time now, although their dad seemed to have a harder time letting go of the dream. He was often on his son's back to practise more and he rarely missed a match — whether a school fixture or for the club Jamie played at on weekends.

He was one of those annoyingly vocal parents who would spend most of the time bellowing advice to the players or berating the referee. Lisa knew from personal experience of him watching her play hockey. She'd eventually asked him not to come any more, confessing that she found it embarrassing and off-putting. Luckily, he hadn't taken offence, probably because it freed him up to watch more of Jamie's football.

Her brother was now singing Boyzone's 'Love Me for a Reason' in her doorway in a ridiculous high voice. Lisa gave him her death stare. 'Why can't you leave me alone? Just because you haven't got any Valentine's cards.'

'Who says I haven't?' Jamie replied, stopping his stupid singing. 'I found one slipped into my locker at school on Friday, actually. So stick that in your pipe and smoke it.'

What? Where the hell did he pick up these sayings?

'To be honest, Jamie, I really don't care. But if you don't go away and give me some privacy, I'm calling Mum.'

'Ooh, not that,' he replied, quivering like a jelly in a way that almost made Lisa crack a smile. 'Anything but that!'

Reminding herself that she was annoyed with him, and laughing would only encourage more nonsense, Lisa said: 'I warned you. Muuum! Jamie's winding me up again. Can you get him to leave me alone?'

He scampered off back to his own bedroom. So when Christine appeared halfway up the stairs, he was nowhere in sight.

'What's the matter, Lisa?' she asked, running a hand through her hair. 'I was trying to catch up on some marking. What are you two squabbling about now?'

Christine had recently started teaching Junior Three at Aldham Primary. Previously, she'd been a Junior One teacher at another school around ten miles away. She'd avoided teaching at the same school that Lisa and Jamie attended, as she didn't think it was fair on them to have their mum around all the time. However, she had always wanted to teach at her local primary and — as luck would have it — a vacancy had arisen to start there last September, right after Jamie had left.

It was the first time she'd ever taught that particular year group, which meant she'd had to do more work from home than usual as she found her feet. She looked tired this morning and Lisa felt bad for calling her.

'It's all right, Mum. He's gone now, but he was doing his usual — winding me up.'

'What about?'

'Nothing. It's fine.'

Christine sighed. 'I do wish the pair of you would make an effort to get along better. I thought you'd have grown out of this constant quarrelling by now.'

'It's never me that starts it,' Lisa protested. 'If he'd leave me alone, rather than coming in my room and annoying me all the time, there wouldn't be any rows.'

'Maybe your brother likes spending time with you. Have you thought about that? It would be nice if you gave him the time of day once in a while.'

'You always take his side. It's so not fair.'

'I'm not taking anyone's side. I'm piggy in the middle, as usual.' As if to prove this, Christine trudged up the remaining stairs and knocked on Jamie's bedroom door before going inside and having a word with him.

Lisa didn't hang around to listen to what was said. Instead she shut herself in her own room and concentrated on the exciting task of opening her Valentine's cards.

★ ★ ★

That afternoon, on her way to the village shop to buy a magazine — either *Sugar* or *Just Seventeen*, depending on which issue looked best — Lisa passed Elliot's home and bumped into his mum. She was unpacking food shopping from the boot of her car.

'Hello, stranger,' Wendy said with that lovely smile of hers.

'Hi, Wendy. How are you?'

'I'm very well, thanks. And you?'

'I'm good.'

'What about Jamie and your parents?'

'Yes, they're all fine, thank you.'

'Doing anything exciting over half-term?'

'Not really. I've got loads of homework to keep me busy.'

'Yes, Elliot says the same. They work you hard at those schools of yours. Why don't you come in for a cuppa? You've not been round for ages. I know Elliot would be glad to see you.'

'Um.' Lisa hesitated. Things between her and Elliot hadn't been great recently, which was why she hadn't been to his house for a bit. But maybe now was a good time to bury the hatchet.

'Go on,' Wendy said. 'Listen, I know you two had a bit of a falling out. Elliot told me. But I also know that he misses you, as do I. What's the worst that can happen?'

'Okay.'

'Brilliant. Now make yourself useful.' She handed Lisa a couple of the shopping bags and they headed inside together.

'Elliot!' Wendy called from the kitchen, winking at Lisa. 'We've got a visitor.'

'Who is it?' his voice replied from afar — presumably up in his bedroom.

'Oh, just a gorgeous girl I spotted walking by.'

'Are you winding me up again, Mum?'

'No, I'm serious.' Wendy turned to Lisa. 'Why don't you pop upstairs and say hi while I unpack the shopping and make us that brew. Tea or coffee?'

'Tea, please.'

'I'll give you a shout when it's ready.'

Lisa felt itchy and out of breath as she climbed the stairs, the patterned red carpet somehow looking more garish and old-fashioned than she remembered. She'd been up and down here countless times previously, but not for a while. Even before she and Elliot had their argument, she hadn't been to his house for some time. That was part of the problem.

Her mind jumped back to that snowy day near the end of the Christmas holidays, when Elliot had been the visitor in her house — her bedroom.

★ ★ ★

'Why don't we go outside and build a snowman?' Elliot suggested. 'It's beautiful out there.'

'Aren't we a bit old for that?' Lisa concentrated on filing her nails from her sprawled-out position on the bed.

'Who cares? It's fun. Or we could have a snowball fight, if you prefer.'

'No thanks, El. I'd rather stay here in the warm. But don't let me stop you. I'm sure Jamie would be up for joining in.'

She looked up when her friend didn't answer

303

and saw that he had his back to her, staring wistfully out of the window.

'Did you hear that?'

'Yep,' he replied.

'I won't be offended if that's what you want to do.'

'Right.'

'Have I said something wrong? You look annoyed.'

Elliot sighed. 'You don't seem to want to do things together any more, that's all. We always used to be outside having fun. Now the only time I see you is on the bus and when I come round here. When was the last time you called to see me at my house?'

Lisa wasn't sure how to reply. It was a fair point.

'Where's this coming from?' was the best she could come up with — a feeble attempt at deflection.

'You don't seem to have time for me like you used to. You're always off playing sport or out with someone else.'

Lisa sat up. 'Sean, you mean? He's my boyfriend, Elliot. What do you expect? I know you don't like him, but — '

'So you're going out with him again, are you? On, off. It's hard to keep up.'

'Yes I am, as you know. And we've only split up twice.'

'And why was that again? Oh yeah, because you found out that he'd cheated on you twice — that you know of — and both times you went running back to him. I bet you'd build a

304

snowman if he asked you.'

'You've never liked Sean. That's been obvious from the start. Yes, he's made some mistakes, but I love him — and as my friend you should accept that. I know he's not like you; that he's into rugby and stuff. But so is Neil Walsh and you've always been friends with him.'

Elliot screwed up his face. 'Um, you're comparing Sean to Neil? They're like chalk and cheese. Rugby is about the only thing they have in common, apart from . . .'

'Apart from what? Go on, say it.'

'Apart from you.'

'As I recall, you didn't particularly like me going out with Neil either.'

Elliot shook his head and turned away, so he was looking out of the window again. He let out a long sigh. 'So it's all my fault, is it? Of course. I should have known.'

'I can't believe you're even having a go at me for playing sport, just because you're useless at it. Pardon me for having a life. Maybe you should get one too.'

As soon as the words had left Lisa's mouth, she regretted them, but it was too late.

Elliot's deep blue eyes widened with rage behind his glasses. 'So we're being brutally honest here, are we? Fine. You're right. I've never liked Sean, even before the cheating. I think he's a mindless cretin, like his pal Samo. You thought he was an idiot too once, like when he forced my head down a toilet. I used to think that Sean wasn't good enough for you. But now I'm not so sure. Maybe he's exactly what you deserve.

You're welcome to each other.'

And with that, he stormed out.

★　★　★

As she stood at Elliot's bedroom door, taking a second to compose herself, Lisa could still picture how her friend's face had looked that day in early January. They'd not seen each other or spoken again until a few days later, when they'd returned to school, and they'd never properly made up.

Lisa supposed she'd been waiting for Elliot to say sorry, which he never had. Perhaps she should have been the one to offer an olive branch.

It wasn't that they'd ignored each other after that. Things had just cooled between them. They'd only interacted when necessary and not made any effort to see each other at all outside their bus journeys.

It had been obvious to those around them that something had changed, but Lisa for one had never discussed it with anyone. Especially not Sean, who she'd now broken up with — for good this time — after learning that he'd been two-timing her yet again.

On this occasion it was with some skank neighbour of his, since well before Christmas, apparently. According to Lisa's hockey pal Hayley, he'd even bought them the same cheap perfume as a gift. After learning this, Lisa had hurled her bottle out of her bedroom window, only to be ordered to clear up the broken glass

306

by her dad. It smelled disgusting anyway.

She wondered if Elliot knew about Sean. Surely he did. If anything, the disastrous way that had unfolded was one of the reasons Lisa hadn't apologised to him, because she was embarrassed that he'd been right all along. It seemed so stupid now she thought about it.

She took a deep breath and tapped gently on his door.

'Come in.'

Lisa offered a bashful smile as their eyes met.

Elliot was at his desk. He was hunched over the keyboard of the computer Wendy had bought him for Christmas — the monitor displaying line after line of what looked like gibberish to Lisa. He'd told her about this gift, which he'd been shocked and over the moon to receive, but she'd never actually seen it before. She was sure he'd also mentioned what type it was, but she couldn't remember the name.

She and computers didn't get along. Unlike Elliot, whose favourite class at school was Computer Studies. He'd been dying to have his own machine for as long as Lisa could remember. It was a second-hand model, which Wendy had bought via his computer teacher at school, but they still didn't come cheap. By the looks of things, he was definitely making the most of it.

'Surprise!' Lisa said. She found herself doing jazz hands in a bizarre and desperate bid to make light of the moment.

Elliot gave her a blank stare, before bursting into laughter. 'What on earth are you doing?'

307

She laughed too. 'What can I say? I needed an icebreaker.'

Somehow the mere fact of her being back in Elliot's bedroom made all the difference. After a couple of minutes, any remaining awkwardness between them had lifted. They were back to chatting like they always had.

Lisa, feeling guilty now that she hadn't called round of her own accord, was the first to offer an apology.

'Listen, El. I'm really sorry how things have been between us since that stupid row. It was wrong of me to say what I did and you were right what you told me: particularly the bit about Sean.'

Elliot rubbed a hand over his face before replying. 'Yeah, I heard that you two had split up. You know I think you're better off without him, so there's no point in me saying otherwise. But I'm sorry for what you must have been through.'

'He was two-timing me again. I can't believe I didn't see it coming. He always seemed so genuine when he promised not to do it again, begging me to forgive him; telling me how much I meant to him. You probably won't believe this, but he actually cried when I told him it was over for good. I really thought I loved him, but . . . ' She sighed and shook her head, perched on the edge of Elliot's bed.

Elliot took off his glasses, placing them on the computer keyboard, and walked over to Lisa. He sat down beside her and put his arm around her shoulders. 'I'm sorry for what I said too, Lise. It was wrong of me to lay a guilt trip on you about the sport and stuff — and for not trying to make up with you. I can't believe we've both been so stubborn. Can we go back to the way things were? I've really missed you.'

'I've missed you too,' Lisa replied, a wave of emotion catching her unawares. She couldn't stop the tears coming and, before she knew it, Elliot had pulled her into a hug. It felt so nice to be in her friend's arms; the tears kept flowing.

'I'd better get you some tissues,' he said eventually, pulling away and walking back to his desk. Then he was kneeling before her, his face a few centimetres away from hers, and dabbing at her cheeks. She smiled and found she was staring into his eyes. They were so big and blue; he looked so different without his specs on.

For a moment she thought they might . . .

The sound of Wendy's voice cut through the silence. 'There's a cup of tea and a biscuit for you both down here.'

Elliot pulled back, running a hand through his curls. 'Okay, Mum. We'll be down in a sec.'

If he'd felt the same thing she did, he didn't let on. He handed her a couple more tissues and asked if she was all right.

'I'm fine. Sorry to be such a crybaby. I don't know what happened. I guess I'm relieved to have things sorted between us at last. We mustn't ever fall out like that again.'

'Agreed.'

It was only then that Lisa spotted two Valentine's cards on the windowsill. How had

309

she not noticed them before?

'What are these?' she asked, walking over to them.

'Oh God,' Elliot replied, his face turning a matching red. 'One is from Mum: the one with a question mark. She does it every year, but I usually hide it out of the way before anyone sees. She even tries to disguise her handwriting, but I can always tell.'

'What about the other?' She picked it up to have a nosy before he could stop her. The handwritten message inside read:

> To Elliot,
> Thanks for asking me to be your girlfriend.
> I'm so glad we met.
> Humongous hugs!
> Lots of love,
> Claire
> xxx

Lisa was gobsmacked. 'You've got a girlfriend called Claire? How do I not know about this?'

Elliot shrugged. 'We've barely spoken for the past six weeks or so, have we? What can I say? I took your advice.'

'What do you mean?'

'You told me to get a life, so I did. Well, I got a hobby.'

Elliot explained how he'd joined an outdoor pursuits club that his mum had heard about at the hospital. It was for kids of secondary school age and ran every Saturday from a place about ten miles away called Skelton Country Park, which included a big lake, a series of woods and lots of open space.

'We do all sorts,' he said. 'Canoeing, orienteering, windsurfing, abseiling. I was a bit dubious when Mum suggested it, but it's turned out to be really good fun.'

'And this Claire goes too?'

'That's right. We both started at the same time. Because neither of us knew anyone else, we got chatting and — well — it turned out we had loads in common. She's even really into computers.'

'Where's she from?'

'She lives and goes to school near Bolton, so not that close, but at least we see each other once a week at OP.'

Lisa, who took a moment to realise that OP stood for 'outdoor pursuits', was shocked to find herself feeling jealous.

She'd never known Elliot to have a girlfriend before and, especially after everything the two of them had been through recently, it threw her. It felt like he'd replaced her or something, although she knew how ridiculous that was, since she'd never been his girlfriend.

She used to get the feeling that Elliot fancied her, from the way he looked at her and so on. She'd never minded. If anything, she'd found it sweet. She'd just never thought of him that way — and, what's more, he'd not given her that impression for some time. So why did she feel like this now?

It even smarted when Claire was mentioned again, once Lisa and Elliot had joined Wendy downstairs for the tea and biscuits. Commenting how nice she seemed from the brief few times they'd met, Wendy said: 'Elliot's not invited her over here yet, but I'm hoping he will do soon.' She added in a mock whisper directed at Lisa: 'I'm not that embarrassing a mum, am I?'

'Of course not. You're lovely.'

She meant it too. She'd always enjoyed visiting Elliot's house; the friendly welcome she got from the ever-glamorous Wendy, with her fantastic fashion creations and immaculate make-up, was a big part of that. Thinking about this, remembering all the good times they'd had here, was what shook Lisa out of her momentary spell as a green-eyed monster.

Soon she found herself chatting away about her own three Valentine's cards, all of which had been signed with a question mark and bore a Westwich postmark on the envelope. Other than the fact they were probably boys from King George's, she had no idea who these admirers were and nor did Elliot. She was flattered to have received the cards, though, especially considering she hadn't sent any herself. Secretly, she had a couple of candidates in mind who she hoped they might be from. She was single at the moment, but perhaps not for much longer.

When she got home, having forgotten altogether about buying a magazine, the only thing on her mind was how happy she was to have made up with her friend. Well, at least until Jamie turned up at her door singing Boyzone again.

30

NOW

Wednesday, 25 July 2018

Lisa parked the Octavia on the road outside what used to be her old school. 'Here we are. There's a sign over there for the show apartment. Shall we have a look around?'

El gave her a toothy grin before opening his door. 'Definitely.'

'Give me a second to fix my make-up.' Lisa pulled a compact mirror, lipstick and eyeliner out of her handbag.

Standing on the pavement, his car door still open, Elliot ran a hand across the silver paint on the bonnet. 'Smooth ride. Not like the Skoda cars of old. Remember the jokes about them and Ladas when we were kids?' He winked at Lisa before adding: 'What do you call a Skoda with a sun roof?'

'A skip,' she replied in a flash. 'How do you double the value of a Skoda?'

'Fill the tank. Sorry, it's naughty of me to bring that up, Lise. You can take it, right?'

'Of course. It was Mike's choice, anyway, not mine.'

'I wonder what your dad would think.'

'He'd turn in his grave, for sure. It was part of the reason I agreed to get one, if I'm honest.'

'How do you mean?' Elliot climbed back inside the car as the rain started up again.

'Well, he didn't exactly provide for us when he died. It was unexpected, since he had a heart attack, but all he left us with was a load of gambling debts. There were no savings or investments. Mum's only option was to sell the family house. He was selfish. If he'd looked after himself better, for his family's sake, maybe he'd still be around.'

Lisa's fears about Mike going the same way were on the tip of her tongue, but it felt like saying those words to Elliot would have been a betrayal, so she stopped herself.

'Buying a Skoda was your way of getting your own back?'

Lisa puffed. 'Maybe. A little bit. Let's just say I'll never buy a BMW. What do you drive in Australia?'

Elliot shuffled in his seat and cleared his throat. 'Um — '

'Don't tell me. A BMW?'

'Sorry,' he said, wincing. 'An M4 Convertible.'

'I don't even know what that means. The main thing I care about in a car is that it doesn't break down. But I guess that's a fancy one?'

'What can I say? I always admired your dad's ever-changing cars as a kid.'

★ ★ ★

Looking around the show apartment was weird, particularly for Lisa. El had never spent much time in the girls' school, so it was harder for him

314

to put things into context. But Lisa had been a pupil there for the best part of seven years, from eleven to eighteen.

Some parts, like the main entrance and the corridors, were instantly recognisable in spite of the conversion. Overall the building still retained its air of grandeur. However, the living space had been changed beyond recognition. It was a nice roomy flat with a contemporary feel and all the mod cons, but there was little to remind Lisa of her years studying there.

The estate agent soon cottoned on to the fact that Lisa was a former pupil.

'I bet I'm not the first, am I?' Lisa said.

'Not by a long way,' the woman replied, flicking back the floppy fringe of her short red hair. She raised the corners of her mouth for the briefest of moments — a haughty almost-smile probably reserved for timewasters — then pulled out her mobile and turned to make a call.

'I think she knows we're window shoppers,' Lisa whispered.

'Let's have some fun, then.'

Elliot spent the next fifteen minutes or so bugging her with all manner of questions about the complex. These covered everything from the exact types of locks, windows and insulation materials used, to predicted rates of utility bills and home insurance for the various different sized properties available. By the end, she appeared firmly convinced that Elliot and Lisa were genuinely interested in making a purchase.

'Would you both like a coffee while I put some numbers together for you?' she said, beaming at

Elliot. 'Cappuccino? Latte? It's the real deal. Not the usual instant stuff.'

Lisa jumped in. 'Thank you, but we really need to get going.'

'My wife's very choosy,' Elliot said with a wink. 'But don't you worry. I'll work on her. Do you have a business card?'

'Of course.' She pulled one out from her handbag and handed it over, the white contrasting with the deep red of her perfectly manicured fingernails. 'Could I possibly take a contact number for you? I could give you a call in a few days.'

'Sure,' Elliot said, reeling off a mobile number, which she duly wrote down.

Before they were even outside, Elliot burst into his seal laugh, which promptly set Lisa off.

'You're wicked,' she said in between giggles.

'She shouldn't have been so snooty.'

'What was that number you gave her?'

'Oh, just one I made up.'

'I knew it,' she said, digging him in the ribs. 'You don't even have a UK mobile number, do you?'

'No. I'm glad to get away from all that, to be honest. I've found it really liberating not using a mobile over here.'

'I didn't think I'd ever seen you with one. What about your work? Don't they need to be able to contact you?'

'They can always get me at the hotel if they need to. Don't forget the time difference.'

'True. But what about the business you came over here for? How's that going? You seem to have been spending a lot of your time with us.'

'Are you complaining?'

'Of course not, but —'

'Leave me to worry about my business, Lisa.'

'Why so secretive?'

'I could tell you, but then I'd have to kill you.'
He grinned. 'So are we going to have a look at
this new amalgamated school, or what?'

★ ★ ★

Despite now being called The Royal School,
Westwich and admitting girls as well as boys, the
former King George's building didn't look
especially different to Lisa. As the two of them
walked up to the front entrance, it brought back
memories of school discos. These were the
occasions Lisa most remembered from the
infrequent visits she'd made to the boys' school
over the years.

'Remember that disco here when I ended up
snogging Neil Walsh all night?'

'How could I forget? It was the first one I ever
went to, after you convinced me. It was also the
time I ended up kissing that poor Nicola girl on
the ear.'

This made Lisa laugh. 'God, I remember you
telling me about that. You were mortified,
weren't you?'

'Too right. I thought she'd tell everyone and it
would be all around the school by Monday
morning, but it was fine in the end.'

'I had a word with her for you.'

'You didn't.'

317

'I did.'

'You never told me that.'

Lisa shrugged. 'Looking out for you was one of my hobbies in those days.'

'You did always have my back,' Elliot said, grabbing her hand and squeezing it. 'I've never forgotten that. Especially — '

Lisa jumped in. 'Oh, look.' She pointed at one of the first-floor classroom windows. 'There's someone in there, I think. Did you see them?'

He shook his head.

'I'm sure I saw a figure moving around,' she said. 'They must have gone. Still, that's a good sign.'

Despite the summer holidays being underway, she and El had already decided there was a good chance of someone being around at the school, even if it was just the caretaker. But the lack of cars parked in the grounds as they walked across from Queen Anne's had led to them wondering whether they might have been mistaken. At least it wasn't raining any more, although the heavy cloud cover gave little hope of sunshine.

She was the first to reach the main entrance — a high wooden door flanked by stone pillars — and before she tried to enter, she asked Elliot what they were going to say to whoever they encountered.

'Let's tell them the truth: that we're former pupils and we were hoping for a quick look around. You never know, it might be someone who remembers us.'

'After twenty years? I wouldn't count on it.'

She grabbed the doorknob, only to find it was

318

locked. 'Dammit.' Striding back to the spot where she'd seen someone inside the building, she looked again, but this time no one was visible. All the same, she cupped her hands around her mouth and called out: 'Hello? Is anyone there?'

Her voice echoed across the empty space at the front of the grand school, an ivy-coated blend of red brick and white dressings, which stretched around them in a U-shape.

Elliot, who'd remained at the front entrance, called out: 'Wait, Lisa. The door is open after all. I think it must have been stuck. The wood's probably swollen or something.'

Lisa was puzzled by this, as she'd given the door a really hard yank. But sure enough, he was standing there, holding it wide open and gesturing for her to follow him inside.

'That's weird,' she said. 'I could have sworn it was locked.'

'Not to worry. At least we're in now.'

Inside, the lights were all switched off and there was a sober, silent air about the place that instinctively led them to lower their voices. The foyer was dull rather than dark, enough natural light seeping through to enable them to see everything, while retaining a definite sense of not being open for business.

'What now?' Lisa asked, her voice little more than a whisper.

El shrugged. 'There doesn't seem to be anyone around.'

'What about that person I saw on the first floor? They might think we're burglars.'

319

'Let's have a quick wander and, if we see them, we can wing it.'

'Okay,' she replied. 'Hey, that's where the discos used to be held, isn't it?'

She pointed towards a set of double doors immediately across from the entrance and Elliot nodded. 'That's right. That's the main hall in there. Let's have a peek.'

The pair of them headed inside the large room, which was considerably lighter than the foyer, thanks to a row of sash windows along the outside wall. The space was filled with row upon row of benches, directed towards a stage at the front, upon which stood a wooden lectern surrounded by chairs.

'Wow. This hasn't changed at all.' Elliot's eyes looked up and lingered on the decorative plasterwork covering the two-storey ceiling above.

'Really?' Lisa scanned the hall. 'It's not at all how I remember it from the discos. Mind you, it was always dark then.'

'And all the benches were either stacked elsewhere or lining the sides of the dancefloor.' He winked. 'For couples to snog on. No, I know what you're saying, but this was how it always looked for morning assembly. We pupils would be down here, with the head and all the teachers facing us from the stage. It almost feels like stepping back in time.'

'Um, sorry to break the spell and all, but I really need to visit the ladies' room.'

He led her down the empty corridor to where the main toilet block used to be, the clip-clop of

320

their footsteps jabbing into the silence. At one point he stopped and knelt in front of a row of wooden lockers standing against one wall. Placing his palm on one of the doors, he declared: 'This was mine.' Then he peered at it, so his nose was a few centimetres away from the wood, adding. 'Yep. There you go. Have a look.'

He got up and gestured for her to take his place. 'Okay, what am I looking for?' she asked. And then she saw it: a tiny 'E.T.' etched into the wood near one of the hinges. 'You rebel. When did you do that?'

'My last day, with a compass.'

'You used full stops, like in the film. I thought you hated being called E.T.'

'Only by Samo. That was my way of claiming it back.'

They continued walking, Elliot pointing out classrooms he remembered studying particular lessons in along the way. They eventually reached the toilets, which were still in the same place but had now been divided into separate sections for boys and girls. They both had to go, but El was already waiting for her in the corridor when she came out.

'Remember that time when Samo and his pals bog-washed me?' he said.

She wrinkled up her nose. 'Was that here?'

He nodded. 'Bastard. Is he still local? Have you ever bumped into him or anything?'

'No, I haven't seen him in years.' She laughed. 'Why? Fancy a catch-up?'

'No, thanks. Hey, you know what I said about reclaiming E.T.?'

She nodded.

'Look at this.' He lifted up his T-shirt, giving her a tantalising glimpse of an extremely well-defined six-pack, and pointed to a small tattoo on his right side, just above his belt, displaying the very same initials in the blue-white colour and font from the movie.

'No way. That's amaz — '

Lisa was interrupted by the sound of a gruff male voice bellowing: 'Oi! What the hell's going on?'

She looked up to see a large bald man standing further down the corridor, frowning and pointing at them. 'How did you two get in here?' he demanded, proceeding to stride in their direction.

Lisa grabbed El's hand and threw him an anxious look. 'Oops. That doesn't sound good. What now?'

'Don't worry. Leave him to me.'

★ ★ ★

'Cheers,' Lisa said, clinking glasses with Elliot, who was sitting across from her on a small table by a window in the Royal Oak — the nearest pub to the school.

'Do you remember the last time we were in here together?' he asked.

'A-level results day?'

'Exactly.'

'Wow. That feels so long ago, although at the same time it could almost be yesterday. Does that make sense?'

Elliot chuckled. 'I know what you mean. Have you been here much since?'

She shook her head. 'Maybe a handful of times. Get-togethers and so on. Isn't there anyone else from school that you'd like to meet up with while you're here? What about Neil Walsh?'

'Last I heard he was living in Denmark.'

'Oh, that's right. Didn't he marry a Danish girl he met at university?'

'I think so.'

'Anyone else?'

'I doubt I'll have time. I'm not sure how much longer I'll be here . . . '

His voice tailed off as he grabbed his chest and bent forward, making a growling noise and screwing his face up in pain.

Lisa jumped to her feet, alarmed. 'What's happening? Are you all right? Do you need me to call an ambulance?'

'No, no,' he groaned, holding forward the palm of his right hand. 'Please don't. I'm okay. It'll pass in a minute.'

It felt like forever as Lisa was frozen in place, anxiously watching her friend suffer. She was on the verge of ignoring his plea and phoning for help when, sure enough, he let out a long sigh and sat back in his chair, his face unknotting itself and slowly returning to its usual calm state.

His eyes silently scrutinised her before he spoke. 'Sorry. That happens sometimes. Nothing to worry about. It's a kind of, um, heartburn.'

'It looked pretty extreme for heartburn. Are you sure — '

323

'Honestly, don't give it another thought. I've felt much worse pain.'

Lisa sat back down but wasn't convinced. 'If you say so. Has it totally gone now?'

'Yes.'

'You were talking about not being here much longer. Does that mean the business-side of your trip has gone well? Surely you can tell me that, at least. I'm sorry, Elliot, but it's weird how secretive you are about it. Everything is all right, isn't it? You're not in trouble or anything?'

'You don't need to worry about me, Lise. You did more than your fair share of that when we were kids. I don't have any specifics yet — truthfully — but it's not going to be too much longer that I'm here, so let's enjoy the time we have. Why don't we spend the rest of the day together, just the two of us? We can do whatever you like.'

Elliot was still being as vague as hell about his business. However, in light of the fact that he wasn't likely to be around for much longer, and not wanting to spoil what little time they had left together, Lisa decided not to push him on it. It really was fantastic to see him again after all these years; to witness how far he'd come from the timid, fragile boy she'd grown up with to the strong, confident man he was now. It was far more than his looks alone that had changed. He was so self-assured and comfortable in his own skin. Like Mike had also been once, before he'd had that ripped away from him.

Elliot seemed to have developed an almost magical power of persuasion too. He'd become a real people person, something Lisa assumed came from running his own company. Whatever it was, the way he'd dealt with that angry caretaker who'd discovered them wandering the corridors at King George's, or The Royal School as it now was, had been something to behold. One minute he'd been shouting at them, threatening to phone the police; the next — after a few calm words from El — he'd transformed into a pussycat, making small talk as he walked them back outside and even wishing them a nice day.

Lisa couldn't help wondering how things might have turned out differently had Elliot been that way when they'd first met. The whole 'being stripped of his clothes thing' would likely never have happened. So how would they have got to know each other? Would they still have become friends? Maybe they'd have even got romantically involved at some point.

The Elliot sitting across from her now, with that six-pack she wouldn't forget any time soon, was a real catch. It surprised her that he was still single; from the little he'd told her, she gathered this was due to him being married to his work. Clearly there had been relationships over the years, but not one that had stood the test of time or been more important to him than his business.

Anyway, the idea of spending the rest of the day with Elliot was appealing. A part of her that she barely dared to acknowledge even found it somewhat arousing — as if it might lead to something happening between them. Not that she wanted that, of course. She was a happily married woman and mum. So why did she have to remind herself of this fact? And why had she dreamt last night of the two of them tearing each other's clothes off before Elliot wrapped those big arms of his around her naked body and threw her across the kitchen table?

'Hello?'

She blinked away the illicit fantasy, only to see El's deep blue eyes gazing across the table at her as he twirled a beer mat around in his fingers and tapped it on the table. 'Sorry,' she said. 'I was miles away. What did you say?'

'I asked if there was anything you fancied doing together this afternoon. Or do you need to get home?'

'Staying out sounds good. I've really enjoyed it so far today. It's been fun doing something just the two of us, hasn't it? Like old times.'

Elliot nodded, grinning. 'Yes, it really has.'

'I'll need to phone Mike first to make sure he doesn't need the car for anything or have any other plans.' She pulled her mobile out of her handbag. 'One minute.'

As Elliot got up to visit the men's room, she dialled home. It rang for ages. She was about to hang up and try Mike's mobile instead when Ben's voice finally answered.

'Hello, love. It's Mum. How are you doing?'

'Fine.'

'Is your father around?'

'No.'

'Where is he?'

'I'm not sure.'

'He didn't tell you?'

'Well, he said he was going out for a run, but that was ages ago. I'm not sure where he went got to.'

'Have you tried his mobile?'

'No point. He left it in the kitchen.'

'Well, I'm sure he'll be back soon. What about your sister?'

'Yeah, she's upset about something.'

Lisa rolled her eyes. Where was Mike when she needed him? 'What do you mean she's upset?'

'She went round to Saima's house, for some reason, and she was in tears when she came back. Wouldn't tell me why.'

Lisa was glad to hear that her daughter had taken her advice for once and gone to see her old friend. But why had she come back in tears? Letting out a silent sigh, Lisa added: 'Do you want to put her on the phone?'

'Hang on.'

'Everything all right?' Elliot mouthed, returning to the table.

She put her hand over the microphone. 'Not really. Mike's gone AWOL and Chloe's in tears. No idea why. Ben's gone to — '

'Mum?' Her son's voice appeared on the line again.

'Yes. Where's Chloe?'

'She won't come to the phone.'

'Why not?'

'I don't know. She barely spoke to me.'

'Does she seem okay?'

'Not really.'

'And still no sign of your dad?'

'No — and that's the other thing . . . '

Lisa steeled herself for more bad news. 'Go on.'

'He was pretty upset when he went out. He pretended not to be, but you know Dad. He's not very good at hiding that stuff.'

Lisa massaged her temples as Ben recounted what had happened with the laptop.

By the time he'd finished, there was only one thing left for Lisa to say: 'I'll be back as soon as I can.'

31

NOW

Wednesday, 25 July 2018

Mike hadn't intended to end up in the pub. Or maybe he had. Why else had he taken his wallet with him on a run?

He had done some running first, at least. Enough to make him sweat and to feel it in his knees and heels: typical weak spots for a man of his age carrying a few too many pounds. He'd be forty next February and it was all downhill from there, right? Even his bladder was showing its age, requiring him to visit the toilet far too frequently when he was drinking pints, as he was now.

This was already his third visit to the gents, nauseating urinal cake smell and all. He splashed some water over his face and stared at his reflection in the mirror. What a bloody waste of space. Who was he kidding? He was never going to write a successful screenplay. It was pie in the sky. He couldn't even bang out a plot synopsis without breaking his laptop.

So what the hell was he going to do with his life? Teaching was out; he'd never get another driving job after the last disaster. What options did he have?

Continuing to rely on his wife being the sole

breadwinner was out of the question. It wasn't like he was even any good at being the one at home. Lisa still did most of the cooking and cleaning, which had been the source of plenty of arguments in recent times. Understandably. So why didn't he pull his weight more? Goodness knows. That awful term 'house husband' certainly didn't help. It never failed to make him feel utterly worthless and miserable. And once a black mood set in, he often found himself crippled. Hours could pass by while he stared at a wall, lost in a battle of mental self-torture.

This wasn't something he was able to explain to Lisa. How could he, when he didn't understand it himself? It was like part of him had been lost — and he had no clue how to find it again.

Plus, he had a good idea what she'd say if he did tell her. After Liam Hornby's charges against him had been dropped and the focus shifted away from the battle to clear his name, she'd suggested he ought to see a therapist or counsellor to help him move on from the trauma.

'He's the one who needs help, not me,' had been Mike's reply. He wasn't good at talking about such things to his own family, so the idea of telling them to a total stranger — a 'shrink' no less — terrified him.

But somehow he needed to get his life back together. Things couldn't go on like this. Money was tight at home. Everyone was feeling it — and it was his fault. This year it was a missed summer holiday. What next? What would happen when the kids wanted to go to university? He had responsibilities.

He'd been a catch at university, when he and Lisa had got together as postgrads studying to become teachers. Being a year older than her — literally a man of the world following his globetrotting gap year — she'd looked up to him. He'd been her rock when she'd unexpectedly got pregnant while still on the course, standing by her and proposing, rather than running scared.

He'd supported his new family by working as a teacher while Lisa took time off to have Ben and then, almost four years later, to have Chloe. Eventually, once he became a deputy head, his salary had grown, giving them extra financial freedom and, potentially, a head teacher's pay packet one day in the future. But that had all changed. Instead, he'd become the opposite of a catch: a release, a let go, a loser.

He'd left himself wide open to someone like Elliot waltzing in and sweeping Lisa off her feet. Maybe that was happening right now, at this very moment, while the two of them were off together visiting their old schools. He could be on the brink of losing everything.

Mike knew that getting drunk wouldn't help — not in the long term. If anything, it would only make matters worse. And yet, for the time being, it would numb the pain. And that was what Mike needed today.

'Could I get another pint and a shot of whisky, please, Alan?' he said to the burly landlord of the Swan, who was tending bar. The only other staff member working at this quiet time was a frail-looking, elderly chap called Edgar, dressed in jeans and the same black pub-branded polo shirt as his boss. He was currently making his way around the pub, wiping down tables and rearranging beer mats.

'Whisky?' Alan replied, raising a bushy eyebrow. 'Celebrating something, are we?'

'Quite the opposite. Don't ask.'

'Oh dear. Any particular brand?'

'Honestly, I don't care, as long as it burns on the way down.'

* * *

Mike had lost track of how long he'd been in the pub, slumped on a bar stool, when the two cocky young idiots came in.

From what he overheard, they were decorators who'd finished a job locally; still in their paint-covered work gear, they took up a spot on the opposite side of the bar to where he was seated. They both looked to be in their mid-twenties.

'I'll have whatever that bloke's on,' the shorter of the two, who was barrel-chested with spiky ginger hair, said to Alan with an unpleasant grin, nudging his pal and pointing at Mike.

He was feeling pretty hammered by that stage: drunk enough to block out the smell of bleach and stale beer. The comment didn't particularly bother him, although he knew that was the intention. In a bid to clear the air, Mike raised his pint glass in their direction and said: 'Cheers, lads.'

He thought that would be it, but after getting their drinks, they moved along the bar and stood next to him.

'All right, buddy,' the taller one said. 'How's it going?' He had shaved brown hair with a white patch the size of a golf ball just off centre; his face reminded Mike of a rat.

'Fine. You?'

'What was that?' Ginger snapped. He was the one closest to Mike and he reached out to pat his back in a patronising way. 'You're slurring your words, buddy.'

'I said I was fine.'

'Nope,' he said, winking at Ratface. 'Still not getting that. How much have you had?'

Alan was changing spirit bottles at the other end of the bar, leaving Mike alone with the two wise guys. There had been a few other drinkers in earlier, but they'd all gone. Mike considered moving — finding a table in a quiet corner — but his pint was already half empty, meaning he'd have to return to the bar soon anyway. Besides, he'd been here first.

'Very funny,' he said, staring straight ahead. 'You should be a comedian.'

'What was that?' Ginger replied, patting his back again but harder this time. 'Still can't understand a word you're saying.'

Mike sighed and took a swig from his pint.

'Do I recognise you from somewhere?' Ratface asked him next.

'I doubt it.'

'Eh?' Ginger piped up, shrugging dramatically. 'It's like he's speaking a foreign language.'

'Ignore my pal,' Ratface said. 'He never knows when to let things lie. Seriously, though, I'm sure I recognise you from somewhere. I never forget a face. We haven't done a job for you, have we?'

Not bloody likely, Mike thought; he said he didn't think so.

'It'll come to me in a minute . . . You're not on TV or anything like that, are you?'

In his booze-numbed state, Mike couldn't tell if this guy was taking the piss or not. Was he winding him up in a more subtle way than his pal, or was he serious about recognising him?

He simply shook his head and went to visit the gents — again — where Edgar was almost done mopping the floor and warned him to be careful not to slip.

When he returned, he was glad to see that the two lads had abandoned the bar for a nearby fruit machine. Great. Hopefully they'd leave him alone now.

Alan, who had moved on to drying glasses with a tea towel, nodded at him as he sat back down on his bar stool. Then Mike noticed that his drink was gone.

'What happened to my pint?' he asked the landlord.

'It was empty, Mike, so I took it away. Can I get you another?'

He nodded, puzzled. There had definitely been beer left in that glass. One of those two idiots must have either poured it into a drip tray or drunk it. Bastards. He glanced over and caught Ginger sneering at him: that annoying grin again, just begging to be wiped off his face. This confirmed his suspicions. But now that they'd moved away, and hopefully grown bored of winding him up, he couldn't see any point in saying anything.

Instead, he hoped that they gambled away all their money and left. Of course that didn't happen. No sooner had he thought it than the pair of them let out a loud cheer followed by the clunking, chinking sound of coins pouring out of the bottom of the fruit machine.

Moments later, to his dismay, they rejoined him at the bar and ordered more drinks.

'Once a winner, always a winner,' Ginger said, winking at him. 'I'd have treated you, mate, but I see you've got a fresh pint. You shouldn't have rushed through that last one.' He shook his head and tutted.

Mike clenched and unclenched his hands, breathing slowly to try to calm the seed of rage he could feel growing in his belly. He focused on the sight of Alan pouring two fresh pints of lager, but Ginger was still there, smirking at him in his peripheral vision.

Then Ratface's voice cut through everything else, like a dagger in the gut. 'Shit. I remember who you are now. You're that psycho teacher. The one who attacked a pupil. You were all over the papers.'

'No way,' Ginger added. 'I remember hearing about that. Was that really you?'

Mike didn't answer. He could feel himself losing control and was fighting to stop it.

But of course Ginger wouldn't let it lie. 'It was you, wasn't it? So how come you're in here, drinking? Shouldn't you be behind bars?'

Mike's hands were locked into tight fists now, ready to strike. He was breathing fast and heavy.

'I asked you a question,' Ginger said.

'Several questions in fact,' Ratface chipped in. 'And not one answer. That's rude.'

'You're right,' Ginger went on, starting up with the tutting again. 'It is very rude indeed.'

'What's going on?' Alan asked as he brought the two pints over, eyes darting from the idiots to Mike and back again.

'Nothing, pal,' Ratface said.

'Yeah, just a bit of banter,' Ginger added.

Alan looked to Mike for his take on the situation when the phone behind the bar started ringing. He went to answer it and got drawn into a heated discussion about some issue with a delayed delivery.

'Edgar, can you keep an eye on the bar for a minute?' he called over to his employee, who replied that he would while lugging the mop and bucket he'd used on the toilet floor into a storeroom. Alan disappeared into the back, amid talk of checking something in the cellar.

In the meantime, Ginger started up again. 'It must be him. Otherwise he'd have denied it.'

'Oh, it's definitely him,' Ratface said. 'No doubt.'

'So why did you do it? Why turn on a helpless little kid? Is it because he wouldn't suck you off?'

The two of them burst out laughing at this — and Mike's simmering rage, fuelled by the potent cocktail of pent-up frustration and alcohol, finally boiled over.

Everything that happened from then on was a blur. Ratface started saying something else, but to Mike it made no sense, as if his voice had been slowed down to a fraction of the usual speed. Like it was travelling through water.

Because the floodgates were open.

So he lunged.

And time was sluggish.

Until it wasn't any more.

There was a sudden mad rush of shouting and swearing and flying fists and elbows and sweat and pain and then . . . Elliot.

32

NOW

Wednesday, 25 July 2018

Chloe's phone pinged. Her first temptation was to hurl it across the room, but she managed to stop herself. Instead, she levered her head up from her tear-soaked pillow and glanced at the screen to see who the message was from.

Saima.

She threw the mobile facedown back on to the bed.

But soon, devastated as she was, curiosity got the better of her. Maybe Saima wanted to confess to making the whole story up. Perhaps she was about to admit that she was the one behind the nasty texts after all, and she'd only said what she had in an attempt to get away with it.

She flicked on the screen.

How are you?

Stupid question, Chloe thought, tossing the phone away again. She was awful, obviously. What did Saima expect? Her so-called best friend had been bad-mouthing her behind her back; it also looked like Holly had been the one sending those horrible messages all along.

Things certainly hadn't gone to plan when she'd visited Saima's house that morning.

338

Having convinced herself that she was the one behind the texts, Chloe had expected her to crumble when she turned up — or at least to look awkward and embarrassed, thus confirming her suspicions. Instead, Saima had welcomed her with a big hug and invited her in without question. Her mum had been equally friendly, offering her a drink and a snack; saying how they'd missed having her around the house.

'It's really great to see you,' Saima said once they were alone upstairs — not a hint of guilt showing in her warm smile. 'I've missed you.'

Chloe was tempted to point out that they'd seen each other less than a week ago, on the last day of term, but she knew what Saima meant. They hadn't really talked to each other or spent any time together in ages. Not since Chloe had got friendly with Holly, who'd convinced her that Saima was dull and immature. The three of them had hung around together for a short while at the start of the school year. But the 'two's company, three's a crowd' saying had turned out to be pretty accurate, with Saima being the one to pay the price. They'd ghosted her, effectively, until she got the message that she was no longer wanted. Things had culminated in that one big row and, until today, they'd barely spoken since then.

It was nasty. It was cruel. Chloe knew that, which was why she'd become so convinced that Saima had been the one sending the texts. She had every reason to want to hurt Chloe. What better revenge than this?

But as she asked Saima the question, instantly

darkening the room, she already knew the answer.

It wasn't her.

Saima wasn't like that.

Like them.

Like Chloe and Holly.

She didn't bear grudges. She just missed her best friend, which was why Chloe also knew she wasn't lying when she told her what she'd heard. It made sense when you had all the facts.

Chloe had known Saima for years at primary school. Holly, on the other hand, had only come on to the scene when they'd started at Waterside High last September. And as close as they'd become in that time, Chloe knew that her friend had a vindictive streak. Unfortunately, she'd seen how calculated Holly could be in exacting revenge against those she considered to have 'dissed' her or let her down in some way. Chloe had seen her turn on girls she'd known for years, starting nasty rumours about them, for instance. In one especially memorable case, she'd put posters up around the village proclaiming that an ex-friend of hers was a 'back-stabbing bitch'. Somehow, though, she had a persuasive way of making such actions seem normal — even justified — to those still on her side.

Now that Chloe had had her eyes opened, she realised that the nasty text messages had Holly's fingerprints all over them. How had she not seen it sooner? Well, for one thing, she'd never before been on the receiving end of Holly's wrath. Plus she hadn't given away any clue about being annoyed with her.

Lying on her bed in the present, she picked up her phone. Saima had asked how she was doing.

C: Not great.

S: What are you going to do?

C: I'm not sure. I haven't told her yet that I know.

S: I really am sorry. It sucks to be the messenger. I'm here for you. You know she's a total bitch, right? That's not you, Chloe. She just sucked you in with her BS.

This last comment surprised Chloe a little. It served as a reminder that Saima had a lot more going for her than Holly would like people to think. She was whip-smart and had a real edge to her personality that she only shared with those who knew her best. Her judgment was usually spot-on.

But Chloe needed to talk to someone else about it: someone, unlike Saima, who wasn't twisted up in the whole nasty mess.

Curiously, there was one person who immediately sprang to mind: Elliot.

33

THEN

Saturday, 6 July 1996

Organising a huge house party like that was asking for trouble, but no one could have guessed how much.

People had been talking about it for weeks: Aidan Bloor's sixteenth birthday bash. And yet Lisa had never heard of Aidan before news of the do reached Queen Anne's.

He was in their year, but Elliot barely knew him either.

'He's not in my form and I've never had any classes with him,' he'd told her. 'Since announcing this party, Aidan's gone from being nobody to the most talked about boy in school. It's not even his birthday. That was in May, apparently.'

It was an open invite — everyone welcome.

'Are you going?' Lisa had asked El.

'Yeah, I'm staying at Neil's, which is nearby. What about you?'

'I'll see if I can stay at Hayley's.'

It was a miracle that Aidan's parents hadn't found out what he was planning. They were in Italy for a fortnight, Lisa had heard. His grandparents had moved in to look after him. But this weekend they had a trip of their own planned to London, meaning he was home alone.

The house was massive. It was a three-storey Victorian mansion in one of Westwich's most desirable neighbourhoods, with large walled gardens front and rear.

As she approached it, Lisa wondered what the hell Aidan was thinking. Why invite so many kids to such a fancy place? There was bound to be lots of underage drinking going on — hardly a good combination. As it happened, Lisa was on antibiotics for a bladder infection that had only recently started to clear up, so she was steering clear of alcohol. She had considered dropping out, but such a buzz had built up around this party, she couldn't bring herself to miss it.

Plus there was a boy she was hoping to see. Jake Prentice was a sprinter on the King George's athletics team. He was in her year but had only joined the school in January. He'd previously lived in Hertfordshire, but his family had relocated due to his dad's job: something Lisa understood from her own experience of moving.

It was this subject that had sparked their first conversation, at an athletics meet a couple of weeks earlier, and they'd spoken by phone several times since. She felt a flutter in her stomach every time she thought about him, with his mischievous grin, high cheekbones and piercing gaze. She'd also had the pleasure of seeing him with his top off after he'd won his last race.

She entered the house with Hayley and two

other girls from her class. Aidan opened the door. Eyes glazed with cider, judging by the bottle in his grip, he made a show of welcoming them, kissing each of their hands and proclaiming how beautiful they looked.

At that stage, before it got busy, Lisa noted how immaculate everything looked, from the well-appointed kitchen to the luxurious cream lounge carpet.

A couple of hours later, by which time the front door had been wedged open and the party had spilled over on to the front and rear lawns, Aidan was like a different boy. He was tearing around, from one mishap to the next, pulling his hair out as he realised how quickly things had spiralled out of control.

He was still drunk. That was obvious from the way he was slurring his words and flailing his arms around, having a go at people.

'Someone's going to end up punching him in the face,' Hayley said, sipping on a bottle of Hooch in the kitchen and then cheering as 'Roll with It' by Oasis thundered on to the stereo.

'What did he expect?' Lisa shouted into Hayley's ear. 'Of course people are going to spill things and be sick in the bathroom. It's a party.'

Not that Lisa had attended a party quite like this before. It reminded her of something out of an American movie: one of those high school comedies from the eighties like *Teen Wolf* or *Pretty in Pink*. There might not have been any kegs of beer, but there was plenty of lager, cider and alcopops.

It was weird, in her sober state, seeing the

others inebriated. She'd only briefly spoken to Elliot so far, but he'd arrived with a pack of beer. From the loud, confident way he'd been talking, she assumed he'd had some on the way.

As for Jake, who'd said he was looking forward to seeing her here, she'd not run into him yet.

'I'm going for a wander,' she told Hayley. 'You coming?'

She shook her head, nodding towards an indie kid by the stereo and puckering her lips.

Entering the lounge, where a different stereo was pumping out the electronic sound of The Chemical Brothers, Lisa winced at a large pinkish red stain in the cream carpet, which someone — surely Aidan — had covered in salt. She felt a hand on her shoulder and turned around to see Neil Walsh smiling at her. 'Don't worry, Lisa. It's not blood. Someone thought it would be funny to open a bottle of Aidan's dad's best wine. That happened as he tried to wrestle it off them.'

She and Neil had remained friends after their brief relationship had fizzled out. This was no doubt partly because of Elliot. Plus, more than three and a half years had passed since then. It was ancient history.

Ducking her head and looking furtively from side to side, Lisa mocked: 'Our host isn't in here any more, is he? Last time I spotted him, he seemed ready to blow a gasket.'

Neil laughed. 'No, the coast is clear for now. He's probably relocating the rest of the wine to a top secret location.'

'Is Aidan a friend of yours?'

'I hardly know him, to be honest.'

'That's what Elliot said.'

'Yeah, neither of us has any lessons with him. He's usually a quiet guy who keeps himself to himself. I know it's his house and everything, but he arranged the party. You'd think we'd all turned up unannounced by the way he's acting.'

'Where is El?'

'Drowning his sorrows in the back garden.'

'What do you mean?'

Neil grimaced. 'Hasn't he told you yet? Claire broke up with him today.'

'You're joking! How come?'

'She took him to one side at that outdoor club they go to and said she'd started seeing another lad from where she lives. He's gutted, obviously.'

'Nightmare. I'd better find him.'

'How about a quick drink first? I like your outfit. Brings out your eyes.'

'What, my jeans and band T-shirt?' She nudged him with her elbow. 'I see you're still a shameless flirt. Better save it for someone who's not an ex.'

Lisa had kept her outfit simple, despite wanting to impress Jake. She had the feeling that playing it cool, like they were good mates, was the best way to get him interested. So she hadn't called him last night either, despite saying she would. That wasn't to say she hadn't spent ages fixing her make-up and getting her hair just right in pigtail plaits. Plus she knew how much her tight T-shirt emphasised her bust. Neil had barely looked anywhere else.

She headed to the garden to find Elliot,

hoping to bump into Jake on the way.

As she walked through the hallway, which was littered with crisp packets, plastic cups and empty cans, a cupboard door under the staircase swung open into her path.

'Careful!' she said, coming face to face with a wild-eyed Aidan. 'Oh, it's you. What are you doing in there?'

'Please don't say anything,' he whispered, squinting anxiously at a queue of people outside the nearby toilet. 'I was hiding some stuff in the cellar, but I don't want anyone to know.'

'Your secret's safe with me.'

'Have we met before? You look familiar.'

'You let me in earlier. It's Lisa.'

He nodded. 'You're not looking for somewhere to throw up, are you? Please go outside, if you are.'

Before Lisa could reply, his attention was diverted by the sound of another boy calling his name as he ran down the stairs. 'Where are you, Aidan? You need to see this. There's a group of lads from Westwich High turned up at the top of the drive.'

All remnants of colour drained from Aidan's face at this latest bombshell.

'I'd better let you go,' Lisa muttered. She felt guilty as she shuffled away, but what else was she supposed to do?

The spacious back garden was dominated by a well-manicured lawn. This was occupied by various groups of kids sitting in circles, drinking, smoking, chatting and laughing. There were several couples sitting apart from the rest, getting

347

to know each other with their lips inter-locked.

A path of stone slabs wound its way through the middle to an oval fish pond and, beyond, a large shed and green-house. One of Aidan's parents was obviously a keen gardener, Lisa thought, remembering another small, wood-framed greenhouse at the front, next to the driveway.

The high perimeter walls were flanked with an array of shrubs, flowers and small trees. But it was a larger tree near the rear of the garden to which Lisa's eyes were drawn, as she spotted the unmistakeable figure of Elliot sprawled across a broad lower branch, knocking back another can of beer. He'd announced a couple of months ago that he was growing his hair long, but being so curly, this was a slow process. It looked like there was a dense black cloud hovering over his head.

She walked to the foot of the tree and called up to her friend. 'What's going on?'

El peered down at her, eyes red and unfocused, before taking another swig from his can, half of it spilling down his chin and neck. 'Oh, it's you,' he spluttered, sitting up and wiping away the excess beer with one hand.

'Hi. I hear that alcohol and tree climbing aren't considered a good combination.'

'It looked like a nice place to chill,' Elliot slurred, running a hand through his thick mop of hair.

'Better than the grass?'

'Less people.'

Elliot rummaged around in a pocket of his jeans before pulling out a pack of cigarettes and sticking one in his mouth.

'Since when do you smoke?'

'Since now. They help with weight loss, you know. Added bonus.' He searched several more pockets until he pulled out a plastic green lighter.

'They also kill you, El.'

'Hmm.' He lit the cigarette, took a drag, coughed and jerked backwards, like he was about to fall. Lisa's heart was in her mouth.

'Want one?' he asked, having steadied himself. 'They taste okay once you get used to them.'

'No, thanks. It wouldn't exactly help my running.'

'That hasn't stopped Jake Prentice,' Elliot said. 'He's King George's new star athlete. The head was raving about his talent in assembly, but I saw him puffing away a few minutes ago. Have you met him? He's very good-looking.'

Lisa didn't answer. She was already aware that Jake smoked; now she knew he was here, which was good news. But first Elliot needed her. She hadn't said anything to him so far about Jake. She hadn't even mentioned that they knew each other. It wasn't that she was hiding it from him. It was all part of her playing it cool strategy. She hadn't even told her girlfriends yet. Well, apart from Hayley, who'd dragged it out of her when they were getting ready earlier.

Mind you, she and Elliot didn't discuss each other's relationships a great deal these days. It was something they'd both steered away from after their fallout last year involving her ex, Sean Ferguson. Not that they avoided the subject

349

altogether. As friends, that would be impossible, but they didn't tend to dwell on it or go into great detail.

Elliot hadn't given any indication that his relationship with Claire wasn't working out. They'd been together for ages. Lisa had even met her a few times, although she hadn't found her particularly friendly. All the same, she'd been glad to see her friend happy, which clearly was no longer the case.

'Budge up,' Lisa said. 'If you're not coming down, I'm coming up.'

Soon she was perched next to Elliot on the branch, one arm strategically placed behind him, to hopefully prevent any accidents, and the other gripping the thick trunk.

Elliot offered her a swig of his beer, which she declined. 'You seem very sober,' he said.

'I'm on antibiotics, remember.'

'Oh yeah. Are you feeling better?'

'I'm fine. It's you I'm worried about, El.' She paused before adding: 'I was talking to Neil. He, um, told me what happened with Claire. I'm sorry. Do you want to talk about it?'

'Not really. I think I'd rather drink and smoke some more, although . . . . I actually feel a bit — '

Elliot bent forward, dropping his beer and vomiting all over the grass below. He narrowly missed one of the couples, who'd taken a break from snogging to walk hand in hand back to the house.

'Sorry,' Elliot mumbled.

The girl, a pretty blonde Lisa recognised from the year below at Queen Anne's but couldn't name, turned around and looked up at them, frowning. 'Yuck! That's gross and it almost landed on us. Can't you puke in a bush like a normal person?'

When the boy walking with her turned around too, Lisa's heart skipped a beat. 'Jake,' she exclaimed.

'Hi, Lisa,' he replied, the calmness of his voice doing nothing to douse the flames of fury raging through her mind. 'What are you doing up there with Turner?'

Lisa, who would never get used to the way so many of the boys called each other by their surnames, forced herself to smile. 'We're just having some fun.'

It was a comment designed to give Jake the wrong idea: a desperate attempt at retaliation.

Jake smirked. 'Looks like he's had enough.' Blondie stood on her tiptoes to whisper something into his ear. Then they continued towards the house.

'So you do know him, then,' Elliot said.

The last thing Lisa wanted now, feeling sorry for herself and stupid, was to tell Elliot the full story. She was racking her brains trying to work out what had happened. Had she played it too cool, not giving enough signals that she was interested? Was it because she hadn't called Jake yesterday? He'd seemed so keen for her to come to the party, and yet he hadn't looked remotely guilty at being 'caught' with another girl. Dammit.

Realising that Elliot was staring at her expectantly, waiting for an answer, she replied:

'Yeah, I've spoken to him a few times at athletics. Are you friends?'

'We have a few classes together. He's okay; a bit full of himself. Who was the girl?'

'I don't know.'

'She doesn't go to Queen Anne's?'

'She does, but I don't know her name. She's in the year below. You're very chatty all of a sudden. Feeling better?'

'Yes.' He paused to hiccup. 'Although I'm still totally depressed about Claire. Bitch.'

She offered him a chewing gum, which he accepted. 'Are you going to tell me what happened?'

'She found someone better: a guy from her own school. She's been seeing him for a couple of weeks.'

'Someone else,' Lisa said, giving her friend a gentle hug, careful to keep them both steady on the tree branch. 'But definitely not someone better. It's her loss, El. If she doesn't realise how great you are, you're better off without her.'

Elliot sniffed, hiccupping again and wiping away a tear. 'Thanks. Doesn't feel like that, though.'

'What do you say we continue this conversation on the ground?' Lisa wasn't exactly comfortable perched in the tree, fearful that a sudden boozy move could send them both tumbling.

'Why? It's like old times. How long is it since we've climbed a tree together?'

'A while. I still remember the first time. It ended with me racing that idiot across the field

352

to get your clothes and shoes back.'

Elliot half-laughed, half-hiccupped. 'Now here you are again, helping me. I'm like the damsel in distress in this relationship, aren't I? And you're the knight in shining armour, always saving me.'

Lisa shook her head. 'What are you on about, El? Come down with me and I'll show you a great way to get rid of those hiccups.'

'I will. But let me say one thing first.'

'Go on then.'

Raising his right forefinger dramatically, he said: 'One day — mark my words — I will be the one to save you, Lisa Benson. Maybe not today, maybe not tomorrow, but — '

'Come on with you, Humphrey Bogart. Let's get down.'

Lisa went first, making it to the grass in a few nimble moves. Elliot, in his inebriated state, slipped and fell the last bit, ending up flat on his back at the foot of the tree trunk.

Lisa knelt at his side, surprised to see that his eyes were closed. Even though common sense told her it wasn't high enough to do any damage, she felt her heart race. 'Elliot? Are you okay?'

Her face was right in front of his when his eyelids popped open and, before she knew what was happening, he raised his head off the ground and kissed her full on the lips.

Time froze for an instant as their eyes met and the kiss lingered.

Then Lisa came to her senses. 'Eww, you just puked,' she said, pulling away. 'And you've been smoking.'

'That's why I didn't open my mouth,' Elliot

slurred, wearing an inane grin. 'I even held my breath.'

Lisa wanted to tell him that it still didn't taste nice — and to query what he was thinking, kissing her in the first place — but she didn't have the heart.

'Come on. Let's go in the house and get you some water. You need sobering up.'

She got to her feet and, turning away, subtly wiped her mouth with the back of her hand.

There was a loud noise from the front of the house, like an engine revving. It continued for several seconds, only to be replaced by a brief screeching, then a crash and the unmistakeable sound of shattering glass. Lots of it.

'What on earth was that?' a boy nearby said. But before anyone could answer, there was more revving and screeching, followed by what sounded like a car racing full throttle into the distance.

'Get out!' a high-pitched voice yelled from inside the house. 'All of you — get the hell out!'

Lisa looked at Elliot, who was back on his feet, and bit the side of her lip. 'That doesn't sound good.'

His eyes were stretched like CDs, trained on something happening behind her.

She turned back towards the house and gasped. Aidan was standing in the back doorway, his mouth twisted into something halfway between a manic grin and a snarl. He was brandishing a cricket bat.

He scanned the gawping crowd for a long moment. Then came that high-pitched voice

354

again, raw and animalistic. 'I. Said. Get. Out. Everyone. Now!'

No one moved. They were all in shock, Lisa guessed, trying to process what was going on.

Aidan let out a guttural war cry and, swinging the bat wildly from side to side, ran into the middle of the lawn. Suddenly everyone was pouring back into the house and following the hallway out through the front door.

Lisa grabbed Elliot's hand, pulling him along with the rest of them. She remembered hearing about the group of high school lads turning up earlier, guessing that this had to be significant.

As they exited the front door, Lisa had to blink to confirm that what she was seeing was real. The greenhouse near the driveway had been smashed to pieces. It had been demolished, razed to the ground. All that remained was a heap of glass shards, broken wood from the framework, smashed terracotta pots and various squashed plants. Bizarrely, there was also a colourful selection of women's clothes — everything from party dresses to petticoats — piled on top of a bush at the very front of the house.

'What?' Elliot said, looking from one unbelievable sight to the other, shaking his head and rubbing his eyes.

'I have absolutely no idea.'

The clothing, presumably belonging to Aidan's poor mother, must have been thrown out of an upstairs bedroom directly above the bush. For although the large sash window was now closed, a bright yellow skirt and pink bra remained trapped in it, flapping against the brickwork in the breeze.

Lisa spotted Jake and Blondie among those still mingling, bemused in the front garden. Dragging Elliot with her, and careful not to step into any debris from the greenhouse, she approached them. 'What happened?'

Jake shrugged. 'These pissed-up lads from the high school arrived and got into a row with Aidan and some of the others. They had history, apparently. A couple of them got inside and went upstairs, ransacking his parents' bedroom; throwing all that stuff outside. Then some older lads arrived in a blue Volvo and rammed the greenhouse before they all made off. It's mental.'

Lisa didn't know what to say. How had she and Elliot missed all of this?

Blondie was tugging on Jake's hand, saying they needed to leave before the police arrived.

'Has someone called them?' Lisa asked.

'Aidan said he had,' Jake replied. 'That was what finally got them to leave. Well, him swinging that cricket bat around like a lunatic probably had something to do with it too. They'll never get away with it. Not with all these witnesses.'

'I wouldn't want to be Aidan when his parents get home,' Elliot added.

As Jake and most of the others disappeared down the driveway into the street, Lisa convinced El to help her pick up the clothes. It felt like the right thing to do.

Gingerly, they carried them inside. They found Aidan sitting on the bottom of the stairs, head in hands and the cricket bat at his feet. He appeared to be the only one left in the house.

Lisa cleared her throat, causing him to look up. 'Should we take this stuff upstairs?'

The fire had gone out of his eyes, which were red with tears. 'Thanks,' he rasped. 'Leave them there, please.'

'Can we help with anything else?' Elliot asked.

'No. I want to be alone.'

Lisa nodded at the bat. 'You might want to put that away before the police get here.'

'I didn't really call them. I'm in enough trouble already.'

As the pair turned out of the driveway on to the street, discussing how best to catch up with the friends they were each staying with, Elliot slipped his arm around Lisa's waist. 'Thanks for earlier. Sorry about, um, you know — '

'It's fine. Are you feeling less drunk?'

'I think so. My hiccups have gone.'

'A bit less sad about — '

He raised a hand. 'Don't say her name.'

'Fine, I won't. At least you're not Aidan, though.'

'True.'

'God, what a nightmare. How long do you think he'll be grounded for?'

'At least a few years, I reckon. Plenty of time to practise his batting skills in the garden.' He laughed in that seal-like way of his.

Lisa giggled. 'You're evil.'

34

NOW

Wednesday, 25 July 2018

Elliot arrived at The Swan in the nick of time. Well, a moment too late really, but soon enough to stop things getting badly out of hand.

Walking through the door, he was greeted with the sight of Mike taking on a couple of men at the bar. Fists were already flying — although not necessarily landing where intended — while an elderly staff member looked on open-mouthed, apparently clueless how to deal with the fracas.

The fight appeared to have just started, based on the fact that a staggering Mike was still standing, despite being outnumbered by younger, fitter guys who clearly hadn't drunk as much as him. He was a bulky guy, but Elliot didn't fancy his chances in this particular bout.

There was only one thing for it.

'Oi!' he shouted, loudly enough to get the attention of all present, upon which he waved a hand in their direction and commanded: 'Stop fighting right now, all of you. Mike, sit down. You other two: get your stuff and leave straight away. Don't come back.'

They did as he asked, of course, while the old guy shuffled towards the bar, shaking his head but saying nothing.

Once the two young men had gone, Elliot picked up a bar stool that had been knocked over in the scuffle. He took a seat next to Mike. 'So are you going to tell me what's going on?'

Mike reached for his pint, which had somehow survived the fight unscathed, with a shaky hand. He took a long swig.

Elliot realised the pub probably wasn't the best place to talk if he wanted to get any sense out of him. 'I think you might have had enough, mate.' This drew a scowl from Mike. 'Hey, I'm not judging you,' he added. 'We've all done it, but you nearly got your head kicked in then.'

'I could have taken those two idiots.'

'Maybe. Maybe not. Why the hell were you fighting them at all?'

'They were asking for it. Winding me up. How did you get them to leave? That was weird. You walked in and — '

Elliot shrugged. 'I guess I have a look of authority about me.'

A thickset man with an easy confidence that marked him out as the landlord appeared from a backroom behind the bar. 'Right, I'm done in the cellar,' he told his elderly employee, who was still shaking his head, looking dazed. 'What's up? You look like you've seen a ghost.'

'Come on, let's get out of here,' Elliot said under his breath, not wanting to be around when the pub boss found out what had unfolded in his absence.

He took the lead, glad to see no sign of Mike's new 'friends' outside.

'Why are you heading that way?' Mike asked,

coming to a standstill as Elliot set off in the opposite direction to home. 'Aren't we going back to the house?'

'I told you, we're going for a walk.' His hand twitched, ready to assist if necessary, but he held back, preferring not to force the issue. He hoped that in his inebriated state Mike would be compliant, particularly in light of just being rescued.

Elliot pressed on along the pavement and, sure enough, Mike followed. 'Wait up,' he said. 'I thought you meant the walk home.'

'No, better you steer clear for a bit.'

'How come?'

'Lisa's not best pleased about you going AWOL. If you turn up in that state, you'll get yourself into more trouble.'

'She's not the boss of me,' he declared, nearly tripping over his own feet. Hiccupping, he added: 'And what exactly happened between the two of you today? You better not have tried anything, or — '

Elliot steadied him. 'Easy, tiger. Of course I didn't try anything. That's not why I'm here. Lisa is your wife and the last thing I'd ever want would be to come between you. She's just dealing with a couple of things at home, that's all.'

'Like what?'

'I'll fill you in as we walk,' Elliot said, changing the subject to buy himself some time. 'I hear you had some problems with your laptop.'

'How do you know that?'

'Ben mentioned it when Lisa and I got back

360

from visiting our old schools. He asked me to have a look.'

'It's ruined, right?'

'No, I don't think so. I managed to get it working again.'

Mike's eyes lit up. 'Seriously?'

'Seriously.'

'But I didn't save — '

'The document you were working on?'

'Exactly.'

'It didn't happen to be a plot synopsis for a screenplay, just shy of two thousand words, did it?'

'Yes! Was it still there?'

'It had auto-saved, lucky for you. I saved it properly and backed up a copy.' Elliot handed him a USB stick.

Mike gawped at him before taking it. 'There's a copy on here?'

'Yes. I hope you don't mind, but I read a little. It sounded very interesting.'

Mike patted him on the back, thanking him repeatedly and beaming as only a happy drunk can. He was doing a decent job of keeping up with Elliot now, following him without hesitation as he turned from one street to another. 'So you liked it?'

'I did, Mike. Is that what you want to do: write screenplays?'

'I'd love to. I've always been interested in it, but . . . I don't know, it's a pipe dream, isn't it? Where are we going, by the way?'

'You'll see. Why's it a pipe dream? Every first-time writer has to start somewhere. A wise man once told me that you can achieve anything if you want it badly enough; the main obstacle is yourself. He was the one who convinced me to follow my dream of starting my own tech firm. He's a very persuasive man, Ian, my stepdad.'

'He's Australian, right? Lisa said he was the reason you and your mum moved there.'

'Yep. As I said, he's very persuasive — one reason he's so successful. He was visiting on business when he met Mum. He fell and broke his leg during the trip. She was his nurse and, well, the rest is history. We'd only known him for a few months when we first went out there. It was a leap of faith. Plenty of people thought we'd be back soon enough, tails between our legs, but Ian and Mum are still very happy. They're perfect for each other.'

Elliot stopped talking and looked at Mike, who was trailing behind him again, staring at the ground. Shit. It dawned on him how that might sound to Mike: like his visit now was similar to Ian's all those years ago; like he was hoping to persuade Lisa to move to Australia to be with him. He knew Mike saw him as a threat, but he wanted to change that today, not make it worse.

He needed Mike on board, so it was time to let him in on the truth — some of it, at least.

'Here we are,' he said, stopping outside a small dormer bungalow. There were plenty of little changes and modernisations from how he remembered it: new windows and doors; different coloured paint and a front garden packed with far more shrubs and flowers than there used to be. He'd seen it like this before

362

online, although it still felt weird in person, bringing back a sea of memories, both good and bad. He'd nearly come here a few times during his visit, but he'd always found a reason not to, until now.

'I don't get it,' Mike said. 'Where's here exactly? It's just another street in Aldham.'

Elliot took a deep breath. He looked over at Mike, hoping he wasn't too drunk to understand what he was about to say. Never mind. If he was, he'd repeat himself until it sank in. 'This is where I used to live; the home I grew up in.' He gestured towards the modest house, thinking how tiny it looked compared to how he remembered it and to where he'd lived for the last two decades.

'This is where Lisa saved my life, which is the reason I'm back now. I'm here to repay that debt.'

35

THEN

Saturday, 21 February 1998

'You look nice,' Elliot told his mum as she walked into the lounge, having spent ages upstairs getting dolled up.

'Thanks, love,' she said, her eyes sparkling.

'Is the dress one of your creations?'

'Naturally.'

She did a twirl, making Elliot smile.

'You really like this guy, don't you?'

Wendy held a hand up to her mouth to hide her excited grin. 'Is it that obvious?'

He chuckled. 'Yep, but I'm glad for you.'

Her face turned serious for a moment as she held her cool palm up to Elliot's cheek. 'That means a lot, darling. It really does. You like him too, right?'

He smiled. 'You know I do, Mum. You make a great couple. Now how are you getting there?'

'Ian's sending me a car.'

'A taxi?'

'Something like that.' Blushing, she turned her head to look out of the window. 'It'll be here any minute, so I need to get my shoes and coat on. Is Lisa coming round?'

'Don't think so.' He pulled a face. 'She has a date. She said she might call in afterwards, but

364

I'm not holding my breath.'

'Ooh, who's the date with?'

'Some guy called Alex who works for her dad. He's new: a nineteen-year-old hotshot car salesman. He asked her out last night while she was waiting for her dad to finish work at the dealership. He's taking her for dinner at that new Italian on Manchester Road.'

'Really? He has Graham's approval, then?'

'Yeah, right. Lisa hasn't even told her dad yet. It's anyone's guess where he thinks she's going.'

Wendy shook her head. 'You know how much I love Lisa, but she shouldn't lie to her parents. You'll never do that to me, will you?'

'No, Mum.'

She winked. 'Good boy. Why don't you go and see one of your friends from school? You can borrow the car, as long as you promise to drive carefully.'

'Thanks, Mum, but I'm happy to stay in and watch TV.'

She squinted at her son. 'You're not still pining over that Sarah girl, are you?'

She was talking about his ex-girlfriend, if you could call her that. They'd met at a party a few weeks ago and had been out a couple of times — once to play mini golf and then to see *Titanic* at the cinema — before she lost interest. She was in the year below him at Waterside, the local comprehensive where Jamie went to school. She was gorgeous, which was why he'd taken it so badly when she'd dumped him by phone last weekend. She'd blamed it on having too much school work and no time for a boyfriend, but

Jamie said he'd seen her holding hands with another lad this week, so that was clearly a lie.

He'd never been out with someone that fit before. She was beautiful — way out of his league — and he'd quickly become besotted with her. He'd been blown away when she'd shown an interest in him at the party; even more so when they'd ended up spending the last hour snogging in a corner. He'd made the mistake of bragging about her to his schoolmates, which had backfired when she'd finished with him. He hadn't got around to telling any of them this last part, but he knew he'd have to — sooner rather than later — or risk getting found out and looking even more stupid.

All of this plus the fact that she'd never met her was why Wendy called her 'that Sarah girl'. At least his mum was happy. She was head over heels in love with 'this Ian bloke', as Elliot amused himself by thinking of him.

'What are you grinning about?' she asked him when she returned in her coat.

'Oh, nothing.'

She'd only met Ian Kay, a scarily wealthy Australian businessman, at the start of January, but things had moved really fast between them. He'd been inspecting some building site when he'd fallen and broken his leg. Ian had been rushed to the nearest hospital, where he'd spent the night on a ward, nursed by Wendy. There'd been an instant attraction between them, despite the fact he was nine years older. He'd even refused to be moved to a private hospital in order to stay close to her. And by the time he came to be released, he'd decided to extend his trip to the UK for an indefinite period while his leg healed.

He and his assistant — a man called Larry, who was rarely far from his side — were now living in a rented house in the countryside, a short drive from Aldham. It was a mansion really, with tennis courts and an underground swimming pool. Elliot didn't know exactly how wealthy Ian was, but his actions spoke for themselves.

Wendy had liked him from day one, and it was nothing to do with his money. She hadn't stopped talking about how much he made her laugh with his little jokes and funny comments. Ever the professional, though, she'd refused to entertain his advances — politely rejecting flowers and other gifts — until he was no longer her patient.

She'd had a few short-lived relationships in recent times, but Elliot had never heard Wendy talk about any of them with such enthusiasm. So it hadn't surprised him when she and Ian became romantically involved. What had surprised him was the mansion, because he didn't have a clue about Ian's extreme financial status until then. Wendy had never mentioned it.

Elliot had met Ian several times now and he also really liked him. A tall, tanned chap with short white hair, who looked in great shape for his forty-seven years, Ian had a magnetic personality. He was full of warmth and always smiling; never rushed, despite Larry permanently fending off phone calls for him. Most importantly, he treated Wendy like a queen and spoke to Elliot like an intelligent adult whose opinion he respected.

The only thing that bothered Elliot about the relationship was what the future held. How would his mum deal with Ian's inevitable move back to Sydney, where his home and business were both based?

He'd asked her this a few times, although her response had always been to brush it off with comments about having fun and living in the now. Elliot hadn't said anything, but he'd noticed that she'd recently started wearing her wedding ring on her right hand rather than her left. It was the first time he'd ever seen her do this, which spoke volumes about the serious nature of her feelings for Ian.

There was a knock at the door. 'That'll be my ride,' Wendy said. 'I feel bad about leaving you all on your own. Why don't you come? Ian won't mind.'

'Don't be silly. I'm seventeen years old, Mum. I'll be fine. What are the two of you doing tonight, anyway?'

She shrugged. 'I've no idea. It's a surprise.'

Elliot stood up to give her a farewell hug and kiss. 'Have a great time. Don't do anything I wouldn't do.'

This made her giggle. 'You silly sausage. Love you. See you later. I'll try not to be too late.'

Peering around the curtain to check out her ride, he wasn't entirely surprised to see a white stretch limo. Ian certainly enjoyed grand gestures.

Not that Elliot was jealous. He had plans of

one else was likely to be outside, he wondered whether hiding here was strictly necessary. But better safe than sorry.

Even more lightheaded than normal after a fag, thanks to the JD, he went back inside. He put the extinguished cigarette butt in the kitchen bin, making a mental note to take the bag outside later to cover his tracks.

He poured some more JD into his glass, added a couple of ice cubes and plenty of cola, and took the drink back to the lounge to watch TV. Not that there was anything good on, unless you liked *Noel's House Party*.

If only they had Sky, like Lisa did. Then he could have watched MTV or any number of cool channels. But Wendy wasn't interested. She said it was a waste of money they didn't have and five channels was plenty.

So he turned the video player on and stuck in *Goldfinger*, his favourite James Bond film, which he'd recorded last time it was on the box.

Settling back on the couch, he took a big swig of his drink, which definitely tasted much better with cola. For the first time that week he felt relaxed and, dare he think it, happy. Sarah dumping him had even overshadowed his recent Mock A-level results: two As and a high B. Wendy had been almost as excited by this as she had when he'd got all As in his GCSEs, despite him emphasising that mocks counted for nothing. She'd wanted to take him out for dinner to celebrate last weekend, but he'd pretended not to feel well, although he had a feeling she knew the truth. Anyway, he was celebrating now on his own terms.

He just had to be careful not to get too drunk or he ran the risk of getting caught when his mum got home. Mind you, she probably wouldn't be back until late.

Plenty of time to enjoy himself, in other words.

36

THEN

Saturday, 21 February 1998

Lisa leaned over towards the driver's seat to give Alex a peck on the cheek before he got any other ideas. 'Thanks for dinner.'

'You're welcome,' he replied with that smarmy, self-satisfied grin that had been plastered across his face all evening. 'But wait,' he added as she reached for the door handle. 'Aren't we going to have a cheeky snog?'

'No, I never kiss on the first date,' she lied. This was a courtesy because Alex had paid for dinner. It wasn't to spare his feelings, as she got the distinct impression his confidence was bulletproof.

He winked. 'Yeah, right. So why did you ask me to pull in here, rather than in front of your house?'

'For your sake. Dad would fire you if he knew we'd been out together.'

Alex raised an eyebrow. 'You didn't tell him?'

'You don't know him very well yet, do you?'

He winked, making her squirm as he placed a slimy hand on her knee. 'He loves me. I'm his number one salesman.'

'Well, let me tell you, he loves his daughter more. Sorry, got to go.'

She opened the car door and slid out, glad to escape that hand before it had the chance to travel elsewhere, the thought of which made her want to vomit. Like she'd ever snog him, with that custard breath he had. No, she'd had quite enough of that over dinner.

She pursed her lips into a tight almost-smile. 'Goodnight.'

'It's been fun, Lisa. We should do this again. You do kiss on the second date, right?'

Ignoring this last comment, she walked slowly towards her house. Then once he'd driven away, she turned and headed for Elliot's place, where her parents thought she'd been all night.

She wished that she had been with Elliot all night. It would have been far more fun that an evening listening to Alex's 'hilarious' tales of car sales. It was like being out with a younger version of her dad, for goodness' sake. She'd only agreed to it in the first place because he was quite fit. The problem was that he really knew it. She'd even caught him checking out his reflection in the restaurant window several times during the date. Plus he'd been so busy talking about himself that he'd barely asked her anything.

No, Lisa was definitely never going on another date with Alex. She'd just have to avoid the dealership for a bit. It probably wouldn't take him long to move on, anyway.

She looked at her watch: 9.56 p.m. She hoped that El would still be pleased to see her at this time. Surely he wouldn't have got through all of that JD by himself. She'd be happy to help him with a glass or two, as long as there was a mixer involved.

She huddled into her thick winter coat as she walked along the pavement. Her gloveless hands were buried deep in the side pockets and her mouth was tucked under the top of the zip, slowly blowing warm air on to her icy chin. Lisa was nearly there now. She couldn't wait to get out of the cold. The pavement was already white with frost and everyone's parked cars were iced up. Roll on spring, she thought.

The lights were on in the front room at El's place, with the curtains only partially closed, so for fun she sneaked up to the window and peeked through to see what her friend was doing.

'You lightweight, El,' she said, laughing to herself, when she spotted him asleep on the couch. His face was partially covered by the unruly mop of his shoulder-length curly hair, which for once wasn't tied back in a ponytail. There was a half-drunk glass of what looked like JD and cola on the coffee table.

She tapped on the glass and called: 'Wake up, loser! It's time to get this party started.'

He stirred at this, shifting into a new position on the sofa, but despite Lisa knocking again, he didn't wake up. He must have got pretty drunk already. For a moment she considered calling it a night and leaving him to sleep. But then she thought of the trouble El would get into if Wendy got home and he was still like that, with the bottle of JD and, most likely, a pack of cigarettes left out for her to discover.

People who passed out from drinking could also choke on their own vomit, couldn't they? Oh God. There was no way she could leave him now.

Lisa turned and walked down the side of the house to the back door. It was unlocked, as usual. When she opened it, her heart stopped.

Shit. The house reeked of burning and a grey-coloured smoke was curling out of the kitchen into the hallway. Lisa hesitated for a moment at the open doorway, racking her brains for advice she'd heard about fires, but nothing came.

'El!' she called at the top of her lungs. 'Elliot, wake up, there's a fire!'

There was no reply. No indication that he'd heard her.

Dammit. Should she go in or call for help?

Where would she even get access to a phone?

She'd have to bang on one of the neighbours' doors — and then God knows how long it would take before the firefighters arrived. El could be trapped or dead by then.

She could still see all the way through the hallway to the lounge, where she knew he was sleeping.

She needed to get him out of there . . . while she still could.

Her whole body was shaking, but she knew she had to do this.

Her gut told her it was the right move. And yet another voice in her head was screaming not to deliberately enter a burning building.

There's not that much smoke yet, she told

herself, coughing nonetheless. Just do it. Do it now. Every second counts.

Spitting out every swear word she could think of, Lisa unzipped her coat and threw it to one side.

She turned her spinning head away from the open door, sucked in a deep breath of cold air, pulled the bottom of her jumper up over her mouth and nose, and started running.

She tore straight past the kitchen door, which was also open, glancing to see the cause of the smoke as she passed — and immediately wishing she hadn't. Bright orange flames were licking out of the metal litter bin beneath the window; they were starting to spread to the curtain hanging above it. She considered shutting the door, but fearful of doing anything that might make matters worse, she ploughed on through the hall to the lounge.

It was smokier than expected.

Her eyes were already stinging and watery as she ran up to Elliot's side, grabbing his shirt and shaking him, yelling his name.

His head lolled to one side and his eyes opened slightly, but they were glazed and unfocused. 'Wassgoinon?' he slurred. 'Try-intsleeep.' Then he started coughing, which turned into him vomiting all over himself, some of it even splattering on to Lisa.

'Bloody hell!' she shouted, slapping him around the face in a desperate attempt to rouse him. 'How pissed are you? There's a fire. We need to get out.'

But his eyes kept opening and shutting, rolling

around with no sign of any comprehension behind them.

At this point Lisa knew there was only one way she was getting him out of here alive — by force. Dragging him was likely to be too slow and thus too risky, so carrying him was the only option. There was a reason they called it a fireman's lift, she thought, kneeling in front of the sofa, grabbing her friend under the armpits, pulling him towards her and over her shoulder, and then fighting to stand up.

God, he felt heavy. Twice Lisa's knees buckled as she tried to stand up with him, gasping for breath but finding only dirty air entering her lungs, which weakened rather than strengthened her, making her cough and splutter. But finally, with a determined, animalistic cry, she did it. She got to her feet, Elliot slumped over her right shoulder, and stumbled back to the hall, using her free left arm to steady herself against the wall.

The smoke was thickening, but thankfully Lisa could still see her way through to the back door. She focused on the thought of that cold, clear air outside and, ignoring El's drunken gurgling, she lumbered on.

Passing the kitchen again was the really scary part, as the flames had spread right across the curtains now, which were well ablaze. The smoke was pumping out thick and fast, and the heat was rising to sauna levels.

She couldn't get past it and out of the back door quick enough, almost tripping in the process. But somehow she managed to stay upright.

And then they were outside.

The icy air felt amazing on her face.

Her body was crying out to drop Elliot now, but she needed to get him to a safe distance first, while she had some momentum. So she kept going until she reached the pavement, and then into the next door neighbour's front garden, where finally she let Elliot drop on to the frosty grass and took a moment to catch her breath.

'Are you all right, El?' she asked, kneeling over him and still panting from the exertion. Her shoulders and back felt light in the absence of her friend's weight but ached from the strain she'd put them through.

There was sick all over his clothes and in his hair. Barely conscious, he gurgled something she didn't understand. At least he was outside.

The smell of smoke was everywhere now. She looked up and could see it billowing out of the open back door. Shit. She had to raise the alarm before the whole house went up.

'Stay here,' she told Elliot, who clearly wasn't going anywhere. 'I'll be back for you in a minute.'

She raced to the neighbour's front door and frantically rang the bell, thumping her fist against the wood and shouting for help.

Finally the outside light came on and then the door opened. They were both there — the elderly couple that Lisa recognised from retrieving balls and so on from their garden. Their faces were angry until their eyes landed on her and they saw that something was seriously wrong.

'Next door's on fire,' she said. 'I got Elliot out, but he's in a state. There's flames and smoke and

I don't know what to do. Please get help.'

As she said this, in one long garbled breath, the man dashed to the phone to call the fire brigade.

His wide-eyed wife started asking Lisa questions, but it was too much for her to handle. Her legs gave way and she crumbled on to the doorstep, erupting into a coughing fit.

Kneeling down and helping her into a sitting position against the door, the woman said: 'You poor thing. You're shattered. Come on, we need to get you inside.'

'No,' Lisa panted, trying but failing to stand up again. 'First Elliot.'

In desperation, she pointed at her friend's body slumped in the garden; the woman, noticing him for the first time, held her hand up to her mouth and gasped.

'Don't panic. I think . . . he's just drunk,' Lisa said, hoping she was right. And then, without warning, the tears started to flow. 'I couldn't wake him up,' she sobbed. 'I was so scared, I — '

'The fire brigade's on the way,' the husband said. 'Any idea how it started?'

'I'm not sure,' Lisa replied. 'I just turned up, saw all the smoke and ran in there to get my friend out.' She remembered seeing the kitchen bin well ablaze and had a bad feeling it might have been something to do with El smoking and leaving a fag butt in there, but the last thing she wanted to do was point the finger of blame.

All of a sudden, Lisa felt dizzy and nauseous. 'I think I'm going to . . . '

Everything went black.

37

NOW

Wednesday, 25 July 2018

'So Lisa carried you out of a burning building?' Mike asked Elliot for a second time, shaking his head in disbelief.

'Yep,' Elliot replied. 'Right here. I was overweight then too. It was some feat.'

He'd intended to speak to the new owners, hoping for a quick look around his old house, but he'd knocked on the door and there was no one home. Probably as well, seeing as Mike stank of booze. But he would have liked to see what it looked like inside now: especially his bedroom.

He had at least got a peek through the front windows, although this had drawn the attention of a curtain twitcher next door, where Lisa had carried him all those years ago. Elliot didn't have the energy to speak to them, knowing that the neighbours he remembered had long since moved away, so he'd retreated to the pavement to avoid looking like a burglar.

'I can't believe Lisa's never mentioned it,' Mike said. 'A big thing like that: you'd think she would have told me.'

'It was a long time ago — and it really shook her up. Me too, of course, but less so since I don't remember any of it. It wasn't until the next morning that I grasped what had happened. And all of it was my fault. If I hadn't got so wasted and flicked a fag butt in the kitchen bin without stubbing it out first, there wouldn't have been any fire. I never smoked again after that.'

Still on the pavement in front of his old house, Elliot looked over at Mike, who was staring into the distance. 'Sometimes it feels like I don't know Lisa at all, even though we've been married sixteen years.'

Elliot frowned. This wasn't what he was trying to achieve by telling Mike the story. He wanted to bring them closer together, not further apart. 'Listen,' he said. 'If it's any consolation, she's barely spoken about it to me. Back then she said it was so traumatic and terrifying that she wanted to forget it had ever happened. She was a true hero that day. She's always brushed that off, saying she did what any friend would do, but she risked her life to save mine. The firefighters reckoned I'd have been a goner without her. The place was in a terrible state. We never lived there again.'

'Where did you go?'

'We moved in with Ian. He was renting a house nearby at the time and there was more than enough room for all of us. Soon after, he surprised everyone by proposing to Mum and inviting us to return to Australia with him after my A-levels.'

'Weren't you bothered about leaving your friends behind and stuff?' Mike asked.

'I was hesitant at first. Mum too, but like I said, Ian's very persuasive. He convinced us what a great opportunity it was. Plus most people were heading off to university, anyway. I had a place at Durham to study Computer Science, but I managed to get it deferred for a year, in case. Then once I was over there, I got accepted for uni in Sydney. I'd fallen in love with the city by then — and Mum was the happiest I'd ever seen her.'

'What about family?'

'That wasn't much of an issue. Mum was an only child and her parents were both dead. My dad, also an only child, had died when I was little and his parents had turned on Mum afterwards, like it was her fault, so they weren't in our lives either. Plus our house was a wreck, thanks to me, so it was a no-brainer.'

Noticing the curtain twitcher watching them again, Elliot suggested they should continue on their walk.

'We're not going back yet?' Mike asked, crestfallen.

'Soon. If you could humour me a little longer, I have one more place I'd like to visit. You know Vicky Lane, right?'

'Of course.'

★ ★ ★

Elliot led the way along the rough, moss-laden tarmac of Victoria Street, to use its correct name, where time appeared to have stood still. It was just as he remembered it: the wild plants and bushes; the tall trees; the occasional dog walker; and children laughing somewhere out of sight.

383

He scoured the opposite side of the stream as they walked along, making occasional small talk but holding back on the important stuff until they reached their destination.

'Right, I think this is it,' Elliot announced. 'Yes, I'm pretty sure. How are you feeling, Mike? Sobering up?'

'I'm fine.'

'Good. So you're up for jumping over the stream and having a sit down?'

Mike looked at him like he was crazy. 'I guess so. Can I go home after that?'

'Sure.'

Elliot found a grassy spot on the other side. It was dry despite the earlier rain, thanks to tree cover; he sat down cross-legged and, with a smile, gestured for Mike to join him.

'I need to tell you some important things. But no need to look so concerned.'

He started with Lisa. 'I love her, Mike, but not romantically. It's never been like that between us. Did I fancy her when I was a boy? Sure, for a time, when my hormones got the better of me. But then I grew up and saw things clearly. Lisa's like the sister I never had. It's been amazing to reconnect with her — to meet you and the kids — but . . . ow!'

Damn. That pain again, stabbing into his chest. He doubled up, gritting his teeth and doing his best to supress the desire to yelp.

'Are you all right?' Mike asked, leaning towards him, his brow furrowed with concern.

'Give me a minute,' Elliot whispered, willing this latest attack to pass quickly.

'Is there anything I can do?'

'No.'

Once it was over, Elliot wiped away the sheen of sweat on his forehead and exhaled. 'Sorry about that.'

'It looked painful. What's going on?'

'Listen, Mike, I can't tell you everything, but I'm going to tell you as much as I can. More than I've told anyone else, as long as you do something for me.'

'Of course. But what — '

'I have to leave, Mike. It's going to be soon and, well, I won't be coming back. Not because I don't want to; it won't be possible.'

'You're sick?'

Elliot nodded slowly.

'How bad is it?'

'As bad as it gets.'

'But you look so healthy.'

'Looks can be deceiving. Anyway, the reason I brought you to this spot is because it's where Lisa and I met. We were both aged eleven. Some bullies had stolen my clothes and my glasses. I was in my underwear, struggling to see anything; scared and embarrassed; hiding behind that bush there.

'Then along came Lisa. She was new in the village and we'd never met before, but she rescued me. She ran home to get me clothes to wear and, afterwards, she made sure the boys who'd done that to me never did it again.

'For years after that, right through secondary school, she was like my guardian angel, up to the point when she actually did save my life by

385

rescuing me from that fire. Now . . . the shoe is on the other foot. I'm desperately trying to return the favour.'

Mike interrupted. 'But I don't understand. Lisa's fine. She doesn't need saving.'

'So she'd have everyone believe. But she's not fine, Mike, because she lives for her family and you're not fine; neither are Ben and Chloe.'

'Wait, what are you on about? Who are you to talk like that about my — '

'Stop.'

Instinctively, Elliot reached forward and placed a hand on Mike's forehead, causing him to instantly fall silent.

'Be calm,' he said, feeling Mike's frown disappear from beneath his palm. Up until this moment, Elliot's plan had simply been to talk to him, to try to help him overcome his issues.

But now, somehow, he knew that he was able to do much more: that he had the ability to relieve Mike of his burden once and for all. However, he sensed that this was a higher-level power than the other tricks, skills, or whatever they were, which he'd performed so far. It would require more of him than he'd given previously. This would drain him — accelerate things — bringing on the start of the end. It had to be worth it. He had to trust that he'd already done enough for Ben, Chloe and Lisa.

Elliot looked inwards and the answer was clear: this was the right move. Fixing Mike was the key.

★ ★ ★

When Elliot had set out to find Mike earlier, this had partly been to check he was okay. But there was more to it than that. He needed to stop him rolling home drunk at the wrong moment. Because when Elliot and Lisa had got back from their trip down memory lane, things at the house hadn't exactly been calm.

They'd already known about Chloe being upset. That and Mike's disappearance had been the two main reasons for cutting short their trip out. But even Elliot hadn't foreseen Ben's issues also coming to a head today.

That particular drama had unfolded while he'd been with Chloe in her bedroom, talking through her problems. Lisa had tried speaking to her first, while Elliot rescued Mike's screenplay file. However, she'd refused to talk to her mum, requesting him instead.

'I'm not being funny, but why does she want to talk to you?' Lisa asked. 'She barely knows you. What's wrong with me?'

'We've had a couple of chats before, Lise.'

'When?'

'I ran into her on the way back from the barbecue yesterday, for instance.'

'What about? Was she upset then?'

'Not that she said, but I got the feeling something was bothering her. Listen, why don't I go and see her? It's good that she wants to talk, right? Sometimes people find it easier speaking to an outsider than a close family member.'

'Fine. Seeing as it's you, El. But I wish you'd said something sooner and I do find it weird. I didn't even know that you two had had a proper conversation until now.'

He leaned towards his old friend and planted a kiss on her forehead. 'Trust me.'

So Chloe told him all about what had being going on with the nasty texts — and how she now believed them to be coming from Holly, her supposed best friend.

'Do you have any proof Holly sent these?' he asked, having read through the messages on Chloe's phone.

'No, not as such. Only what Saima told me. But it makes sense.'

'So Saima claimed that Holly had been saying nasty things about you behind your back? Is that right?'

'Yes. She said she overheard her several times at school. Holly was slagging me off to some other girls and saying she had a plan to get her own back. It was all to do with me supposedly trying it on with Kyle, this boy she likes. He's in my History class and we were partners on a project, so we had to spend some time together, but nothing happened. I told Holly that. I don't understand why she's never said anything to me, or why she'd do something so nasty. We're supposed to be best friends.'

'How do you know that Saima's telling the truth? You suspected her first, didn't you?'

'I did, yeah, but I've known her for years and it's not her style to do something like that. She'd even discussed the situation with her mum.'

'And Holly is the kind of person who'd do such a thing?'

Chloe started crying again, which made Elliot

fidgety. He didn't feel that it would be appropriate to give her a hug, although she looked like she needed one. Instead he handed her a box of tissues from her bedside table.

She sniffed as she wiped away her tears, then blew her nose. 'You must think I'm a right drama queen. I'm sorry to put all this on you, Elliot, but I couldn't face telling Mum. She's never liked Holly and this proves she was right all along.'

'You should give your mum a chance. She loves you a great deal and she's so proud of you. I know she wants to help.'

'Maybe. But I don't like to bother Mum and Dad with my stuff, anyway. They have enough on their plate.'

'Is that why you didn't tell them about the text messages?' he asked, getting a shrug in response.

'That's a lot to deal with on your own, Chloe. Whatever they have going on, I know your parents wouldn't want you to keep important things like that from them. It's their job to help with this stuff. What about Ben? Does he know?'

She shook her head. 'I did tell someone,' she said, bursting into tears again. 'I told Holly.'

They mulled over the situation for a while together. At one point the front doorbell sounded. Chloe sat bolt upright on the bed, wide-eyed. 'Who's that?'

Elliot guessed that she feared it might be Holly. 'Don't panic. We won't let anyone in that you don't want to see.'

But the next thing they heard was Lisa answering the door and shouting to Ben that he had a visitor.

Eventually they agreed that Chloe would visit Holly's house that afternoon to confront her. She looked terrified at the prospect, so Elliot offered to accompany her. Thankfully she declined, although she did make him promise not to say anything to her family yet.

'One thing at a time,' she said. 'I'm worried enough about seeing Holly.'

'Relax,' he told her. 'What's the worst that can happen: that your friendship comes to an end? If a mate of mine did that to me, I don't think I'd miss them. Plus there's always Saima. It sounds like she'd be delighted to get close again. Whatever happens, Chloe, will you promise me that you'll tell your parents about it later today?'

'Fine.'

He left her to compose herself and went to find Lisa. While descending the stairs, he heard muffled voices coming from the lounge, the door of which was shut.

Drawing closer, he recognised the sound of Ben talking to a male voice that he couldn't pinpoint. He tiptoed past the door, torn between minding his own business and an urge to eavesdrop. When he reached the kitchen, he found Lisa sitting at the table, reading a magazine. She looked up. 'At last. How did you get on?'

He nodded. 'Pretty good. She's upset. It's to do with her friend Holly, but she's asked me not to say anything — '

'What? Come on, El. I'm her mother.'

'I know, Lisa, but I promised her.'

'I don't care. I want to — '

'Listen, I got her to agree to tell you later on. But first she wants to see Holly to make sure she has her facts straight.'

'I knew that girl was trouble the moment I laid eyes on her. She was the one who drove a wedge between Chloe and Saima.'

'I think Chloe knows you feel that way about Holly already.'

'What's that supposed to mean?'

'Just something Chloe said. She's fragile. I'd tread carefully.'

Lisa slammed her magazine on to the table. 'Tell me you're not giving me parenting advice.'

'I'm trying to help. Don't shoot the messenger.'

'Sorry, I didn't mean to snap. It's hard being the one trying to hold everything together in this family, that's all. My daughter's upset about goodness knows what, my husband's gone AWOL, and my son's having a secret discussion in the lounge with a strange man I've never seen before in my life.'

It suddenly dawned on Elliot what might be happening with Ben. 'Yes, I heard someone at the front door. What's that all about?'

'No idea. It was a guy in his late twenties, I'd say: small, skinny, balding. He introduced himself as Henry, but Ben appeared before I could ask any more details. He didn't exactly look happy to see this guy, but he whisked him into the lounge and asked me to stay out.'

'Did you hear what they were talking about?'

'I caught a little at the start.' Lisa lowered her voice, holding a finger up to her lips. 'Ben asked how Henry had found him and he said something about an IP address. That's a computer thing, isn't it?'

Elliot nodded.

'Do you think I'm okay leaving them alone?' Lisa asked. 'It seems a bit weird.'

'Better here than somewhere else.'

'Exactly.' She paused. 'Do you know what? No, I shouldn't . . . '

'Go on. If you were thinking it, you might as well say it.'

She lowered her voice further still. 'Don't say anything, but I've always wondered whether Ben might be gay. If this Henry hadn't been so much older . . . the vibe between them. It almost seemed like, you know.'

'What makes you think that?'

'I'm his mother. You pick up on certain things. Mike and I have discussed it a few times. We've agreed to wait and see if Ben brings it up with us.'

At that moment the lounge door swung open and Ben came out, a deep frown on his forehead, followed by his visitor, whose eyes were glued to the floor. They both appeared flustered and neither looked in the direction of the kitchen, disappearing towards the front door.

'What's going on?' Lisa mouthed, unable to see the hallway from her seat.

Elliot shrugged, peering in that direction but seeing nothing helpful. He did, however, hear

392

Ben tell the man to 'never come here again'. Then there was the sound of the door opening and closing.

Shortly afterwards, Ben appeared at the entrance to the kitchen.

'Everything all right?' Lisa asked him.

He gave a half-hearted nod.

'Henry didn't stay long.'

'No.'

He gave Elliot a look — brief yet intense — before announcing that he needed to speak to his mother.

Elliot got the idea. 'I'm going to pop out for some fresh air,' he said, spotting a good opportunity to hunt down Mike.

As for Chloe, she was still in her bedroom. He popped his head in, only to find she was ready to go, so they headed out together, leaving Ben and Lisa alone for what Elliot hoped would be a very productive chat.

38

Wednesday, 25 July 2018

'Stop.' Elliot reached forward, placing a hand on Mike's forehead. 'Be calm.'

And just like that, the red mist surging through Mike's mind was evacuated.

He'd had a short fuse as a child. They'd even nicknamed him Hulk for a while at primary school after he'd lost it with a bully and chased him around the yard in a rage. It had been much less of a problem as an adult — until bloody Liam Hornby came along with his belligerent behaviour and career-wrecking false accusations.

Ever since then, it didn't take much to make Mike angry. Like the fight Elliot had saved him from in the pub. Like his nasty, cringeworthy behaviour towards Lisa in the restaurant last Friday. Alcohol made it worse. Mike hated himself when he got like that, but once the scales tipped, it was as if he was someone else: a creature led by his emotions rather than rational thought.

Sitting there cross-legged on that grassy spot near the stream, Mike tried to remember what Elliot had said to make him angry, but he couldn't. It was gone. All that remained was calm. And clarity, he realised: the alcohol's effects puzzlingly wiped away.

Elliot's hand was still pressed against his forehead, eyes locked on his, like searchlights probing his soul. Mike stared back, wanting to ask what was happening, but he found he was unable to speak or, come to think of it, to move. This was certainly odd, but he was too calm to be concerned.

Elliot started speaking. His voice was serene, warm and soothing, its measured rise and fall enchanting; almost . . . pleasurable.

'I'm here for you, Mike. I can help you, if you trust me. I can relieve you of your burden. But you have to tell me. You have to let me in and share the heart of it: the poison eating away at you, stifling you, holding you back. I need you to tell me everything, Mike, without reserve. Then I'm going to take away your pain, so you can move on with your life.'

'It's no big secret,' Mike said, his tongue moving freely again. 'Even those idiots in the pub knew about it, thanks to all the press coverage.' He found he wanted to explain things to Elliot; for once, he was able to do so — to think about that awful time — with detachment. The fury didn't rise up in his chest like usual.

'Liam Hornby is what happened to me. His lies wrecked my career and now there's nothing left for me. I'm burnt out and useless. Teaching is the only thing I'm qualified to do and I can't do that any more. I tried something else, driving the van, and look how well that turned out.'

'You could still teach,' Elliot replied. 'You were cleared of the charges. Leaving the profession was your choice. It wasn't forced upon you. Why did you feel unable to continue?'

Mike thought about this. It was strange to be able to consider the topic, which usually made him so riled, in a disconnected way, as if it was someone else's life rather than his own. His official line, which he repeated now to Elliot, had always been that the lack of support from the head and his other colleagues had been the final straw. There was truth in this. After he'd been suspended on full pay, he'd barely heard from them. Although they'd said to his face that they believed his version of events — and had no doubts about his innocence — it hadn't felt that way. Rather they'd seemed to distance themselves from him. He'd felt like a gangrenous limb being tied off in preparation for amputation.

The other thing he mentioned was the way he'd felt judged by the court of public opinion. Again, this was nothing new. He'd said so countless times before to whoever would listen. There was also truth here. Look at those men in the pub. They thought he was guilty, apparently unaware of the fact the charges had been dropped. Even those who had read or heard about him being cleared probably thought there was no smoke without fire. It was easy to think the worst of people. The media encouraged this with its sensationalised reports and headlines, dragging his name and reputation through the gutter while his accuser remained anonymous, thanks to his age.

If he was to start afresh at a new school, how long would it be before some parents got wind of what he'd been through? Probably a matter of days. It would only take one curious person doing an Internet search to find out. And once that happened, would they feel sorry for the terrible ordeal he'd endured? Doubtful. More likely they'd ring the headmaster to voice their concerns about the 'child beater' teaching their little poppet. Then how long until some innocuous thing he did got misinterpreted in light of his 'colourful past' and someone made another false allegation?

There was no way on earth that he or the rest of his family could relive that hell again: the media intrusion; the rumours and name-calling. At a particular low point he'd been spat at in front of his children, for crying out loud.

Elliot, whose hand remained glued to Mike's forehead, nodded as he listened to all of this. When Mike stopped there was a long pause, as if Elliot was processing the information. Usually Mike would have found the silence awkward, particularly in light of the hand on his head and the way he was being scrutinised. But it wasn't like that. He remained calm, like a theorist analysing some abstract concept from the comfort of a recliner.

It did occur to him that if anyone was to walk past while the two of them were like this, the situation would appear very odd. Not that he cared.

Finally Elliot spoke. 'I understand everything you've said to me, which makes sense, but it's not what I'm looking for. What's truly holding you back lies deeper.' His eyes fluttered shut as he took a deep breath and slowly exhaled. 'I believe it's something you've never told anyone before. You may never even have admitted it to yourself. I can sense it, but . . . the details aren't there. You need to take me back to when it happened: this moment between you and the boy, when you were alone in your office. I want you to imagine yourself there again and describe it to me.'

'Fine,' Mike replied. How often had he relived that time in his dreams before waking in a cold sweat, sleep banished by a single intrusive thought: what might he have done differently to avoid that horrendous outcome?

★ ★ ★

The little psycho, fresh from telling Mike to go screw himself, now had the gall to feign innocence while grinning at him. He'd been caught red-handed attacking his classmate with stinging nettles, for God's sake.

'Don't give me that, Liam. You knew exactly what you were doing. I asked you where the nettles came from. Well?'

A shrug in reply — all the more infuriating considering the nastiness of the incident, which was surely premeditated. Mike was struggling not to lose his rag.

'What do we have to do to get through to you? Why are you so determined to cause trouble at every opportunity? It's not for my good that you come to school, Liam. It's for your own. You're the one — '

The eleven-year-old was leaning back in his chair and yawning now. What the hell was the point?

'You're a — '

He was saved from saying something he'd later regret by the ringing of his desk phone. 'Hello?'

Beth, from the school office, needed the key for the safe. He decided to take it to her to allow himself a moment to cool down.

'Stay where you are,' he told the boy, whose large frame and arrogance always made him seem so much older than he was. 'And don't touch anything. I'll be back to deal with you in a moment.'

He was only gone for a couple of minutes, but when he returned . . . Damn, how could he have prepared himself for that?

His office had been completely ransacked: files and paperwork all over the place; his computer knocked to the floor. And that smell! The bastard had pissed all over the carpet. And there he was, sitting back in his chair, a wide grin slashed across his face, like it was the funniest thing in the world.

Mike was literally shaking with rage. 'What the hell have you done?' he yelled.

★ ★ ★

'Stop,' Elliot commanded, snapping Mike back into the present. 'That's it.'

Mike was confused. He didn't understand. He'd not even got to the part when Liam had smashed his own head down on to the desk,

399

breaking his nose and spraying blood every-where. Or later when he'd received that fateful phone call from the kid's dad, who'd called the police and vowed to fight tooth and nail to ensure Mike 'went down' for what he'd done. Surely that was the moment when his world had come crashing down around his ears; when he truly realised the gravity of the situation.

'What do you mean?' he asked Elliot, although as he said this, a little voice in the back of his mind was whispering something else: a message meant for him alone. It was warning him to keep his trap shut or else.

Or else what?

Mike felt his heart starting to race, the calmness ebbing away.

'I felt it,' Elliot said. 'I saw it in your mind's eye. It was there for an instant — and then it was gone. Did you see it too?'

'Um, I'm not sure.'

'Think yourself there again, Mike. Picture exactly what you saw, what you could smell and what you felt like when you walked into your office and witnessed the devastation.'

'Okay. I'll try.' Mike cast his mind back again. He remembered handling the cool metal of the long, chunky safe key as he passed it to Beth. She smelled of hairspray and fags. Next he was walking back to his office, a hint of bleach in the air, mixed with the familiar scent of stale gym kits from PE bags on pegs along the corridor. He was wondering what to say next to Liam and feeling a lot more calm, thanks to those couple of minutes away from him.

Then bang.

That awful scene of devastation again.

The lovely office he'd worked so hard to earn.

His personal, private space.

Wrecked.

And that smell.

The ammonia-laden reek of urine taking over the entire room while that shit grinned at him.

'Yes, that's it.' Without warning, Elliot jerked his hand away from Mike's forehead. 'Now how do you feel?'

'I'm devastated. Shocked. Furious. Raging.'

'And? Set it free.'

'I want to . . . ' He let out an exasperated sigh, the syllables refusing to form themselves.

'Yes? Don't stop now. Keep going.'

'I want to . . . I want to . . . ' He was struggling to control his breathing now, panting like a woman in labour. Beads of sweat ran down past his temples.

'Come on, Mike. There's nothing to fear.'

'I want to pick up that little shit and throttle the life out of him. I want to punch him so hard that his face caves in. I hate that bloody arsehole!'

As soon as the words had left his mouth, Mike gasped. He threw a hand up to his lips, wanting to cover them; to stifle the terrible thing that he'd uttered; to somehow take it back.

But it was too late.

He'd said it now.

The truth was out.

'I didn't actually do any of that . . . He really did — '

'It's okay, Mike.'

'No, it's not. I'm a teacher. I mean, I was a teacher. How could that thought have even crossed my mind? I really wanted to hurt him in that moment, Elliot.

'God, I've never told anyone that before. Not even Lisa. If he hadn't have done what he did to himself, maybe . . . I don't know. What if that's something I'm actually capable of? How could I ever teach again knowing that possibility?'

He paused for a couple of seconds before adding: 'Maybe I actually am the monster I was accused of being.'

Elliot shook his head. 'Thoughts and actions are two very different things, Mike. You need to focus on what happened, not what went on inside your head. And as I promised, I can help with that. Hold on tight.'

Hold on tight, Mike thought. What did he mean?

But before Mike's brain could formulate an answer, quick as a cat, Elliot pounced on him. He came with both of his hands this time, clamping one on either side of his head.

Mike recoiled as an ear-splitting, high-pitched screech sounded, like electric guitar feedback right inside his skull. Then there was a blinding white flash.

39

'Well, forgive me for stating the obvious, Elliot, but you're back.'

'I am.'

The room was the same bright, box-like blank space as before: cream walls, no windows, white metal door.

Again they were sitting opposite each other at the table.

Elliot wondered if it was the same room, before recalling what he'd been told last time about people perceiving it differently. So it wasn't a room at all, right? He guessed that meant it was some sort of an illusion.

He'd originally imagined it being somewhere near Sydney. Now he knew better. Such concrete terms could never apply here.

The man called Will, in his funeral-style black suit and tie, was watching him closely. Was he actually a man, though?

'So how did it go?' Will asked, his northern English accent sounding far softer to Elliot's ears following his trip home. He looked around the same age as him, maybe a little younger. He'd initially thought older, due to the grey hair and matching stubble. But Will's pin-sharp blue eyes and youthful complexion told another story.

'Okay, I guess. How do you think it went?'

'Very well. You should be proud of yourself. I see you put to good use several of the, er, abilities you were granted.'

'Hmm. I didn't do it for myself. I did it for Lisa.'

'Well, you carried yourself admirably and it hasn't gone unnoticed. They're calling you a natural.'

'A natural what? And who are *they*?'

'That's a conversation for later. I've already said too much.'

'Whatever. Listen, I thought there would be time to say goodbye. What must Lisa think of me, leaving without explanation?'

The last thing Elliot remembered of his visit was sitting by the stream with Mike. He'd sensed that relieving Lisa's husband of his burden would be costly to himself in terms of time remaining. It was the same to a lesser degree on every occasion that Elliot had used one of his special skills. Each instance had appeared to tap away at whatever power was allowing him to be there, speeding up the countdown, as indicated by those awful pain attacks he'd experienced. Will confirmed this, reminding him of his initial guidance to use his gifts wisely and sparingly because everything had a cost. However, Elliot had expected at least another chance to talk to Lisa.

Will picked his tablet up off the desk, keeping the screen facing away from Elliot. He frowned, tapped something into it, frowned again, swiped, tapped some more and then nodded.

'There will be an opportunity for you to make contact one more time, if you'd like that. However, I'm afraid you'll only be able to speak to one of them and it won't be for long.'

'Really? How does that work?'

'You decide who and then — '

'Lisa. Definitely.'

'No problem. I can arrange that.' He moved to stand up.

'Can I ask you a question first?'

'Of course.'

'How are things going with my, er . . . body?'

'Right. The doctors in Sydney have met with your mother and stepfather to discuss turning off the life support machine. They're still weighing it up. It's a horrendous decision to have to make, obviously, but having heard the overwhelming evidence that there's no longer any brain function, I think it's only a matter of time.'

'I see.' Elliot had known this was coming. They'd discussed it in detail last time. But that didn't make it any easier to hear. It broke his heart to think of the torture his mum must be going through, seeing his battered, lifeless body lying on the hospital bed; having to make this terrible decision. He wished from the bottom of his heart that he could be there for her. It felt so cruel that he'd been taken away so abruptly, without any warning and at such a young age, especially after the heartache she'd already experienced when his father died in that motorbike accident so many years earlier. Thank goodness she had Ian.

'How's Mum doing?'

Will pursed his lips, creating dimples in his ruddy cheeks. 'She's in bits. Ian too, although he's doing his best to hold things together.

405

They're both heartbroken.' His voice seemed to falter as he added: 'It's incredibly hard for any parent to have to let a child go.'

'I don't suppose there's any chance of me, er, seeing her, is there?'

Will sighed, running a hand through his windswept hair. 'I'm so sorry, Elliot. I wish there was, believe me, but there isn't. I did explain this last time we spoke. I'm afraid seeing your mother isn't even an option I can offer you instead of speaking to Lisa. The only reason that's possible is because you've already spent time with her.'

Elliot nodded in silence, feeling his eyes start to well up. He was picturing his grief-ridden mum breaking down at his funeral and the image scorched itself into his mind's eye. If only he could have had the chance to tell her and Ian how much he loved them both; how he appreciated all they'd done for him in his life. But it wasn't meant to be.

He gulped. 'So what happens to me after the machine is turned off?'

'Once your body dies, your soul is free to move on. A guide will lead you across to the other side.'

Elliot sat up in his chair. 'A guide? Someone other than you? I thought — '

'Please, there's nothing to be concerned about. My task is to help you through this transitional period, while your body remains alive.'

'But why can't you be my guide?'

'We all have our roles to play. It's above my pay grade, if you like. You'll be in safe hands, though. I've pulled a couple of strings and arranged ... ' He lowered his voice. 'I'm probably not supposed to tell you this. Honestly, I've not been here long enough to know; I'm still learning the ropes. I'll say it anyway. She was my guide when I passed over. Her name's Lizzie. She's lovely and far more experienced than I am.'

'So you were human once? When did you die?'

'September twenty sixteen.'

'Really? That's not long ago. And now you're an angel?'

Will smiled. 'Me? Far from it. We're on the same team, but they're considerably higher up the pecking order. I'm not even allowed in the field.'

'What about this Lizzie, then? Is she one?'

Will shook his head. 'No, only a special few get selected to become angels. It's a huge honour, as you'll soon — ' His tablet bleeped. 'Sorry, I need to arrange that final meeting with Lisa.'

'Could I just ask you a couple of things first?'

'Sure.'

'What happens after I've gone? Once Lisa and the others find out the truth about my visit, how will they make sense of it?'

'Don't worry. Their memories will slowly fade until they no longer recall you being here. The same goes for anyone you've had dealings with in these last few days. Take the staff at your hotel, for instance. They've already forgotten you. But it'll be a more gradual process with Lisa and the family. That doesn't mean the good you've done will be any less effective. They just won't remember your involvement. It's a simple protection mechanism to keep everyone sane. Does that answer your question?'

Elliot nodded. 'There is something else that's been bothering me about my trip. I don't suppose it's important, but it would be nice if you could clear it up.'

'Go on. I'll do my best.'

'Who's Sandie?'

'Sorry?'

'That strange woman I met in Manchester. The one who had Ben's wallet. After she grabbed hold of my hand in the car, it was like she knew the truth about me being there. I was afraid she was about to spill the beans in front of Ben and Chloe.'

'Oh, you mean Cassandra.'

'Yes, right. She said that was her actual name. Is she one of your, um, team or — I don't know — something else?'

Will shook his head, pursing his lips. 'She's just a normal person, apart from the fact that she has a natural psychic ability. She inherited it from her mother, who was quite a well-known fortune teller in her day, apparently.'

Elliot raised an eyebrow. 'Seriously? That stuff's real?'

'Well, there are a great deal more charlatans out there than genuine psychics, mediums, or whatever you want to call them. But yes, some of them are real, for sure. Like you, most people these days don't believe they have any genuine ability, which tends to make things easier for us.

We do keep them on our radar, though. I looked her up when you ran into her. As far as I know, it was just a coincidence that your paths crossed.'

'I see. Fair enough.'

'Okay, I'll get on and sort out that meeting then, shall I? Back soon. Don't be alarmed if someone else comes to talk to you in the meantime.'

'This Lizzie, you mean?'

'No, it's too soon for that.' He winked and looked upwards. 'Think big. You're on the radar of some important folks here.'

40

NOW

Friday, 27 July 2018

Lisa was worried about El. No one had seen him since Wednesday. This was all she could think about as she emptied the dishwasher that evening, the others busy elsewhere in the house.

Mike had been the last of them to spend time with him, on Wednesday afternoon, but he'd returned alone.

'I think he's gone back to his hotel,' he'd said at the time, although he hadn't seemed entirely sure. Mike had reeked of booze, admitting yet another trip to the pub, but strangely he hadn't behaved drunk at all.

'So where did the two of you go?'

'For a walk around the village. Elliot showed me where he used to live and where the two of you first met. What he said was quite illuminating: particularly the bit about you pulling him out of a house fire. I can't believe you never mentioned that before.'

Lisa wondered what else Elliot had told her husband that day, because there was definitely something different about him since then. He was behaving like a man who'd had the weight of the world lifted off his shoulders. She hadn't seen him smile so much in years and he was being kind and affectionate to her, like he used to. They'd had sex for the first time in ages last night and it had been fantastic. She'd actually had to bite down on the quilt to stop herself from screaming the house down. Yesterday he'd spent hours on his laptop working on the screenplay he'd been talking about forever. Then he'd mentioned the possibility of finding private tuition work via a website he'd come across.

This was incredible. She'd given up on Mike returning to teaching in any form, so hearing him utter these words was a huge corner turned. It had even made her forget about him disappearing to the pub again on Wednesday. She hadn't dared to make too big a deal of the turnaround, for fear of jinxing things, so she'd not asked Mike any probing questions. However, she was desperate to speak to Elliot to find out more. And if it was something he'd said or done, of course she wanted to thank him.

Then there was everything that had been going on with the kids.

Ben had come out, for a start. He'd admitted to her that he was gay. He'd not gone into much detail about his mysterious visitor, and she hadn't wanted to push. But as she understood it, this nasty little man — Henry — knew Ben's secret and had threatened to tell people. Ben had claimed not to be overly concerned by this. Dismissing it as a bluff, he'd said that he could share worse things about Henry with the world. (Lisa didn't even want to think what these might be.) However, Ben had decided it was time to tell his family now.

Afterwards, she embraced her son and held him tight. She told him how much she loved him and thanked him for trusting her enough to tell her. This brought them both to tears — happy ones, at least — followed by more hugs, kisses and kind words.

'Are you surprised, Mum?' he asked. 'Or disappointed?'

'Of course I'm not disappointed. Why would I be?'

'I don't know, because of weddings and children and stuff.'

'Oh, darling. Being gay doesn't preclude any of those things any more.' She ruffled his hair like she used to when he was little. 'You're a silly sausage. As for being surprised, not entirely. Your father and I have discussed it a few times as a possibility.'

Ben's eyes popped out. 'Really? I thought no one had a clue. Do you think my friends at school might know too? I'm not sure I want to tell them yet.'

'Don't worry about that, love. One thing at a time. I'm your mother, don't forget. I carried you in my womb. Just because I guessed, it doesn't mean anyone else would. Your dad didn't see it straight away. It was only after I said something.'

Ben screwed his face up into a knot. 'I'm worried about telling Dad. Do you think he'll be okay with it?'

'He'll be absolutely fine. I promise. We both love you unconditionally, Ben. And don't worry about Chloe either. You might not realise it, but she worships you. She'll accept it in a flash.'

And they both were fine about it, of course, when he told them over dinner on Wednesday evening. Seeing her son's hands shake and hearing him choke up when he made the announcement brought tears to Lisa's eyes. But it was fantastic to see the look of relief on his face afterwards.

Mike jumped up and gave him a hug, told him he loved him and reiterated how proud he was to be his father. He also reassured Ben that he wasn't 'one of those old-fashioned dads' who'd have any kind of issue with it. Chloe was surprised, having no clue beforehand, but it clearly didn't bother her in the slightest. She was soon berating him for not telling her sooner and asking if he had a boyfriend.

Meanwhile, Chloe had her own issues to deal with. She'd now told the rest of the family what had been going on with Holly. That nasty piece of work had been secretly sending her malicious messages from a pay-as-you-go phone, as well as badmouthing her to whoever would listen. It was over some boy Holly liked. She'd asked him out, only for him to tell her that he preferred Chloe: an innocent party in the whole thing.

Rather than taking the rejection on the chin and moving on — maybe even talking to her supposed best friend about it — Holly had turned on her. She'd convinced herself that Chloe had engineered the whole thing, despite the lack of any evidence, so had set out to make her life miserable in return.

Recounting her confrontation with Holly to

Lisa, Chloe had said: 'She invited me into her bedroom like normal, as if nothing was wrong. She even asked me, pretending to be a friend who cared, if I'd received any more nasty messages. So I came out with it: I told her I knew she was the one who was sending them.

'She denied it, but I was ready for that. I had the pay-as-you-go number programmed into my phone, which Elliot had suggested. I called it there and then. Luckily, the phone was turned on. It rang from a drawer in her bedside table, and she was suddenly apologising, trying to explain; saying that she was in love with Kyle and hadn't been able to stop herself.

'But I'd heard enough by then. I told her we were done and to stay out of my life for good. Then I walked out of there. I still can't believe she did that to me. I hate her, Mum.'

Lisa, following El's earlier advice, had resisted the temptation to say that she'd never liked or trusted Holly. Instead she'd focused on Saima, suggesting that Chloe should concentrate on rebuilding that friendship.

The last few days had seen some major developments for everyone in the family except Lisa — and Elliot appeared to have played a key role in every one of them. Even Ben had let it slip that Elliot knew about him being gay before she did. Goodness knows when, but El appeared to have talked it through with him, encouraging him to tell his family the truth.

It was weird, because although she was thankful for what El had done, she also felt a bit left out. How come he'd spent so much one-on-one time with them during his visit and yet, apart from the daytrip to their old schools, not with her? She was the one he'd come to visit, wasn't she? So why did he seem more interested in the others? And where the hell was he now?

When he hadn't come back with Mike on Wednesday, Lisa hadn't been concerned. She'd assumed he was tired and, as Mike suggested, had returned to his hotel. She hadn't even given it too much thought when he'd not shown up yesterday, assuming he was catching up on some of the business he was supposed to be here for. But now, having heard nothing for more than forty-eight hours, she found it strange.

After finishing up in the kitchen, Lisa walked through to the lounge, where Mike was busy typing on his laptop although it was nearly 9.30 p.m.

'I'm worried about El,' she said. 'Do you think something might have happened to him?'

Mike looked up from his screen and rubbed his eyes. 'Um, I don't know, love. Why do you say that?'

'It's strange not to have heard from him in more than two days. Are you sure he didn't say anything when you last saw him? He didn't mention that he was going anywhere on business?'

'Sorry, no. Why don't you give him a call?'

'I don't have his number.'

'Oh. Does he have a mobile, actually? I can't recall ever seeing him with one.'

'He must have an Australian mobile, but he

415

never gave me the number. He always just turned up here.'

She decided to ask the kids, who were in their bedrooms, but neither had his number. Ben said El had mentioned leaving his mobile in the hotel safe, which gave Lisa the idea of calling him there.

'Hello,' she said to the bored-sounding girl on reception at The Grange, who answered after a couple of rings. 'Please could you put me through to Elliot Turner's room?'

'Is he a guest here?' the receptionist asked in a monotone voice.

'Yes.'

'Do you know his room number?'

'No, I'm afraid not.'

'One minute, please.'

She put Lisa on hold. A tinny version of some classical tune she vaguely recognised kicked in. The wait seemed to go on forever. She was on the verge of hanging up and dialling again when the receptionist came back on the line. 'I'm sorry. There's no one of that name staying here. Are you sure it's right?'

'Yes, of course I'm sure,' Lisa snapped.

'Well, there's no one of that name staying here. Is there anything else I can help you with?'

Lisa racked her brains, desperately trying to work out what was going on. Surely he wouldn't have checked out without telling her. Could he be staying there under a different name, perhaps? But why would he? It made no sense.

She told the girl what he looked like and that he was an important businessman from Sydney.

She added that he was originally from Aldham and had an unusual accent, somewhere between the two. Surely no one else of that description could have stayed there recently.

'I'm sorry,' the girl said, without sounding apologetic. 'I don't remember anyone of that description. Is there anything else I can help you with?'

Somehow managing not to swear, Lisa asked to speak to a manager. After being placed on hold again forever, the same annoying voice returned. 'I'm afraid the manager is currently tied up with something. Can I get him to call you back?'

'Yes, thank you,' Lisa replied, forcing herself to remain polite, even though she felt like shouting. 'Could you emphasise to him that it's important, please?'

After giving the girl her details and noting down the manager's name, Lisa hung up. She decided to give it half an hour and, if she hadn't heard back by then, to go to the hotel in person.

Something didn't feel right.

She was in the process of recounting the story to Mike when the phone rang.

'Oh, good,' she said, racing back to the landline. 'Hello?'

'Lisa?' a shaky voice asked. It was a woman, but definitely not the receptionist she'd spoken to earlier.

'Yes, speaking. Who's this?'

'Um, sorry to call at this time. I know it's late with you. It's Wendy, Elliot Turner's mother,' the voice replied, totally catching Lisa off-guard.

'Wendy? Oh my God. How on earth are you? How lovely to hear from you after all these years. Is everything all right? Are you looking for — '

'No, I'm afraid everything isn't all right. I'm . . . ' There was a pause during which Lisa heard a muffled sobbing and then, away from the handset, Wendy's voice again: 'I'm sorry. I don't think I can do this.'

'Wendy, what's going on?' Lisa asked, her heart thumping in her chest. 'What's happened?'

An Australian man's voice came on the line. 'Lisa, love? It's Ian, Wendy's husband. I don't know if you remember me?'

'Yes, of course. What's the matter with Wendy, Ian?'

He sighed into the phone. 'She wanted to do this herself, love, but I'm afraid she's not up to it. It's too soon. Everything's still so raw.'

'Sorry, I don't understand. I don't know what either of you are saying. Is this about Elliot, because I — '

'I'm afraid it is. There's no easy way to say this, Lisa. Elliot was in a terrible accident just over a week ago.'

'I'm sorry, what? I don't — '

Lisa felt the room start to spin as Ian's voice continued.

'Bear with me, darling. This isn't easy. Please let me finish. He was out surfing in some pretty wild conditions and, well, he got into trouble. They found him washed up on the beach, unconscious and in a really bad way. His head had taken a pounding on some rocks. The docs did everything they could for him, but there was

418

no brain function. We eventually agreed to let them turn the life support off and . . . we stayed with him as he slipped away. He's gone now, love.'

Ian kept on talking. He was saying something about how important she'd always been to Elliot and about his will, but Lisa could no longer process the words. She couldn't comprehend what was going on. This had to be some kind of trick. Or maybe she was dreaming.

How was any of this possible?

She fell back against the wall and slid to the floor, the receiver tumbling out of her hand. She felt woozy and lightheaded — and then she passed out.

41

NOW

Friday, 3 August 2018

Lisa woke up feeling awful. It was 8.03 a.m. She'd barely slept. She hadn't been able to turn off her brain, which had been thinking the whole time about Elliot, whose funeral had taken place overnight.

It had been in Sydney, of course: his adopted home; the place where he'd made his life for the past twenty years; the place where he'd died. They were nine hours ahead there, so the 1 p.m. service had occurred at 4 a.m. local time, when Lisa had been tossing and turning in bed.

A week had passed since she'd learned the impossible truth about Elliot and still she couldn't get her head around it. Of course she couldn't. It made absolutely no sense. How could Elliot have been here in England with her and her family when he was actually lying in in a hospital intensive care unit in Sydney following the horrific surfing accident that ultimately took his life?

The whole thing was crazy. It was like something out of an old *Twilight Zone* episode, except — as little sense as it made — she knew that somehow it was real. It had definitely happened, because she and her family had all

420

experienced it; they all remembered Elliot being here.

So how was it possible?

This was the question Lisa had been asking herself nonstop ever since that devastating phone call from Wendy and Ian last week. The only logical explanation she could come up with was that it hadn't been Elliot at all but rather an impostor. He'd certainly looked and behaved very differently from when she'd last seen him, so to begin with this was a possibility her rational mind had clung to, although her heart told her otherwise.

Then she'd looked up his death on the Internet and found an Australian TV news story that included recent video footage of Elliot being interviewed about his successful educational app. The man she saw and heard was, without question, the same person who'd cooked a roast dinner in her house a few days ago; who'd saved Ben from choking and done so many other things to help her family during the course of his short visit.

So how was it possible?

It wasn't. And yet it was.

Either that or Lisa had gone insane.

Or maybe this was some long, convoluted dream that she'd suddenly wake up from and her life would be normal again.

The only other person who knew the truth was Mike. He'd found Lisa passed out on the floor after hearing the news from Ian, so of course she'd had to tell him. He'd thought she was winding him up at first, or at least someone was winding her up. When the manager from The Grange had called back, Mike had been the one to speak to him. The next day he'd insisted on visiting the hotel in person. But no one there had remembered Elliot, even when Mike had used his phone to show them that video online.

Now Mike seemed more ready to accept it than Lisa. He said it somehow made a strange kind of sense after what he'd been through with Elliot on his final afternoon. He claimed that Elliot had done something to him then: helped him in a way that he couldn't exactly remember but which had made him feel an awful lot better about his life in general, infusing him with a new sense of purpose and an ability to move on from the whole Liam Hornby thing.

Obviously Lisa had probed Mike about this, keen for more information, but he genuinely appeared to have forgotten. He said the last thing he remembered was walking down Vicky Lane with Elliot and him pointing out the spot where Lisa had first met her old friend, all those years ago, hiding behind a bush in his underwear. Then he was walking home alone, feeling happier than he had in ages.

They'd decided not to tell Ben and Chloe for now, fearing it would be too much for them to comprehend. So Lisa had had to hide the awful grief she was feeling from them, which hadn't been easy.

They'd already told them that Elliot had needed to rush home unexpectedly. Now the plan was to wait a few weeks before breaking it to them about the surfing accident and the fact

Elliot had died, only skipping the details that made no sense. Because how could they tell the kids everything? How could she explain that the accident had taken place before Elliot came to visit them and — as a result of some miracle — a healthy, vibrant version of the man lying broken in hospital in Sydney had turned up here on the other side of the world?

Sometimes as a parent you had to protect your children from the truth. Right or wrong, that was what she and Mike had decided to do. Ben and Chloe had enough on their plates without having to get their heads around this. The plan wasn't flawless, bearing in mind the information available online, but it was the best they had.

Mike stirred next to her in bed. 'Are you awake, love?' he asked.

'Yes.'

'Did you manage to get much sleep?'

'No.'

He leaned over and kissed the end of her nose. 'I'll make us a cup of tea.'

Mike had been incredibly supportive about the whole mind-bending situation. He'd been her rock over a difficult few days. It was like her husband of old had returned to take charge at the very moment she needed him most, wrapping a strong arm around her and guiding her through the minefield she'd been dropped into.

'Do you think I can ring Wendy now to see how the funeral went?'

Mike looked at the alarm clock. 'Um, five past eight here, so that makes it . . . five past five in the afternoon there. The funeral was at one, right? And the wake is at their house?'

'Yes.'

'Should be fine.'

Lisa took a deep breath. 'Okay. I'm going to do it. Shut the bedroom door, would you? I don't want Ben or Chloe to hear anything.'

'Of course.'

Once she was alone, Lisa picked up the phone and stared at it for a long moment before dialling the number. She hadn't told Wendy or Ian about Elliot's visit here. How could she? They'd think she was loopy. She had discussed flying over for the funeral, but they'd talked her out of it.

'That's lovely of you, darling,' Wendy had said when Lisa phoned her back the day after the initial call, having gathered her thoughts. 'But you really shouldn't fly all that way. It's not what Elliot would have wanted. He'd rather you remembered him how he used to be. He's not here any more. His body's an empty shell now. His soul is free. You don't need to come here to say goodbye to him. You can do that in Aldham, where there are so many happy memories of the two of you together.'

Wendy was calmer that time. She was more philosophical, although she confessed to being constantly up and down, saying that Lisa had happened to catch her at a good moment.

Today it was Ian who answered the phone. Wendy was in a bad way, he said. And although the wake was still in progress at their house, she'd retired to bed.

424

'Poor thing,' Lisa said. 'Give her my love, won't you?'

'Of course.'

'How was it?'

He let out a heavy sigh. 'Difficult, of course, but everyone was lovely. There was a fantastic turnout and . . . you know. It went as well as these things can.'

'I wish I could have been there.'

'Don't be silly. It wouldn't have made any sense for you to fly all this way. No one expected you to, Lisa. Oh, and thank you for the lovely flowers you sent. They arrived first thing this morning.'

'It was the least I could do.'

Ian cleared his throat. 'You meant a great deal to Elliot. I know you hadn't seen each other for a long time, but that was only because of the distance. He often spoke of you and how you were always coming to his rescue as a nipper. And none of us will ever forget how you saved him from that fire.' His voice wavered as he added: 'He might not have lived a long life in the end, but you more than doubled what he did get. I know he always planned to return to Aldham one day to see you and your family. It's such a shame it didn't happen. He never forgot about you, though. I can promise you that, love. That's why we called you so soon after he died.'

After Lisa had hung up, promising to phone again tomorrow, Mike returned with two cups of tea. 'Did you speak to Wendy?'

'No, she was too upset. She'd gone to bed, apparently, but I had a word with Ian. He said

425

everything went well.'

It felt so weird to be talking about this like it was a regular funeral, when nothing about the situation was normal. She and Mike had discussed it so many times over the past week, there was little more to say. It made absolutely no sense — but it was what it was.

'Do you think we'll see him again?' she asked her husband.

He sat down next to her on the bed and gave her a reassuring hug. 'It would be nice to think so, wouldn't it? I guess anything's possible in light of what we now know about Elliot.'

'But he was still alive — well, his body was at least — when he came here. Do you think that was the key?'

'Honestly, I don't know. If you'd asked me that same question a month ago, I'd have feared for your mental health. But look where I was a month ago, compared to where I am now. I feel like a different person, like I've found myself again, and so much of that is down to him.'

Lisa couldn't argue with this. Mike's new calmness and understanding had been a godsend. His rediscovered tenderness and affection had also done wonders for their relationship, which had flourished both physically and mentally in recent days.

'However he did it, Elliot came to us for a reason,' Mike continued. 'He helped all of us in different ways and we're much better for it as a family. I think we need to focus on that and try to forget about the inexplicable stuff, because we'll only tie ourselves in knots. You, Ben, Chloe and I: we all need to appreciate how lucky we are to be here and to have one another.'

Lisa knew that her husband was right. Previously, before learning of Elliot's death, she'd found herself envying the time he'd spent with the rest of her family rather than her. She recognised how incredibly selfish that was now. But still she yearned for some closure. She couldn't help but wish that she'd got the chance to say a proper goodbye to her old friend and to thank him for everything.

★ ★ ★

That afternoon Lisa, who was feeling the effects of her lack of sleep the night before, told Mike she was going for a nap upstairs.

'No problem, love.' He barely looked up from his laptop, typing enthusiastically at the kitchen table.

It was a sunny afternoon and the kids were both out with friends. In Chloe's case it was Saima, who she was getting on well with, now that horrible Holly was out of the picture. They'd been meeting up daily and Chloe seemed to have put the whole nasty messages thing behind her for now.

Ben was with Oliver, a boy he'd been friends with since primary school, who Lisa had always liked. He was shy but polite. She had a feeling Ben might be warming up to telling him about being gay, although the official line was that he didn't plan on sharing the information with anyone outside the family yet. All in good time.

The important thing was that Ben seemed far more happy and relaxed since telling them. Lisa doubted it would all be plain sailing. When was it with any teenager? But at least he could now be open and honest with them.

Up in the bedroom, Lisa opened a window to let in some air and drew the curtains. She didn't bother undressing, opting to lie down on top of the quilt. A moment later, she was asleep.

★　★　★

She found herself back in her childhood bedroom. She was lying on the single bed and everything was just as it had been when she'd first moved to Aldham, before they'd had a chance to change the manky brown carpet and cover the 'bogey' green walls, as Jamie had loved to call them.

Madonna and Prince were staring down at her from the walls; there was a healthy pile of well-thumbed *Smash Hits* and *Jackie* magazines, alongside her old pink radio-cassette player. She sat up and walked over to the dressing table, which was covered in the kind of hair and beauty products she used to love as a girl. Then she looked in the mirror and, staring back at her, she saw the reflection of her eleven-year-old self.

There was a knock on the closed bedroom door.

'Hello?' she said, walking over and opening it a tiny crack to see who was there.

Her heart skipped a beat when she saw a bespectacled, curly haired, overweight young

428

Elliot flashing a wonky grin back at her, looking exactly like he had when they'd first met.

'Are you going to let me in then, or what?' he asked.

'Of course,' she replied, swinging the door open. 'Is it really you, El?'

'It sure is,' he replied in his high-pitched boy's voice. 'How are you, Lise?'

She pulled him into an embrace and held him tight. Then she let go and looked him square in the eyes. 'Is it *you* you? The one who came to visit us somehow, despite the fact it was impossible?'

He nodded. 'The very same.'

'So why did you leave without saying goodbye? How on earth were you there in the first place? And . . .'

She paused as her mind caught up with her mouth. In a quieter voice she added: 'So you're dead?'

'In human terms, yes.'

For the first time, the hard truth of this fact really dawned on her. It was too much. She fell back on to the bed and the tears started to flow. 'Are you okay? Will I ever see you again, like you were, for real? I've only just got my best friend back and now . . .'

Elliot took a seat next to her and pulled her into a hug. Despite the boyish tone of his voice, Lisa still recognised the man within as he spoke. 'Listen, we don't have long.' He took a deep breath. 'And after this, I don't know if or when we'll see each other again.'

His words only increased the flow of Lisa's

tears. She'd feared this was coming, but that didn't make it any easier to accept.

'There are things I need to say to you,' he continued, sounding short of breath, 'but I have very little time. I know you must have a million questions, but I need you to listen. Please? I'll tell you what I can.'

Tenderly, Elliot placed a hand under her chin and looked at her for confirmation. She nodded.

'I'm not able to explain exactly how or why I came to you like I did.' He shrugged. 'That's a condition of me being here now. And honestly, it's not something I fully understand myself. Let's just say that there's more to our existence than life and death.'

'But what does that — '

'Please, Lisa.' Elliot's big blue eyes glistened in the light. 'For so long I've wanted to pay you back — to thank you for what you did for me when we were younger. There were so many things over the years, but carrying me from that fire was . . . incredible. You put your life on the line to save me that day and I'll never forget it. I'll never forget any of the times you came to my rescue. You were and always will be my best friend.'

He gave Lisa a warm smile, using a finger to gently wipe away some of her tears, while blinking to clear his own. 'It may seem like I spent more time with the rest of your lovely family than I did with you. I'm sorry if that's the case, but I only ever wanted to help. I had to do what I felt was best.

'You're such a strong, amazing person. But

you were crumbling when I arrived, Lisa, from trying to carry everyone else. I did my best to help the others, hoping to help you. As an outsider with a few special tools at my disposal, I tried to make a difference.'

Lisa nodded, swallowing several times despite the huge lump in her throat. 'I understand that now, El,' she said. 'You've made such a difference to all of us, especially Mike. He's like a new man. I can't thank you enough. I realise how lucky I am to have him and Ben and Chloe; to be alive when you're . . . ' Her voice fell away. 'It's not fair what's happened to you. You're still so young. I — '

'It is what it is. Things don't always work out like we think they will. I can't complain. I'm so glad I got the chance to reconnect with you. I should have come to visit years ago, but I always thought there would be time later. Don't ever make that mistake. Live your life in the present.'

'I will, I promise,' she replied. 'And every time I think of you, which will be a lot, I'll use that as a way to appreciate everything I have in life.'

Elliot looked upwards and squinted as if concentrating on something. 'Please hug me again,' he said, turning back, his voice cracking with emotion.

'Of course.' Lisa wrapped her arms around her friend and squeezed tight, wishing the moment could last forever. Their tears ran into a single stream as their cheeks pressed together. Lisa felt her heart racing and her lungs short of breath. It all felt so real.

'Is this a dream?' she asked, squeezing her

friend tighter to steady her quivering limbs. 'It doesn't feel like that, but how can it not be?'

'Trust your feelings.' Elliot lowered his voice to a whisper. 'It's more than that — and I'll prove it to you. A letter will arrive in the next few days. It'll be from me, written before I died. It's my final gift to you. Please accept it, enjoy it and live a wonderful life with your fantastic family.

'One more thing. You mustn't worry about me. However it might look to you, my life is far from over.' He shook his head, chuckling. 'Honestly, if I could tell you what they have lined up for me — who I've spoken to — it would blow your mind.'

'What do you — '

Elliot frowned. 'Sorry, Lise, time's up. Goodbye. I love you.'

'I love you too.'

★ ★ ★

Lisa woke up for a moment, her head still woozy with sleep, blurring the lines between what was real and what wasn't. She glanced at the alarm clock and realised she'd only been in bed for a few minutes, although it felt much longer.

Still shattered, with no energy to think of what she'd been dreaming, she rolled over on to her side, snuggling into the duvet, and her eyes slid shut.

Epilogue

NOW

Monday, 13 August 2018

'Post, Mum,' Ben said, dropping three or four envelopes on to the kitchen table where she was drinking a cup of coffee and making a shopping list.

'Thanks, love.'

She didn't actually look at the letters until ten minutes later.

One, addressed to her, immediately stood out due to the fact it had an Australian postmark. It looked official, but when she opened the envelope, the first thing she saw was a handwritten letter, stapled to the front of several other printed documents. Intrigued and slightly nervous, she picked it up.

Dear Lisa,

If you're reading this, something has happened to me. I'm not sure what that is, since I can't see the future, but seeing as I've instructed my solicitors only to send this out on the occasion of my death, it can't be good.

Anyway, let's not dwell on that. I don't want this to be a morbid letter 'from the other side'. I want it to be a pleasant

433

surprise: a gift, from one old pal to another. This is my way of saying thank you for saving my life when you pulled me out of that house fire and for being the best friend a boy could have growing up.

I know we've not seen each other for years, but that's my fault more than yours. I'm the one who upped and left to the other side of the world and then became a workaholic with no time for holidays back to the UK. Don't get me wrong; I've really enjoyed my life here. I have plenty of friends, but no one like you. How could anyone else ever come close?

You may know that I've done pretty well for myself in Sydney. My business has taken off and I've made some good investments. But money is no use to you when you're dead.

There's no point in me leaving loads to Mum and Ian, assuming they've both survived me, because they're comfortable already. I have no significant other or children, so there's only one person I can think of that I want to leave my fortune to: you.

Now don't get too excited, Lise. It's not everything. I do of course have business responsibilities and so on, and I can't totally cut out Mum and Ian, who have been brilliant to me over the years. That said, I am leaving you a significant, life-changing amount, details of which should be attached.

Please do whatever you like with the money. It's yours now — and believe me, you deserve it. I wouldn't have been alive to earn it if you hadn't saved my life.

I knew you were special the moment we met down Vicky Lane — me in my pants and socks, hiding behind a bush, and you helping me without hesitation. You went on to prove that again and again as we grew up.

Life's short. (Don't I know it?) Be happy. Be grateful for loved ones and never forget the importance of family and friendships, for it is them that bring real meaning to our lives and make us what we are.

Now don't you dare be proud! It's only money — take it. Enjoy every penny with your husband and children and everyone else that matters to you. All I ask in return is what you asked of me when we were eighteen and said goodbye to each other at the airport: don't forget me. I know I'll never forget you.

Lots of love,
Elliot
X

Acknowledgements

Thank you to everyone who has supported me on my writing adventure so far, especially my family, friends and readers. Here we are at book three and I couldn't have made it without you. Extra special thanks to:

The best wife, daughter, sister and parents that anyone could ever wish for.

My fantastic literary agent, Pat Lomax, and the rest of the team at BLM.

Editor extraordinaire Phoebe Morgan and everyone at Avon HarperCollins.

We do hope that you have enjoyed reading this large print book.

Did you know that all of our titles are available for purchase?

We publish a wide range of high quality large print books including:
Romances, Mysteries, Classics
General Fiction
Non Fiction and Westerns

Special interest titles available in large print are:
The Little Oxford Dictionary
Music Book
Song Book
Hymn Book
Service Book

Also available from us courtesy of Oxford University Press:
Young Readers' Dictionary
(large print edition)
Young Readers' Thesaurus
(large print edition)

For further information or a free brochure, please contact us at:
Ulverscroft Large Print Books Ltd.,
The Green, Bradgate Road, Anstey,
Leicester, LE7 7FU, England.
Tel: (00 44) 0116 236 4325
Fax: (00 44) 0116 234 0205

Other titles published by Ulverscroft:

DEAR MRS BIRD

A. J. Pearce

Emmeline Lake and her best friend Bunty are trying to stay cheerful despite the Luftwaffe making life thoroughly annoying for everyone. Emmy dreams of becoming a Lady War Correspondent, and when she spots a job advertisement in the newspaper, she seizes her chance — but after a rather unfortunate misunderstanding, she finds herself typing letters for the formidable Henrietta Bird, the renowned agony aunt of *Woman's Friend* magazine. Mrs Bird is very clear: letters containing any form of Unpleasantness must go straight in the bin. But as Emmy reads the desperate please from women who may have Gone Too Far with the wrong man, or can't bear to let their children be evacuated, she decides the only thing for it is to secretly write back . . .

THE MAN WHO DIDN'T CALL

Rosie Walsh

Imagine you meet a man, spend seven glorious days together, and fall in love. And it's mutual: you've never been so certain of anything. So when he leaves for a long-booked holiday and promises to call from the airport, you have no cause to doubt him. But he *doesn't* call. Your friends tell you to forget him. However, you know they're wrong: something *must* have happened; there *must* be a reason for his silence. What do you do when you finally discover you're right? That there *is* a reason — and that reason is the one thing you didn't share with each other: the truth.

THE ROAD TO CALIFORNIA

Louise Walters

Proud single parent Joanna is accustomed to receiving phone calls from her fourteen-year-old son Ryan's school telling her that he's in trouble. When he hits a girl and is excluded, Joanna knows she must take drastic action to help him. Ryan's dad Lex left home when Ryan was two years old. Ryan doesn't remember him — but more than anything, he wants a dad in his life. Isolated, a loner, and angry, he finds solace in books and wildlife. Joanna, against all her instincts, invites Lex to return and help their son. But Lex is a drifter who runs from commitment, and both Joanna and Ryan find their mutual trust and love is put to the test when Lex vows to be part of the family again.